W9-BEC-597

RANDOM
HOUSE
LARGE
PRINT

The Fortune Men

The Fortune Men

★

NADIFA MOHAMED

RANDOM HOUSE
LARGE PRINT

Published in the United States of America by Random House Large Print in association with Alfred A. Knopf, a division of Penguin Random House LLC, New York, and distributed in Canada by Penguin Random House Canada Limited, Toronto.
Originally published in hardcover in Great Britain by Viking, an imprint of Penguin General, a division of Penguin Random House Ltd., London, in 2021.

Documents from ASSI 84/135 are licensed under the Open Government Licence v3.0 from The National Archives, London.

Image on page 446 is from **The South Wales Echo**, used with permission from Reach Newspapers, London.

Front-of-cover art by © Howard Grey / Bridgeman Images
Cover design by John Gall

The Library of Congress has established a Cataloging-in-Publication record for this title.

ISBN: 978-0-593-60778-7

www.penguinrandomhouse.com/large-print-format-books

FIRST LARGE PRINT EDITION

Printed in the United States of America

1st Printing

This Large Print edition published in accord with the standards of the N.A.V.H.

For M.H.M. and L.V.

Naf yahay orod oo, arligi qabo oo, halkii aad ku ogeyd, ka soo eeg.
Oh soul, go run to your homeland and look for it where you knew it.

—AHMED ISMAIL HUSSEIN,
"Hudeidi," written in detention in
French Somaliland, 1964

Remember the green glow of phosphorous,
on a bow waved warm tropic night,
the wonderful wild roaring forties,
when you fought the storm at its height.
The scent of the spices off Java,
a frigate birds cry to the moon,
the sound of the anchor chain surging,
when we stayed in that crystal lagoon.
No requiem plays at your passing,
no friend there to bid you goodbye,
who knows that the sea birds are grieving,
and perhaps a fool such as I.

—HARRY "SHIPMATE" COOKE,
excerpt from "The Last Tramp Steamer"

The Fortune Men

Kow

[One]

Tiger Bay, February 1952

"The King is dead. Long live the Queen." The announcer's voice crackles from the wireless and winds around the rapt patrons of Berlin's Milk Bar as sinuously as the fog curls around the mournful street lamps, their wan glow barely illuminating the cobblestones.

The noise settles as milkshakes and colas clink against Irish coffees, and chairs scrape against the black-and-white tiled floor.

Berlin hammers a spoon against the bar and calls out with his lion tamer's bark, "Raise your glasses, ladies and gentlemen, and send off our old King to Davy Jones's Locker."

"He'll meet many of our men down there," replies Old Ismail, "he better write his apologies on the way down."

"I b-b-b-et he wr-wr-wr-ote them on his d-d-d-eathbed," a punter cackles.

Through the rock 'n' roll and spitting espresso machine Berlin hears someone calling his name. "**Maxa tiri?**" he asks as Mahmood Mattan pushes through the crowd at the bar.

"I said, get me another coffee."

Berlin catches his Trinidadian wife's waist and steers her towards Mahmood. "Lou, sort this troublemaker another coffee."

Ranged along the bar are many of Tiger Bay's Somali sailors; they look somewhere between gangsters and dandies in their cravats, pocket chains and trilby hats. Only Mahmood wears a homburg pulled down low over his gaunt face and sad eyes. He is a quiet man, always appearing and disappearing silently, at the fringes of the sailors or the gamblers or the thieves. Men pull their possessions closer when he is around and keep their eyes on his long, elegant fingers, but Tahir Gass—who was only recently released from Whitchurch asylum—leans close to him, looking for friendship that Mahmood won't give. Tahir is on a road no one can or will walk down with him, his limbs spasming from invisible electric shocks, his face a cinema screen of wild expressions.

"Independence any day now." Ismail gulps from his mug and smiles. "India is gone, what can they say to the rest?"

Berlin makes his eyes bold. "They say we got you by the balls, darkie! We own your land, your trains, your rivers, your schools, the coffee grains at the bottom of your cup. You see what they do to the Mau Mau and all the Kikuyu in Kenya? Lock them up, man and child."

Mahmood takes his espresso from Lou and smirks at the exchange; he cares nothing for politics. While trying to straighten his cufflinks a drop of coffee runs over the rim and falls on to his brightly polished shoes. Grabbing a handkerchief from his trouser pocket, he wipes it off and buffs the stain away. The brogues are new and as black and sharp as Newfoundland coal, better shoes than any other fella here has on his feet. Three £1 notes burn away in his pocket, ready for a poker game; saved through missed lunches and nights spent without the fire, mummified in his blankets. Leaning over the bar, he nudges Ismail. "Billa Khan coming tonight?"

"Me come from the jungle? I wish I come from the jungle! I said to him, look around you, **this** is the jungle, you got bushes and trees everywhere, in my country nothing grows." Ismail finishes his joke and then turns to Mahmood. "How would I know? Ask one of your crooks."

Kissing his teeth, Mahmood throws the espresso down his throat and grabs his fawn mackintosh before stalking through the crowd and out of the door.

The cold air hits his face like a spade, and despite urgently forcing the jacket around his body the bitter February night takes hold of him and makes his teeth chatter. A grey smudge hovers over everything he sees, the result of a hot chink of coal flying from a furnace and into his right eye. A pain so pure that it had hoisted him up and backwards on to the cooling clinkers behind his feet. The clatter of shovels and devil's picks as the other stokers came to his aid, their hands tearing his fingers from his face. His tears had distorted their familiar faces, their eyes the only bright spots in the gloomy engine room, the emergency alarm clattering as the chief engineer's boots marched down the steel staircase. Afterwards, two weeks in a hospital in Hamburg with a fat bandage wrapped around his head.

That smudge and a bad back are the only physical remnants of his sea life. He hasn't boarded a ship for near to three years; just foundry work and poky little boilers in prisons and hospitals. The sea still calls, though, just as loudly as the gulls surfing the sky above him, but there is Laura and the boys to anchor him here. Boys who look Somali despite their mother's Welsh blood, who cling to his legs calling "Daddy, Daddy, Daddy" and pull his head down, mussing up his pomaded hair for forceful kisses that leave his cheeks smelling of sherbet and milk.

The streets are quiet but the news of the King's death drifts from many of the low-slung windblown terraces he passes. Each wireless set relaying the broadcast discordantly, either a second ahead or delayed. Passing the shops on Bute Street, he finds a few lights still on: at Zussen's pawnbroker's where many of his clothes are on hock, at the Cypriot barbershop where he has his hair trimmed and at Volacki's where he used to buy seafaring kits but now just bags the occasional dress for Laura. The tall grand windows of Cory's Rest are steamed up, with figures laughing and dancing behind the leaded glass. He peeks his head through the door to check if some of his regulars are there, but the West Indian faces around the snooker table are unfamiliar. He had once belonged to this army of workers pulled in from all over the world, dredged in to replace the thousands of mariners lost in the war: dockers, tallymen, kickers, stevedores, winch men, hatch men, samplers, grain porters, timber porters, tackle men, yard masters, teamers, dock watchmen, needle men, ferrymen, shunters, pilots, tugboatmen, foyboatmen, freshwater men, blacksmiths, jetty clerks, warehousemen, measurers, weighers, dredgermen, lumpers, launch men, lightermen, crane drivers, coal trimmers, and his own battalion, the stokers.

Mahmood turns away from the wreathed and porticoed splendour of Cory's Rest towards the docks, from where a red mist tints the raw, uncooked sky. He enjoys watching the nightly, industrial spectacle: the dirty seawater appearing to catch fire as vats of rippled, white-hot furnace slag from the East Moors Steelworks tip into the lapping evening tide. The railway on the foreshore bank clanking and screeching as carts shoot back and forth between the billowing steelwork chimneys and the angry, steaming sea. It's an eerie and bewitching sight that catches his breath every time; he half expects an island or volcano to spit out from that bubbling, hissing stretch of petrol-streaked water, but it always cools and returns to its morose, dark uniformity by morning.

The docks and Butetown cover only a square mile but for him and his neigbours it's a metropolis. Raised up from marshland the century before, a Scottish aristocrat built the docks and named the streets after his relatives. Mahmood had heard a rumour that the world's first million-pound cheque was signed at the Coal Exchange.

Even now, in the morning, a different calibre of men come bowler-hatted to work at the Mercantile Marine Office or the Custom House. At both the Marine Office and Seaman's Union you know which door to use if you don't want trouble, and this goes for the labouring white men as well as black. Beyond the financial district, the neighbourhood is for everyone, all of them hemmed in and pushed close by the railway tracks and canals cutting them off from the rest of Cardiff. A maze of short bridges, canal locks and tramlines confuse the new visitor; just before his time, Somali sailors would wear the address of their lodging house on a board around their neck so that passers-by could help navigate them. The canals are a playground to young children and once, when two went missing, Mahmood had spent a blue, insomniac night searching the muddy water for any sight of them. They had been found in the morning—one white, one black, both drowned. But his boys are still too young to go wandering, **alhamdulillah**. One day, when they are older, he will show them around this port town with its Norwegian Church and kosher abattoir, its cranes, booms and smoking chimneys, its timber ponds, creosote works and cattle yards, its three broad thoroughfares—Bute Street, James Street, Stuart Street—criss-crossed with ever-narrowing terraces. The flags and funnels of the world's shipping fleets crowding the pierheads and sprawling across the dock basins.

Mahmood silently plans the future but now, defeated by the icy chill sneaking itself through the gaps between his coat buttons, he decides against another night of poker and heads home to Adamsdown, where the real fire in his life burns.

Violet collapses heavily into the wooden chair and waits for Diana to set the table. "Where's Gracie?"

"Just finishing up her extra schoolwork, she'll be down in a minute."

"I think she's working too hard, Di, her little face looks haggard."

"Don't be ridiculous. She is barely putting pen to paper, spent most of the evening going through my high heels and jazz records. I went up to chivvy her along and her face was smeared in Max Factor Sunset Shine. She thinks she's set for Hollywood, that one."

"The cleaner said that when she was changing her bed sheets she found a photo of Ben in his flight suit under her pillow."

"I know." Her smile stiffens and she turns her back to Violet.

Violet squeezes Diana's forearm. "Strength, Sister. **Koyekh.**"

"Come on down, Grace, we're waiting for you!" Diana shouts up the stairs, ripping her apron off and folding it over the back of her chair. The pounds she put on over the Christmas holiday still show on her muscular body and her green wiggle dress strains across the back. Her black hair folds into loose waves over her shoulders; she needs a haircut but Violet likes it like this, it gives her sister a Mediterranean look.

"You are a perpetual motion machine."

"Not by choice, I tell you. Maggie got Daniel to drop off the chicken as I had so many customers earlier. Every last one of them wanted to put his money on a horse with some kind of association with the King: 'His Majesty,' 'Balmoral,' 'Buckingham Palace.' I don't know if it's their way of paying their respects or just superstition but I've never seen anything like it."

"I saw one of them cash his advance note of pay with me and then go through to you. A fool and his money . . ."

"Oh, that's poor Tahir, he's not right in the head. One of the sailors told me that he was 'misused,' as they say, by Italian soldiers in Africa. He tells me he's the King of Somalia and killed thousands of men in the war."

"Which horse did he put money on?"

"The Empress of India," Diana says, splitting her red-lipped mouth with a loud laugh. "I suppose he thinks that's his wife."

"Goodness gracious. Let me go wash my hands quickly." Violet smiles, looking over the spread on the table: roast chicken, pickled gherkins, boiled potatoes, carrots with red onion and beetroot, and a pile of poppyseed bialys. She returns from the sink and slips her stockinged feet out of her black orthopaedic tie-ups, stretching her serpentine spine, scoliosis having made a puzzle out of her ribcage and shoulder blades. She is paler than both Diana and Maggie, her face their father's down to the deep furrows on either side of her mouth, a nun-like purity to both her dress and to her pink-cheeked face. Her hair is still dark but the promise of a white widow's peak suggests itself above her sparse eyebrows. She gives the impression of someone who has always looked older than her real age and is now at the point of inhabiting a body tailored to her: the modest Cardiff shopkeeper.

"Turn on the wireless, Di, I want to hear the rest of the news. Imagine Princess Elizabeth—sorry, **Queen** Elizabeth—getting the liner back, knowing she has to give up her calm little life with her husband and babies to take the throne."

"No one is **making** her. She can stay in Kenya and declare the end of the monarchy for all I care."

"You have no sense of duty. How could she do that when a whole country, a whole empire, is waiting for her?"

"You would say that, you daddy's girl. You make me laugh, Violet, Da leaves you this shop and you take it as seriously as if he had left you the entire world. I can imagine your face in the papers today, talking about your solemn pledge to rule 203 Bute Street to the best of your power, with the help of Almighty God."

"This shop is my life, and if I had just sold it in '48 what good would that have done? A widow, a spinster and a little girl, jumping from home to home and job to job."

"We could have gone to London or New York."

"To start again? No, Diana, you're still young enough to get married and have more children. I couldn't."

"Of course you could. Maybe not the kids, but you could certainly get married."

"Should I go rooting through the rascals and charlatans who would only want me for my business?"

"Fine, fine. Your choice." Diana raises her hands in surrender and then hollers at the top of her voice, "Grace! Get down here this instant."

"Coming!"

"Just come! Aunty Violet is tired, and the food is getting cold and slimy."

Thuds pound down the winding staircase and then there she is—the centre of both of their worlds—four feet five of undiluted hope and promise.

She kisses Diana and Violet on their cheeks and then wriggles into her chair. Grace's soft round face is changing shape, Ben's square jaw pushing itself out and her nose taking on a fine Volacki curve. Ten summers, ten winters without him, thinks Diana, casting a glance over her daughter's freckled face.

"Did you get any of your exam practice done, petal?" Violet asks her, cutting into the chicken and putting three slices on to Grace's plate.

Grace takes a big bite from a bialy and smiles mischievously. "Well, Aunty, I did start to, but then . . ."

"Hmm?" Diana rolls her eyes. "My make-up bag proved more interesting?"

"You shouldn't have left it out, Mam, you know how easily distracted I am."

"You're a cheeky one, Gracie," laughs Violet.

The wireless announcer forms a fourth companion at the table; a rich male voice from London that sounds clothed in tails and a white bow tie and dress shoes from Bond Street. The tinkle of their knives and forks merges with sonorous choral music and the clang of bells ringing, from Big Ben to a medieval kirk at the furthest reaches of the Hebrides. The land beyond their dining room is in mourning, the stars frozen in their stations, the moon shrouded in black.

"Take these dishes to the kitchen, then get ready for bed, Grace."

"Yes, Mammy." Grace swigs the last of her raspberry cordial and then organizes as many plates as she can in her arms, as she has seen the waitresses in Betty's café do.

"One at a time, you can't carry all of those," says Diana, relieving her of some of the pile and following her into the kitchen.

Violet is desperate to lie flat in her bed and fall asleep but she still has to write up the day's takings, secure the front door—upper and lower bolts, two deadlocks, Yale lock—and then the back door, before carrying the metal cash box up to her bedroom. The weight of it all pins her to the chair before she forces herself up and walks mechanically back into the adjoining shop.

Even at this late hour music pounds through the walls from the Maltese boarding house next door—rock 'n' roll with insinuating saxophones and thrusting drums—and Diana bangs her fist against the plaster to make them quiet. An explosion during her time with the WAAF in the war has deafened her a little in one ear but the Maltese play their music loud enough to wake the dead. With her daughter asleep in bed, Diana changes into her nightdress and slips under her quilted silk eiderdown. It was Violet's wedding present to her, and for some reason one particular corner still smells of Ben's cologne. The night always makes the presence of him blur his absence. She draws out his journal from under her pillow and holds the small blue pad carefully to stop loose pages falling out. The lamplight makes the pages look translucent, his fine, even handwriting floating in the air like a chain of dragonflies. She blinks twice and brings the journal closer to make the words still. The entries have stopped reading like the words of a dead man and instead allow her to believe that he is still out there, in Egypt: sheltering from sandstorms, wandering through the souks of Suez and Bardia for souvenirs to bring home, before the night-time sorties in the Wellington with "his boys" in 38 Squadron. She hadn't realized before the war what a beautiful writer he was. Even his empty days, spent reading whatever books he could get his hands on, were written in a way that made her feel the stifling languor of his tent. Now, the deserted

Italian positions littered with abandoned trucks, motorcycles, jackboots and binoculars are as familiar to her as the steam-powered fairgrounds of her childhood. The mercury incandescence of the Mediterranean lit up by a full moon more worthy of a place in her memory than the turgid Irish Sea.

It takes Violet a moment to understand what the sound is. Her nightmare is still live, filling her mind with images of hands banging on the windows of a synagogue as the entire white structure sweeps up into flames, the night sky shimmering green and blue from the Northern Lights, the cries of men, women and children lifting up to it unheeded.

An alarm.

An alarm ringing.

Not for those dying inside the **shul**, but for her, in her own home. She sits bolt upright in bed and holds her head in her hands, her heart pounding louder than the metallic rattle of the burglar alarm. Edging her feet into her slippers, she picks a silver candlestick up from the dressing table and switches on all the lights. Hearing footsteps on the landing, she holds on tight to the doorknob and feels almost ready to faint. It would be easier to just die here quietly, she thinks, than to face whatever is on the other side. Leaning her forehead against the door, she closes her eyes and slowly turns the knob.

"It's alright, Violet, the window's busted but there's no one down there." Diana is standing at the top of the stairs, a torch in her overcoat pocket and a hammer in each hand. Seeing her sister's bloodless face, she stomps over and pulls her into her arms. "Don't be getting into a state, Sis, everything's fine. Whoever it was chickened out."

Shaking, Violet holds on to Diana and tries to gather her nerves together; it's not just the break-in, or the one before, or the one before that, but the letters that land on the doormat, counting the relatives murdered in Eastern Europe. Names that she barely remembers from her childhood, figures she can just about identify from black and white family portraits now come to her in her dreams, crowding her dining table and asking for more food, more water, a place to rest—please, please, please—pleading with her in Polish, **kuzyn, ocal mnie**, cousin, save me. Nowhere feels safe any more, it is as if the world is trying to sweep her away, her and everyone like her, creeping through locked doors and windows to steal the life from their lungs. Avram dead, Chaja dead, Shmuel dead. In Lithuania, in

Poland, in Germany. More and more names to add to the memorial plaque at the Temple. The facts still seem unreal. How could they all go? The letters from Volackis in New York and London pile up but make less and less sense, rumours of who perished and where, when and how, a drip feed of death with a little happy news forced in at the end—a birth in Stepney, a graduation in Brooklyn.

"Which window is it?" she finally asks.

"The little one around the back. We'll call Daniel in the morning and get him to brick it up. I've put boxes up against it for now. Come on, get in with Gracie, and I'll keep an eye on things."

Nodding obediently, Violet creeps into her niece's room and slides into bed beside her; gathering the child's sleeping body up in her arms, she feels even smaller and more vulnerable than her. There is an atlas on the floor beside the bed and Violet reaches for it, flicking through; the red of the British Empire tints the pages. She's had to learn so much more of the world recently, learnt the names of places that sound fantastical—Uzbekistan, Kyrgyzstan, Manchuria. The strong young men and women who had hidden in forests and survived Hitler are scattered, running, running, running from the catastrophe, going further and further east, as if looking to jump off the edge of the world. It's become the work of spinsters, who don't have the excuse of husbands or families, to round up these waifs and strays, these communal children who trust no one but take whatever is given. She sends money to these distant relatives and even to their destitute friends through banks in Amsterdam, Frankfurt, Istanbul, Shanghai, never knowing if it has got to them in time, or if they will come to their senses and turn back to civilization, if it **is** still that. Violet drops the atlas back on the floor. The rhythm of Grace's inhalations and exhalations calm her but not to the point of sleep; her ears are fixed on the sound of Diana sweeping the glass away downstairs, her feet marching up and down the floorboards, fearless and strong, until finally she pounds up the stairs as the first birds call up the dawn.

Daniel arrives while they are eating breakfast, the fear of the night veiled by the homely scents of coffee and toast. Violet blushes as he leans over to grab a crust from her plate, his deep, foreign-accented voice thrilling her and his bearlike body filling the dining room. She snatches a glance at his pale, wide-eyed face lost in the black fur of his beard and astrakhan hat, crumbs catching in his moustache. Musky cologne emanates from his damp sheepskin coat as he pulls it off and hangs it up in the hallway. He belongs to Maggie, their middle sister, but desire and envy have crept into Violet's heart. Her body is flush with yearnings stronger than she has ever felt before, and Daniel is the focus of them, his tall and broad frame like a sepulchre for her hope of some day bearing children. He is in her waking dreams: his lips, his hands, his pink nipples lewd and raspberry-like against his snowy skin. The fire in her womb suddenly flaring before the change moves the heat somewhere else. She looks forward to the end of it all—anything rather than this lovelorn, girlish infatuation with a man who sees her as a sister.

"Maggie is worried about you girls, she thinks the street is getting worse. I tell her it nothing, cost of the business, but she like a chicken this morning, pacing, pacing. She wants me to get you a gun!" Daniel pulls up a stepladder and eases the remaining glass out of the window frame. "It must have been a little fella who think he can come through this window."

With his back to Violet, she cannot help but look at his backside straining against his trousers. She looks quickly away when she sees Diana smiling at her.

"No need for that," Diana replies. "Me and Vi have agreed that we couldn't stab a burglar but we could certainly batter one. Vi came out of her room ready with a candlestick last night, I'm sure she would have made mincemeat out of him."

Daniel's laugh booms out and then it's just the grind of mortar mixing, the scrape of metal on stone, and the **tap-tap** of bricks piling one on top of the other. The rectangle of light quickly extinguished and another barrier placed between the world and Violet.

After Daniel departs for the gentleman's outfitters he owns with his brothers on Church Street, Grace kisses them goodbye and strolls the few minutes to St. Mary's primary school, which sits beside the church where most of the locals are baptized, married and laid to rest. Diana sets up her table as a turf commissioner in the small, damp outbuilding in the yard, the radio turned on to follow the day's major racing fixtures. Her nails, painted so thickly scarlet they look dipped in vinyl, are the only colour in the room. Her face will be slowly made-up throughout the day, like a photograph developing in a darkroom, until at 5 p.m. she will look ready for a red carpet; the transformation from young widow to aged starlet complete. Violet, on the other hand, is habitually bare-faced and clean-nailed, she wears a simple navy calf-length dress and her father's silver war badge pinned to her brassiere for courage.

One display is still how their father left it; full

of expensive compasses and ivory-inlaid hipflasks that are beyond the reach of their customers but still distinguish the shop from the others on the road. The rest of Volacki's is engorged with cheap and popular items: wellington boots hanging off hooks, black school plimsolls crammed into wooden cubbyholes, cotton dresses hanging ethereally from a rail near the stockroom, woollen blankets wrapped in tissue paper and stored on the upper shelves. This shop is a "padded cell" in Diana's eyes, a place of madness whose method only Violet knows, the merchandise piling around her in small, unstable heaps. She sells knives, razors, rope, oilskin hats and coats, good strong work boots, sea bags, pipes, tobacco and snuff, but the real money is in cashing advance notes of pay for departing sailors. The heavy hand-cranked till collects more than a hundred pounds a day in its deep trays—and is only touched by Violet—never mind the safe or drawer where she keeps larger notes. The last customers arrive after the official closing hour, knocking discreetly yet impatiently on the glass panels to buy an urgent box of matches or cigarettes; everyone bending the law a little to make life easier.

Laba

[Two]

The plump, fat-marbled kosher mince begins to sizzle and brown in the pan and Mahmood shakes a teaspoon of chilli powder into the oil. He had bought kosher all the time in East London because he had a good butcher only a few doors down, and kosher is as good as **halal**, religiously speaking, but now, for some reason, it also tastes better to him. Holding the mysterious Hindi-labelled spices up to his nose, he picks out cumin, turmeric and ginger—good enough—and spills a teaspoon of it over the lamb. He'll eat some mince with a side of tinned sweetcorn for lunch and then mix the remainder with the last of the rice in the evening. This is as much good eating as he's capable of now, even though he had learnt how to steam, stew and roast while a ship's pantry boy, and to bake from the little kitchen job he'd had in the Somali boarding house he'd roomed in last year.

Mahmood still can't accept that he is just another uncared-for man eating from a plate on his lap in the solitude of a cold rented room. He had always helped Laura in the kitchen—what other husband would have? He'd had to, because she had no sense of what good food tasted like; he'd managed to get her to use herbs and spices, but still her carrots would be undercooked, her potatoes mushy, her meat dry and gasping. Now, meals are just another thing he has to do by himself, for himself. Everything with just his own damned hand.

Mahmood has to remind himself that he doesn't **hate** Laura. That he is not **better off** without her. That those red thoughts that jut into his mind as he's walking down the street—telling him that her tits are too small, her arse too flat, her face too long—are not what he really believes.

Laura has fixed him in this longitude and latitude. He's only living in this house—with black men he has no common language, culture or religion with—so that he can stake her out, and keep things rolling between them until she comes to her senses. He watches the company she keeps and crosses the road to see his sons every few days. In many ways it's a come-up from that derelict Somali boarding house he was told to leave after the mosque business. He has a room to himself with a lock on it rather than that attic room sprawling with camp beds. He doesn't have to put up with the all-night coughing, or gossip, or damp laundry dripping from the lines suspended across the ceiling. All of the other seamen were lazy beggars, rolling around in bed waiting for someone else to get the stove hot in the mornings. Mahmood remembers the yellowed list of regulations pinned up above his head that Warsame had read to him before telling him to pack his bags.

1. The Seaman's Lodging House keeper shall not sell or be engaged in the sale of intoxicating liquor, or be engaged or interested in the business of a Clothier, Outfitter, or a Slop-dealer.
2. The Medical Officer of Health, officers of the Board of Trade, and Police have right of access and inspection to his premises at any time.
3. He must provide at least 30 cubic feet of air space for each person in his dormitories, and not accommodate at any

time a larger number of lodgers than has been authorized by the Council.

4. He must follow out certain provisions regarding sanitation, water closets and washing facilities, and general hygiene. He must affix in a prominent place a copy of the City's Byelaws in this respect together with his scale of charges, and not make a higher charge than is provided by the scale.
5. He must not admit or fail to exclude from his premises any thief, reputed thief, prostitute, or reputed prostitute, or any other person of immoral or improper character.

Mahmood had laughed when Warsame got to that last rule. So he was no better than a prostitute? **Ajeeb.** He packed his trunk and vacated his 30 cubic feet of air space; moving into Doc's place that very same afternoon.

Red brick and leaded glass, the smell of bleach and defeat. The Employment Exchange has the atmosphere of a church; job notices flutter from the wall like paper prayers, and mean council workers dole out state relief with the aloofness of priests placing wafers into indigent mouths. Out-of-work miners, dockworkers, drivers, handymen, barrel boys, plumbers and factory workers mill around, their eyes avoiding each other. The pinewood floor is dented from the tramp of work boots near the counter and littered with cigarette butts and matches.

"WELDER NEEDED"
"TEN YEARS' EXPERIENCE NECESSARY"
"UNDER 21 YRS?"
"APPRENTICESHIPS"
"CARPENTERS NEEDED"
"GRAVEDIGGING"

Mahmood shoves his hands into his sports jacket and paces from one notice to another, looking for boiler or foundry work. He has only shrapnel in his pocket, having lost the rest at poker. There is nothing worth trying for; none of the usual firms that can be relied upon to take coloured fellas are advertising. He looks again at the gravedigging notice. It's for Western Cemetery, the pay not half bad, but the thought of shovelling hard, damp earth and filling it with stiff corpses makes him shake his head and mutter, "**Astaghfirullah.**"

Pulling his homburg hat low over his eyebrows, he takes a yellow ticket stamped with a 9 and waits his turn for the counter beside one of the heavy coiled radiators. The heat from the cast iron blasts through his thin trousers and teases his skin, somewhere between pleasure and pain, and he rocks his body back and forth, letting the heat rise and dissipate. On the last tramper he had taken, the owners had installed new boilers and all the brass fittings had shone gold in the white light of the furnaces. He had stepped back to admire the conflagration, before shovelling more coal in and turning the white light into an almost sentient, colourless gas that roved backwards and up the chimney like a **jinni** escaping a lamp. He had birthed that fire and nurtured it, from yellow to orange to white to blue and then that colour that had no name, just pure energy. He'd wondered what it would be like to step forward the few inches that separated him from it, whether, like in **cadaabka**, his skin would just fall from his flesh like a sheet. He had been formed by those fires, turned from a puny pantry boy into a knotted-muscled stoker who could stand at hell's gate for hours at a stretch, his face roasted and grimy with coal dust.

"Number nine come forward."

Mahmood takes the chair in front of Counter 4 and places his hat on his knee, before handing over his grey identity card.

The woman in front of him is in a brown tweed suit and maroon lipstick, her hair done up with a net over the large bun. She looks at Mahmood over the rims of small wire-framed glasses. "What can I do for you, Mr. Mattan?" she says, examining the card.

"I need national assistance, no job good for me."

"What work can you do?" she asks, lengthening each word.

"Boiler work. Quarry."

"Let me see if there is anything else that we are yet to pin up."

She looks through the files on her side of the partition; her manner is good, better than some of the other clerks, who seem to resent him, whether he is looking for work or drawing dole.

"There is one foundry job here but I don't think you will be suitable," she says, leaving the rest unsaid.

He meets her gaze, swallows a bitter smile.

She stamps his card in the right places and counts out two pounds and six shillings.

"Have a pleasant day, Mr. Mattan."

"And you, madam."

Mahmood rises and folds the £1 notes into his pocket book, before putting on his hat and leaving the melancholia of the Exchange for the thud and clamour of the racetrack.

The turf at Chepstow is turned up nicely; drizzle lifting the smell of soil, grass and horseshit into the air. Mahmood had had a tough morning at the greyhound track but is feeling better now that he is on to the horses. Hooves thundering, the ground shaking, his heart thudding, the other punters shouting or whispering, "Come **on**, come **on**!" Gasps as a rider is thrown off and then, with no breath escaping his lungs, his horse breaks clear from the wave of undulating muscle and mane and is whipped, whipped, whipped, head daggered forward, across the finishing line. The confetti of betting stubs thrown to the wind is confirmation that he was one of the few sharp enough to take a risk on the stallion; over ten pounds in winnings on a horse with 20/1 odds. Mahmood had changed his bet at the last moment, after catching sight of the horse in the paddock; he was a fine-looking black thing, and Mahmood could have sworn that he had nodded to him as he passed by on the groom's reins. A lucky name too, Abyssinia. Names beginning with an A are always good to him—and he has visited Abyssinia too, another sign. He should lean more on the As, he thinks. So far he has won on:

Achtung
Ambitious Daisy
Apache
Artist
Angel Song
Artois

Arkansas's Pride
Atlantic Revelry.

He should also hand over £5 quickly to Doc Madison for the lodging room in Davis Street, before it slips through his fingers and the codger gets on his back. The rest he will spend on the boys and Laura, treat them now that he has paid off the court fine. It had been a mistake, that last time—not just theft but sacrilege on the charge sheet—he had taken things too far, and it had turned them all against him. The shoes piled up outside the **zawiya** on Fridays seemed to be fair game—you could come with one pair and leave with another, with no real bother—but the **zakat** money was truly **haram**. He can't ask any of them for nothing now, apart from Berlin.

Passing the cinema, he looks up to see what pictures they have on: **Double Dynamite**. Still. And **Quo Vadis** and **The African Queen** as the new releases. He will watch **Quo Vadis**, but turns his nose up at **The African Queen**. He spends too much of his money on the pictures; it's one of his chief vices but also his school. Where else could he learn so much about this place he's decided to call home? Its dreams, its history and its myths? In that dark, flea-ridden hall he's learnt how to romance girls, how to talk real English, and examined how his neighbours see themselves and how they see him. Films have made him realize it's hopeless to expect the Adamsdown biddies to change their ways; they'll only ever see him like one of those grimy coolies in loincloths, or jungle savages, shrieking before their quick, unmourned deaths—or at best, a tight-lipped houseboy proudly taking punishment in place of his white master. It makes him marvel that Laura was able to ignore all that shit and see him as a man like any other. Was it because her family, with its hunger, cussing and bitter wisdom, was not like the rich, chattering ones shown in the pictures? She is part of the servant class, he knows that now, who might just as easily stamp a black man into the dirt as offer him a hand up like a brother. Whatever it was, the navy money in his pocket had certainly helped.

Mahmood stumbles over a loose cobblestone and corrects his balance self-consciously, looking left and right. He is paranoid that his steps look strange, flat-footed; his shoes are a size too big, to allow room for the painful corns on his feet. You cannot look like prey here. You cannot show weakness or your days are numbered, like those of the Somali drunk the police beat to death last year. Mahmood had learnt to do the black man's walk early on in Cardiff: to walk with his shoulders high, his elbows pointed out, his feet sliding slowly over the ground, his chin buried deep in his collar and his hat low over his face, to give nothing away apart from his masculinity, a human silhouette in motion. Even now, he flinches when passing gangs of Welshmen when they've been at the boozer on rugby days; everything might seem calm, normal, when suddenly a fist comes into his face as hard as concrete, the shock of it knocking all words out of his head. The laughter as they pass on, the attacker giddy and loud with self-congratulation, the shame hotter than a furnace. Other black sailors keep a knife or razor in a pocket, but for him the risks are too high. The police know him by name, they might search for a stolen watch and find the razor or knife—and then what? Two years for an offensive weapon. Instead, he has perfected not being seen. He knows people call him "the Ghost" and it satisfies him; it helps with the work and reminds him of the characters in the American comic books he picks up for his eldest boy:

Absorbing Man
Black Bolt
Chronomancer.

· · ·

It's late by the time Mahmood reaches Berlin's; he had gone home to change, ignoring Doc's calls for rent, before darting out again in a three-piece suit and dark overcoat. Berlin brings out his self-doubt; he always looks so polished, like Cary Grant or some other star. Smoothing his moustache down, Mahmood pushes the heavy black door. Calypso music fills the room and somehow makes it feel busier. There are only a few customers on this Monday night: students in black turtlenecks sitting on stools, a white couple dancing awkwardly beside the jukebox, their hips moving in an uncoordinated staccato. Berlin is standing fixed behind the bar, his arms stretched out either side of him, hands clenching the counter, his head bowed. Lost in this reverie, it takes him a moment to notice Mahmood settling into the bar stool in front of him; he finally lifts his head and his distant-seeming hazel eyes settle ambivalently on him. His face is reminiscent of a shark's—a hammerhead—with his flat skull and wide, dark lips. He is handsome but in a dangerous, bloodless way. He never loses himself or allows people to lose themselves in him. Mahmood knows that he abandoned a daughter in New York and a son in Borama; he speaks of them easily, but with no guilt or regret. He likes this lack of emotion from Berlin. It means you can tell him anything, and it is like speaking to a wall: no shock, no moralizing, no pity or disgust. Berlin has low expectations and a worldly acceptance of even the greatest tragedies. His own father had been murdered before his eyes in a raid on his clan by the dervishes, and watching that dagger run across his father's throat must have taught Berlin not to cling too hard to life.

"So the wind has blown you in again?" he asks in Somali.

"The wind has blown money into my pockets, **sahib**." Mahmood drops a handful of coins on to the bar. "Get me a pasty and a black coffee."

"Good day at the races?"

"Not bad at all."

"You missed some action tonight. The police found a couple of Chinese sailors running opium from a lodging house on Angelina Street. Using it themselves, too, so they were walking on noodle legs to the police car, them and this little bebopper from the university. It gave the reefer boys a laugh to see the police busy with someone else."

"The Chinamen are good at keeping their secrets. Someone must have told."

"Like they said in the war, the walls have ears. Nothing is secret for long in this whore of a bay."

Mahmood finishes with his pasty after just a couple of bites. It's greasy and stale, but luckily his stomach has become a small, easily satisfied thing. On the ships he could throw down whatever was put in front of him and go back for more, now he eats just enough to trick his mind into thinking he's had a meal.

"You think that new Somali from Gabiley is telling tales to the police? Something about him smells bad to me."

"Who? Samatar? You got the wrong fella there. His knees start knocking if he even sees a police car. Wrong man to be an informer."

"Grass," Mahmood says, unconvinced, rolling the word in his mouth like a lost tooth. He hates grasses even more than coppers. You can be sitting down with a man, playing poker or warming your hands on a mug of tea, and the next thing you know everything you said is repeated back to you in the police station; no matter how much trash you were talking, or how tipsy you were, it goes down against you. You deny it and the police grab your neck and say they know it's so.

"I know an informer when I see one and he ain't it," Berlin repeats. He is quieter when away from the others; he doesn't need to get up on a stepladder and perform the role of bossman, the man who made it, the man who beat it all. It's getting late and he's burning down like an old wick; wiping the counter in slow, deliberate circles, rubbing his eyes. Despite the gleaming black hair and straight back, he is in his fifties and age is starting to catch up with him; he no longer attends the rent parties, and makes excuses to stay at home on weekends.

His gaze fixes somewhere over Mahmood's shoulder and his eyes track someone or something.

"What is it?" Mahmood asks, turning around.

"Just that Jamaican bastard, Cover. That carpenter who stabbed Hersi last year, just over there by the jukebox it was. If anyone is an informer it'll be him."

Mahmood squints at the small figure walking along the opposite side of Sophia Street. Doesn't look like the kind of man who could give trouble; his arms swing as he walks and the pipe in his mouth sends neat puffs up into the cold air.

"What makes you say that?"

"He cut Hersi three times with a razor and then stuck him with a broken bottle."

"Why?"

Berlin lifts his hands to the sky. "He hates Somalis? Who knows? Hersi was nearly killed, he was in hospital drinking one blood transfusion after the next, but listen, the Jamaican go to court and get off scot-free, a pat on the back and home to bed. He's never coming back in here. Informer." Berlin looks like he wants to spit the word.

"These West Indians hate us for no reason. That snake landlord of mine always wishing me harm."

"The ships are where the troubles start, and then they follow us on to land. All of us fighting over crumbs. You are a fool to live there. You need to stay with your own people. That Cover will end up in jail one day, but not before he kills somebody."

The carpenter disappears from view.

"You're still set against going back to sea?" Berlin asks abruptly. "Might be good for you to let all that noise about the **zawiya** cool down, give the sheikh time to forget."

"Why should I? I want to keep seeing my boys."

"From across the street with a pair of binoculars?"

"Better than across an ocean or two," Mahmood replies, curling his lip.

"She don't want you bringing money in, or what? You can't take these young girls so seriously. They go to the pictures and think marriage is going to be one long song-and-dance number. All kissy-kissy, lovey-dovey. What, she's twenty? Twenty-one? What does she know of what a father needs to do? You don't want your sons to see you out of work and broke all the time."

"What makes you think I'm broke?" Mahmood jumps from his stool and slams his pocketbook on the table. "Look inside, you call that broke? I live better than those sailors with their Salvation Army coats and fingerless gloves."

Berlin rolls his eyes and slides the pocketbook

back towards Mahmood. "You stay in Cardiff until the last trumpet call. It's not my concern. You want another coffee, big man?"

Mahmood nods and wipes his hand over his brow. His heart is racing and he can't explain why he fears that he will end up boarding a ship soon, unable to keep his promise to his sons. Behaving like all the others do, just floating debris with no ties anywhere.

"You're a gambler, you know that sometimes you just have to let fate take over." The coffee machine hisses and steams as the last drops fall into the white cup. "Did I tell what happened to me when I went to New York, in 1919?" Berlin asks, smiling.

Mahmood shrugs.

"I went there from Barry Docks, had done good service in the merchant navy during the Great War, was still a young boy but felt that I was some sort of hero with my chest puffed up and my moustache just coming in. The ship spat out its cargo in New York and then went into dry dock, so I march off with my pay burning a hole in my pocket. I see all these beautiful coloured girls in furs, stockings cut low on their calves, ribbons in their slick hair, and I say what! What have I been doing stuck inside boiler rooms with stinking men? I have wasted my whole life already! The girls were from the south of the country, they tell me to go to Harlem, that all the swellest, most giddy-up places are there and that it's a Negroes' paradise. I say take me there now. We ride a taxi because I want to show off and we stop at a diner to feed. The food is all their food—pig this and pig that—but I find something to chew on, and one of the girls she's a real doll, face made for kissing, and she's leaning into me and laughing and I lean back and laugh too, **kekeke**, showing all my teeth, and I have forgotten all about any ship or curfew or anything. I hadn't been near a woman in months . . . and the girls are singing for me and ordering more and more and they see friends passing and call them in, and I'm still leaning and laughing. We finish up and they say, there's a party! Let's go! Louis will be there and Fats and rich ofays with good smuggled whisky. I pay for everyone and we take another taxi, as my girl says her feet hurt, and we go to this party on Lexington and I don't see Louis or Fats but there's low light, swinging music, sharp drink. I'm getting woozy, I lose my girl in the crowd and it looks like people are dancing on top of me, like I'm falling through the floor. I can take my booze, you know that, and I'm wondering what kind of American drink is **this** that makes me lose my head. I wanna find my girl and hold on to her feet, and so I crawl through the crowd, thinking I'll recognize her red shoes, but I can't and in the end they drag me out of the party. I wake up in the street, and you know what? Those girls had picked me clean—nothing but my seaman's card in my pocketbook—drugged then cleaned me out. I drifted downtown, close to the port but too ashamed to show myself to the captain, all of these deep holes in the ground where they're building this new block and that new skyscraper. I sit, sorry for myself, looking out over the water, holding my head, when someone push me from behind. I jump to my feet, thinking it's time to fight. The man laugh and I say whatcha laughing at? My fists up already. You don't know me? Why should I know you? Hamburg '05, he says. I step back and think it can't be, he pretends to pull back an arrow and shoot me and his name hits me instead. Taiaiake."

Mahmood feels like he is back in **dugsi**, watching his Qur'anic teacher pace back and forth, the stories washing over him in great waves. "Who was he?"

Berlin's eyes glint and he pauses to throw an espresso down his throat before starting again.

"We'll have to go right back to nineteen-oh-five. To Hamburg, Deutschland. Me and a hundred others crossing sea and land because we were told there was good work in Europe. Recruited by a Somali **dalaal** who scouted across the Habr Awal territory and the Garhajis and Warsangeli for people like us willing to go with him. I was a boy with no father and when I heard so many of my clanspeople were going away there was no way my old mother could hold me back. Our cattle had died, we couldn't go near our old wells because of the dervishes so the camels had only a couple of weeks in them, there was nothing she could give me. There we were: the decrepit, the just born, the **wadaads** and the weavers, the **suldaan** and his servants, the potter and the poets, all on a **dhow** to Aden. The **dalaal** gave us all this sweet talk, that the Deutsch were so impressed when they heard about the brave Somalis that they demanded to see us in the flesh, all we had to do was show them our way of life and they would pad our pockets with gold. Beneath us in the **dhow** we had everything—our saddles, spears, prayer mats, headrests, cooking pots, all that we had! The minute we arrive in Hamburg there is a photographer waiting for us on the docks. His flash exploding and making the babies cry. We met the big boss, Hagenbeck, and he takes us back to his mansion and tells us to make up our camp in his long green garden. I fell asleep on the grass while watching the women tie the wooden frames together and when I woke up small white faces were peering through the fence, giggling and whispering to each other. I took a fright at these white-haired little **jinns** and ran into one of the completed **aqals** and stayed there while more and more **gaallo** arrived to stare at us."

"**Astaghfirullah**," laughs Mahmood, "it's still the same when you cross the railway bridge."

"No . . . no, this was something else, they were not looking the way you would at a stranger, because their features or clothes are strange to you, they looked in doubt of our real existence, **wallahi**. Their eyes like this . . ." Berlin stretches his upper and lower lids wide open, "watching every movement we made. They looked at us as if we were creatures of their imagination, as if they might be hallucinating altogether."

"So what about that man in New York?"

"I'm coming to him! We stay in that garden for a few days and in the end we can see more white faces than leaves on the trees. We are ambushed but told to live normally, as if back in Africa. Africa? Where is that? I ask. I had never heard of the place. We had a hidden area to do our business, but what do we find? Deutsch boys my age, and men who should have known better, climbing up trees to watch us as we did it. When Hagenbeck tells us to pack up we say '**subhanallah**' and do it gratefully, but we are not going home, no, we are going on tour. We walked to the train station with our enemies running behind us, touching our skin to see if the black come off on their hand, pulling the hair of the children, grabbing anything we drop and stealing it. Savages. There's a special train waiting for us and on the platform there are zebras, elephants, monkeys, Asians, Africans, Native Americans, Australians gathered together as if on Judgement Day. We were part of some kind of carnival, pulled together from every corner of the earth, to be exhibited in Berlin. They counted us on to the train to make sure no one had got lost, but inside there was complete chaos. A madhouse of languages, half-naked people, and screaming children. I pushed through, looking for a seat, leaving the other Somalis behind, until I finally found a quiet carriage. Sitting around me were men with only a strip of hair running down their heads, and in front of me a fella around my age with a bow and arrow in his hands. I wrapped my three metres of cotton closer around my shoulders and sat up, real tough, hardening my eyes, but the boy smiles and holds his palm out to me, and I take it."

"He was the one who found you in New York?"

"That's right, Taiaiake, a Mohawk from Canada. We did everything together in Berlin, we sat side by side as they measured every inch, and I mean every **inch**, of our bodies, took pictures of us sitting and standing up, looking this way and that, poured plaster on to our faces so they could keep casts of us. It was unlike anything else! We felt like kings. We competed against each other in the games they put on and stared as the girls walked past for the beauty contest. **Allah**, we didn't realize then that they saw us as little different to the elephants and zebras on parade. Some of the Inuit died there and the Germans took their bodies, boiled off the flesh and put them on display in a museum. You couldn't even die in peace. Later, Taiaiake went to America and took to the sky to dance along steel girders, and me to the sea. There wasn't land anywhere that we could call our own and live well."

"So you think I should take to the sky or sea?"

"You're a man of the sea, aren't you? You shouldn't cling to this piece of flint they call a country. Warm yourself up beside a nice furnace somewhere in the Indian Ocean and come back with a clean slate and money in your pocket."

"I'm not going anywhere. The devil looks after his own," Mahmood smiles.

"**Doqon iyo malaggiisa lama kala reeb karo**, a fool and his fate can never be parted," sighs Berlin. "Off you go then, **roohi**, I need to close up."

As Mahmood slides off the stool and reaches for his hat, Berlin abruptly turns and thumps a palm to his forehead. "You see how I'm getting old? Telling you stories from a thousand years ago but forgetting to give you this." He pulls out a blue airmail envelope from the jumble of papers inside a small drawer.

Mahmood Hussein Mattan, c/o Berlin Milk Bar, Cardiff reads the neat, blue writing. A five-shilling monochrome stamp with the dead King's face and a map of British Somaliland makes clear the sender.

Mahmood sits down heavily again. "**Hooyo**," he sighs defeatedly.

"Mothers always catch you, even if you run to the ends of the earth," Berlin laughs. "You want me to read it for you?"

Mahmood waves a hand in acquiescence. Neither he nor his mother can read or write but somehow she still finds a way to pour her words into his ears across all that space and time. He can picture her sitting in line for one of the scribes near the Public Works Office, her rough-hewn stool holding up her fragile bones, her long robes somehow falling just a millimetre above the dusty ground strewn with eucalyptus leaves. The memory of her is like a boulder on his back and he slumps forward on the bar, hiding his face.

"Shall I do her voice?"

"You want me to stick a knife in your back?"

Berlin chuckles but then clears his throat, rips the thin envelope open, and intones.

"My lastborn, my heart, my knees, my liver, the final blessing of my womb, I pray for you five times a day, I plead with God that he may show you his most merciful face. I bless you. I bless you. I bless you. Say **ameen.** I have consulted the fortune-teller and he tells me that you are safe and that your three beautiful boys are in good health, and their mother too. **Ameen. Ameen.** I have seen more sailors from Cardiff in Hargeisa than I can count on two hands and they tell me you move regularly. May Allah still your feet and give you comfort until he reunites you with me. When will the boys be grown enough to see my old face? Not that there is any beauty in it but there are blessings to be found in the company of the aged. I do not know how much more of my allotted time I have ahead of me but I will fast and pray until the last breath. My son, do not forget your **deen**, I am an unschooled woman but that is **cilmi** I can pass on with certainty; there is no harbour or shelter apart from Allah. Never forget that. Your brothers send their greetings and wish me to tell you that they have put in a bid to win the first cinema concession in Hargeisa. I do not know if it will be granted to them, or to one of those cut-throats on the other side of the ditch, but if you have anything to contribute, **manshallah**, otherwise I will tell them it is impossible. Some of these sailors return with such good fortune, son, and I hope that one day it will be you stepping out of a car with your suitcases and children and happy wife.

Now, **nabadgelyo iyo safar salaama.**
Your mother."

Berlin folds the letter and pushes it under Mahmood's nose. "Some men may call themselves poets but your mother is the real article."

"She uses words like arrows."

"Poetry is war, what else you expect?"

"A truce."

"You really don't want it?"

"No, you keep it."

Berlin rubs his thumb along the crease of the letter before pocketing it. "You'll know one day . . . when your mother is under the earth, and no one prays, weeps or cares for you in the same way. Then you'll warm your heart with letters like this."

"Until that day, then . . ." Mahmood says, pulling the brim of his felt hat over his forehead.

After turning the sign on the door, Berlin perches on a stool and lights a cigarette, his silhouette appearing and disappearing with the flashing juke-box lights. The floor is mopped, the till emptied and the coffee machine cleaned, just enough time to savour a last cigarette before Lou begins hollering for him to come to bed. He tries to empty his mind but thoughts gallop up and down—bills that need to be paid, a court summons for street gambling, a memory of his long-dead mother's incense suddenly as strong as the cigarette smoke, another of his American daughter's downturned infant mouth. He rises and opens the drawer behind the bar; pulls out an old postcard of the Empire State Building in a blizzard, postmarked ten Decembers ago. Taiaiake had written a short message in block capitals on the reverse, wishing him a good new year and telling him that he thinks he saw Lucille in a playground in Boerum Hill, and that she looked well and was climbing the frame as well as any steelworker. The postcard has been in the drawer since it arrived, Berlin thinking that any day now he will reply but somehow never managing to do it. Brooklyn is lost to the past, to the man he had been before the Johnson-Reed Act had cleansed America of men like him. He struggles to keep old worlds alive; friends, lovers, even children seem to deliquesce when he turns his back, appearing in fragments in his dreams and quiet moments to stake their claim on him.

. . .

Mahmood stands on Davis Street, looking up through the torn net on the sash window as his family prepares for bed. She stands, spare and angular, with Mervyn on her hip, rocking back and forth to soothe him, her brown hair aglow under the orange lampshade. Her mother is beside her and they converse in their abrupt, hand-waving fashion. Omar and David are in their vests and underpants, jumping on the bed and making a mess. If he were to walk in there, they would clamber all over him, like monkeys in a tree, laughing like maniacs while their mother tried to incinerate him with her eyes. She was, **is**, a formidable foe, able to argue that dark is light and light is dark, and so furious with him that she would unleash Old Testament plagues if she could.

He had failed. That pane of glass between them expressed the distance that had grown imperceptibly but undeniably in their five years of marriage. He knew—no, maybe not knew, but felt, yes, felt—that she was going with another man. He thought he had seen her coming out of the picture house with a black fella, a light-skinned man with a thin moustache; he hadn't seen the girl's face, that's true, couldn't keep up with them, but she had the same build and hair colour as Laura. She had changed so much over the last five years: hips, a little bit on top too. She wasn't a plank-bodied young girl any more, but the tongue had remained, and could lacerate any man's pride faster than a cat o' nine tails. The first time they had met had been in a café in town, her hair drizzled with rain, her skin not far off the colour of the marble counter. Her foolish sister was sleeping outside the furriers so she could be the first to buy a fake mink or chinchilla when the sale started in the morning. Laura had ordered a couple of teas when she felt him staring at her. Her seaweed-green eyes flashed a glance at him and then back to the clasp of her purse. He hadn't known what to say, his English was still engine-room basic then, but he didn't want her to leave without even trying to get her attention. He liked her red hat, the way her hair curved around her jaw, the hardness of her nose above her soft, pink lips, the way she wore her cheap, oversized clothes with style. Eventually, with a croak, he asked, "You wanna come pictures?" She would tease him about this long after, imitating his accent and awkward invite, but she had agreed to the date, and three months later they were married. They had kept the courtship quiet. She only told her sister, and he didn't bother telling the other Somalis at all—what for? Just for them to say that she would leave him broken and shoeless?

Or that she would turn around one day and call him a dirty nigger? Or that she wouldn't know how to look after his children and would feed them pork and choke them on boiled potatoes?

On their wedding day, he had taken a detour to buy a white carnation for the lapel of his brown suit and had arrived at the registry office to find Laura red-eyed and stiff-necked. Her grandmother had come limping down from the Valleys to put a halt to the wedding but it hadn't worked, so she sat on a wooden chair at the back of the room, reading her Bible and hollering "Lord have mercy on our souls" throughout the ceremony. It had been too quick and messy, in hindsight, he should have gone to visit her parents to show them that he wasn't some cannibal who had a pot waiting for their daughter, he should have bought her a ring and given her more money to tide her over while he went to sea. He thinks that, deep down, she has never forgiven him for leaving directly after the hasty consummation—in a borrowed bed—of their vows, or for spending eight months away, jumping from Kenya to Ceylon to Malaysia to Australia and back again. The most lucrative signing of his life but, man, had it cost him something too.

They are still friendly, in a sense, go for the occasional walk, and he is still welcome to visit when he wants. But they had nearly done it, nearly confounded all the doomsayers. Who else had breached a white home like that? Walking in through the front door with a suitcase and a smile. Laura had made that happen. There could be no denying the force that lay within her sleek, lithe body. She was a gangster. Closing the door to the box room they shared, and knowing everyone could hear. It made him love her even more. Meeting her father at night on the landing, both of them in their shorts, was the worst thing about living there; he looked like he wanted nothing more than to push him down the stairs. But even he had relented in the end, finding boiler work for Mahmood, and telling Laura that she had made her bed and had better lie in it when she'd said she wanted a divorce last summer.

Saddex

[Three]

"Oh, would you look at this one!"

"What? Show me."

Diana opens the newspaper wider and swivels to show her older sister.

DIVORCE GIVEN TO WOMAN WHO FOUND HUSBAND IN LINGERIE.

"The silly beggar!"

"I don't know why people get married if they make such a lark of it, I really don't," Violet says, her eyes rushing greedily through the print.

"Listen to this bit, close your ears, Gracie! The lingerie was a combination of the wife's undergarments and those bought especially by the husband."

"Oh, the shame of it, how could he do it to her?"

"And this bit . . . she had become suspicious when her top drawer grew emptier and emptier." Diana unleashes her cackle, making Grace drop her knife in alarm. "Take the paper, I know how much you love these stories." She flaps the **Echo** towards Violet and picks up her knife and fork.

"I don't **love** them but they don't half make me glad that I never married."

"Well, you know you've picked a wrong 'un when you land up in the **Echo**."

"Do you think any of our men are getting up to these sorts of tricks?" Violet whispers, holding the newspaper between herself and Grace.

Diana raises her eyebrows. "I'd put money on it. Men are men are men. There's no end to the tomfoolery they get up to."

"Even the **frum**?"

"Especially them! I might trust a religious woman but I never trust a religious man. They're just better at hiding it all, if you ask me."

"But Ben wasn't like that, was he?"

"No, but he was a saint. Sentimental to the hilt

too, wasn't able to keep secrets or lies for long, a funny one like that."

"This one is even worse . . . a woman, this time! She's asking for a divorce even though she'd moved her husband into a shed in the garden and brought the lodger into the marital bed. The judge threw out her petition for desertion and told her she'd done the deserting. Cheeky mare."

"The **chutzpah** of that one."

"Oh no . . . another gelignite robbery in London. A diamond mounter's in Mayfair, no sign of forced entry but blew open the safe and stole thirty thousand pounds, sixth attack by this gang in twelve months."

"I know where your mind's going, Violet. What would a gang like that want with the chickenfeed in our safe? It wouldn't even pay for dinner at the Savoy."

"Or a local outfit to get the same idea? You think gelignite is so hard to come by, so close to the war? There'll be stashes of it all across the country."

"Your mind is like a submarine, there's no depth of paranoia it can't reach."

Violet turns her head slowly to give her sister a contemptuous look. "And you're naïve, this world is only getting worse, you can either ignore it or do what you can to protect yourself."

"The last thing **I** am is naïve. I just choose not

to dwell on knife-wielding maniacs, jelly gangs and every imaginable catastrophe, but on happier things. Speaking of which . . . Purim!"

Grace's head flips up from her plate and she seems to reanimate after a long silence. "Mam, will you teach me how to line dance? And did you get the velvet for the skirt? Aunty Violet has already made me the crown."

"Not yet, I've been looking for purple but so far only found red or blue. Don't worry, I'll get it in time, and I've kept enough sugar back so that we can have three cakes at least, made with real eggs too, from Mrs. Llewellyn."

"You'll look better than the real Queen, I bet." Violet smiles.

"I hope so! Sarah is going as a queen too, and I want to look better than her."

The seaside postcard is peeling away from the side of the cabinet; the tape attaching it to the varnished rosewood has become yellow and desiccated. It is so familiar that she sees only its shapes and colours: the fat man and the thin girl, the bag spilling out gold coins, the speech bubble hanging between them. Her father had placed it there, tickled in some way by its casual contempt for men like him, pawnbrokers and moneylenders. She hated it, but to remove it was to also remove the fingerprint he had left imprisoned between the tape and the glossy blue card, and the sound of his laughter puffing out in spurts from his scarred lungs. These precious relics are necessary to remind her that the shop isn't a prison but a sanctuary, teeming with markers of her life and those of her family. She pulls a bolt of expensive white taffeta towards her, and remembers her father saying softly how much he'd like to cut into it for her wedding dress, but like her it had remained untouched, leaning against the wall with the other premium fabrics. She unwraps the cellophane packaging and examines its condition; the silk is slightly brittle and lighter at the edges, and has a smell of damp that has been absorbed from the walls, but no holes, thankfully. It was another one of her father's impulse buys, to satisfy his eye for beauty rather than to put money in the till. She rubs the fabric between her fingers and considers making Gracie's Purim dress from it; better than letting it all go to waste, she thinks. Their customers have no money for these fancy goods. She opens one of the tiny drawers in the haberdashery cabinet and finds mismatching glass beads, mother-of-pearl buttons, paillettes and ribbons. She could stitch a pretty, embellished bodice from cheap navy velour and then just use the taffeta for a full skirt. It would have made her father smile to see Grace dressed so lavishly, when he dressed in the same tweed trousers and waistcoat day in day out, and darned his long johns until they were a patchwork. They were not the type of people to treat themselves; only baby Diana had learnt the art of dressing well, a consequence of a childhood spent in hand-me-downs, no doubt. It's another six days until Purim, she will have enough time on the weekend to complete the dress and surprise her niece with a pair of enamel bangles.

A tram rattles along Bute Street and sends a small thud of air against the glass windows. One large pane is original Victorian glass that pitches a distorted reflection on the wall as the sun sets. The other pane had to be replaced in '47 when a soldier threw a brick into the shop, avenging, in his mind, two British soldiers who had been hanged by the Irgun in Palestine. The fool clearly not realizing that one of the soldiers was a Jew himself. It had been even worse for the Rosenbergs, in Manchester. The pubs had shut on that bank holiday due to a beer shortage, and some hooligans had used the pictures of the dead Tommies on the front of the newspapers as an excuse to tear up as many Jewish shops as they could find on Cheetham Hill. The shock of their own glass shattering that summer night remains with Violet; her nerves tuned up and jangling at any unexpected bang or crash. She hates closing time, when the street fills with male cries, the sound of bottles smashing and curses as fights break out between the sailors, dockers and trawlermen.

This patch of earth, reclaimed from marshland and still liquid, deep beneath the foundations, is all the sanctuary they have. The damp, however, crawling up all the buildings, nibbling at them, warns that they don't belong here either; that one day the sea will take back their home.

It never seems to stop raining and tonight it's heavier than usual, rivulets of it sloshing down on to the pavement from the sodden shop awning. She looks through the glass door and a taxi drives past, its windscreen wipers scraping back and forth; inside are a well-dressed couple, kissing passionately, eyes squeezed shut. She opens the door and stands in the fresh air for a moment; even in this weather a gang of Maltese sailors stand outside their lodging house, talking loudly. Down the street Mr. Zussen is leaning out of his pawnbroker's, peering worriedly at the overflowing drain in front of his shop. He looks like a character from the Bible, a long white beard hanging down to his navel, his tall, nervous, rumpless body seemingly centuries old, his hangdog face usually looking out impassively—decade in, decade out—from his glass service hatch. She loves him and all the characters she has grown up with, loves their solidity and earthiness. The wind picks up and blows, wet and cold, against her cheeks. Another day over, she whispers to herself, and then shuts the door.

Looking at her wristwatch, she sees the minute hand shiver towards 8 p.m., and just as she is about to lock the five locks, two young women in flashy make-up step in out of the rain.

"A devil of a night! And I've only gone and left my brolly at home. Can we pop in for a second, Miss Volacki?"

Violet recognizes them both. Café girls. All peroxide and rouge. "Oh, I shouldn't, not with the Closing Act and all, but quickly, come in, come in."

"Thanks, love," says Mary.

"What can I do you for?"

"Scarf, please, haven't gone to the trouble of setting my hair only to look like a wet dog when I get to the pub."

"It's a marvellous do," smiles Violet, looking at the peroxide halo around Mary's head. "Come and pick one you like."

While Mary tries different styles in the mirror, Margaret approaches the counter. "You know, Miss Volacki, I might as well pick up a pair of shoes for me eldest, it's like she sticks her feet in fertilizer every night."

"Leather?"

"Oh no, canvas ones will do her, I expect she'll be needing another pair before the month's out."

"They'll be towering over us soon enough," Mary says, chipping nail varnish from her fingers with a thumbnail.

"What size is she?"

"A one, I think, or a little less."

Violet's girdle pinches her stomach as she bends over the boxes she has pulled down from the shelf. She hadn't organized them, hadn't found time to, and so now must check through the randomly sized plimsolls. "I'm not seeing a size one, Margaret." Violet straightens her back with a loud sigh and climbs to her feet. "But I'm sure I've got some in, come back in the morning and we'll have found them for you."

Mary fixes her new headscarf around her face in the mirror and checks her teeth for lipstick before throwing a full-wattage smile at Violet. "I'll grab some grips and a box of matches while I'm at it," she says, handing over the coins.

"Alright, Miss Volacki, I'll bring her in the morning and we can try them on, there and then. Sorry to have been a bother," Margaret calls out.

"Don't be soft, it was no bother at all. Be careful you don't get soaked out there, girls."

"We'll be alright, just going down the pub to meet our fellas."

They pull the door open and the night steps in: the splash of tyre on wet tarmac, the stink of sesame oil and broiling meat from Sam On Wen's Chinese restaurant, the tinny clatter of calypso from a record player, the lean shadows hunkering near the bus stop.

"Night, Miss Volacki."

"Goodnight."

"How much coal did you put on the fire, Diana? It's like the tropics in here." Violet fans her face as she steps from the shop into the adjoining dining room.

"Put this foot out first and then let the other one follow, oops, try again . . ." Diana holds Grace's hands as she wobbles in her mother's high heels. "To get your balance you have to stand up straight, but don't lock your knees."

Hank Williams plays loudly on the wireless and the fire crackles as a red-hot coal disintegrates and hits the grate.

"I asked Mammy to teach me to line dance," Grace shouts over her shoulder as she trips over her mother's feet.

"Don't do yourself an injury, Gracie, there's plenty of time for you to be trotting around in all sorts of uncomfortable footwear." Violet squeezes past them to the kitchen and washes her hands.

"Gracie, let's stop to eat now." Diana lifts her daughter out of the T-bars and sits her on a chair at the head of the table.

"Is there any of that beef left over from yesterday?" Violet asks, wiping her hands on a tea towel.

"No, sorry, I put it all in G's sandwiches this morning."

"No bother, I'll manage with what we have." The table is a little sparse tonight but there is custard powder in the pantry and some pears in the fruit bowl.

As Violet sits down, the shop doorbell rings.

"Oh, leave it. It's ten past already. Let them come back in the morning." Diana sighs.

Violet hesitates for a moment but then rises. That bell and that shop have a hold on her that she can't resist. "It must be a regular. Let me just see who it is and what they want."

"Don't let your food get cold."

"I won't."

Grace leans dangerously back in her seat to watch as her aunt strides across the dimly lit shop and opens the locked front door directly ahead. Diana catches the chair just before it tips backwards. "Sit properly and eat your food."

They glance for a couple of seconds at the coloured man standing in the rain on the porch before Diana slams the dining-room door against the cold draught.

Afar

[Four]

"Missus, do you mind turning the music down?" asks a uniformed policeman panting at the dining-room door. He holds his black helmet close against his stomach and his eyelids flutter as he speaks.

"Turn off the wireless, Gracie. How can I help you? Is that burglar alarm playing up again?"

He looks confused. "No . . . there's been an incident. Your sister."

"What?" Diana looks past him and sees other men inside the shop. "Excuse me," she says, gently pushing him out of the way.

Grace kicks off the high heels and in her white ankle socks follows behind her mother.

"What is going on?" Diana looks from one unfamiliar face to another.

The men turn and seem to size her up. "Mrs. Tanay, my condolences. We've just arrived. She was discovered by this gentleman who was after a pack of cigarettes." The detective points to an ashen-faced old man in a flat cap.

The front door swings in the cold night air and it's only after Grace has walked around her mother towards the till that Diana notices the blood on the floor, seeping up the sides of Grace's frilly socks. "Stop!" shouts Diana.

She pulls Grace back and then marches around the corner to the north side of the shop. Violet lies face down, illuminated by the low light from a glass cabinet, blood sprayed up the white walls around her. "Violet, get up! What's happened, love?" Diana reaches down to rouse her sister, thinking she has hit her head and swooned, but as she brushes the hair away from her face she catches sight of the wide cut to her throat. She falls back on her heels and screams, "Who did this?"

The uniformed policeman pulls Diana up and asks her to take Grace back to the dining room. "Did you really not hear anything, Mrs. Tanay?"

"No! No!" Diana searches around frantically to

find Grace in the crowd, but she is still by the till counter, picking one foot up and then another to examine the red on her feet. "Don't look, baby, don't look!" She covers Grace's eyes but cannot help looking back herself, to the smear of hand- and kneeprints leading back to the alcove where the shoeboxes are kept, where Violet's own thick-soled shoes lie upturned.

Be careful, Gwilym, you're tramping through the blood you are. Time of death estimated between 20:05 and 20:15. First man on the scene goes by the name of Archibald. No, make that A.r.c.h.b.o.l.d. Came for a packet of cigarettes. Not a peep heard from the next room. Her sister is a bit deaf and there is a seal around the dining-room door to keep out the draught. Bloody forensics taking their time again. Ah, we've got the Detective Chief Inspector pulling up. Put an embargo on any ships that think they're leaving the docks tonight. Next of kin eating dinner through it all. Thinks she saw a black man on the doorstep just after eight. A few break-ins recently. No men in the house, you see. No shout, must have let him in. I only saw her a couple of days ago. May the Lord rest her soul.

. . .

HaShem! HaShem! Maggie, Maggie, look what they've done to our Violet. They've cut her throat. Where's Grace? Here, Diana, she is right here. There's too many bloody police in there. Why won't they let us see her? How did you not hear anything? Go upstairs and get brandy from the cabinet. On the right side. Drink this, Di, please. Stop rocking. Violet. Violet. Violet. Violet. Violet. Violet. Violet. Violet. You must come to stay with Daniel and me tonight. Never, never, never. How could this happen? God turned his back, didn't he?

There's a crowd outside rubbernecking, Chief. Push 'em back. The family saw some darkie in the porch just before it all happened. Visit all the coloured boarding houses. Stop any ships from leaving the port. They ain't half keening next door. It's their way. Have you got all the photos you need? She tried to get away, look at these smears. We got a real mean bastard on our hands. They'll want to bury her tomorrow, you know. Autopsy first. No real mystery though, is there, Chief? Great big slashes to the neck. Anything missing? Can't tell yet, but must be. The car is here from the mortuary.

. . .

Baruch dayan ha'emet. Patience, Diana, the Lord will console you. You really believe that? Grace, come here, sit on my lap. Your skin is so clammy, darling. Close your eyes and rest on me. I've called them all, they're all coming. Oh God. Rabbi Herzog is on his way from Rhymney. They'll drown me. I won't be able to keep them away. There's someone at the back door. It's the cantor, Joshua.

"May the Almighty comfort you among the mourners of Zion and Jerusalem."

"I can tell when a man be hypnotized."

"How, Doc?"

"You should know, Monday! Don't be a damn fool. You got obeah men in your country, de Gambia, don't you? Can't be just bongos and jungles."

A flash of annoyance lights up the Gambian's slanted eyes. He is the best-educated man in this house, having left his missionary school at sixteen, yet Doc won't stop talking down to him. He exhales and rubs the lumpy keloid scar on his neck where stray wiry hairs have grown inward, spiralling into his skin like miniature drills. Monday's head in the low light appears covered in a dense brown cap; the hairline trimmed into severe angles around his temples and neck, and broaching his forehead, until it stops abruptly a few centimetres above his unruly brows. "Me thought hypnotism were different. Something those geezers in white coats do."

"It don't need be. It can be a vaudeville ting or a white-coat-strap-you-down-and-make-you-confess ting, you see what I'm saying? It's a mighty powerful ting. When you under, you **under**."

"So, how can you tell, Doc?"

"De paper have it 'ere in white and black. 'Pallor, a moonstruck visage, enervated responses,' and I've seen men at sea who just about do any ting and after dey can't explain dem selfs for fudge and now dis Frankenstein doctor trying to bring it to de New Theatre." Doc Madison reaches over to the bedside table for his clutch of 8 p.m. tablets. His iron-post bed piled high with pillows and floral quilts has the look of an oriental throne, a still point of majesty and judiciousness, while his purple silk pyjamas just add to his regal air. He had left the merchant navy, bought this run-down terraced house in the street behind the prison, and then taken to his bed; brazenly flouting the white man's law by taking public assistance while renting out the rooms. Doc lives and sleeps in the front room with Jackie. The tenants joking that the two of them in bed must be like cadavers in a medical school: this is what a young heart looks like, this is what happens to an old sailor's liver, here is a plump healthy womb, and an ancient woebegone scrotum.

"What they tell him?"

"Take it someplace else! Dey ain't crazy."

"You could hypnotize a fella or lady into doing anything, handing over their pocketbook or the keys to their house, get into a girl's drawers without her saying her daddy kill her or asking how much you got. Mighty powerful."

"He think he a real tap-a-di-tap too, cos he a medical doctor to boot, but what doctor asks for money at door and want an interval? A shyster, dat who. Put another coal on de fire, bwoy, me feeling a chill with dis damn rain falling all night."

Monday shoves the poker through the orange embers and then takes a large cube of coal and tosses it towards the back of the grate.

The slam of the front door beside Doc's room shakes his thin sash windows and sends a fierce draught through the rotting wood of the Edwardian frames. The whole house is as sickly as its owner: creeping damp crawling up the peeling walls, the bowels of its plumbing congested and rumbling, the leaky and bandaged pipes exhaling gas.

"God damn him to hell! Why he need to thump de door so?"

Monday kisses his teeth contemptuously and squirms back into the spaces his muscles had pressed into the red velvet armchair, his body concealing its threadbare and skeletal parts. With footsteps on the bare pine of the hallway, both men look to the door with glares in their eyes.

As expected, the brass handle turns and Mahmood steps in, his black wool coat glossy and sequinned with rain, his homburg trickling droplets on to the only carpeted room in the house.

"Eh-eh, 'ere he come, like da Grim Reaper heself." Monday stares at Mahmood, from the fine hairs of his receding hairline down to the sabre points of his winkle-pickers.

"You gonna keep smashing my door till it break? You know how much it cost to replace door?"

"Relax yourself, Doc, that piece of wood ain't going nowhere." Mahmood's long strides cut through the room and he takes a seat on a small tweed sofa. He has to strain sometimes to understand Madison's strong Jamaican accent.

"Mind you don't get that cloth wet!"

Mahmood shoots a look at his landlord before removing his coat and placing it, inside out, on the armrest beside him. "You got the **Echo**?"

"You 'ave any luck today?" Doc asks as he throws the newspaper to him.

"A little." That is all he ever says to that question; he doesn't want any man's nose in a business so delicate as his **nasiib**.

"A little mean you can pay upfront for next week's rent."

"No, that would be if I win a lot." He moves slowly from page to page, looking at the pretty girls in the adverts, moving from the back page to the front as if it were an Arabic journal.

"That a new coat." It's a statement rather than a question as Monday's eyes turn from Mahmood to the coat. He puts the floral saucer in his hand to his mouth and slurps the over-spilt tea.

"It be old."

"I thought I saw you go out this morning in that little sports jacket of yours?"

"I changed."

"You be like Cinderella, all you need do is twirl around and you got a fresh suit of clothes on your back?" Doc chips in.

Mahmood smiles. "What you make of tomorrow's races?"

"Interesting horse at fourteen hours, sired by Old Tabasco, good Scotch jockey and all."

Mahmood scrolls down the list; he can't read much English, but he likes to pretend, and can recognize a few familiar names and all of the numbers.

"That rascal Rory Harte was in the paper again, on a drunk and disorderly charge," Doc rolls out all his crocodile teeth, "he tell de judge that he 'ad only wanted to push de boat out," he laughs through his nostrils, "and de mighty judge ask him, 'What's to stop you pushing it out again?' and you know what Harte tell him?" the laugh explodes out of his mouth and hits the walls, "de boat's sunk. **De. Boat's. Sunk.**"

All three men laugh at the docker's wisecrack.

"Man, it take an Irishman to say that to the judge!" Monday whinnies and chokes on his tea.

Collecting his coat, Mahmood uses the distraction to leave the room before Doc starts on again about the rent, or the door, or the coal that doesn't walk in by itself off the street, or the milk splattered on the kitchen table.

In his bare bedroom, Mahmood strips off his pinstripe suit, before manipulating jacket and trousers on to a misshapen wire hanger. His fine socks are wet at the toes and heels but he keeps them on in dread of the cold bed, which always seems to have been doused in ice water. He had tried to meet that Russian woman earlier, the raven-haired thief who had caught his eye in the Bucket o' Blood pub. She is older than him, wiser and meaner, and there is a dangerous chemistry between them. He had promised himself he wouldn't see her again but then he'd ended up at her red door. She wasn't home anyway; probably out courting some other fool. He needs to just cut it off and make sure that Laura never hears about her.

Taking a deep breath, he dives under the woollen blankets, his sinuous arms and legs shivering as the cotton sheet tries to steal what little body heat he has. He pitches around in the bed, trying to get his blood going, but the cold is stronger than him. Punching his musty ancient pillow into a decent shape, Mahmood is startled by a loud **rat-tat-tat-tat** on the front door.

Too late for anything good, too insolent for anyone but the police.

Monday's heavy steps and then the creak of the door.

"Hello, hello, apologies . . ."

"Inspector! Please, please."

They haven't got anything on me, can't have, thinks Mahmood. It must be something to do with that new Jamaican upstairs—Lloyd, or whatever his name is—calls himself a boxer but never trains or competes, just upstairs blowing reefer smoke out the window.

Doc has put his outside voice on, Mahmood hears him clearly through the wall.

"Detective Lavery! What brings you out on dis malignant night? I try my hardest to keep a steadfast, Christian establishment and I'm aggrieved, truly aggrieved, dat any of mine would be the locus of your suspicions."

"Nothing to unduly worry you, Mr. Madison, yours is not the only lodging house we'll be attending tonight. Are all of your tenants at home?" Lavery has a strong Welsh accent and together their voices are those of a lord and his gamekeeper on a radio comedy.

"I should think so, Detective, but we have a new man upstairs and he is the kind to keep he-self, pardon me, himself to himself."

"We'll need to speak to everyone, Mr. Madison."

"He in, he in," Monday reassures.

"Let's start at Mattan's."

They are on him before Mahmood has even had a chance to put his trousers on. "Who is it?" he yells.

"Police." They ambush him in his drawers and vest. Familiar faces. Morris and Lavery.

"What do you want?" Mahmood stands square in front of the pair of them.

"Where have you been this evening?" Lavery asks, while Morris runs his eyes over everything, his fingers already on Mahmood's coat.

"To the Central."

"What pictures did you see?"

"Korean War and cowboys."

"What time did you leave the Central?"

"Half past seven." Turning to Morris, Mahmood says sharply, "You got a warrant?"

Morris ignores him and carries on searching through the pockets of the overcoat.

"Which way did you come home?"

"Past the baths."

"You alone at the cinema? See anyone you know?"

"Yes. No."

"Have you been down Bute Street this evening?"

"No."

"You carry a knife, Mattan?"

"No."

"We are going to search your room, Mattan."

"What for?"

Morris pats the pockets of a jacket on the back of the chair and finds a broken razor.

"I used to shave with it. It broke a long time ago."

"You have another razor?"

Mahmood points to the dresser.

Lavery removes the safety razor from a drawer and examines the blade. He puts it back without comment.

"You have any money?"

"No."

Morris holds out the few silver and bronze coins he's found in the coat.

"Where did you go after the cinema?"

"I come straight home." Mahmood tenses up as Lavery and Morris paw through everything. "What are you looking for? Why you come to my room? You have no warrant."

"Don't get cheeky, we don't need a warrant, there's been a serious incident in Bute Street tonight and a coloured man is believed responsible."

Mahmood scoffs. "Why a coloured man?"

"You need to tell us the truth as to where you've been tonight, Mattan, this is more serious than your shoplifting."

"I don't talk to you." Mahmood grabs his trousers, swirls the fabric straight and then rushes his legs inside.

"A woman has been killed." Lavery looks him in the eye.

"You lie. All police are liars."

"You better watch your loose tongue. I'm asking you again, where were you tonight?"

"I don't tell you anything."

Morris touches both pairs of shoes near the bed and rubs his fingers to feel for moisture.

"If you hear anything, you come down to the station and talk to us, understood?"

Mahmood stands guard near his door until they leave and then sits heavily on the bed. The calm of the night wrecked. What woman murdered? No end to the lies they tell to make a black man's life hard.

Hearing a commotion, he ventures back to the door and slips his head out. The upstairs Jamaican is wrestling with a uniformed policeman and getting the better of him. Lavery and Morris come hammering down the steps and enter the fray. Turning to Monday, who stands dumbstruck in the hallway, Mahmood shrugs and closes his door against the chaos.

Somerton Park greyhound stadium. Newport. Mahmood kisses the betting slips in his right hand and goes to the window of the tote to collect his winnings. The pound notes slam down one after the other until there are twenty of them between him and the teller in his flat cap. Ten weeks of wages sitting there, fat and easy, the edges crisp enough to cut your fingers. Enough for rent, Laura and the children, and his keeping for a little while; the wad is so thick he has to cram it into his starved pocketbook.

"Looks like you've had a good day, Sam," says the pipe-smoking man dealing out his winnings.

"Sam? My name ain't Sam."

"I call all you boys Sam."

"All you boys. What you mean by that? You think you funny calling us Sambo? I'll break your skull." Mahmood slaps the counter and the man jumps back in fright.

"I didn't intend any offence," he says, holding up his hands.

"You bite first and then you want to cry. Always." He shakes his head and then throws the coins into his trouser pocket and looks back to the track. Another race is about to start, new dogs lined up at the gates, steam streaming from their panting mouths, and he feels the excitement all over again, the anticipation somehow more intoxicating than the victory. No, no, don't be a fool, he tells himself, wills his feet to keep moving, and soon enough he's back on the empty road, heading for the bus stop.

On the 73 to the Royal Infirmary, he passes through Cardiff city centre, looking out the grimy window as if at the pictures; totally insulated from the war-beaten and monochrome misery. Its patched-up spires, wooden handcarts, haggard chickens and bloodied rabbits hanging from butchers' windows, mothers pushing baby carriages with fierce abandon, the broad ivory dome of the town hall blackened with soot, shop fronts drooping loose letters like earrings, teahouses with tuppence specials on buttered bread and a cuppa, boarded windows, fenced-off bombsites. It's a difficult place without money in your pocket; he'd be happy if they tore the whole place down like the council wants to do to the docks. He doesn't know how they can look down on Butetown with so little to show for themselves. The Bay emerges out of the industrial fog and sea mist like an ancient fossilized animal stepping out of the water. You might walk along the docks and find sailors carrying parrots or little monkeys in makeshift jackets to sell or keep as souvenirs, you can have chop suey for lunch and Yemeni **saltah** for dinner, even in London you won't find the pretty girls—with a grandparent from each continent—that you just stumble into in Tiger Bay.

The other Cardiff to him means that circuit between factory, home and pub that feels as leaden as the perambulations of a workhorse. He can't, no, won't be broken into that. Getting cheated by a pound every week by some crook that thinks you should be grateful for any kinda work at all. Sweeping, cleaning, not getting anywhere near the machines because then they'll have to pay you a man's wage. The shame of the canteens, men touching you like a slave on an auction block and asking if you're black cos you came out of your mother's arsehole, laughter sickening into a swell that brings bile to his throat. The pink corned beef and boiled potatoes served with a side of "an Englishmen, an Irishmen and a nigger walk into a bar." The white men unhappy, bitter, frustrated of their own accord but treating you like you're the final insult. He isn't like the other Somalis, who once slept out with the camels and have only known life to be a bed of thorns and rocks. No. He had always slept in comfort as a boy, on an Indian mattress, with a cup of sugared milk ready for him in the morning, and his mother pouring lines of her own poetry into his ear, praising him. He can't feel their gratitude. Take the 2s 5d with a nod and a smile though his back is breaking, his nostrils choked with dust, his knuckles stiff and bleeding. White men are nothing special to him, he has known them from a young age, dropping off canvas bags of sugar and tea at the colonial club in Hargeisa and collecting tennis balls on their drought-desiccated court. He can look them in the eye and talk back but it is still hard. Hard.

"You get outta my house."

"What you talking about, Doc?"

"I ain't 'bout to start no debate wid you, you 'ave a fortnight to pack your belongings and find other lodging."

Monday sits on the armchair, smirking.

"You know what me just about to do, man? Pay you upfront for the next eight weeks. Pay good money for your damp fucking room."

"Damp? It good enough for everyone else, what make you tink you so high and mighty? You bring trouble to me door from de minute you come. How many time de police knock looking for you?" Doc kisses his teeth in disgust. "You lifting my blood pressure, bwoy, you got your notice, now leave me in peace."

"It not **me** they were looking for last night," Mahmood says, peeling off notes from his stack to cover the next two weeks before he throws them on to the bedside table.

"And de other times?" Doc snaps.

Mahmood shrugs and stalks out of the room.

He passes Doc's girlfriend in the kitchen as he heads to the toilet in the yard. "What rattled his cage?"

She's elbow deep in flour, kneading bread, her flower-printed dress straining at the biceps and her thick eyebrows dusted white. She is a tall, broad gal, the way the old-timers like 'em, as simple and maternal as a cow. She was in the papers last year, he'd heard, because Doc went to sea and left too little housekeeping to tide her over, and so in his absence she'd sold his furniture and lived it up. Doc had taken her straight to the police station on his return and pressed charges, but somehow they were still together.

"A man came round from the council to inspect the property this morning, now he thinks you reported him. Did you?" Her eyes are bright and innocent-seeming.

"Why would I?"

"That's what I told him, but you know what he's like when he's got a notion buzzing round his head. You hear about poor Violet Volacki? Murdered last night in her shop by a coloured."

"That her name? They took away the Jamaican last night, he the man?"

"Don't look like it, he's upstairs snoring away, they found the mari-je-wana in his room, that's what got him in trouble."

"Stupid man." Mahmood spits, he hates dope-heads, hates their laziness, their sleepiness, their refusal to understand this world needs all the alertness and force you can muster.

"Must have been a tussle, she was a sturdy little thing and lived on the docks all her life, doubt she would have been a pushover." She slams the dough on to the table.

"He probably just got her from behind like this." Mahmood wraps his arm loosely around her neck, smelling the sweet sweat and lavender water rising from her café au lait skin.

"Stop it!" She giggles awkwardly and squirms in his grip.

He doesn't see the grimace on her face, so continues. "Then all he have to do is take a razor and cut her throat like this . . ." He strokes two dark, tapered fingers across her rigid neck and releases his grip, gliding back on the linoleum to restore the distance between them.

Her eyes are wide, shoulders frozen high, startled by his touch and worried that Monday or Doc might enter and misconstrue the scene. "Ah, get away with you! You made me jump."

"No need to fear." He smiles and holds her gaze for a second too long, just enough to communicate that he is lithe and smoky-eyed and half Doc's age.

It is a rare day when Mahmood catches any sunlight, so nocturnal has his life become. Some nights he arrives at his makeshift home at 4 or 5 a.m., finding more amusement in the night than he does in the day. Lacing up his shoes, he swears he will leave Billa Khan's by midnight, or 1 a.m. at the latest, and head to the Labour Exchange in the morning. It's been months since he's had a decent job; the last was at the airfield where he worked as a caretaker, a good, clean job. From blue sea to blue sky, that's how he's travelled, drawn again and again to these machines that make the world seem so small and navigable. He'd kept the job for months, turning up on time and keeping his mouth shut, but somehow it had still fallen through his fingers.

Adjusting his homburg hat—the hat his mother-in-law says reminds her of funerals—low over his eyebrows, Mahmood realizes that there are too many people he doesn't want to see on the street: the Nigerian watchmaker chasing after a watch he'd snuck out of his pocket, the lanky Jewish pawnbroker who had taken in his bedclothes when he'd had nothing else to pawn, that Russian woman from one of the cafés who he both wants to see and dreads seeing. He takes a deep breath and steps out.

The A-boards outside the newsagents are still plastered with photographs from London: the flag at Buckingham Palace at half mast, Churchill in his stovepipe hat paying his respects, the new-minted Queen in the back seat of a car with her eyes fixed ahead. The King's death is turning into a Hollywood production when everyone knows he was a weak man, pampered from birth, unmanned by wealth and too much ease.

He jumps over the low brick wall surrounding Loudoun Square and cuts across the scrappy grass, the trees hung with swing ropes by children, who have also left behind sweet wrappers and chalk marks on the stone path. Mahmood squints ahead, at a heavy shape between the tree trunks, and softens his footsteps. He approaches and finds a man sunk into the bench, his head downturned in sleep, with a greasy paper bag clenched in one of his grey-knuckled hands. The face frozen between scarf and woolly hat is middle-aged and West African, lost to the world. Mahmood stands over him, watching. He's not homeless, his clothes and boots are in too good a condition, but why is he out here in the cold with his coat pockets gaping? A worker. Exhausted. Dormant between shifts. "Leave him," orders a voice inside Mahmood's skull, "leave this motherless child." Mahmood turns and continues on to Bute Street.

This spot beneath his feet, on the corner of Angelina Street, always catches his attention. This gambling corner is where Khaireh raised a gun to the back of Shay's bald head and spilt his brains all over Berlin's shoes. At that exact moment, Mahmood had been waiting outside the Paramount Club in London for a blonde who had stood him up; he'd waited two hours, thinking he must have got the time wrong, but the traffic lights flashing on the wet road were all the company he had that night. He should have been here, could have witnessed something he had only ever seen in films—pure, blind, bloody vengeance. Shay was a difficult man, had been warned too many times already about taking the savings lodgers left with him, but no one could have known that Khaireh was **that** kind of man. To do it in public like that, with a gun and with all those witnesses! It took some balls. He was willing to hang for the sake of his pride. Berlin said afterwards that his legs had almost given way beneath him from the shock, that he'd cradled his dearest friend's head in his lap as the life left him, that he'd had to wipe that white curdled mess of memories and thoughts from his shoes, that all the street gamblers around him had whispered **al-Fatiha** as he closed Shay's eyelids.

Mahmood raps his cold knuckles against the glass panel, once, twice, three times, rain spitting down as Billa Khan waddles slowly downstairs. He can't be seen outside this illegal poker club when he's on probation, so he punches the glass irritably just as Billa Khan swings the door open.

"**Masla kya hai?**" Billa Khan pushes a flop of his heavy, oily hair from his eyes and glares up at Mahmood.

Mahmood barks back in Hindi. "**Janam mein yeh kaam khatam hoga ya nahin.**"

He waves him in. "**Jaldee karo, bhai.**"

Another seaman who has stopped going to sea, Billa Khan runs poker nights in his rented room and earns a living that way, taking a pound from each player. He refuses to speak English, so they communicate in the Hindi Mahmood picked up in Aden. Mahmood closes the front door and silently follows the Indian's wide rear up the stairs. Khan's bowling-pin-shaped body always amuses him; his fashion of wearing trousers hitched up to near his nipples just exaggerating his narrow shoulders and feminine hips.

The fire spits, cigarette smoke gathers thickly under the fringed lampshade hanging from the ceiling, and Mohammed Rafi croons a Hindi playback song from the small record player. This is Mahmood's chosen world and it's enough to bring a smile to his face. He cases the room. Six men, two big money players: next door's Jewish landlord and the Chinese laundryman. He nods and they nod back.

"They have given us her back. We have her back."

Her skin cold, her lips grey, that wide slash around her neck turned a dull, wrinkled pink and half hidden under a high collar. The coffin Diana has picked out for Violet is a deep walnut with a fine layer of cream silk inside. It looks almost bridal; the quilted silk embossed with flowers along the trim. She had never wanted nice things for herself, always too practical, had worn black widow weeds despite never having had a husband to lose, but now she'll be carried to her grave in an ostentatious box that has no purpose but to rot with her. The men wanted everything to be kosher, for Violet to be wrapped in a plain white sheet, but she went out and bought the coffin alone. The house is covered in lilies, blaring scent from every vase, jug and mug that could be mustered. Violet, however, had always hated their cloying smell and the orange pollen that dusted and stained all of her French linen tablecloths. Old friends who had refused to ever cross the bridge into Butetown have come in large defensive convoys under their umbrellas; bearing dainty bouquets and dishes wrapped in old rags. Violet's murder—those two words seeming so bizarre and ill-fitting still—proving right all the fears they harboured of the Bay, yet somehow emboldening them to come see the terrible place for themselves. The housewives of Canton, Penarth, Ebbw Vale, St. Mellons all coming to gasp at the street gamblers, half-caste children and tumbledown bars with tumbledown women chatting outside. The broad windows of the Volacki shop blinded with black crêpe, the "**Closed**" sign turned permanently to the world, the Maltese lodging house and Cairo Café, on either side of it, trying to keep the noise and music to a mournful level. Diana could easily drench the whole thing in petrol and torch it: the shop, the house, the street, the city, the world. Why did it deserve to stand? When a harmless woman who had only ever worked and tried to look after her own was slaughtered like an animal in an abattoir. Bleeding to death while her family cut their roast potatoes and asked for the salt in the next room. Why hadn't she gone to check on Violet when she'd seen that man on the doorstep? He wasn't someone she recognized but it's hard to tell a face, especially a dark one, at night under a hat, isn't it? She should have left that damned dining-room door open so she could have **seen** or at least **heard** what was going on. Not closed it like a fool. What kind of people was she living amongst if he could do that, knowing how close they were? Fearless, merciless, brazen. Violet was right to be afraid. Diana grinds her jaw as she washes plates and cutlery at the trench-like Belfast sink. She is rough with the cloth, and the tines of the forks stab into her skin. There is an immense storm of violence brewing in her, sometimes thinning into mist but other times gathering into a dark, lightless mass that chokes her lungs. She could kill someone in that mood, take a little butter knife and plunge it deep into the eye of the next man she sees; only men are the targets of her rage in these lightning-quick fantasies, big, hulking men who need cutting down.

Inside the toy store, the thick furry bear hangs limp from a large hook on the wall, a red spotted bow tie tight around its neck. Mahmood lifts the chin and sees two yellow marble eyes and a flat smile stitched into the muzzle. It is more than three feet tall, including the immense head with its little boater hat perched between the ears. He wraps his arms around it and lifts it free, his face engulfed in the softness of the fine fur, the bear so well made he almost expects to hear a heart beating inside it. The price is extortionate but it's been too long since he bought the boys something, and it's the little Eid in a couple of days. Their mother will probably say that they need new shoes or cots instead but he can't resist buying them the kind of fripperies he never had as a child: train sets, toy soldiers, drum kits, wind-up monkeys with clashing cymbals. The boys will love the bear, he's sure, clambering over it the same way they do him. Laura will be satisfied by the navy trench coat that he's hidden in the canvas bag hanging over his shoulder. It is a double-breasted, double-seamed, satin-lined coat with a nice thick belt to cinch in her trim waist. He had slipped it into the bag, unseen by the half-blind proprietor of A. & F. Griffin. It's a magic trick that he has perfected under even better scrutiny. The timing, technique and departure all as important as each other, the tiniest hesitation or fumbling and it was all over, the moment lost, or the coppers on your back.

He is not sure the coat will fit Laura's small island of a body. After their marriage he had explored her as inquisitively as Ibn Battuta, her green veins showing through her mottled skin as clearly as branching rivers and streams. Her breasts firm and goose pimpled under his hard grip. Truth be told, he had hurt her that first time, a mistake caused by forgetting what it was like with a virgin, but also because he had been an angrier man then; he was using her body to avenge himself of every laugh, "nigger" and slammed door. Driving himself into her without being able to meet her unblinking eyes. Just before meeting Laura, he'd docked in America, in New Orleans, where even black and white shit had to be separated, and where any white woman could make you carry her bags, or have you killed for catching her eye.

Things had changed when he had come back from sea and felt the thump of his child inside Laura; first, irrational panic that this white body contained something so precious to him, that his sixteen-generation **abtiris** would be passed down to a child mingled with the blood of Welsh miners and Irish refugees. The heaving as the baby turned somersaults and thrashed like a sea creature beneath her taut hot skin amazed him. Then it became his haven, her body, somewhere private and sanctified that allowed the stresses and humiliations of the day to fall away. Her scars, smells and private parts becoming as familiar to him as his own until she complained that she wanted to be left alone, that she was sore and constantly pregnant and wanted a break from it.

They could only find black-walled, squalid places to rent as a mixed couple in Cardiff, and had no chance at a council house, so they had decided to start afresh. They moved to Hull to live together properly, as a family, until one day, home from a shift at the steelworks, he came back to an empty house. Boom! She had packed up a suitcase and returned to Cardiff with the boys. First complaining that she couldn't stand living with her family and then running back, crying, saying she was lonely without them. Just like that, Laura had pulled her body away from him, had deported him from it, and slowly all they had to talk about was the children, or money, or what her mother or father had said. Laura no longer the teenager who had so easily told her parents no but now a woman who seemed to delight in telling **him** no. No, no, no to everything. Awake in his cold bed at Doc's place, hearing her voice telling him no, no, no: to getting back together, to trying for a girl, to moving to London. He can't accept the possibility that another man might one day be pawing at her, filling her with his seed, desecrating his temple. Everyone laughing at her, saying she's too stretched out for a decent white man; and her moving from black man to black man, like they do, growing slack and pliant. Falling for someone who might beat her or pimp her out. Using black men like knives to hurt herself with, like some end-of-the-line white girls did, proof of how far they had fallen from redemption. No, she isn't that type, he reminds himself; if anything, she is the blade that he has cut himself on. They need to stay married to keep her respectable; those old heifers on Davis Street can only say so much while they are properly wedded. But if she slides they **will** finish her.

Mahmood had known before Laura that their marriage was a kind of death for her, and he understood that she needed time to grieve. He had swallowed his pride and let her name their firstborn son after her favourite brother, who had moved out of the house in disgust at their marriage. Now, he can see that she is growing alert to status and all its tiny degrees: she keeps the boys away from the Qur'anic school, uses their Welsh names, wants them baptized and raised just like their cousins. She is retracing the steps they had taken together. He had arrived at their house not long ago, and found his boys sat around the table, eating boiled pig's trotters. Almost retching at the slick oil on his sons' lips, he'd got so angry that he'd just picked up their plates and thrown them into the backyard, **akhas**!

Mahmood had also blown his top another time, when he had told her mother that he would kill her dead if he saw her with another man. Laura had heard him from the landing upstairs and bellowed a stream of cuss words at his departing back. Course, he didn't mean it, she would know that, but love can drive a man to madness. This place, too, had a way of making you demented. Look at that poor Sikh bastard, Ajit Singh, waiting for the hangman in his cell at Cardiff jail. Go stir-crazy after a white girl threw him over, so he shoots her outside a hospital in Bridgend with a thousand witnesses to hand the black cap to the judge. A damned foolish end to a life.

Diana watches from the bus stop outside the shop as the main Eid al-Adha procession troops down from the canal all the way round Loudoun Square and ends at the **zawiya** on Peel Street, while Sheikh Hassan's competing but smaller group dawdle up from the docks. Children dressed in Yemeni **thobes** and headdresses, with tin discs and red embroidery on the bodices, lead the adults in song and step. Even Christian, Buddhist and Jewish children have joined their friends, dressed in nativity costumes of Mary blue and shepherd check, miming the verses of the Arabic **nasheeds** and raising their voices at the choruses, "**Ya Allah, Ya Allah, Ya Allah kareem.**" A **darbouka** keeps the beat and is added to by the pounding footsteps of hundreds of celebrants. Up front is Ali Salaiman, proprietor of the Cairo Café, holding one side of a navy banner stitched with Holy Scripture by Cardiff's convert wives. His own wife, Olive, stands outside their café handing out meat **sambusas** and paper cups of Vimto cordial. Aproned matrons, flat-capped gamblers, ruined rummies, yapping dogs, fresh-faced bar girls and leather-jacketed teenage delinquents watch from the pavement and wave out of windows. A few tatty Union Jacks, left over from VE-Day celebrations, flap about. The giddy children delight in what they call Muslim Christmas and take cellophane bags of boiled sweets and gobstoppers greedily, without knowing or caring what the day commemorates. The story she knows well enough from the Torah: sacrifice of a child as small and innocent as them. Isaac's throat reddened by the blade but miraculously not cut; his silence in Abraham's arms as, weeping but steadfast, the prophet obeyed God's command; the ram then sent down at the last moment to replace Isaac and deliver God's mercy. Both the trial and deliverance celebrated. Diana knows the Muslims tell it a little differently.

The stumpy dome of Noor ul Islam **zawiya** comes at the end of a row of brick chimneys on a plain grey terrace on Peel Street. The original mosque had been destroyed in the Cardiff blitz of '41, Mahmood had heard, and this stark white building with its pointed-arch windows had replaced it; the black paint along its edges giving it the look of a child's pencil drawing. The voices of boys in prayer caps and turbans chanting religious verses in lilting Welsh accents stream out of the window, the one-legged Yemeni teacher holding a cane to the blackboard, the wall behind him covered in medallions of hand-painted Islamic calligraphy and leather-bound **kitabs**. Mahmood wipes his feet before entering and then takes his shoes off in the small vestibule leading to the prayer hall. The **qibla** glows with neon Arabic letters along the niche's crest. It's sometime between '**asr** and **maghrib** prayers and the hall is empty apart from one old soul clicking his **tusbah** beads, his yellowed soles tucked under him and his slouched spine heaving to the right. The names of Allah come in whispered fragments from him: The Witness, The Friend, The Evolver, The First, The Last.

Along the stairs, worshippers' footsteps have already worn away the dark varnish to reveal the pale whorled pine of each steep step. Mahmood skips up them, his keys jingling in his pocket as he leaps over two at once. He stops at the first floor where there is a meeting room decked in Persian rugs and low Arab cushions. He sees their legs first, socked feet splayed out before them, as a silver samovar steams to a boil, fogging up the bare window. Their cheeks bulge with **qat**, brought over frozen from Aden so that it is now dry and acrid—still chewed, however, for the sake of custom if not pleasure.

"**Ya salam!** Look who has returned," says the mosque caretaker, Yaqub.

"**Assalamu alaikum, kef haq?**" Mahmood spreads a wide smile over his face. "Getting an early start on the chewing today?"

There is a delay before anyone responds. "Liverpool docks on strike so no work today." It is Ibn Abdullah, the one-time alcoholic who now has a dark callus on his forehead from pressing it so often against a prayer mat.

"You have no shame, Ibn Mattan? You come back to the scene of your crime." It's Yaqub again; he rises to his feet and blocks Mahmood's view of the suitcases and steamer trunks lining the far wall. They are preparing for a **hajj** to Aden, the luggage full of "charity": nylon shirts, cotton underpants and bras, boxes of penicillin and aspirin, baby milk powder, English dictionaries and children's textbooks. Mahmood wonders how much of it will reach the poor that it is intended for and how much will be gifted to their families. Yaqub follows his eyes to the suitcases and recites a **hadith** cursing thieves to the lowest **cadaab**.

"It was a loan."

The Yemenis laugh. "**Kebir, oh kebir, ya Iblis!**"

"And I always pay my debts." Mahmood reaches for his pocket.

"You need to be careful, Mahmood, the devil on your left shoulder will soon collapse from exhaustion writing all the trouble you get into, have mercy on him."

"Well, let him strike off this one thing at least," he raises the cash in his hand over his head, "you all see this?" then he slaps it hard into Yaqub's palm, "I've put in a little more for my donation." Mahmood strikes a pose in the middle of the circle, chest out, chin up and mock salutes the portrait of Imam Ahmad bin Yahya over the fireplace. It's so poorly executed that the bulging-eyed, drug-addled, minuscule King of Yemen looks more goblin than the **jinn** he is reputed to be; the **jinn** who has escaped untold assassination attempts by jealous relatives, republicans and fanatics.

Stepping out into the cold air, Mahmood's conscience is lighter but so is his wallet, noticeably so, worryingly so. This is what always happens. A big win that haemorrhages into nothing overnight. There is a strong smell of incense on his jacket that he hadn't noticed inside the mosque. His mother had always said it was a sign of evil not to enjoy the sacred smell of **oonsi** but it remains a headache-inducing odour to him.

. . .

It felt ridiculous lugging the teddy bear down the narrow street, the small distance between numbers 9 and 42 Davis Street punctuated by twitching curtains and urgently slammed doors. The atmosphere of Adamsdown is cooler and meaner than that of Butetown, with the few black and brown residents corralled into a handful of run-down boarding houses. It is where Irish dockworkers, hunchbacked deliverymen and sleep-deprived factory workers live with their families, in brown-brick terraced houses bought with council loans and paid off within fifteen brutal years, the spectre of compulsory purchase and demolition hanging suspended somewhere over the sea. So far, the only objectionable thing that the sea had actually blown in was the foreign seamen. It always tickled Mahmood that Laura's mother, Fanny, had told his wife as a young teenager to cross the street if a foreign man ever tried to talk to her, and when Laura asked what she should do if he followed, the answer was to scream. No one screams at the sight of him but they are generous with muttered insults, evil stares, laughs, dishwater splashed in his direction by the women, and pebbles thrown by their young sons. He lives here because Laura lives here, with her parents and youngest siblings, in a house hit by shrapnel from a German bomb during the blitz, which left behind a leaking roof and a spiderweb-cracked bathroom window. Mahmood knocks the brass knocker of the blue door and gathers the bear and bag up in his arms. The sound of David's small feet pounding up the hallway quickens his breath.

"Mammy, Mammy! Daddy's at the door!" he shouts out, pressing his nose up to the frosted glass and leaving a wet smear.

Mahmood laughs at the sound of his son's voice and every tight, gnarled sinew of his body slackens, the constriction of his lungs only perceptible now that it has lifted.

"Wait for me," he hears Laura call out, but David is grabbing for the door, stretching his body on tippy toes and struggling with the lock.

At last, he's managed it and Mahmood is both proud and afraid.

"Daddy!" David trills, overcome and wriggling as his dad lifts him up with one arm.

"**Aabbo**," Mahmood corrects in Somali, "call me **aabbo**," but the words fail, just the nuzzle and smell of him is everything.

"Bear mine?" he asks, pawing at the huge stuffed toy.

"For you and your brothers, yes."

"No, mine!"

Mahmood places David back on the floor and gives him the bear to hold but it's too big, he loses his balance and sinks under it, as if assaulted, but happily so.

"Where am I meant to put **that**?" Laura steps out of the front room, cradling Mervyn to her bare breast.

"Anywhere you want, my girl." Mahmood smiles.

She rolls her eyes and pads back in a pair of men's woollen socks to the settee. "Shush, Omar's sleeping upstairs."

Mahmood follows her, helping David carry the bear as its head drags on the floor.

The fire's burning but she's there alone, with a mug of tea and the newspaper balanced on the settee's wooden arm. "Where are your parents?"

"Bingo. The water's just boiled, go and get yourself a mug if you want." She looks gaunt and fatigued, her wristwatch loose and restlessly circling her fine bones.

"I haven't come for no tea." Mahmood swings the canvas bag in his hand so that it falls at her feet.

"What's that?"

"Look yourself."

Pulling the groggy baby away from her breast, she languidly tugs her brassiere back into place, the large raspberry-like nipple receding slowly from his view. She rests the baby's head on a cushion and sighs before bending over and opening the bag.

He watches every small muscle of her face for a reaction; imagining that he can see the pupils of her large translucent eyes expanding and contracting as she looks the coat up and down. She strokes her hand over the fabric and flips open the satin lining. Small appreciative sounds escape her lips but nothing coherent or unambiguously grateful.

"It's nice," she says finally.

"It's **real** nice," he corrects.

Folding the coat up in her lap, Laura turns to her estranged husband and asks, "Where did you get it from? It looks and smells brand new."

"A shop up in the town, I paid good money for it, got lucky at horses, at the races," he fumbles.

Laura has perfected a glance when it comes to Mahmood that signifies scepticism, amusement and a "let's leave it there" finality.

"I can't accept this, Moody."

"Who says you can't? God? The King?" He paces the carpet in front of the fire. "You get given a present, you can't give it back."

"I can't be encouraging you . . . please! Just sit down, you're giving me a headache!"

David looks up from the teddy bear he's been wrestling with and his eyes flicker back and forth between them, afraid there is going to be another row.

Mahmood sits in her father's high-backed, uncomfortable armchair and closes his eyes for a second, defusing his rising temper. He opens his eyes and lets them rest on the wallpaper, patterned with tendrils of lilac leaves that seem to float.

"I cannot believe you stole from the **zawiya**," she says softly, carefully, bitterly.

"I had to," he says, resting his temple between thumb and forefinger.

"What kind of a devil of a reason is that? You had to?"

"I had to pay your maintenance, didn't I? You think the court just writes it down for a laugh?"

"You have missed too many of those payments for me to buy that excuse."

David snuggles up between his father's legs and sucks the knuckles of his right hand, his foot scratching nervously at his calf; his eyes are anxious and beseeching.

"I was broke. One hundred per cent skint. Will you accept that?"

"I will because it's the truth." Laura smiles, part victory, part love. "I could write a book about being skint, Moody, it's nothing new to me, I don't let it get under my skin. But stealing, I've sat too long in Sunday school to think **that's** alright."

"Well, I never went to Sunday school but I went and sat with the **macalim** under a tree on Fridays and he told me that thieves' hands should be cut off. Real life teaches us something else."

Their voices are still soft and it's a relief to both of them that the tension has quietly dissolved. Mahmood runs his long fingers through his son's curly brown hair, massaging the scalp. David's whole skull fits neatly within the span of his own large hand.

"You are your father's boy, ain't you, David?"

David smiles in contentment.

"I paid them back, you know, the **zawiya**, gave them more than I took."

"That doesn't surprise me, Moody, that's the kind of man you were when I married you."

"I've never changed."

"Oh, yes, you have."

"All of it was always inside me."

"Hmm, that's probably true, but who wants to search out every last thing hidden within them? Certainly not me. There's some things you keep the door closed on."

"That's women's talk, men have to go out in the world and see what it does to them, you can't sit at home like a virgin."

"Go under that canal bridge and you'll find enough women with that very same attitude."

"Even you, Laura . . ."

She baulks at the suggestion.

"No, no, that ain't how I meant it." Mahmood kisses his teeth. "I meant . . . you were told that marrying someone like me was the worst a girl could do—worse than stealing, by miles—and yet, you did it, didn't you? Your brother stopped talking to you."

"I was a fool for love." She smiles.

"No, not a fool . . ." Mahmood rises from the armchair and lifts David into it. He crosses the rug and kneels beneath Laura, taking her warm hands in his own. "You are the best thing God ever gave me, you and these three boys. I would steal the stars out of the sky for you."

"Don't get soppy on me now." Laura blushes and tries to slip her red, eczema-wrinkled hands from his grip but he holds on.

"It's true, I swear on my life."

"So change, then. Mahmood, change! Don't be so soft in the head. Get rid of this jacket—and that infernal bear too, if you managed to pinch him an' all—and just give it a break, for Christ's sake."

"The bear's legit, he's not going anywhere, but I'll take the jacket back if it makes you happy."

"It does. It will. Get a straight job, Moody. Until then, I don't want to hear any more smooth talk."

. . .

Mahmood paces up and down a dim and derelict corner of the docks, where the railway tracks stop and a row of storage depots begin. Although overlooked by ships' funnels, cranes and rattling chutes tipping tons of grain into the holds, in the evening when the dockworkers have clocked off and the sailors amble uptown to sink a skinful, there is not a soul about, apart from the occasional copper whistling by on his four-hour patrol. He has found a job starting in the morning, in a rubber hose factory, but he just needs to offload this coat and then he can relax and begin that clean, legal life again. The Maltese fence he had agreed to meet with, Alfredo, had stood him up earlier, when they were meant to meet at their usual spot in a yard behind The Packet pub. He was usually good for his word but Mahmood had given up after fifteen minutes of waiting. There's another guy who he's done business with a couple of times before, another Maltese but shabbier and more dubious than Alfredo, who uses this patch. The last time they'd met, Mahmood had a wristwatch that he'd finagled off a Nigerian watchmaker, which he was trying to offload, a good watch that just needed repair. Should have got him eight pounds but the fence didn't offer even half that. Hearing distant footsteps approaching, Mahmood straightens his hat and pulls the belt of his mackintosh tight. There is a street lamp about ten yards away but on this moonless night he can't see anyone approaching. He doesn't like stepping out here when mobs are negotiating and deciding deals; it doesn't pay to see something you're not meant to. Whisky, opium, seamen's clothing allowance cards and tobacco are the real money-spinners, lucrative but controlled by a few gangs: British, Maltese or Chinese. He would never get a look-in. Now and again a fight breaks out between them, and maybe a dead body is dredged out of the canal or the sea, but otherwise it is a quietly efficient world.

The footsteps are close now, rebounding off the metal storage depots and brittle, frosted iron railings. He peeks out again and sees two thickset men, wearing long black overcoats that give them the bearing of undertakers, with just their pale chins visible under the shadows of their hats. They step closer and closer, the **snap**, **snap**, **snap** of their soles biting the glittering cobbles. Mahmood steps back into the confusion of carts, barrels and diesel stores, wishing his dark skin would absorb all the darkness of the night, his breath leaving his nostrils in two thin white streams.

The men stop, confer and then briskly stride to Mahmood's inadequate hiding place. The taller man stops just a yard from Mahmood and with a gloved hand pushes the brim of his trilby further up his forehead. With a small pause and a smile he pulls out a pair of gleaming handcuffs and reaches for Mahmood's wrist.

"Mahmood Mattan? You do not have to say anything but anything you do say may be taken down and given in evidence against you."

Shan

[Five]

Diana had at first fled 203 Bute Street, sending Grace to Maggie's house and staying there for a few nights to settle her in but now things have to be arranged. She locks the door to the shop and then sits, back aching, on Violet's stool behind the counter. The last few days have been evil; a vortex of black clothes, bleak appointments, harried sandwiches and sleepless nights. The funeral took place on the weekend, the cortège leaving from the shop at 2:30 p.m. exactly with a large crowd of locals trailing it to Cardiff's Jewish Cemetery. White flower wreaths, two blinkered horses with black plumes on their heads, the coffin in a glass carriage, the roads lined by men holding their hats at waist height, children walking too close to the horses so as to touch their flanks, the coach driver in top hat and greatcoat using his whip to nudge them away. Grace had walked the whole way, neither crying nor grumbling, her hand squeezing Diana's tight. Her face framed by a black scarf that made her look older than her years. There must have been more than two hundred mourners from all districts of Cardiff: black and white, Muslim and Christian, Old Jewish families and **greeners**, lawyers and butchers. It was a good send-off, with no caution to expense, but it passed by like a silent film, unreal and unmemorable. Violet had been so quiet, so reclusive, that few knew how to eulogize her, they just kept saying, "She was a good girl, a real **mechayeh**." They didn't know that she kept a scrapbook of actors' portraits, or spent hours of her Sunday in the bath reading crime novels, or had taught herself how to waltz, foxtrot and cha-cha by following printed guides.

Blood. Blood. Blood. The floorboards have seams of red varnish running through them where blood has pooled and dried. The white wall will need to be repainted to remove the faint spray of oxidized blood, but that won't be her responsibility. The property is already on the market, the Volacki's sign that has been up for forty years destined for the scrapyard. Her sister's blood will remain there as long as possible to remind everyone of her absence. She pushes the stool back to stretch her legs and then glances to the left, where the safe is: the cause of all this heartache. She had little knowledge of Violet's financial affairs but the police keep pursuing it. Diana kept out of the shop and avoided work talk over dinner. How much was in there? When did she go to the bank? How much float did she keep? How much did she take in a day? She could only guess the answers. Violet was as self-reliant and secretive with the business as their father had been, and the turf commissioning kept Diana too busy to ask any questions. Fortunately, the shop girl, Angela, had her head screwed on and could give a better sense of the figures; she was adamant that from looking at the little accounting book Violet kept, there must be about a hundred pounds missing from the safe. The value of a life proven not to be immeasurable but easily rounded up to one hundred pounds sterling. Enough to buy a second-hand car, or three cases of Château Latour wine, or a second-tier racehorse, or the land under a ruined house. Whatever the devil spent it on, she hoped it would be cursed, would never bring him or his people anything but pain.

Daniel has already moved as much of the clothing stock as can be resold to his shop, so now only the small domestic and maritime goods remain on the shelves and in the displays. Coiled ropes, waterproofs, matches, gumboots, blades, small tin trunks; just enough supplies to take a boat out to sea and sail away with Grace.

Diana is still trying to be sensible, appropriate, holding back the torrent of expletives she wants to scream at regulars who turn up at the door, pushing at it and standing there, stupefied, when it doesn't open. Even if they know what's happened, they ignore the black crêpe and still come by force of habit to cash an advance note of pay or buy a pair of socks.

She has been the tough one in the family for so long that she hasn't felt the scale of her own helplessness for years. "Such a trooper," "Hard as nails," "Did you see her in the paper? Didn't she look powerful in her uniform?" Corporal Diana of the Women's Auxiliary Air Force, who had given up her home and business to enlist straight after **Kristallnacht** with her Scout leader husband, who only returned to Cardiff because she was pregnant with their first, and in the end only, child. Tough Diana, the tomboy, who became her father's long-wished-for son, given a car for her eighteenth birthday, unlike her sisters with their ballgowns, who decided to raise her daughter alone rather than risk the unsure affection of a stepfather.

Corporal Diana is imploding, she is cracking up, but so deep runs the hard exterior that only she can notice the fine fractures running along her bones. "It'll be Whitchurch asylum for you if you don't pull yourself together," she reminds herself regularly, but it's no fix. She can get through the next few days, weeks, maybe even months, if she just lets go of everything. For the first time in her life she will let the men decide what to do: with the case, the shop, and her child. She'll make herself as pliant as possible so that she doesn't crack any more. The tide of it all just pulling her in and pushing her out, the shipwreck slow and ongoing until maybe, one day, she will wash up on some distant, unknowable beach, hopefully with Grace still beside her.

Grace, Grace, Grace, Grace. Darling Grace. Already Tough Grace, who will take the entrance exam for Howell's despite everything, who said that Aunty Violet would have wanted her to. How can she continue to love this child so hard when life has made it clear that no one really belongs to her? That she can so easily be left behind in the ruins of their life. Diana covers her face with her hands and tries to rein in her quickening breaths.

Grace says she saw him too, the man on the doorstep, when she had peeped into the shop from the dining-room door. It is one of the few things that confirm he wasn't just a figment of her imagination; a phantasm of what a murderer must look like, a black shadow with a mouth of gold. Grace thinks he looked Somali but Diana is not sure, sometimes some of the West Indian men are long and lean and have those gaunt faces too. She cannot remember his features precisely, but at night, in bed, flashes come back of his leather gloves, his pointed shoes, and the brass buttons of his overcoat. Extraneous details that just taunt her. The pain of sitting, eating, dancing while her sister was murdered a few feet away is something that claws at her, that makes her feel stupid and worthless. She did not hear anything; that is the cold truth. Nothing to make her think Violet was in danger or needed her aid. Now her heart races at the thought that she might fail Grace too.

Purim arrived five days after the murder. It was agreed that it would be inappropriate for Grace to attend any parties but it feels as though she is already being marked out, tainted by tragedies that she can't help but be tied to. They had seen children dressed as clowns, bats and fighter pilots, gathered outside the Methodist Hall assembly room, and watched for a few moments before the children had recognized Grace, waving for her to join them. After they had started to walk away, Grace had looked back only once before turning her head to the ground, and she didn't speak a word of the missed party when they got back to Maggie's.

She has spent the whole day cleaning, her knuckles scored and red from scouring away the policemen's dirty footprints, ink markings and tea stains. It was meant to be a solitary task, but Angela and her mother, Elsie, had appeared early in the morning with buckets and cloths and refused every kind of no she proffered.

Tall and elegant, born of a Nigerian sailor father and a mother who'd run away from her husband in Sheffield, Angela wears a velvet hairband and ties her Afro hair into a faultless chignon each day. She had started to work in the shop soon after her sixteenth birthday, just like Violet had, and despite their dissimilar looks they were almost like mother and daughter in their mannerisms and reticent speech. Maybe one day she would have taken over the daily duties of the shop, if Violet had ever decided there was a life beyond work, giving Angela a position she would have enjoyed and deserved. Their presence today, in the end, was fortunate, their chatter and gossip suspended the desolate sense that they were wiping Violet away; removing not just the neat handwritten reminders she taped on to drawers, the floating strands of her brown hair, or the smear of her medicated hand lotion on the switches of the cash register, but the very fact of her existence. Violet Volacki, Spinster, Dead at forty-one years of age. That is all the papers write. But when will even those bare details be put aside? By the time the soil over her grave has settled and can bear the weight of a headstone? Or not until her "silent killer" is executed and forgotten himself?

Maggie had appeared after lunchtime, when the shop was in complete tumult: dust thick in the air, chairs and stools stacked precariously in a corner, all the display-cabinet doors wide open. She had brought rubber gloves and pulled them purposely out of her handbag, her red-rimmed eyes dry for the moment.

"I can't leave all of this to you, Diana," she said, grabbing a sponge from the counter and wringing it over the mop bucket.

Understanding that her sister might need to occupy her hands as much as she did, Diana shouted, "Go for it, Maggie!" and turned back to sweeping the stockroom.

When she returned to the shop floor, maybe ten minutes later, her sister was leaning against the wall, grey-faced, the sponge twisted in her hands.

"What happened?" Diana asked, rushing over.

Angela held out a photo. "She found this. She looked like she might faint, so Mam's gone to get her a glass of water."

Diana glanced down at the black and white snapshot and then shoved it quickly into her pocket. Disentangling a stool from the pile, she ordered Maggie to sit and then took the sponge from her. "You shouldn't have come!" she said, her voice loud and harsh. "You're just making it more difficult."

Maggie looked up through the tears, her wide and helpless eyes those of a housewife unfamiliar with tragedy.

Diana's anger was quickly subsumed by pity and regret. She kissed the parting of her sister's smooth hair and apologized quietly. "Just sit there, Sis, help when you feel up to it."

Elsie returned with the glass of water but it remained untouched in Maggie's hands as she stared, tears coursing silently down her cheeks, at the three women rushing to and fro.

Angela and Elsie had stayed until five and then insisted on walking Maggie home. Angela had brushed away payment but Diana had already hidden two £1 notes in her handbag in anticipation of the refusal.

The doorbell rings and startles Diana; she checks her watch and is barely able to make out its face in the gloomy room. The grey clouds have hardened into night without her even noticing. She snaps the table lamp on and finally she can make out the time—6 p.m. It must be him.

The journalist from the **Western Mail**. Bastard. He had insisted on meeting her in the shop, for "colour," he said, but "to gawp" was what she heard. That conversation with him on the telephone had bothered her all night, it was the reason she had arrived so early in the shop, to disrupt any ghoulish pleasure he might find in witnessing "the murder scene." He had wanted to bring a photographer but she had refused, there would be nothing to capture now beyond a shop in full spring-clean disarray. Maybe he thought there would be a chalk outline on the floor, like in a gangster movie, or bloody handprints, or some telling clue to the identity of the culprit that he would be the first to discover. The doorbell rings again and Diana slowly approaches the door.

Before turning any of the locks she yells, "Who is it?"

"Parry from the **Western Mail**, Mrs. Tanay."

Her sigh is heavy enough to burst her lungs. **Click, clack**, the locks go, like small bones breaking.

"Good evening, Mrs. Tanay, I trust you're well." He steps into the shop before she has even opened the door wide, her "come in" trailing after him.

He's a young chap with narrow trousers and a weaselly face, he moves lithely and with complete entitlement around the room, his tight-lidded blue eyes darting from one corner to another while he writes notes on a small pad. "You're not still living at the property, are you?" he asks.

Diana shakes her head and pulls a chair to the counter. "Sit," she orders.

"You sound like a sergeant."

"Corporal."

"Pardon me?"

"Nothing."

"First of all, let me offer you my condolences on this most terrible of losses."

She shouldn't have agreed to this.

Daniel had kept on at her. "The rabbi said it was a good idea, and so did the solicitor," he said.

"What about the butcher? Did you ask the rag and bone man too?" she had replied.

"Mrs. Tanay."

Diana lifts her eyes from the floor.

"Could you tell me as much as you know of the circumstances of the . . . crime?"

"There is not much to tell at the moment, it must have happened just after eight p.m., we didn't hear anything, and she was found about twenty past eight."

"You heard nothing at all? 'Silent killer' indeed." He sounds delighted, jotting frenetically, his shorthand like the sequences of an ancient language. "Where were you at this time?"

"With my daughter."

"Upstairs?"

"No, in the dining room through there, teaching Grace to dance." Diana nods towards the internal door.

"A matter of yards."

"I suppose so." Diana blinks rapidly and then looks back to the adjoining door.

"Would you say that Miss Volacki had any enemies?"

Diana laughs out loud, surprising herself as well as the journalist, a single incredulous honk of a laugh. "I can say with complete confidence that she didn't have any enemies."

"No rough sorts with a grudge? No disputed debts?" he pursues. "Moneylenders are not known for their universal popularity, are they?"

"Violet was not **just** a moneylender," Diana says bitterly. "People **knew** her, they bought little odds and ends from her and were given credit when they needed it. Even the seamen treated her with respect, she helped them."

"But there must be so many foreigners! Seamen from Bongo Bongo Land and God knows where, violent men, men who are not used to our laws and the way things are done here."

"I don't know anything about that."

"The police are looking for a Somali, aren't they? I have a note of the police telegram: 'Somali, approximately thirty years of age, five foot seven, moustache, a gold tooth.' Did you see this man yourself?"

"Yes . . . no . . . I don't know. I looked through the door but I can't be sure. My daughter thinks she saw a Somali."

Finding a crack in her apparent assurance, Parry hesitates a moment before asking, "Was Miss Volacki . . . ah . . . interfered with . . . at all?"

Diana's eyes widen in shock but then in a loud, clear voice she replies, "No! And you better make that damned clear."

"Understood, understood."

"Ridiculous!" Diana hisses under her breath.

"Didn't mean any offence, Mrs. Tanay, it's the readers, you see, they want to know absolutely everything."

"I think we should end the interview now, Mr. Parry, but there is just one last thing I want to say. The police are doing a sterling job and have sent extra officers, from London to Glasgow, but they are struggling to identify a suspect. To that end . . ." Diana removes a folded piece of paper from her pocket and flattens it out against the counter. Looking like a child slouched over her homework, she focuses hard on Daniel's extravagant handwriting and reads. " 'My brother-in-law, Mr. Daniel Levy, an outfitter of Church Street, Ebbw Vale, decided with the family yesterday that we would be prepared to pay the sum of two hundred pounds to anybody who gives information which will lead to the conviction of the man. A cheque for that amount will be deposited with the family solicitor, Mr. Myer Cohen. The solicitor, in conjunction with the police, will decide who is eligible for the reward if a man is discovered and convicted.' "

"Oh, sensational!" Parry looks ready to shake her hand in gratitude. "What a generous reward that is! That will definitely put the cat amongst the pigeons. This story will run on the front page tomorrow, I'm sure of it."

Diana rises and leads him to the door.

"Good evening, Mr. Parry."

"And a very good evening to you, Mrs. Tanay, I'll be following this case very closely, I assure you, very closely indeed."

Diana fakes a smile and then slams the door behind him.

Chief Detective Inspector Powell takes a sip of scalding black tea from his glazed blue mug, an old raffle prize from his rugby club's Christmas party, and waits a moment outside the interview room. He hears Lavery going over and over the same details in his monotonous drone and the suspect mumbling back in broken

English; Mattan doesn't know that they have been following him for almost a week. He twists the handle and then throws the door open, his bulk almost darkening the room. After a dramatic pause he nods to Lavery, who slides from his seat and offers it to him wordlessly.

The room is stuffy, and sweat quickly gathers between his shoulder blades and under his arms. Powell pulls the plug on the two-bar heater positioned beneath his feet and rubs his palm over his bald pate. Mattan, the small-time thief, sits opposite him, cocky as anything.

"How do you do?" Powell says, offering a handshake across the plywood table.

"How do you do," echoes Mattan, squeezing his hand hard.

"Let's make this simple, shall we, son? We're all busy men here, aren't we?" Powell laughs.

Mahmood murmurs something non-committal and tries to maintain his poker face.

"Simple larceny. You're no virgin when it comes to that charge, we all know that, but there is something else I'd like us to chew the cud over."

Mahmood waits impassively, his fingers knitted together into a ball on the table.

"You see, we have many witnesses who say they saw a Somali outside the Volacki shop on the night that Violet Volacki had her throat cut."

Mahmood raises his eyebrows in bewilderment.

"You not notice how many Somalis live on that road? Why you ask me this question?"

"When was the last time you went to Bute Street?"

"I can't remember, too many months ago."

"So why did the Indian, Mubashir, say you called him out of a café the night before the murder asking him to sell you bread from his shop?"

"If I'm in café why I'm asking him to go to shop for bread?" Mahmood laughs.

"Don't laugh, lad, don't laugh." Powell holds Mattan's gaze hard until the Somali blinks and lowers his eyes.

"Why has your landlord, Madison, said that you arrived home at eight thirty on the night of the murder while you claimed to have got home from the cinema a full hour before that?"

"I know what time I got home."

"How do you?"

"Because I looked at the clock above the paying box at the Central when I come in, four thirty, and when I left, seven thirty."

"Who did you see at the cinema?"

"I see many people I know."

"Did you talk to them?"

"No."

"You been to Bute Street after the murder, then?"

"No, I don't go there."

"At all?"

"No."

"Witnesses tell us they saw you there on the day of the funeral."

Mahmood rolls his eyes in exasperation. "You say this man said this and said that but I do not believe you. I no read what you write down. You fetch them and I will see if they say these things."

"That can be arranged, I dare say. Your wish is our command. Inspector Lavery, bring Madison or Monday here."

Mahmood watches the door open and close as Lavery leaves, and then grimaces for a moment: this interview is strange, these coppers unpredictable, the coat long forgotten, but all this talk of the dead woman instead.

"Don't worry, we'll furnish you with a sandwich and a cup of tea in a while," Powell says, misunderstanding the suspect's expression.

Mahmood glances at Powell. He regrets saying that he didn't believe him so bluntly. His plan was to say as little as possible and to stir truths and untruths together until they both dissolved into one convincing story. He shouldn't have spoken with **af-buhaan**, he needs to rein back his temper and smile a little, especially as this detective looks like he could easily punch his fist through a wall. A Welsh bull, that's what this man Powell reminds him of: dense, compacted meat squeezed into an old-fashioned suit with two small, unblinking eyes in his large-boned face. Well past fifty, but his muscles probably galvanized by age rather than weakened.

Powell yawns. “Pardon me, I’ve been barely catching a wink this past fortnight, working twelve-, fourteen-hour shifts,” he says, as if to an empty room.

Mahmood nods his head lightly in false sympathy.

The policeman recording the interview on a typewriter in the corner looks between them, and waits with fingers stretched expectantly over the keys.

Lavery returns and whispers into Detective Powell’s ear, and then both take up positions, facing Mahmood across the table.

“Did you ever tell Mr. Madison how you thought the woman in Bute Street was killed, and did you show him by actions how you thought it was done?”

“I doesn’t speak to anybody about how the woman was killed. I don’t know this woman. I don’t bother her. She don’t bother me. She don’t tell me nothing. I don’t tell her nothing.”

“Well, we’re hearing the complete opposite. It’s put us in something of a quandary. Either you’re lying or Madison and Monday are.”

“Believe what you want, I tell you true, **ruunta**,

I tell you truth." Mahmood stumbles, his English is fracturing, words of Somali, Arabic, Hindi, Swahili and English clotting at once on his tongue. He runs his hand over his hair and takes a deep breath. "Monday say whatever Madison tell him, if he says jump he say how high."

"In your country how do they slaughter animals?"

"What you mean?"

"Well, how do you do it? What makes the sacrifice holy?"

"You say **bismillah** over the animal."

"And you run a dagger across its throat, do you not? Did you ever do that in your country?"

"I never butcher."

"I've seen it here in Cardiff, on your feast days, you've never taken part?"

"I like my clothes too much."

Powell scribbles something on his notepad and then rises slowly from the table, leaving the room without a word.

Smoking his pipe and pacing up and down the dark hallway, Powell collects his thoughts: Mattan is wilder than he expected, a real rogue with no respect for authority, a covetous darkie of no fixed abode. He'd read somewhere that for Somalis every man is his own master. They aren't like the jovial Kroo boys or anglicized West Indians, but are truculent and vicious, quick to draw a weapon and unrepentant after the fact. This one must have become bold after the soft sentences he'd received in the past; remembered to wear gloves, dispatched the victim without a peep, disposed quickly of the murder weapon and stolen cash. Dangerous but now unable to keep his lies straight. A good substantial case, something his son should be helping out on, instead of faffing around in Ryton College, wasting his time on amateur dramatics, civics and English literature. What does an inspector need with all that gobbledegook? The police service is surely losing its way. He's been in the job gone thirty years and he's learnt everything he's needed to know by thinning his boots out on the streets. Talking to the dregs of society. Knowing their habits better than they do. Holding your dinner down when confronted with their bestial acts, that's the knack to this job. Not to say that there isn't some place for book learning, forensics, but it's still down to that relentless knowledge and pursuit of the wolves who live within the flock. The perverts, lunatics, desperadoes, lovefools, sadists and Jekyll and Hydes that he's interviewed and shared a cigarette with before sending them on to the gallows. It's usually the sluts and nigger-lovers that bear the brunt of it, shot down if they're lucky or dragged naked out of a blood-soaked ditch if they're not. Respectable women like Miss Volacki should be inviolable, must be. He'd known her for decades, known her father too. She was a minuscule woman, wouldn't even reach as high as his chest, obviously not a Christian but sober, industrious and straight as a die. Tiger Bay needed people like her, otherwise it would go completely to the dogs. He'd catch her killer, he was sure of that; he didn't need the papers or the councillors hurrying him. They'd spoken to every seaman docked that night, every pub landlord, every thief, every dopehead, every whore, the milkmen and road sweepers, the shopkeepers and café owners, the pastors and sheikhs, the moneylenders and their debtors, the street dice-throwers and the kids who watch them, and to police forces across the country. If the local cats, dogs and horses could talk he would have pulled them in for questioning too. The younger men might get excited working the docks, but for him it was just depressing what the country had come to. Spending almost every night this past fortnight on the Bay had disheartened him; it was crawling with queers, darkies, hoodlums, communists, and traitors of every description. You could smell the dissolution in the air, from the oily stink of spices pumping out of the eating houses to the wisps of marijuana smoke coming from loud house parties. Was this the country that so many good men and boys had died for? "The ports are our broken skin," that's what his first Chief Constable had said, way back in the twenties, and it was still true. No one had listened when Wilson suggested outlawing mixed-race marriages then, and here lay the consequences.

Footsteps clatter towards Powell and he raises his head from the floor. "Sir, Monday is here to see you."

"Good, good, bring him in, and call in that useless Jamaican, Cover, too. He said that asylum case, Tahir Gass, was the Somali he saw outside the shop, didn't he?"

"Yes, sir."

"Well, let's see if we can't jog his memory a little bit. Gass has already hot-footed it on to a ship."

"Mr. Mattan says that you have made a mistake in the time that you have said he came into the house that Thursday night. Would you tell me now what time he came in?"

Monday stands by the door, holding his hands behind his back, and nods sombrely, avoiding Mahmood's face. "I will.

"I was sitting on the sofa in Mr. Madison's room, talking about racing and pools. This man . . ."

Monday points disdainfully at Mahmood, "came in about quarter to nine. He sat down on the sofa by me. He didn't say anything. I gave him the paper but he didn't look at it. Just stared in front of him."

"I doesn't, I doesn't, you say everything Madison tell you to say."

"What is this? Why can't you tell the man the truth? You know what time you came in that night."

"Bastard!"

"You call me a bastard? You call me a bastard in front of the policemen?" Monday raises his palms to the ceiling as if testifying in church.

"And a liar! Big liar! You tell them untruths. I no show you nothing about how woman was killed, you lie."

"Settle down now, gentlemen." Powell smiles.

"On my dear mother's life I swear that he told Madison that it would be easy to attack her and that you just put your arm around her neck and cut her throat with the other hand. I saw it."

"**Qaraac! Ibn Sharmuta!**" Mahmood curses.

"Big fool! You son of a perverse and rebellious woman."

"That's enough. Take him out of here, Lavery."

"You are Madison's slave, his dog, he care nothing for you, why lie for him? He just angry because I report him."

"That's enough, I said." Powell beats his fist on the table until Monday is safely out of the room.

"Did that satisfy your doubts regarding our witness statements, Mr. Mattan?" Powell asks, raising a bushy eyebrow.

Mahmood wipes saliva from the edges of his mouth and tries to shake the anger out of his skull. "British police is so clever. I tell you I kill twenty men. I kill your king. This I tell you if you like, you think that right?"

Lavery visits him in the piss-walled police cell.

"Why you keeping me here? Just send me down to the Magistrates."

"You forgot it's a Sunday tomorrow?"

Mahmood rubs at a new stain on his trousers. "So Monday?"

"That's right. Now, Mattan, do you have any objection to standing in a line of men, all Somalis, and several people—some ladies and perhaps a man or two—would be asked to see the line. Do you understand what I mean?"

"I understand. It is up to you—I don't care."

"Very well, I shall try to arrange it for the morning. Do you want me to send for any friend of yours to be here? Do you want me to get any special clothes for you to wear? That suit looks like a miner's been rolling around in it."

Mahmood listens, at first apathetically, but when he sees the snare they are trying to catch him in, he snorts with laughter. "I understand, you tell them what I am wearing so they can pick me out. No, I don't want special clothes, I don't want no friend, I don't need anything, and I won't be in your parade either, you can't force me." He smiles a smug, beatific smile.

Lavery's face, long and gloomy at the best of times, hardens but he just nods and closes the cell door softly behind him.

On Monday morning he is taken to be photographed. The camera flashes close to his face, his eyes fluttering so much that the felt hat-wearing photographer takes another to be sure. He also takes two more shots, of left and right profile, and then holsters his weapon. Mahmood puts down the board with his chalked-on name and moves away from the wall. Out of the corner of his eye he sees half a dozen people walking slowly past the open door. He recognizes an old grocer he used to buy from, then behind him, catches sight of a Maltese poker player who'd dealt him a loaded hand once, then, no, it can't be! The Nigerian watchmaker he'd tussled with once over a watch. What kind of gathering is this? All of these disparate faces from his past coming to peer at him as if at the new lion in the zoo, guilty curiosity in their eyes. There is a white-socked, brown-haired girl trailing after them, she's around twelve years old, sucking her sleeve absent-mindedly. She looks at him hard, neither blinking nor embarrassed, just boring into him with another set of glacial blue eyes. She whispers something to an older woman in a headscarf and then shakes her head, turning back to Mahmood for one long last look before they disappear.

The ride in the back of the police car reveals the first frothy buds of cherry blossom and magnolia, warmth or something like it in the air, birds trilling and bickering. They've given him a collarless khaki shirt and brown trousers to wear and he now waits his turn at Cardiff Magistrates. The gloomy, wood-panelled waiting room is noxious with beeswax and Brasso and Mahmood is relieved when a clerk comes hammering down the steps to announce they are ready for him.

Like a game, Mahmood's head turns this way and that as the subject of his freedom is batted around the courtroom.

The charge is larceny.

Understood.

The value of the coat £12 12s.

Understood.

Does the accused want to apply for bail?

Yes, sir!

Then the game changes. "Certain formalities need to be completed," "We want to keep him for five days," "A more serious matter."

What is that fool Powell doing here?

"He is a seaman in possession of a seaman's discharge book. He has been evicted from his lodgings and is now of no fixed abode."

Madison. Again. May that man burn and burn.

"What do you mean by 'more serious charges?'" the magistrate asks, leafing through the pile of documents before him.

"We are not at liberty to say more about it at this juncture."

The magistrate looks at Powell and frowns. "If that is the case, I can only grant a remand until Wednesday."

The clerk turns to Mahmood. "What do you want to say?"

Mahmood clears his throat but his words still emerge in a whisper. "I wish to say nothing."

It's with a sigh that Mahmood passes through the gates of Cardiff Prison. The Victorian building is so close to his former lodgings in Davis Street that its shadow used to keep his room dark for the first half of the day, until the sun managed to vault over its three storeys of muddy brick. He's in the van, handcuffed, wondering who will collect his trunk and meagre possessions from number 42. Whether Madison and Monday are rooting through his things right now, reading his letters and filching what they want. It's a headache, constantly looking for new lodgings; when he's out, he'll have to move out of Adamsdown, there's no way he'll be able to face those two without starting trouble. The fourth move in twelve months and still no prospect of Laura, the kids or a home anytime soon. He's sick of dealing with the police, feeling the rattle of their bracelets around his wrists, sharing mattresses with the city's vagrants and derelicts. He's too old for this and they, the police, are beginning to hate him; there's something personal brewing there, they speak his name too freely, and want to believe he is capable of anything. He won't let them use him as the rag they soak up spilt blood with.

At the processing desk they give him a blanket, a mug, a basin, a new uniform. Just two nights here and then release. They enter A Wing and it smells of boiled cabbage and unwashed men. A teenage prisoner, on his knees with a dustpan and brush, looks up and whispers for a cigarette. Mahmood pulls out his empty trouser pockets as an answer. Sunlight streams down from the high windows and bounces off the metal barriers, grilles and staircases, almost blinding him. The screw leads him up to the third floor. The prison cells, he remembers, are so cramped that with outstretched arms you can touch both walls at the same time.

After he's already walked two paces into the cell, Mahmood jumps back on seeing another man already there: a black man lounging in the bottom bunk, his big feet hanging over the edge of the narrow cot.

"Me ain't no duppy, you na 'ave to jump outta your skin, man."

"What you doing here?"

"I'll leave you chaps to get acquainted," the screw says, before locking them in.

Mahmood dumps the objects in his arms on the upper bunk and glances down at Lloyd, the mysterious boxer at number 42.

"Dangerous Drugs Act, anyting else?" Lloyd laughs.

"But they let you out."

"And den dey find more on me and call me come back in."

"Bad luck."

Lloyd chews the end of a matchstick and makes a "no bother" face. "Whatta bout you?"

"Stealing. Raincoat."

"I 'eard you call de Ghost, the sun come out too fast and catch you?"

Mahmood smiles. "You can say so."

"Bad luck to you too." His words come out slow and sonorous, in an accent still strongly possessed of Jamaican cadences. He's a good-looking man, a shade or two lighter than Mahmood and with an American Indian pitch to his eyes and the broad angles of his cheekbones. His hair is close-cropped with a sharp side parting razored into its gleaming whorls.

"I've always had a cell to myself," Mahmood says, pacing the small strip between door and white-barred window.

"Me know, this place sure is far from de Ritz but as long as dey do our washing and bring the boiled food we can't complain to no manager."

"That bastard Madison kick me out of the house."

"He a **cold** man, bitter as an ol' spinstah."

"Fuck him. I'll find somewhere better to put my head and a better pocket to put my money."

"No shortage of rat-infested lodging in dis so-called Tiger Bay."

"I don't sleep any place rat-infested." Mahmood turns his head sharply towards Lloyd.

"Rest yourself, man. Anywhere we go we ain't but a foot away from King Rat, whether he below us, above our head, behind the walls, he never far. Buckingham Palace nothing but a playground to him."

Mahmood stands, looking straight out of the window at the crown of a bare oak tree on the civilian side of the high perimeter wall; at the sky that has cleared to a blazing, radioactive blue; at the sooty backs of the terraces of Davis Street with their weed-choked backyards ugly with upturned wheelbarrows, rusting bicycles, flapping shirts and grey undergarments pinned to sagging washing lines; at the sloping, rain-beaten outhouses about ready to give up the ghost.

"You getting sentimental for ti bed?"

"No, my woman and boys live over there."

"You married a **backra**?" Lloyd smirks.

"What you mean by **backra**?"

"A white gal," he replies, running his tongue over his small, nicotine-stained teeth before giving them a little kiss.

Mahmood glances over his shoulder and for a second it seems as if Lloyd is transformed. He has a peculiar energy, serpentine and shifting, that makes it possible to doubt, for a second, that he is human, that he is solid, that he won't change form before your eyes.

"I thought you Mohammedans couldn't eat . . ." Lloyd stops his joke there when he sees the strange look on Mahmood's face. "You alright?"

Mahmood turns back to the window. "I don't want to talk about my wife."

"Your prerogative, chief."

"I know it."

Lloyd sits up, throws his legs over the side of the bed and plays a quick rhythm on his thighs, his broad yellow palms loud and hollow against the dense muscle. "Ah!" he yells, jumping to his feet.

Mahmood turns quickly, thinking he is about to attack, and raises his fists.

Lloyd laughs. "You wanna spar? Put up dem dukes!" He throws quick, dart-like punches that stop inches away from Mahmood. His eyes bright, his smile wide, he looks suddenly joyful and childlike.

Mahmood mimics him and bounces on his feet, hiding his face behind one arm as he jabs with the other, beginning to laugh.

"Round Two. Ding! Ding! Ding! Joe Louis versus Sugar Ray Robinson. De Brown Bomber gets the sugar man on de ropes! Pow! Pow! Pow!" He pretends to unleash a barrage of blows on to Mahmood's head and then skips back and twirls with his fists in the air. "De uncontested champion of deeee worrrrld!"

Mahmood drops his arms and complains. "You can't make yourself champion."

"All the way from Kingston, Jamaica! De undisputed, uncontested, unquestioned champion of de universe!"

Lloyd wraps his long arms around Mahmood's

shoulders and pats him lightly on the back. "Better luck fi next time, Ghost."

Mahmood shakes him loose but they are both laughing, midday sun shining through the bars. He feels the close walls of the cell recede and the heat of Lloyd's touch warm on his skin.

"Ah, man, de summer, de summer in London, de tings dat carry on make you want to cork up your ears."

Lights out. Both of them on their backs in their bunks. The mattresses so narrow they have to sleep as still and straight as Nosferatu.

"I'd prowl from Notting Hill Gate to Green Park in half-hour easy, dat was my precinct, some fellas just lime between Marble Arch and Lancaster Gate, but de real top sports come out along de railings near Green Park. I kept a coop of five girls—three from de counties, one Irish, one dark little gal from Spain. All wore red shoes, stylish, nah? Dat was my trademark."

Mahmood doesn't reply, he is near sleep and only half listening to Lloyd's sleazy tales.

"I kept them in style, it be their own money but I bought class: royal hat-makers, French stockings, Italian shoes, dey looked like dey step out of **Vogue** magazine. I was part loverman, part boss, part fairy godmother. Not dat dey all understood what dey were receiving. One of me English sports would roll up her mink stole and sit 'pon it in de winter if de bench too cold, what do you do with a gal like dat? Not much. But summer, no man can get vex in a London summer, you cool off in de Serpentine and den lie back, eyelids red, on de grass, knowing dat you were born for dis and no one can break de spell. I came all de way from Jamaica so it ain't de sun dat I'm chasing, but der is someting about how dis country change when der is some warmth to sweeten dese Anglo-Saxons and Celts. How all dose grand buildings on Whitehall, Pall Mall and Regent's Street look like dey tanning too as dey lose der grey and turn gold. Man, even de pigeons in Trafalgar Square start to strut and get sex crazy, it just pouring out of ev'ry fountain, ev'ry bar tap, ev'ry sweaty armpit. De same madness."

Mahmood knows what he means. He had met Laura in the early summer of '47. At that moment when you can go from umbrellas and woollen coats to short sleeves and ice creams in one day. He'd wait under the railway bridge at the top of Butetown at 5:30 p.m. sharp, just after her shift at the paper factory had finished, always fearing that this time she'd stand him up, but then she'd come along, neat scarf tied under her chin, her mother's old coat cinched in with a plastic yellow belt. "Alright, Moody?" she'd ask in her deep voice. Then he'd take her bag from her, to look gentlemanly, her metal sandwich tin chiming along with their steps, as they headed to the cinema or a milk bar. He had signed on to a ship headed to Brazil the week they met but had then passed the job along to another Somali, there was just **something** about her that made him want to dilly-dally. She had made him wait—that he liked—for her, it was marriage or nothing. She also had grit, didn't give a penny damn about what anyone else thought about anything.

"You know sometimes you see a fancy car sliding along and assume dey after one of de gals? And den you realize it's you dey checking out. First time it happen, I say to meself, 'Jesus!' I afeared it must be some pansy out for dark meat but den der's a woman in de goddamn passenger seat. She lower her sunglasses and look at me outta de window of de Rolls-Royce, real cool, you 'ear? I swear she look just like Marilyn Monroe, a hoity-toity Marilyn with big pearls 'alf choking her neck. De man curl his finger and call me over. 'Good evening, good evening, isn't the weather fine?,' 'Oh, certainly is!' We talk de English way and den he tell me dey about to 'ave a party and would like to invite me, no, he say 'to extend an invitation.'" Lloyd chuckles. "I say I would be most delighted and get in de back of de car, pale fine leather, smell real good, enough room to stretch my legs out real straight, and we go to der pad in 'Olland Park. I spare you de details but it were a kind of party I never been to before but have known since, went back to de park with three pounds in my pocket too and de gals asking where I've been."

Mahmood grimaces. He remembers once, early on in Cardiff, that a man coming out of a pub, a bald man squeezed into a three-piece suit, had grabbed his arm and said that his wife would like to say hello. They walk up to his gaunt wife. Black bouffant hair, powder-white face, she look embarrass and try to hide her bad teeth. "Say hello!" the man order and she look down and mutter something like hello. Mahmood pull his arm free and start to walk away. "Don't go," the man plead, "do you have somewhere to stay? We've got a spare bed going to waste." He hadn't understood then why they were so eager to take him home when many wouldn't even look him in the eye. It had taken time but he eventually understood that for some men it was a real thrill to watch their woman done over by someone else, and a black man gave the biggest thrill of all. It was like learning that he was surrounded by cannibals, his mind couldn't unwrap it, how could a man do that to his wife? To his children? To himself? It made him feel as if he had gone too far from home, too far to understand anything.

"Man gotta hustle while he still can, no shame to it."

Mahmood exaggerates his breathing in reply, feigning sleep, but Lloyd drones on until he sends him to sleep for real.

Berlin must have browbeaten the **badmarin** to pull a pound from the lint of their pockets because in the morning a solicitor turns up, asking to see Mahmood, says that he has been sent to represent him. He's a youngish fella with a sharp widow's peak and arched black eyebrows that remain high up his forehead as he speaks. He barely meets Mahmood's eye but just points with a ridged thumbnail to different lines on which he should sign. His careful **M. H. Mattan** still awkward-looking and crimped like a child's. The solicitor—was it Morgan? Mahmood barely caught it—stuffs the documents into a large yellow envelope, the "REX" scored out and replaced with "REGINA" in fresh black ink, and leaves with a curt farewell thrown over his shoulder.

The prison hums like a train station, every little noise made loud and metallic by the bare brick and criss-crossing metal railings. Laughter, spoons clinking against enamel bowls, warders' whistles, and from one table a man with a baritone voice singing a sorrowful Welsh hymn towards the blank wall. A crew of Maltese prisoners huddle together, their tan skin and neat dark moustaches making them seem healthier and somehow more dangerous than the pale, untrimmed horde of white inmates. There are a few other dark skins that he can see; a couple of West Africans with small nicks to their cheeks, a scrawny Arab with dark half-moons under his eyes, a thick-necked Chinese with tattoos on the backs of his hands, a handsome, preening Indian. The porridge was dished out only minutes ago but already there is the smell of cabbage and boiling meat coming from the kitchen. A day in prison rushes by so fast, as if the warders are eager to put the prisoners to bed and then have the run of the halls and yards themselves, sliding down the bannisters and doing trapeze walks along the railings.

"You coming?" Lloyd nudges him and leads the way to the exercise yard.

The yard is not for exercise as much as it's for standing up, taking in fresh air and looking at the sky without a smudge of soot and bird shit fouling the view. The men circle each other in concentric rings, the eldest in the middle, their shoulders knocking each other, tobacco the main topic of whispered conversation, crimes unspoken and backgrounds unknown.

"Get a load o' him!" says a man, and suddenly the yard is a-shiver.

"Who?"

"What you on about?"

"Where am I supposed to look?"

"Singh!" hisses the first man, his flat bald head now visible as he points up to an external staircase leading to one of the far wings.

Mahmood cranes his head over the others, resting a hand on Lloyd's shoulder so that he can gain some height.

An Indian man in a pale blue turban appears between the black spears bristling along the top of the yard's brick walls. He's broad, as long-bearded as a prophet, and moves with the lumbering gait of a dancing bear, his hands cuffed as he trots, up-down, up-down, behind a warder, until they disappear through an arch and out of sight.

"Fat fucker, isn't he?" someone shouts and then after a second's delay, the prisoners in the yard laugh all at once.

"It'll take more than a rope for 'im! Chain more like, greedy bastard."

"It's worth gettin' a capital if they feed you so well."

"Oi, Judge, I'll put the black cap on myself, but just remember I like my steak well done."

"He won't be having a steak, boyo, he's a Hindu! They'll just have to pay out on rice and spices."

"He's a Muslim, you fool!"

"You're all imbeciles, the man's a Sikh! You can tell it by the name! Ain't none of you served with them?"

"I have. Who wants to know what you call a Hindu that's done everything? Bindair Dundat . . . you don't have to pay me for that one, chaps."

Some men groan, some chortle, but the mood, the strange chill that Mahmood had felt on seeing the condemned Ajit Singh, is gone, evaporated by the prisoners' refusal to feel it.

"How de English put it?" Lloyd nudges.

"What?" Mahmood asks, scrunching up his eyebrows.

"Dat man, he look like . . . his goose well and truly cooked."

"His fate bring him all the way here from India, imagine."

"How long you think you stay here?"

"Man, I'll be out 'fore de week pass."

"Me too."

"You say so?"

"By God, man, I finished with this place."

"You certain dey ain't got nuttin' else on you?"

Mahmood stops pulling at the loose skin

around his thumbnails and lies back on the bed. He thinks back over the last few weeks and, apart from one time when he pickpocketed an old fella at the Newport races, he's clean. "Nothing."

"You 'ear about de Jew woman who got rob an' kill in her shop in ol' Bute Street?"

"Who hasn't?"

"She had a nice big safe in der. Big prize."

"You think so? Look to me she sold only small pieces."

"You step inside her place?"

"Many times. Got some shirts, dresses for the wife."

"I hear she a nasty woman, a real Jew, de kind dat hear pennies jingling in your pocket as you pass de street."

"Once she tried to sell me a bundle of shirts with a couple missing."

"Oh, you see what I'm saying, den? She probably messed with de wrong person. Dey tussle, she die, and den he think why should I leave de place empty-handed? Manslaughter dey call it."

"Who tussles with a woman and pulls out a knife?"

"It was a knife? I didn't read dat."

"Or a razor, whatever it was, you can't find no justification."

"If a man give a good case to de police, I bet dey would go easy on 'im."

"Where you been where they go easy on any man unless he got money or know the right people? I seen them wake their own white beggars with a kick to the head."

"Nah, man, you gotta learn how to sweet-talk dem, dey simple boys in uniform, cops and robbers need each other, you give meaning to der life and dey to yours."

Mahmood is incredulous, what kind of **gabay** is this? "They not no simple boys and I **don't** need them in my life."

"I'm just saying . . . whatever a man done in his life der is a way of putting your best foot first."

"And that way is by telling them nothing, nothing or just lies, that is the only way to talk with police. Keep your mouth shut or lead them far away from where they want to take you. If you don't understand that you should go back to your own country."

Lloyd laughs. "Don't rush me, man, I know when I go back. January the first, 1960. Dat be de date I promise myself and dat de date I'll go, not a moment 'fore, unless de Almighty got someting to say 'bout it."

"Why 1960?"

"Cos dat will be ten full years of Blighty, a decade, and den I can say I saw it, lived it, and left it. You planning on going back to your piece o' desert?"

"I can't think about it until my boys grown, there is nothing for me anywhere they don't be."

"I bet you some kinda prince, or chieftain's son, or second cousin to Selassie heself."

"Who me?" Mahmood laughs a laugh that seems to catch in his throat. "You kidding, we had a little shop in Hargeisa, maybe ten camels grazing out in the desert with the rest of our clan's. Nothing to rush back to . . . my father was short like Selassie, that the only thing same about them."

"So you come here to try your luck like de rest of us? My schoolmates dey tell me dat Old Blighty on her knees and dat I should come take her from behind," he cackles.

"I am a gambling soul. Even as a small boy if someone say to me, 'Oh, I know you won't do that or you can't do this,' I look them in the eye and just do it. I take everything life give me and throw it in fate's face. My mother sent me on a lorry with traders to Dire Dawa and in the hills I fell out the back and hurt my arm. My arm look like this, you see?" He twists his arm awkwardly at the elbow and stretches it out so Lloyd can see it from the bottom bunk. "The men tell me, 'Go home, go see a bone-setter, you can't carry on with us now,' but I just force my arm straight and climb back on to the lorry, go all the way to Dire Dawa. No one can tell me no. I will just tell them yes."

"Dat's a mouth of big talk, bwoy, you expounding your philosophy?"

"What that word?"

"What? Philosophy?"

"No, the other one."

"Expound. Dictionary word. It mean to sound off, fancy word for explain."

"Yes, I'm expounding. Listen, let me tell you the first time I was arrested. Rhodesia. 1945. I had started my journey down to South Africa to join the merchant navy. Already made it through, let me think . . . Kenya and then Tanganyika . . . when I crossed the border into Northern Rhodesia and then those uniformed dogs got me the minute I hit that red soil. Arrested me for illegal entry and threw me in jail, first time in my life, I was still a young boy, all bones and no sense. No water, nowhere to lie down, just fifty black men in a cell sleeping standing up, shitting into an empty milk powder can. Men coughing and you feel their TB on your neck, your face, enough to make you sick just thinking about it. Somehow, I still don't know how, a Somali butcher from my clan, his name Haji Ali, heard that I was in jail in Lusaka and he put up twenty-five pounds bail, he don't know me from Adam but he bailed me out and I was deported south, where I was heading anyway. From the first pay packet from my first ship I sent him thirty pounds. You don't forget. Good or bad. That is also in my philosophy."

"Yes, Jehovah! Dat is de righteous way. Whatever sins we commit we leaven dem wit godly acts."

"We try, we try, we listen to the angel on our right shoulder and the devil on the left."

"Dat how you Mohammedans see it? Well, Amen, dat's something I can live by."

Mahmood hadn't really sent any money to Haji Ali, but he had intended to, still intended to, and liked the idea of being the kind of man who did things like that. A just outlaw.

In the showers, where the water is so aggressively cold that Mahmood's heart is thumping in his chest, and the green, medicated soap keeps slipping from his trembling hands and thudding against the cracked white tiles, something strange happens. At first, the sound merges with the splutter and shush of water through the old, cantankerous pipes, the splatter of feet through puddles, the slap of palms against wet skin, but slowly it separates and becomes distinct. The naked prisoners, head bowed and in a uniform of soapsuds, hiss, Sssssss, first softly then rising to a barbed crescendo. The message is clear, there is an informer within their ranks, Mahmood flicks his head left to right, he catches Lloyd's eye and he begins to hiss too. Only Mahmood is quiet, ignorant of who the target of the shaming is.

Wednesday arrives. Magistrates. A change again into civvy clothes. Dark grey trousers, green shirt, green waistcoat, they don't give no tie or collar, so Mahmood feels like Charlie Chaplin in a pair of oversized suede shoes. He catches sight of his hair, frizzed up in crazy waves around his head, and tries to flatten it with his hand and a bit of spit, like his mother used to irritatingly do when he was small. In the police van, his thoughts briefly settle on "the more serious matter" that the inspector was trying to conjure up: whether it might be the Maltese and their fencing rings or if the shopkeeper, hoping to swindle his insurance, had said he robbed more than just the raincoat. They have nothing on him either way.

The skin on his face and hands is taut and has turned grey and ashy from the harsh prison soap. At home—not home but the lodgings—he would put coconut oil all over his body to keep it supple and to massage away the knots on those days he worked at the quarry. He'll do it later today, when he's found new lodgings, he thinks.

They arrive at the court and he lets the two older prisoners in the back leave the van first.

Two policemen march them up the tall stone steps, through the arch and then they slip through a side door to wait their turn.

Standing before the two magistrates, Mahmood's gaze keeps going up to the gallery. Laura. Laura is there, sitting beside her mother, both of them looking smart in navy suits. Berlin, too, and Dualleh the Communist, Ismail, and so many strangers. The gallery is packed. Usually there is just one old busybody, whiling away the hours and clacking her knitting needles. There is one, of course, but she is on the edge, pushed out by the newcomers.

"Please, turn this way, Mr. Mattan," the magistrate on the right says.

Mahmood takes a last look at Laura, her face severe under the shadow of the hat, and then turns ahead.

"You are charged with murdering Miss Violet Volacki at her shop in Butetown, Cardiff, on March the 6th. Do you understand, Mr. Mattan?" the clerk of the magistrates asks.

"He understands perfectly, sir," Detective Inspector Powell says, standing up from his chair.

Mahmood does not understand. He feels a cold sweat rush down the length of his spine.

"In view of this man's financial position, I think the question of legal aid might be considered at this stage. Do you want a solicitor to defend you?"

"Defend me for what?" Mahmood snaps, looking up towards Laura so he can confirm the lunacy of what they are saying. But their eyes don't meet, her face is hidden in her hands.

"Defend you on the two charges for which you appear at this court," the clerk replies, surprised at the tone as well as the question.

"I don't want anything and I don't care anything. You people talking crazy. You can't get me to worrying."

"We want to assist you, but it is up to you to ask for legal aid."

"It is up to **you** what **you** do. I don't ask for anything. I have nothing to do with murder."

The two drab magistrates look to each other with displeasure and one of them interrupts the proceedings to say, "We want to help you all we can." He looks benevolently, expectantly at Mahmood.

"I don't want help from anybody."

"You say it is up to us. We are **going** to grant you legal aid and we will **remand** you in custody until March the 25th."

Mahmood hears Laura's deep cry above him, lost in the gasps, as he is led out of the court.

. . .

It all comes together in the journey back to the prison: the strange conversation about the dead woman, the hissing, how he talks of the police as if they are old friends of his, how the warders smirk when they see him. Lloyd is a grass. He's a snake. He talk sweet then poison you. He is the worst kinda black man or any man. Mahmood needs to get him quick before they move him to another wing or get him out of the prison. The cell empty. Mahmood rocks back and forth on the hard mattress. He waits for the bell. Scans every face in the yard. Spots him. Moves slowly. Then pounces. Shoe in his hand.

Thwack! Once. Twice.

"Nigger!"

That foreign word coming from his mouth unbidden, projecting like venom from his lips.

Lix

[Six]

The room is grey, filled with gloomy morning light and faded chintz. Diana, propped up on two frilly pillows, reaches for the lamp switch and turns the stained-glass shade red. Her hair is in her eyes but she doesn't bother adjusting it, just rests a saucer on the pink counterpane and lights a Player. She savours these moments first thing, before the past, present and future have solidified, when time feels timeless and screeching seagulls have safely navigated her from dreams of soundless wailing. She smokes the cigarette with her arms flat on the bed, inhaling and exhaling from the side of her mouth, ash falling square into the saucer. She can feel a wave of "things to do" building up in her mind but she holds it back, back, back; trying to allow herself these five minutes of nothingness. No thought is free now or unfreighted, they each come with entangling duties, fears and sorrows, so she sucks the tobacco deep, keeps everything still and listens to the swoop and shriek of innocent birds.

After washing her face and brushing her teeth at the basin, she strips off her nightie and stands for a moment before the mirror, taking inventory: white strands in her black hair, black moles on her white skin, black eyes surrounded by blue skin, silvery tendrils across her stomach and hips, only the pale pink of her lips and nipples lifts the monochrome. This thirty-six-year-old body of hers is still strong, still shapely, but she has mothballed it, for her daughter's sake, for sanity's sake. Her thoughts drift to those lines from "To His Coy Mistress" that she had once recited in Mrs. Benson's English class.

Thy beauty shall no more be found;
Nor, in thy marble vault, shall sound
My echoing song; then worms shall try
That long-preserved virginity,
And your quaint honour turn to dust
And into ashes all my lust . . .

"My quaint honour indeed," thinks Diana, wondering how Marvell could see a dead woman as just a lost opportunity to get his end away. But there's some truth there: when was the last time a man had touched her? Beyond a handshake or brief consoling embrace? She was once passionate, free. Now what? Fearful? Frigid? Past it? None of those words feel right. Her soul still desires human touch, warmth and envelopment, but there is no time for it now, no place even. "Had we but world enough, and time," she wouldn't be the woman looking back at her from the mirror; a woman who had thought she could refashion the world and her place in it but had been left with chastened, darkened eyes. The world is finite and unyielding, as is time, those eyes say.

Mrs. Pritchard, the landlady, is in the dining room fussing with her rabbit-themed crockery: bunny mugs and coasters, little silver teaspoons with rabbit ears, Peter Rabbit egg cups, embroidered hares skipping across napkins, a ceramic doe nursing her litter on the lid of a tureen. Her whole unappetizing warren strewn across the table.

"Good morning, dear."

"Good morning."

"I have my son stopping by so I thought I would put some welly into it."

The table heaves every morning; Diana and the other woman, the secretary, are barely able to make a dent in it. Today, she manages a cup of tea from the winter bunny teapot and a bite of toast.

"Lift up the lid there, **cariad**, and you'll find a nice bit of smoked mackerel. You can't go wrong with Tenby mackerel."

Diana slides a greasy little fish on to her plate without any intention of eating it.

Detective Inspector Powell had accompanied her to the court yesterday. He'd told her that this man had been at the top of their list from the very beginning, that one constable who'd had previous dealings with him shouted out his name the minute he'd heard about the murder. Everything would move quickly now, the Department of Public Prosecutions would sew together the numerous pieces of evidence against the Somali, and a capable barrister present it all at trial. Powell has a bad habit of talking both down to her and over her, his tall dominating frame and handsome gargoyle face an inch too close, but he also appears genuinely moved by Violet's death, and keeps telling Diana that "if there is anything at all you need, don't hesitate to call at the station" until it almost sounds true.

She had gone to the court against her better judgement. She feared the effect it would have on her to see that man again, whether she might even faint or do something else ridiculous. Sitting up in the gallery, in the back row, she had waited and waited until she felt strong enough to peer down and take a glimpse at him: a thin, harmless-looking young man with a growing bald spot on the crown of his head, nothing more than that. He kept looking up, searching out a face in the crowd, and Diana looked in the same direction at a pale girl in a blue suit, sitting straight-backed in the front row of the gallery. An older woman, presumably her mother, whispered regularly in her ear and patted her narrow back a few times. None of them looked familiar; if they had ever been on Bute Street or in the shop she couldn't say, theirs were just the anonymous faces found amidst the unfortunate, distant-eyed flotsam of Cardiff, their quiet lives sustained by day wages and borrowed rations. Berlin, the milk bar owner, had raised his hat to Diana but she had looked away, blushing, unable to acknowledge anyone in that setting. When the man, Mattan, had been given a chance to speak to the magistrate, his flintiness had surprised her, as did the aggrieved pride in his voice; his English boomed loud and clear, unlike some of the sailors who mumbled and spoke in two-word phrases. She didn't like the pantomime gasps and hubbub as he was led out, but it felt too as if a page had started to turn, that this part of her own ordeal had a foreseeable end.

Up the steps to the flat above the shop, knees creaking as much as the old wood, already a different smell to the abandoned place—damp, mice, stale five-spice from the Chinese restaurant. Daniel has sold all the wardrobes, dressers, chests of drawers and cabinets, and emptied their contents into cardboard boxes and suitcases for her to look through. Violet's possessions spill out of six large boxes in her room, while Diana had managed to keep a tight rein on her and Grace's clutter to the point that their memories can now be carried away in two large armfuls. She kneels on the rug and starts with Violet's clothes: dark, collared frocks, corsets, knitted cardies, girdles, her "fancy" twinsets, rayon slips, an expensive-looking tweed pencil skirt Diana had never seen her wear, the familiar High Holiday wool suits and silk blouses. The shoes: two pairs of black lace-ups for the shop, patent court shoes, a pair of knitted slippers with the backs pressed flat.

It can all go.

Then it's on to her toilette: hair rollers clogged with her fine brown hair, paddle brushes, an untouched tin of pressed powder, talc, Yardley soaps sealed with the golden royal warrant, a large bottle of Revlon perfume, the subdued red lipstick she wore a handful of times a year.

Her books and magazines: piles and piles of **Picture Post**, **Good Housekeeping** and the **Jewish Chronicle**, the collected works of Dickens and Shakespeare, **Jane Eyre**, **Rebecca**, **Pride and Prejudice**, schlocky paperbacks with lurid covers and titles, Teach Yourself guides for bridge, their father's Russian poetry collection, and dictionaries. Diana puts aside one roller, the pressed powder and red lipstick and seals the rest up in their boxes with tape. In large chalk letters she writes "Sally Army" and moves on to the archival collection: birth, marriage, divorce and death certificates in a muddled pile on top of each other, their father's naturalization papers and property deeds, insurance and investment certificates, school awards from the 1920s for each of the three daughters, letters between Violet and Diana while she was in London with the Women's Auxiliary Air Force. She unfolds one letter, written on a blue page torn from a military-issue exercise book, and reads.

21st October 1940
Dear Darling Violet,

Beep, beep, beep, this is London calling, here is the news: I'm terribly sad to have missed your birthday again, but this year I can promise to make it up to you with wonderful news. I'm not going to let Jerry's silly little bombing campaign stop me from returning to Cardiff next month. I've applied for leave already and expect it to be granted, but I won't tell you why just yet. Don't worry about me, Vi, the barrage balloons and fighter pilots are doing sterling work above our heads. I'm sleeping in a bunker deep underground and wouldn't exchange it for a penthouse at the Savoy.

Kisses,
Diana

How many weeks pregnant must she have been then? Eight? Ten? It was still early but getting to the point where people had to be told and decisions made. Ben hadn't heard yet, the letter stuck somewhere between London and Egypt. She knew he would reply with an excited telegram as soon as he received it. What a time that was, a quarter-century of life behind her and seemingly centuries still to go, Grace a minuscule tadpole within her, the story of the Volackis and Tanays commingled and thrown forward into the future. Ben a machine-gunner and sergeant in the Royal Air Force, looking tanned and handsome in his flight overalls and bomber jacket, the effort it took not to boast when girls asked what her husband did.

Diana opens another box and finds the gramophone records she'd wished she had taken to the lodging house with her. The Andrews Sisters, Cab Calloway, Eddie Cantor, Artie Shaw, The Ink Spots, Ella Fitzgerald, Louis Armstrong, Billie Holiday. She pulls The Ink Spots record out of its sleeve and places it on the turntable of the portable gramophone she had bought Violet for her fortieth birthday. First, that beautiful sound of white noise, of captured time, of anticipation and held breaths, then the plodding guitar chords of "It's All Over But The Crying." The early verses so melancholy and sentimental that her eyes begin to well until the song turns around on itself: tempo rising, beat deepening, harmonies quavering, the same despondent lyrics sung over the ebullient tune of a toothpaste advert jingle. Next, the full-hearted sorrow of "We Three." She leans back, spreads her fingers on the dusty floor and closes her eyes.

Ben. London. August 1940. There's still sand in his hair from the Sahara. He has become nocturnal from the night sorties and after they make love he reads by candlelight until dawn. They're in a cheap bed and breakfast in Earl's Court, on a terrace of once-grand white villas that are now flaking and sooty. The French hostess charges too much for her terrible **petit déjeuner** so they walk to a caff in High Street Ken where they eat a good fry-up and listen to the one record the proprietor owns. "We Three" by the Ink Spots, played over and over until they hear it even when the place is silent. Ben could impersonate the lead singer, Bill Kenny, beautifully, batting his eyelashes and puckering his mouth for the hammy falsetto notes. She would take the spoken parts, putting on the deep southern drawl of Hoppy Jones, "Now, I walk wi' my shadow, I talk wi' my echo, but **where** is the gal that I love?" Such childish, irreplaceable joy.

A couple of years earlier, a few days after the bonfires and fireworks of Guy Fawkes Night, they had woken up to the news that would shape the rest of their short married life. **Kristallnacht**. Ninety dead, one thousand and four hundred synagogues burned to the ground, broken glass and jeering crowds. Days and days of it. German Jews incarcerated, forbidden to work or to go to university, or to hold property, yet forced to pay compensation for the very violence that had destroyed their homes and livelihoods. Ben and Diana listened, waited for the British government to react to this barbarism, but only the Americans recalled their ambassador. The

British wrung out their ornate condemnations and wagged a half-hearted finger at Herr Hitler. She doesn't remember the exact moment the notion of enlisting came up, who brought it up or where. They both had the foresight to see that, despite Chamberlain's hesitation, war was inevitable. They might as well have told their parents that they were setting off on a polar expedition, for all the sense it made to them. It was only when they saw the uniforms—brand new and neatly pressed—that they believed it was real. One night, her father arrived at her front door, convinced that he could persuade her to stay behind, even if Ben wanted to give up everything for the sake of strangers. Parked at the kitchen table with mugs of tea, she let him deliver his spiel; describing the charity sales she could organize for **Kindertransport** children, the petitions she could draft and send to the local parliamentarian, the plans the Board of Deputies had in place to persuade the government to accept more refugees. She pushed across that morning's copy of the **Daily Mail**, its headline screeching "ALIEN JEWS FLOODING IN!" and let him read the article that decried Jewish refugees taking British jobs while the native population languished on the dole.

"We either fight this fight now or later, which is better, Father?" she remembers saying.

"They have been saying this all the time I live here, it's no bother," he replied, pushing the paper away with disgust.

"It's different now, Daddy, I can't prove it but I feel it down to my bones. Soon it won't be just Russia we can't set a foot in but the whole of Europe. We'll be marooned on this little island and surrounded by sharks. You left Russia to save your life but still tried to help those left behind, and this is how I want to help."

His hands already had a little tremor then, which he tried to hide by drumming on the table.

She pushed on, wanting to finish this conversation before Ben returned home. "Remember the riots in 1919, when you put on your silver war medal and paced the barricaded shop with a club, me and the girls upstairs, squashed under the iron bed, as Mummy kept watch at the window. You know we fell asleep at our normal bedtime? Didn't matter that we were little 'uns and could hear glass smashing, fires burning, women screaming, men baying for blood, none of it mattered because we had our hero. So now there are little girls hiding under their beds in Germany, men just like you beaten and killed for nothing, a fire lit under their beds, what should I do?"

He had nodded then, defeated, and patted her head with some kind of benediction. "You go, child, I have raised you to have too much courage, now I can only blame myself."

The WAAFs nicknamed the balloons "sausages" but to her they looked like whales, with bulbous silken bodies and three flashing silver fins, floating in the sky as waves of clouds rushed by. Chained to a network of steel cables, the hydrogen-filled balloons were to be winched up to keep bombers from diving or dropping their explosives with any accuracy over London. The instructors warned them of the dangers they would face: lightning could set the gas alight or travel down the steel cables into the winch, while heavy winds could topple the balloons or wrest them away. It took eleven weeks of training to become a balloon operator. Diana remembers standing barefoot and in overalls, painting over interior tears in the nylon balloon fabric with a noxious glue, only thirty minutes allowed inside and then twenty minutes of fresh air. When her time was up she would be hauled out by the arms like a modern-day Jonah. Yet another day, Diana knee-deep in mud as she tussled with a deflated balloon in the middle of Wembley Common; untangling the sharp, slick steel cables with stinging, blue fingers. Diana in a classroom, jotting down how to load a splice wire or calculate a balloon's elevation. Diana having a go as "the bird in the gilded cage," manipulating the winch's gears while simultaneously watching the cables unfurl, calling out "blue line, thirty feet," "tension, four hundredweight," "no slack on drum," "start up winch" or "haul in winch" to the irascible instructor. She had done and survived it all.

Diana lifts the needle from the record and places it back in its sleeve, her reverie over. She stands and brushes the dust off her skirt. She must go downstairs and look through the post to see if Howell's have sent the exam results for Grace. She'll have to get her something nice to celebrate if she's won the scholarship. Try to put all of this out of her mind long enough to buy a nice little jewellery set or a taffeta dress.

She'd had to take Grace along to the identification parade. Mother and child trooping into the central police station. They both thought they had seen a glimpse of the man in the doorway but they couldn't agree on what they had seen: hat or no hat? Coat or no coat? Somali or West African? It would've been funny if it weren't so terrible. Diana thought there would be a line-up of different men but instead they had asked them to stand in a dim corridor while they led the chief suspect towards them. Placed under a large light that made him blink unseeingly in their direction, the suspect's gaunt face looked eerie, glowing as it did under the merciless yellow light. Grace rubbed her face against Diana's hand as she looked and looked. It was not him, they agreed on that, this was not the face in the doorway.

Detective Powell seemed disappointed in them and led them back out to the street with a request they think hard about what they actually remembered.

It had come to her one night, a week or so after everything happened, that maybe it was true that their family was cursed. Her mother had said it intermittently throughout the years but Diana had shot the idea down impatiently. There wasn't a place for curses or lucky heather in the modern world, or so she had thought. Now, there was a strange comfort to the idea that all of this pain was beyond their control, beyond the realms of prayers or intellect or justice. Curses were in the Bible, weren't they? God cursed, the prophets cursed, the angels cursed. Such a multitude of misfortunes: her mother's orphan childhood, the two divorces, their father's bad lungs, Violet's twisted spine, Ben dead before he ever saw his child, Violet killed steps away from where her family ate dinner. A curse with an origin and cause so obscure it could never be lifted, that made more sense than anything else. The men thought that they had God—that they were the special ones who could hear him, plead with him, sing for him, wield power in his name—and where had it got them? They're scrabbling around trying to explain the inexplicable, the newsreels hiding nothing, not even the tumble and crack of Europe's last Jews as bulldozers drove them into mass graves. A curse, the women knew. The mark invisible yet indelible, Diana knows now too. The face of an acquaintance as she announces her pregnancy, the crowds on the steps of a church as the bride and groom emerge, the young romantics canoodling on a park bench—she has no way of sharing that joy any more. She finds herself wishing harm on them—a miscarriage, an affair, a terrible revelation—and then looking away in shame. She can march those cruel thoughts away but she cannot face a lifetime of nodding and smiling as other people's lives glide past hers, everything good falling and staying in their laps.

There is a buyer interested in the property, a hardware merchant from Newport who is trying to drive down the price by a quarter. Diana will probably agree but feels no obligation to be quick about it. He keeps calling Daniel, telling him to make her see sense, which makes her delay even more. He thinks that because there was a murder in the shop he should get a discount. That he's doing her a favour by purchasing it at all. To him it's just property but all of her history is tied up in its bricks and mortar. Her father had bought the building in 1909, first number 203 then, later, number 204, knocking them through to create one large shop. He had enough money left in the bank to hire a maid and to commission a large oil painting, of the girls dressed like Tsarinas, to hang above the dining table. Diana's earliest memories are of exploring the maze of nine rooms upstairs and looking down at the carnival life of Bute Street from the sash windows. A parade of hulking great Vikings with blond beards and ripped shirts bloodied from brawls, of Salvation Army bands looking for drunks to save, of robed Yemenis and Somalis marching to celebrate Eid, of elaborate funeral cortèges for the last of the rich captains of Loudoun Square, of Catholic children clad in white on Corpus Christi, led by a staff-twirling drum major, of makeshift calypso bands busking to raise enough money to tour the country, of street dice games descending into happy laughter or nasty threats, of birdlike whores preening their feathers to catch a passing punter. What an education for a young girl it had been. Safe too, safe enough for Violet or their mother to stroll alone to the bank every week, with hundreds of pounds in takings stuffed into a handbag. Old maligned Tiger Bay, as tame as a circus lion. But she has decided to leave it all behind, to leave the Bay and never return.

Grace has won the scholarship to Howell's. The thin envelope stamped with the school crest was lost in a pile of post Diana had stacked up on the counter a few days ago. She said she would do it for Aunt Violet, and she did. **L'chaim**. Diana hopes she won't struggle there, being one of the scholarship girls and Jewish on top of that, but it's what her father had left Russia for, a chance to become someone through hard work and talent. Maybe life would be different for her. All three sisters had left school at sixteen to start work in trades they expected to remain in until old age. If only she could tell Violet that Howell's had accepted their little chicken, how proud she would be. Maybe Grace would be the first to go to university, to travel, and enjoy an easier life. Diana has never been abroad in her life, even though she has cousins in New York who have told her to visit countless times. She could take Grace. They could even emigrate there, why not? The ground beneath their feet is liquid now. They could become Americans or Canadians or Ten Pound Poms. Live the wandering Jew life. Try to outrun the curse if nothing else. But first, a good education for Grace amongst the daughters of Cardiff's gilded class: barristers, surgeons, shipping barons.

Diana looks up from the letter, thinks she's heard footsteps in the back room and takes a few steps towards it. No sound, so she approaches closer. Looks into the empty alcove where the police think Violet was attacked before she crawled into the open, bleeding heavily, to pursue her murderer. Diana marches around, examining every corner to dispel her fear. Violet is suddenly very present in the shop, her humming and brisk little steps easy to sense. Returning to the counter, Diana rushes to put her coat on, stuffs the letters into her handbag and slings it over her shoulder, then slams the door on the eerie place. Out into the daylight and the ordinary chit-chat of street life, the tram sending sparks into the air, she looks back at the dark melancholy shop front and hopes to never set foot inside it again.

The GP surgery. A yellowed plastic skeleton grins at Diana from a corner of the waiting room while a black child wails in his mother's arms. The place has changed, the old doctor, Something-Lewis, had left the practice in theatrical protest at his loss of income under the National Health Service, and she is glad of it. He was a shameless snob with strange ideas about who should be "encouraged" to breed, which he enjoyed expounding at every visit. He'd usually manage to squeeze a quick, placatory "not that I have any issues with the noble Hebrew race, of course" into his lectures, and Diana would reply "of course," a doubtful smile tickling her lips.

The replacement, Dr. Woodruff, looks to be in her early thirties, and has a boyish cropped hairstyle. Large green eyes and plump red cheeks give colour to her otherwise plain, milk-white face. The brogue as she welcomes Diana into the cosy room is a soft, Edinburgh purr. Yes, she's much better, Diana thinks, as she takes a seat opposite her. She had been hoping to avoid talking about any of this, but now it has started to take a physical toll; no more than a couple of hours' sleep at night, headaches, her monthlies gone, heart racing and jumping all over the place, a constant sense of dread. She gives the doctor all of the symptoms and waits for her to stop jotting them down.

"Do you have any idea what might have brought all this on, Mrs. Tanay?"

Has she not heard? Everyone has heard. "It's my sister, Dr. Woodruff . . ."

"Mmm, what about her?"

"My sister was murdered."

Dr. Woodruff leans back into the vast leather chair she's inherited from Dr. Something-Lewis. "I'm ever so sorry, Mrs. Tanay. I had no clue."

"You must be the only one left."

"I'm afraid I'm not one for reading the newspapers."

"That's probably a medicine of its own."

Dr. Woodruff meets Diana's gaze, holds it with a forceful, maternal insistence. "Do you have any support at home? I understand from your records that you are a war widow with a small child."

A war widow with a small child sounds little better than Tiny Tim, thinks Diana bitterly, but she answers, "Yes, my other sister, my brother-in-law too."

"Well, that is good to know. Let's tackle the insomnia as a start, shall we? Find something that 'knits up the ravell'd sleeve of care,' as Shakespeare puts it in **Macbeth**."

Diana looks down at her hands, doesn't know anything of **Macbeth**.

"I'll write you a prescription for Medinal, take one tablet an hour before bed. You'll have a touch of grogginess in the mornings but it will be worth it."

Diana takes the prescription gratefully. "And the other . . . issues?"

"Time. Your body has taken quite a shock, just as much as your mind has, and it needs time to find its equilibrium again."

"I should just wait?"

"I believe so, but come see me again, in a month or so."

"Yes, Doctor."

Diana sits on the bed of her rented room and places the sleeping tablet on her tongue, washes it down with a glassful of water. She has spread photographs of Ben, Violet and Grace all over the floor and she looks down at them, her eyes skipping from one to the next. The crisp black and white images begin to blur through her tears and she pads a hankie quickly against her cheeks. One of them in particular is painful to see again: a small snap of the three sisters in white smocks and pigtails, as they wait for the ferry to take them to Ilfracombe's sandy beaches, buckets and spades dangling from their hands. Their parents stand awkwardly together to the side. Diana must be no older than ten in the photo, her wide smile full of new misshapen teeth, gloriously innocent of what life has in store for her. What a thing life is, she thinks. Chaos upon chaos. She wants to warn that little girl, "Don't grow up, whatever you do."

The sleeping tablet acts more dramatically than she had anticipated and Diana slides drowsily under the sheets with her eyes already sealed. The world pulls away from her, even the deep sadness she had felt looking at the photos melts away, and she passes out in one . . . two . . . three . . .

The only thing to wait for now is the trial, but the wait itself is a trial. Diana mulls it all over. She doesn't want to sit in the witness box, but she must. She doesn't want to explain how she heard nothing of the murder, but she'll have to. She doesn't want photos of Violet's body paraded before the jury, but they'll see them.

It's an exercise in impotence, like pregnancy, a period of waiting, waiting, waiting, with no control over the outcome. When she was heavily pregnant with Grace and the Luftwaffe attacked Cardiff, there was that same sense of suspended animation; you could look up to the sky all you liked but the minute you looked away death might come. Ben sent letter after letter, all of them arriving in a packet, full of fear and worry and then incredulity that no one was replying to him. Railways down. Telegraph wires cut. Roads blocked by rubble. It had been such an expedition for her, with only two months left before the baby arrived, to scramble to a working Post Office and send a telegram. The stress of it all was playing on his nerves, she could tell by the ever-increasing Xs scrawled across the bottom of the letters and the I LOVE YOU's written in large letters, as if giving a farewell shout.

Then, April arrives and their roles are reversed. MISSING IN ACTION. His pretty script replaced by the typed bureaucracy-ese of the Air Ministry. Ben's Wellington left the RAF base at 11 p.m. on 13th April to attack an enemy airport, and then nothing. No wreckage. No body. As if they had flown straight up and into space. Hope. Hope. Hope for God's grace, if nothing else. That's what everyone said. And she did, with a force that could have raised Lazarus himself. He disappeared on the second day of Passover, an auspicious time, they reassured her. It was even Easter Sunday, God damn it, what other time could you ask for a miracle, a resurrection? She read stories of airmen rescued and nursed by Somali Bedouins or appearing suddenly in distant prisoner-of-war camps. Strange stories, but anything is possible in wartime. The baby was readying itself, stretching little fists and knees against Diana's stomach, just a few more weeks left. The Red Cross sent her a letter: they would contact the Germans and see what information they had on Ben and his crew.

"Hold your nerve," Diana told herself, "all you have to do is concentrate on delivering this baby safely so that when he comes home, injured or not, you will all be together." The birth coincided with another short blitz over Cardiff. It was too dangerous to try for the infirmary so the baby arrived at home, with only Violet to help guide her out by candlelight. With sirens wailing, fire engines shooting along Bute Street, V2 bombs whinnying down, the force of explosions nearby swooping through the house and billowing dust into their hair, Diana dug her face into a pillow and bellowed her daughter into the world.

When morning arrived, Diana padded to the window, Grace swaddled in her arms, to survey the damage from her childhood perch: number 184 had lost its exterior and looked like an open doll's house with colourful beds and chairs on show; silvery barrage balloons bobbed over the charred, broken-boned warehouses on the docks; a cloud of white smoke obscured the low sun. The air burned her nostrils, carrying the smell of burning sugar, explosives and evaporated whisky into the room. A fire engine stood abandoned at the top of the road, its thick tyres molten and pooling like treacle on the ground. Someone had chalked THERE WILL ALWAYS BE A TIGER BAY on to the roof-slate–strewn pavement.

Hearing a cry from the right, Diana turned to see a woman in a gas mask run into the arms of an air-raid warder, sobbing against his shoulder as she pointed a brown finger behind her. The warder sprinted to a pile of rubble under the Marquis of Bute pub and began to dig through the bricks and mortar. Passing dockworkers rushed to help him, and then Diana watched as a green-coated arm and black trousers were excavated from the debris. Then laughter. Squinting hard, Diana saw a decapitated body. The laughter was unsettlingly hysterical now. The woman approached the men unsteadily, her face hidden behind the macabre gas mask. The dockers lifted the body up on to its buckle-booted feet and the poor woman jumped back in fright. Diana recognized the blitz victim as the four-foot statue of the marquis that had stood pompously on the pub's cupola. The scene had made her laugh so much that Grace had startled and begun to wail. THERE WILL ALWAYS BE A TIGER BAY. "Bloody right there will," she thought.

In London, the past year, she had seen THERE WILL ALWAYS BE AN ENGLAND scrawled everywhere: on the ruins of bombed-out homes in Victoria, on the plinth of Nelson's Column in Trafalgar Square, on the grey stones of Waterloo Bridge. It was a kind of talisman, a prayer, and it worked, she never entertained the notion that they might lose the war. The capital city had developed a malevolent romance during the Blitz; the river brooded beneath the bridges, black and muscular; the stars shone and reconquered the night sky; blacked-out streets susurrated with lovers hidden in doorways and alleys. Full of longing for Ben, Diana would meander north and south over the Thames in the few hours she had free from Balloon Command. They were stationed in Green Park, close to Buckingham Palace, but she went east regularly, to Whitechapel, to visit Ben's large, boisterous family. On the journey home once, she had caught two burglars breaking the window of a tall Georgian terraced house. Without thinking, she had yelled and chased the thieves up the street, their figures darting between the plane trees that shaded the pavement. Fit and strong from her work, Diana had kept close behind them, shouting "Thief!" until an air-raid warder and policeman ambushed the pair and got them in handcuffs. She had never told Ben about that adventure but she was proud that at no point had she been afraid: exhilarated, yes, angry, yes, nervous, yes, but never afraid.

The summer came and went without news of Ben. Diana wrote letters describing Grace's smallest changes, the head lifts, smiles, rolls and babbled words that he'd missed, and stored them in a drawer for when he returned. Ben always wrote about the minutiae of his days in Egypt, from the cup of tea his bearer, Mohammed, brought him in the morning to the chatter in the mess room and the books he read at night. By writing, she could kindle some hope that he was still out there, wondering what was happening in Cardiff. The Air Ministry wrote again in November to say that he was now presumed dead, but too much time had elapsed for her to believe that he was just another Jew fallen under Hitler's scythe. She felt deeply that he was somewhere beyond her reach, fighting a never-ending, nocturnal war up in the clouds, his machine gun rat-tat-tatting and spitting fiery stars.

In Queen Street, just as Diana emerges from one of the genteel arcades, juggling a wrapped silk dress for Grace and some treats from Wally's delicatessen, she feels a tap on her shoulder. She turns around and sees an elderly woman in a green headscarf, the wire of a hearing aid trailing down into her collar.

"Mrs. Tanay, isn't it?" she asks, extending a bony hand.

Diana frees her hand from her bags and shakes it. "It is. Have we had the pleasure of meeting?"

"Once or twice, but it was your sister, God bless her soul, who really knew me."

Diana smiles, nods, waits for a chance to get away. "And your name is?"

"Gray, Mrs. Gray. I have a little second-hand

shop on Bridge Street, nothing as grand as yours, mind."

"I daren't call our shop grand."

"You have a buyer yet?"

Diana is surprised by the bold question and murmurs a vague reply.

"Great big place like that, you'll make a fortune."

"I'll be getting on now, Mrs. Gray, I have to collect my daughter from school."

"Righty-ho, don't let me keep you, dear, but one last thing. Everyone and their maiden aunt has been asking me if anyone has claimed that reward yet?"

Diana has already turned away. She picks up her stride and gives the old gossip a faint, "Good afternoon, madam."

"And a good day to you too," Mrs. Gray cries after her retreating back.

Toddoba

[Seven]

So, you say your father is dead?"

"That's right."

"And your mother?"

"Last I heard she still living."

"What was your father's profession?"

"He had a shop, grocer's shop, and he had lorries for transport too."

"Well off, then?"

Mahmood nods vaguely. "Not very rich but not poor, he was a clever man, liked new things, modern, yes, a modern man."

The prison doctor has already taken Mahmood's height, weight, temperature, blood, urine, and now he wants his life story too.

"How many brothers and sisters do you have?"

"Four brothers, all older, no sisters, two girls die as babies and one get sick around seven years old." Mahmood's cell is messy, his prison-issue pyjamas are in a heap on his unmade bed, and he has dumped the morning's bread uneaten into the chamber pot along with the thin, tasteless milk. He might have tidied up if he had known the doctor was coming today, but he doesn't really care. It's his modest protest to show them he shouldn't be here at all.

"My brothers they take over my father's business, they all big men with families. Why do they put me here and not in the normal prison?"

"You're on a capital charge."

"They stupid but soon they'll know I'm innocent. They give men compensation for wrongful jailing, true?"

"That is true. But I have nothing to do with that, I'm a medical officer."

"I understand, carry on."

"When did you arrive in Britain?"

"In 1947. I was a pantry boy on a cargo ship, but later I become a fireman."

"Can you read or write English?"

"No, I only go to religious school in my country. I can read the Qu'ran."

"You read and write Arabic, then?"

"No, I just read the Qu'ran, it's . . . different. Not the same as Arabs write now."

"What languages can you speak?"

"I know Somali, Arabic, English, Swahili and a little Hindi."

"A bona fide polyglot."

Mahmood doesn't ask what he means, puts it down to white-coat talk.

"Do you have any injuries or disabilities?"

"Nothing, just a small problem here . . ." His lashes flutter as he points a finger close to his right iris. "When the sun is too hot, it looks like a small fly is in my eye. Happened at sea when burning coal hit me in the face."

The doctor's handwriting disappoints Mahmood; he might be illiterate but he feels he can still judge good penmanship from bad. "What you write down?"

"Blowback from furnace caused small vision impairment."

"Blowback from furnace caused small vision impairment, yes, that's nice." Mahmood prefers the doctor to the screws. He finds them both oafish and overly sensitive. They cry over every little thing and report him to the governor. The young doctor is calm and handsome, wears a nice tie and cufflinks, he waits expectantly as Mahmood answers his questions and seems intrigued by his replies.

"Have you ever had tuberculosis?"

"No, but they keep the ships so cramped and dirty it be a miracle."

The doctor hesitates and then asks, "Have you ever been diagnosed with syphilis, gonorrhea or any other venereal disease?"

Mahmood leans back and almost shouts, "No! What you take me for?"

"Have you or any family member experienced fits, hallucinations, psychosis or mental illness?"

"We are and always have been sane, thanks be to God."

"Any nervous trouble such as bedwetting, nail biting, fear of the dark, irrational fears?"

Mahmood rolls his eyes so hard the doctor smiles.

"You mean to tell me that men come to prison who are scared of dark and can wet their beds?"

"We get all sorts here."

"Man! That make me wonder about this bed I'm sitting on." Mahmood laughs and makes a show of checking the bedding beneath him.

"What marvellous teeth you have!" The doctor exclaims.

Mahmood clamps his mouth shut, embarrassed, he doesn't like white people talking about his teeth because it's something they only compliment coloureds on, as if it's some kind of miracle that they have something beautiful about them. "What you writing now?"

The doctor finishes the sentence before looking up with his warm brown eyes and replying, "A healthy negroid individual, active, in good health, with excellent teeth!"

"Well, Moody, how are you going to get out of this? You know that this is a hanging offence, don't you?" Laura jiggles Mervyn on her lap as he begins to fuss, but Mahmood holds his arms out over the wide table and takes his youngest son in his arms.

"It is if you're guilty, I ain't got nothing to do with it." Mahmood tickles the boy's full cheeks with his scraggly moustache and coos in his ear. "**Wiilkayga, macaaney.**"

"He usually naps at this time."

Other prisoners hunch over tables around them, talking quietly with their wives or mothers.

Mervyn's large eyes fix on his father's face with a look of alarm, and he claws curiously at his father's nose and lips.

Mahmood laughs as he is manhandled. "He don't know me! Look!"

"Course he does, he's just cranky. Anyway, I bought you these cigarettes . . ." she digs around in her handbag before sliding over a packet of Players.

Mahmood's eyes light up at the sight of the blue wavelets and bearded sailor pictured on the box.

A warder marches over before Mahmood has even had a chance to reach across.

"That's not permitted. He'll get his tobacco allowance like everyone else, Tuesday next." The warder snatches up the cigarettes in his hairy paw and glares at Laura, before returning to his spot by the wall and pocketing the box.

Laura says nothing but gives Mahmood a "rude bugger" look. He smiles and then squeezes Mervyn closer to his chest, trying to hide his shame at having dragged his wife and child into a place like this.

"I spoke to Berlin, he says that they've got the money for the solicitor, at least for the hearings at the magistrates, but that the Allawi Friendship Society at the mosque ain't going to lift a finger to help. The sheikh said that in their charter it says if a fella gets into trouble of his own making they'll take no part in his affairs."

"Yemeni sons of bitches. They take our money when it suits them but don't wanna give nothing in return. How is any of this my own making? I have nothing to do with that woman, that shop, that murder."

"I know that, Moody, I **know** that. It's a misunderstanding. You've never laid a hand on me so how are you going to get up one day and cut a strange woman's throat? But you got too many enemies and too few friends. The sheikh is just trying to punish you for what happened last year."

"How much punishment he want me to have? I pay a **fine**, I'm on **probation**, I pay back the **money**. He want to sacrifice me for Eid too? **Ibn Sharmuta.**"

"Enough, Moody, you'll agitate the baby."

Mahmood rubs his cheek against Mervyn's soft wispy hair. "When will you bring the other boys?"

"I can only manage one at a time. The woman from prison welfare told me off when she saw me carrying Mervyn in, said it was bad for him to be in this environment."

"Forget that."

"I'm not going to pay her any mind, don't worry. I'll bring David next as he keeps asking where you are, asked if you've been naughty again."

"That boy **clever**, nothing pass him by."

"Too clever by half, he tried to stop Daddy entering the house the other night, said that he heard on the wireless that the police were looking for an old man with a moustache."

Mahmood throws his head back and laughs. "No! Can't be my son if he take the police's side."

"He's yours alright, he's still doing that Somali dance you taught him. What's it called?"

Mahmood remembers with pure pleasure the four of them, before Mervyn was born, cosy in their little terraced house in Hull. The coal fire burning and a bedsheet wrapped around his shoulders in place of a **shaal**, a biscuit tin drum in his hand as he taught Omar and David how Somali nomads danced. One, two, three . . . then a missed beat, Mahmood leaping forward with a shout of **soobax** in that gap. He had tied pillow-cases around the boys' waists and they toddled around him, their eyes as wide as moons, moving their limbs in uncoordinated, antic shapes, their high-pitched, mispronounced **soobaxs** completely out of time. Laura watching it all bemusedly from the tweed armchair they had bought cheap from another Somali sailor.

"**Dhaanto**, it's called a dhaan-to." Trying to make the simple word even simpler.

"Duntoo, I'll tell the little beggar when I get home." Laura stands up to reach for Mervyn and quickly kisses Mahmood's fingertips as he lifts him towards her. "Chin up, OK?"

"OK."

. . .

Is it mouth before nose? And feet before ears? Mahmood stumbles over the **wudu** sequence, repeating many steps until he's reassured that he's achieved **taharat**. The other prisoners look at him strangely as they back away from the spluttering taps with little more than a whisper of water on their faces. The last time he had prayed properly was in Bombay, in 1949, at the Jama Masjid, between Crawford Market and Zaveri Bazaar. Ablutions were performed there in an old water tank with goldfish flashing through the bright green water and turtles bobbing intermittently up to the surface. Their ship, the SS **Emmeline**, was docked in the city, disgorging a cargo of British farm machinery and double-decker buses, so he had cajoled the other Somali firemen, trimmers and greasers to head into the sprawling city with him. They quickly ended up in the markets; chomping through mangoes, papayas, stringy tamarinds and dry sugar cane as they idled through the stalls. Nothing you couldn't buy under that tall vaulted roof: fake gold, squawking chickens, embellished rugs, toupees and henna, Hindu gods and technicolour paintings of Jesus and Mary, oily perfumes and incense sticks, defanged cobras and bleating white kid goats. The **masjid** had been a welcome discovery after all of that. The **'asr** call to prayer bounded off the onion-domed building, pigeons and black kites stirred the inert cloudless sky, intricate tiles adorned every surface of the **masjid**. Between two grand pillars, surrounding the wide pool of water, crouched a crew of maimed beggars, eating slowly and politely from a shared platter of rice and watery **dhal**. It was all peaceful enough to move something in him. When a local told them in a mix of Hindi and Arabic that the **masjid** was known as "the ship of the world to come" because it had been built on water, Mahmood had stored away the phrase in the part of his mind where he kept things of beauty.

Now, though, praying is a serious business. He wants God on his side, to weigh fate in his favour. At some point, he thinks, his luck had soured. From birth to twenty years of age everything had gone his way with little effort on his part, but since then, in these last four years, bad luck has surrounded him like a fog. The few small respites at the racetrack or poker table not changing anything substantial about his life or bringing the old luck back. He needs God to hear him, to see him in this squalid jail, surrounded by heartless strangers, and to restore him to his family. The gambling and godlessness will go, that's his part of the deal. Returning to his cell, Mahmood throws his blanket on the floor and plants his feet towards Mecca, as close to the south-east as he can approximate. With his open hands by his ears, he closes his eyes and begins.

"**Allahu akbar, subhaanak-Allaahumma, wa bihamdik, wa tabaarakasmuk, wa ta'aalaa jadduk, wa laa ilaaha ghayruk . . .**"

Then pauses to remember the next part, "**. . . a'auodu billaahi minash-shaytaanir rajeem bis-millaahir rahmaanir raheem.**"

Then the opening **surah** of the Qur'an, "**. . . al-hamdu lillaahi, rabbil'aalameen, arrahmaanir raheem, maaliki yawmideen, iyyaaka na-budo, wa-iyyaaka nasta'een, ihdinassiraatalmusta qeem, siraatal ladheena, an'amta alayhim, ghayril maghduobi" alayhim, waladduaaalleen, ameen . . .**"

The prayer flows from him like a song, like water bubbling up to the surface of a desert. Crouched on his heels at the end of the prayer, he lingers and dives into supplementary prayers. He pulls **surah** after **surah** from the well of his mind: some poured into him at cane-point by the **macalims** of his childhood, some overheard from his pious, fearful mother, others patched together from makeshift funerals for men buried at sea. He will ask the warders for a Qur'an, he decides, turn this captivity into something good for his soul.

. . .

Mahmood lies on his back, his eyes tracing the cracks in the painted ceiling from one corner to another, his head cradled by his interlocked fingers. The cell is bright and he can hear laughter from the exercise yard; he hasn't left his cell since he was charged with murder and moved to this new wing, or opened the Qur'an that a warder pushed through the hatch in the door. He is wary of mixing with the other prisoners in the hospital, expecting to find some in the full flush of TB or, even worse, men who look well but carry an arsenal of poxes, bacteria and viruses that he might pass on to his beautiful sons. He'll ask the doctor if they are contagious and then venture out of the fetid room.

Maybe he should tell the doctor his real age too. It probably won't make a difference, he knows, but perhaps they'll go a little easier on a twenty-four- rather than a twenty-eight-year-old. He should show the doctor that his life isn't cheap, tell him that he was born in **Qorkii**, the year of registration, the year of famine. Delivered safely in the middle of nowhere, between Arabsiyo and Berbera, to a mother well past forty, Mahmood had arrived into a world wet and red from the slaughter of emaciated animals, a world of Indian civil servants under shady trees scribbling nomads on to welfare lists, of sacks of government rice and stewed wild plants. The drought had lasted three years already and had followed an outbreak of rinderpest in livestock imported from Europe. Out of his father's thirty-eight camels, only ten remained, of his seventy-two cattle only five, and as for the sheep, well, their bones would make good fertilizer. The goat hides had gone to Aden for a measly price, the market glutted, the British Customs officials taking their usual tribute of tax.

Mahmood had heard all of this over and over again from his mother, Shankaroon, the **abaar** and **gaajo** she had faced, the many times she had snatched him from the clutches of death, her self-sacrifice, her ingenuity, the frayed rope tied tight around her waist to staunch her own hunger pains. The story of his life recited in the poetry of her melodious, melancholic **buraanbur**. He knew every detail of how she trekked four days to a welfare camp in Bulahar, carrying him in a sling on her back, only to be told by a Yemeni fisherman, as she approached the coast, that no one who entered the camp came out alive. An outbreak of smallpox had cut down those already weakened by hunger, he said. She staggered back in the direction she came, the horizon melting into a yellow mist, only to wake up lashed to the back of a **geel**, Mahmood in the arms of a tall, raven-black woman, feeding at her breast as she marched beside the camel. That woman nourished them both and then deposited mother and child at the nearest settlement, before venturing further into the eroded, skeleton-strewn **miyi**. His mother never mentioned the saviour's name or clan, if she ever even knew it, but gave meaningful looks to suggest it was clearly not a mere human they had encountered. **Jinn**? Angel? Reincarnated ancestor? It wasn't for her to pretend to know.

It made him feel guilty as a child, that she had suffered so much for him, that she loved him so hard when sometimes, when he looked at her beside him on the sleeping mat—weather-beaten, pockmarked, jangling with silver bangles and holy talismans—she frightened him. He had been a frail boy, stunted by that famine, and she had tormented him with every kind of medicine: frankincense suppositories, myrrh mouthwashes, acacia tea, **malmal** sap, amulets tied to his arms and legs to prevent the evil eye, emetic powders from Indian traders, injections and pills from British doctors, the words of the Qur'an washed from a slate and poured down his throat, his stars consulted by a long-haired **faallow**, his wrists and ankles burned with metal to cure chronic malaria. Finally, his mother made fine cuts in his abdomen and rubbed in coarse salt. He'll never forget the yelp that broke from him when she did that, her soft words and tight grip as he fought her off, his stomach burning as if set alight. That last medicine put him on his feet and made a wanderer of him, a **dalmar**, happy to put as much distance between him and his mother as possible.

When his elderly father, Hussein, returned after four years working as a trader in Aden, he had enough ten-rupee notes secreted within his white-bandaged legs that he could afford the rent and licence for a shop in Hargeisa, where many of his clan already lived. Mahmood moved with his four brothers and parents into a one-room mud-brick bungalow while their camels, marked with their characteristic star-shaped brandings, were sent away with an uncle. With the animals went also the turmoil that a season of drought, rinderpest, anthrax or locusts might bring upon the family, and while Mahmood lost the craggy, wild desert he gained the novelty and intrigue of town life. Hargeisa had once been just the widest point of a long watercourse where elephants gathered during the **gu** rains, and nomads watered their beasts, but then the sheikhs had come. A **jamaca** had been established there at the end of the last century, a sanctuary for the devout, destitute or captive, away from the tumult of the Dervish war and the profane harshness of nomadic life. They planted sorghum in the valley, grew bananas, mangoes and pomegranates along the riverbank, built an angular, lime-washed mosque and spent the evenings in prayer. Mahmood arrived after the town had already been coarsened. One paved road, fifteen eating houses, thirty-two general merchandise stores, a half-hearted jail, a basic infirmary and an Irish District Commissioner were all it took to make it the third-largest town in the protectorate.

His father's shop sold tea, millet, meat, white cotton, grey sheeting, rice, sugar, salt, grass fodder and whatever nomads traded with him. The income stretched far enough to employ a young, pretty **jariyad** to do the chores for their mother, who had grown fat, slow and pious with her comfortable life. Mahmood clung around the knees of the long-plaited Oromo maid, Ebado, and would not nap until she had sung to him or rubbed his tired feet with oil. He massaged her thin shoulders in return, then her little brown hands, rebraided the loose ends of her rows and rows of tight plaits, stole handfuls of sugar to gift her. His mother, jealous and vengeful, sent him to a **dugsi** run by the puritanical **salihiyya** order, where the **macalim** rocked back and forth to measure the rhythm of the **kitab** verses, and punished slow learners with vicious pinches that raised bloody welts on their skin. The **macalim** taught Mahmood that becoming a man was like turning wood into charcoal: a process of destruction until something pure and fiercely incandescent emerged. Tears softened the soul while pain toughened it. That was a lesson

Mahmood understood quickly and effortlessly; everything in his life had already suggested it.

When his father was selected by the Governor as an **Akil** to adjudicate religious cases, it was a surprise to Mahmood that the aloof old merchant with his neat columns of rupees, annas and pices had once cared enough about religion to travel to Harar and Jeddah to study the holy texts. His preening mother, on the other hand, clicked her **tusbah** and glowed with pleasure. She attended every court he presided over—the forbidden marriages, the ugly divorces, custody battles, inheritance disputes and compensation demands—muttering her own unforgiving commentary on the proceedings. Strange women appeared at their home, their tearful voices disturbing Mahmood's nap, begging his mother to intercede on their behalf because their husbands had abandoned them, or taken their children away, or insulted them more deeply than they could bear. Boiling up pan after pan of spiced tea, his mother tried to resolve these problems herself, meddling intensely and swearing Mahmood to secrecy. Fortunately for his mother, his father would have greater concerns in the few years before his death.

Mahmood first saw the Haji at the age of eight, during an Eid march by the whole **salihiyya** order through the town. Bearing a small yellow flag with a red star and crescent, Mahmood marched in columns three boys wide, from the livestock market in the north to Sheikh Madar's tomb in the south, past the abattoir, the police station and jail, the small strip of smoky **mukh-bazars**, and the District Commissioner's broad bungalow. At Sheikh Madar's tomb, they prayed and then listened to a sermon by an elegantly robed and turbaned man with a white beard. Standing at the rear of the crowd, Mahmood heard just some phrases and lines of poetry, the unmistakable war poetry of the Dervish. The Haji's rasping, imploring voice must have fixed itself in his memory, though, because when he heard it weeks later in his father's shop, as the two men chit-chatted over Customs taxes, he recognized it immediately. "The Haji is one of our own, a clansman and brother," his father said, apologizing for his son's wary expression, "come kiss the great man's hand." The smooth white smile he gave Mahmood belied the trouble the Haji would bring to their door.

Between that day and the day his **aabbo** died, he doesn't remember a time when his father was not talking about something the Haji had said or done. It was through the Haji that Mahmood learnt Somali convicts were sometimes flogged with nine-stranded whips in the jail, and that street boys dependent on government rations were caned if they refused to clean the streets. He climbed a mango tree, one day, pretending to pick fruit but aiming to see into the jail yard and prove the Haji's report with his own eyes. The sight that met him was more shocking than a pen of shackled, blood-soaked men would have been. Grown men in long shirts and cropped trousers were milling around the brown sand, some watering bright flowers and leafy vegetables, others repairing thick, multi-stranded ropes; under a hibiscus tree a man pedalled a loom while convicts seated around him wove baskets or cut out patterns in leather. The prisoners did their women's work in absolute silence and Mahmood stole down the tree before they caught sight of him. It was worse than a flogging, or was it? He couldn't tell. The British did this to men they got hold of, he had seen that, made them into their cooks, nannies and laundry washers. Beat them like disobedient wives and made sure they could never be respected as real men again. The ragged orphans who had settled in Hargeisa in the hope that some relative would find them, who did the dirty abattoir work, or came from the weakest, poorest clans, were easy targets, but in that yard were locals he had seen before, at that time puff-chested and pugnacious. When Mahmood returned to the shop, he asked the Haji how he knew so much about the British.

The Haji rubbed the black callus on his forehead where his head hit the ground during **salaat**, and tucked a fold of his turban behind his ear. After exchanging a look with Mahmood's father, he leant an elbow on the wooden counter and looked up at the ceiling with his pale brown eyes. "I lived in Berbera as a young man, worked as an office clerk for the infidels, bought my food with the **haram** money they forced out of our nomads and traders. I speak their language well, very well, and I heard them speaking of us as children, but I thought in time we would become a new Aden, with ships coming from all over the world, that we would have trains like India, that they would push the Abyssinians back to their highlands. Nothing, we got **nothing**." He dusted his palms together. "Then I heard poetry so strong it stopped my heart. I followed it out into the desert, into the battlefield, into a world of death and piety. For that I was deported, forced out of my homeland by men from a country we will never see. They sent me to Mauritius, a little island of statue worshippers, where I wandered place to place, known by no one." He blinked, as if about to shed a tear, then regained himself. "Once our leader, our poet, had passed on to **akhirah** they gave me permission, per-miss-ion, **haa**, to come home, thinking I had been defanged, when now I'm pure poison to them."

Once Mahmood had finished with the **dugsi**, at around eleven years of age, he worked alongside his brothers in the shop. He had learnt to recite a third of the Qur'an but that knowledge was quickly submerged beneath the songs, jokes, riddles, **maahmaah**, goods prices, tax levies, **dhow** times and foreign words he had learnt while shuttling between Aden and Hargeisa with his brother Hashi. With all five sons now out buying and selling for him, Mahmood's father set his mind to buying lorries to extend their reach to rural parts of the country. Keeping his plans quiet so as not to arouse competition or envy, their father applied for a transport licence and sent a camel as a gift to the District Commissioner. Perhaps if he had spoken to an astrologer first he would have postponed his plans, as that year his sub-clan almost went to war with the British. It started with a fight over a woman, a flirtatious young thing with thick ankles and pearly teeth. A fight that started with fists ended with a dagger stuck between the ribs of a teenage Eidegalle poet. The assailant fled into the **miyi**, seeking protection within his clan from the Eidegalle. Usually, it would be a matter of time, of cooling blood, then the negotiation of a suitable **diya** payment, but now the British wanted to be the sole adjudicators of murder cases. They said they wanted to teach Somalis the sanctity of life, even if it meant learning it at the end of a hangman's noose. As the weeks stretched on and the boy's clan refused to surrender him, the Haji perceived the magnitude of the moment. This was his clan, his blood, and he would raise the cry of "**tolaay!**" so loud they would hear it in Westminster.

While Mahmood's father chewed his lip nervously, the Haji convened **shir** after **shir** of the clan's elders to encourage them to resist the British demands. Mahmood watched as the Haji, holding a hand over his silk-clad heart, a fire illuminating his strong profile, laid out all the reasons why it would be **haram** to hand the culprit over for execution. Hadn't the Eidegalle already accepted the terms of the **diya**? Hadn't the British paid blood money when a drunken English mechanic had shot and killed a nomad boy? Hadn't they called it "criminal negligence" and paid just a portion of the compensation due? Wasn't it against the very spirit of Islam to cold-bloodedly kill a man when there was still some chance of peace and restitution? He would publicly declare as infidel **any** Muslim who played **any** part in this injustice. The henna-bearded and shaven-headed elders supped their tea and murmured "**na'am**" and "**waa sidaa**," but Mahmood caught some of them exchanging furtive glances too.

One old man, wearing perhaps twenty yards of white cotton wrapped around his stringy body, rose to his feet and shook his head, "You cannot call **kuffar** anyone who in their hearts believes in God and his word. You become the sinner in that case."

The Haji scowled, vexed that he had been contradicted and his train of thought broken. "It is simple, Halane, you cannot clutch to your bosom a man who has declared faith and allegiance to a foreign king. Can a man go in two directions at the same time? Can he ride two horses? Can he be a slave to Allah and to a **gaal** at the same time?" The Haji shook his head with disgust at his own question. "No, **astaghfirullah**, only Allah is worthy of worship and obedience. The British people are a simple, servile people. They are peasants, satisfied working their lords' lands, who cannot understand **xorriyadda**, our love of freedom. I know them, they are never happier than when they meet someone more important than themselves, then they bow and plead, 'Sir, sir, I am your humble servant.' They consider Somalis wild because every man is his own master, but they forget we have one powerful master, **Al-Rab, Al-Raheem**. We need only our land, Allah will be our sustenance for everything else."

The clan, with the Haji as its de facto **suldaan**, held its nerve, until the Camel Corps finally arrived on their grazing lands, just a few dozen miles outside Hargeisa. The news arrived at the shop the same afternoon. A young mud-streaked nomad with a black ostrich feather in his hair had ridden immediately to rouse the town. He washed his face and drank a goatskin of water before breathily recounting the events to the gathered men. A British captain, backed by nearly fifty mounted and armed Somali askaris, had arrived at the Biyo Kulule reservoir and demanded the surrender of the suspect and the three men accused of harbouring him. Speaking through an army interpreter, an elder told them to go find them in hell. Realizing there would be no capitulation to his order, the captain commanded his troops to round up the livestock as forfeited goods. Two men who ran to disperse the camels were shot in the back, and the elder who had spoken bluntly was trussed up and taken prisoner. With tall grain-fed camels, the Corps used their **geeljire** wrangling skills to herd the various animals and drag them away, leaving a few old worthless bulls and calves that wouldn't survive the **jilaal** without their mother's milk.

Mahmood's father advised an immediate surrender of the wanted men, but the Haji won the argument again. "Blood is on the ground, blood is on the ground," he kept repeating, as if delighted by the idea. Another raid on another watering place resulted in five dead and a man known as

Farah of the Hundred losing all hundred of his camels. When the third raid arrived, the nomads were waiting; they had dusted down and oiled the rifles kept hidden after the Dervish war. Shots were fired on both sides and a fork in the road approached; either a return to the bombardment and massacres of the Sheikh's time, or a drawing back of daggers on both sides. After an assembly of all the **suldaans**, **boqors**, **garaads**, **akils** and **qadis** of the whole Habr Awal clan, the youth who had started the trouble was finally retrieved from his hiding place and sent to wrestle his fate alone. Even after the trial, in which the Governor played judge, prosecution and jury, the Haji had one last card hidden behind his back. He had managed to convert an unknown number of Somali policemen to his cause, and one by one they refused to prepare the execution shed. After nine rebellious constables were sentenced to hard labour, the inevitable hanging quietly went ahead and the **sheeko** was brought to a close.

This long episode fractured the relationship between the Haji and Mahmood's father. If there wasn't a distinction in how they perceived their place in the world before, it was now bold and written in red. Although never declared a **kuffar**, Hussein felt there was a mark on his back, and the curt "**salaam**" of the Haji as he passed by the shop always seemed to be followed with some muffled invective. The District Commissioner finally granted the transport licence and Hussein resigned his post as judge with relief. He died of a heart attack two dry seasons later, after enjoying more than his fair share of years and wealth, and with five sons to branch out and strengthen the family name. Those sons had diligently washed and wrapped his body in a single white shroud, and borne him on their shoulders to his final abode under an acacia, resting his left cheek on the mummifying, mica-flecked soil before the shovels went to work. His place in society affirmed by the large crowd at his burial, the Salat al-Janazah was led by the Haji himself.

The Haji had courted the brothers one by one, from eldest to youngest, turning a honeyed **af-minshaar** on them. He offered unsolicited advice on everything, from new merchandise arriving in Berbera, to talented lorry mechanics, popular cuts of fabric and eligible girls they might want to marry. He had learnt to smile again after his defeat over capital punishment, but his grin seemed barbed to Mahmood, the row of gold teeth out-flashing the decayed rest. He was a renewed man, engaged in a campaign of propaganda and quiet resistance against the British. There was no need for skirmishes; nomads held nothing more important than their camels, and all he had to do was shed doubt over the safety of locust bait and veterinary injections. A Public Works official would set locust bait, and a young child or woman would scatter it away from the well. If the Haji thought he could win this war of attrition, he was strengthened by the occasional suicides of colonial officials with nothing but alcohol, destitute women and servants for company, in missions strewn throughout the desolate hinterland.

If, as it seemed, it was true that the British hated their lives in Somaliland, it would go some way in explaining just how quickly they abandoned the protectorate in '41, when the Italians invaded from their colony in the south. Taking their Indians with them, it was as if the British had busted out from a jail. Life became difficult as the Royal Navy blockaded the coastal ports, what with the family shop relying on overpriced fruit and vegetables trucked in from Gabiley and Arabsiyo to keep customers coming. The Italians had their own plantations near the Shebelle and Juba rivers and big-time traders in Mogadishu to provision their troops, so the brothers ended up buying stock illegally from **La Forza** rather than selling anything to them. They were the first to sell spaghetti and macaroni in Hargeisa but the regular customers, unsure of how to prepare the stiff pasta, fed it to their goats in disgust and never returned to purchase more.

The Haji, distraught that his wish for the British to leave had been granted so abruptly and bewilderingly, led the brothers every day for **duhr** prayers at Sheikh Madar's **masjid**. The swollen, expectant congregation waited for some instruction on how to deal with these new infidels, but he had no answer, no plan. Fate had ambushed him.

For Mahmood, the absolute stillness of the town, and therefore the whole world, was terrifying, he seemed to be the only thing moving or growing in it. He was finally taller than his mother, and as he approached his teenage years the first shoots of wiry hair in his armpits and on his chin had begun to appear. Not quite a man yet but certainly not a child, he bristled at the low regard his elder brothers held for him. Never would he be the one to make decisions. Never could he say "let's sell this instead of that," or "employ him instead of the other." He was the "**soo qaado taas**" man, the fetch-it boy. No better than Ebado, who was now in her unhappy twenties and in frustrated love with Hashi. After a relative rush of activity in the morning, the town settled into a sunbaked, soundless, cud-chewing torpor: the rough roads empty apart from black and white goats, the air so static that if one leaf or blossom was stirred from a tree, Mahmood could follow its entire slow, swaying descent to earth. He had a feeling that he could scream at the top of his lungs and no one would hear him.

He walked all over, depriving his brothers of his servitude. From Nasa Hablood to the livestock market, from the police station to the Public Works Office, from the white district back to the native quarter, from his father's rock-marked grave to Sheikh Madar's tomb. He pressed on. The intense heat of that dry season kept even the roughest street boys inside. The town's women and girls had already gone into hiding, in fear of Italian troops, and the few men he passed appeared lost in their own concerns or reveries. When he heard laughter one day, accompanied by strange hooting-tooting music that assaulted his ears, he followed it to its source. His pursuit ended at the threshold of a mud-brick **makhayad**, hidden behind the warehouse of a Parsi sugar trader from Bombay. With the crunch of spilt sugar between his toes, Mahmood crept away from the door and the uproarious men sprawled on tatty divans set out along the four walls. His retreat was slowed by his fascination with the horned machine that the toots and hoots seemed to be spitting out from.

"Who is this little one poking his nose into our affairs?" a reclining man with a henna-bright beard asked the others, on catching sight of Mahmood. "**Kaalay**! Come!" he ordered, reaching his hand out as if to pluck him from a vine. "You got a message for one of us, boy?"

In the murk of the earthen room, clouds of tobacco smoke billowed and drifted from gurgling **shisha** pipes, obscuring which leg belonged to which torso and which face belonged to which body. It was a warehouse of men, piled up indolently on top of each other.

"I've seen him. You're one of Hussein's boys, **sax**?" asked a young man with a Western-style hat askew on his head and a blue **macawis** wrapped around his narrow waist.

"I am."

Senseless laughter.

Mahmood's pride, already weighty and adult-sized, was bruised. "What's so funny about that?"

"Nothing, boy, Hussein was a good man, **Allah oo naxaristo**. We are just silly men who find humour in everything. Get out of that hellish sun and sit with us. Take this." He proffered the metal snakehead of the **shisha** to Mahmood, and then extricated himself from the other bodies to fiddle with the twirling disc atop the music player.

Holding the **shisha** pipe nervously in his hand and seeing no place for him in the throng, Mahmood sat in the doorway and folded his long legs beneath him.

With the burst of another hooting-tooting song, the young man reclaimed the pipe from

Mahmood and kicked away the legs in his path until he was safely in possession of a few inches of divan. "What's your name, Ibn Hussein?"

"Mahmood."

Smiling broadly and switching to smooth English, he placed a hand over his heart and, with eyes dramatically lowered, announced, "And I remain your humble servant, Berlin."

That's how they met and how Mahmood fell in love with Berlin. A love platonic and pure, for sure, but weighted by the close scrutiny the boy put the man under. His bearing, his ideas, his silences, his insults, his desires, his hates, Mahmood would have scribbled them all down if he could write, but instead he memorized them and brought them home like birds caught in his snare. He prowled around the doorway of the tea house, his ear attuned to the sound of Berlin's voice over the din of the others. Seamen. Sailors. Merchant Marines. Stokers. Firemen. Trimmers. **Badmarin.** They called themselves many things but he quickly understood that they were men of the sea, men of the world. As he lurked around the edges of the **makhayad**, protecting his place within their confessional by passing this to one and fetching that for another, he picked up fragments of their histories, their mythologies.

Ainashe, a convalescent sailor with oily, stained bandages on both forearms, was recuperating after his ship went down off the coast of Malaya. Every hour, with wild eyes, he would go over the details of the torpedo attack. How it struck the engine room during his brother's shift, while he was on deck taking the air before his own four-hour watch began. The spume of boiling water that splashed his face as the steel deck erupted beneath him. Feeling a touch on his neck as he sank deeper into the water, he flailed his arms behind him, fearing a shark was circling for a good position to bite off his head. "Christ! I'm only trying to help," shouted the First Mate, as the stoker swore in Somali, pleading with God for a different death. "Come here! Hold on to this, pal." The old Scottish bastard passed him a half-broken crate and helped him find some stability before swimming away to look for other survivors. Bobbing up and down, his broken arms struggling to carry his weight, he felt the flutter of surfacing corpses before he caught sight of them. They came up one by one, like dancers entering a ring, as smooth and limbless as sea cows. Of all the bodies with heads there were only enough eyes, noses, mouths and ears to form one complete face. Surrounded by this school of monsters, Ainashe kicked out until he recognized the scar on one ribcage, a long yellow river of a scar that his brother had earned in a bar fight in New York. Shivering, Ainashe pulled his brother's naked torso to him and spoke encouraging, babyish words to the space where his handsome head should have been. All gone. All gone. Ainashe's **makhayad** audience just tutted sympathetically, sighed "**sabar iyo imaan**" and then returned pitilessly to whatever joke or tall story he had interrupted.

They shrugged off the weight of Ainashe's misery and insanity with an ease that at first shocked Mahmood but then felt right and manly. Through their uproarious laughter, their theatrical disgust, poetic insults and vast worldliness he learnt more than he ever had before. The central philosophy of the **makhayad** school of thought was that **this** didn't have to be the sum total of his life: this vista, this horizon, this language, these rules, these taboos, this food, these women, these laws, these neighbours, these enemies. These were heretical, pulse-quickening ideas, but they slowly made a disciple of him. Berlin, in particular, had fashioned a heart of smooth marble, his blood cooler than that of a dead man. He was about to marry in Borama, to please his mother. A girl chosen by his mother, a girl he hadn't met and would probably never see again. He said it would just need a fine rubdown of his heart to put the whole thing behind him.

When the British returned with reinforcements, six months after they had evacuated the colony, they pushed the Italians back into their own empire and returned to the familiar toing and froing with the Somali clans. With South African, Indian and East African troops to supply, the British Army became the spendthrift customer the family shop had always wanted. They had earned enough by the end of '41 to purchase a second-hand three-ton Bedford lorry to add to the small fleet, and their mother started dropping hints that maybe it would add a little prestige to the family name to send Mahmood away to boarding school. Protesting that they would turn him Christian, make him eat pork and teach him to look down on his illiterate brothers, Mahmood resisted hard. They could send him away but not to Amoud or any other prison-school, let him go to Kenya or Tanganyika, where he could buy stock to send to Hargeisa. He'd only heard of Kenya and Tanganyika from the sailors but they had sold him on slow-blinking, dark-lipped Swahili girls, extravagantly tall and deeply upholstered beds, and ancient, cosmopolitan ports. To his amazement his eldest brother agreed—whether it was to separate him from the delinquent sailors or to toughen him up, he didn't pry—but the thirteen-year-old was to try his own luck as a man. Mahmood would go to Garissa, in the Somali-inhabited north of Kenya, to stay with a clansman, and then the brothers would send a lorry to collect prearranged orders for the shop.

Mahmood had absconded from Garissa within the month, contemptuous of its squat, dusty buildings and tedious familiarity. He dictated a telegram home from the Central Post Office in stentorious Nairobi and then pushed on to the promised amusements of Mombasa. He laboured as a porter, unloading dockside **dhows** and passenger launches, and then found employment with a scholarly Somali merchant based in Zanzibar. He worked behind the counter of the merchant's jewellery and fabric shop in Stone Town and pined after the girls who came into the dim, coral-stone bazaar. Omani girls lost within black **buibuis**, long-plaited Banyali and Sikh brides, grape-skinned Waswahili flirts with pierced septums. He caressed fingers as he squeezed rings past stubborn joints, and shook with nervy excitement as he tied heavy necklaces around their sweat-creased necks. The world felt far away from the serpentine alleys of Stone Town and he passed a whole year without telling his family where he was. It comforted him to know that he was beyond their orbit. He had nightmares in which his mother, with her albatross love and supernatural acquaintance, came hobbling after him, tracking the high arch of his footsteps and turning up at the bazaar. Her sad, black-rimmed gaze more painful than he could say.

As if running away from these dreams, he fled one day to the mainland, to Dar es Salaam. With luck pouring over him like gold, he quickly found a position with another Somali, Bibi Zahra, a Barwani widow from Mogadishu. He had told her that his brothers owned four lorries, and for her that was enough reason to hand over the keys to her white Morris Minor. With a quick prayer Mahmood got behind the broad thin wheel of the car and realized he was too short to see far beyond the bonnet. The widow passed him her valise to sit on but when he started the engine, its rough cough startled him and he yanked out the key, afraid he had broken something. With her shouting encouragement from the backseat and pointing out the switches and gears she had seen her previous chauffeur make use of, they made slow but sure progress to her white, jasmine-entwined bungalow. From the widow, Bibi Zahra, he learnt the art of indolence; her days passed in a molten routine of beautification, dining and promenading. She chattered more than the birds in the large, palm-shaded garden and pulled the servants and gatekeepers into the vortex of her own languid timekeeping. Mahmood could sleep as late as he wanted, knowing that she had probably only drifted into sleep as the sun was rising. He never saw the **sahib** she spent all day preparing for, but he heard him and saw a broad shadow pass across the draped windows. Childless, she filled the house with a clutter of servants, trying to replicate the small, noisy home of her childhood in the narrow alleys of Hamarweyne. Pulled between the ease of the widow's home and the sense that he was slipping back into resentful boyhood, Mahmood began to overeat, chopping and washing for the cook who, in return, let him pick at the fried breads and spicy stews the widow had taught him to make.

There was a girl in the household, a tight-braided Swahili girl named Kamara who appeared twice a week to wash the widow's clothes and bedding, and she became the metronome by which Mahmood measured his days. He had four positions that he could take to monitor her from in the three hours she spent at the bungalow: polishing the car as she arrived in the morning, at the kitchen hut door as she filled basin after basin from a standpipe in the garden, at the smoky window as she pumped her little feet into the sudsy water a few inches away, and finally under the jacaranda tree as she pinned up broad white sheets and expensive clothes. He didn't speak a word to her, but catching sight of Mahmood's surly, lovelorn looks, the greying cook took to singing "**Nashindwa na mali sina, we ningekuoa malaika,**" and patting his empty pockets when she neared the kitchen. It was true

Mahmood had no money, he was kept in such comfort that the widow thought there was no need to deplete her precious inheritance in handing over paper or metal. What kind of bride price would a **dhobi** girl want? He had no idea. All he could offer were secret drives in the car and greasy snacks from the kitchen.

He mulled over his predicament, silently watching a silent girl, until many months later he noticed the oblong mound under her shift dress, the impertinent point of her distended belly button. Eyes wide, he scrambled up from under the jacaranda and walked out to the car with tears in his eyes. He felt like a beggar ogling a half-eaten plate. He cursed her while his inner consciousness berated him for thinking he had any claim on her. He was as wretched as the gaudy fat eunuchs that came to the bazaar in Stone Town, haughtily spending their master's money as if it was their own, talking of weddings and women as if they had ever had one. He didn't want to have to play with himself like some madman or monkey, but the situation was very bleak indeed. He stuffed his mouth, drove the widow from shop to shop, and went to bed every night with good but frustrated intentions.

One day, parked outside the Post Office, as Bibi Zahra telephoned her sister in Mogadishu, a stranger thumped the glass window and jolted

Mahmood from his nap. "You!" smiled a young man, his face sweaty and bright above his white button-up shirt.

Mahmood frowned and rolled down the window to tell him to go to hell. "Is this your car? How much you pay me for it?" he barked.

"Don't get sharp with me. I know who you are, Mattan. Your people have been looking for you everywhere, street boy."

Mahmood blinked rapidly, squeezed the wheel tighter and felt for the accelerator with his foot. "What do you mean?" he said weakly.

"You know what I mean," the man scoffed. "Your mother is asking every merchant, sailor or soldier in Africa and Aden if they have seen you, even if it's your rotting, stinking body. You have the police on your back? Why did you run from your family? Allah will get you for it. No one ever taught you that heaven lies under the feet of your mother, **yaa**?"

"I'm working, I'm going to send money to them," Mahmood lied, his voice high and childish.

He could smell Bibi Zahra's heavy perfume before he could see her.

"What is the matter, Mahmood?"

"He's been caught."

"Caught? By you? What has he done?" she screamed, turning back and forth between them.

"Nothing, my mother is looking for me," he said, addressing the steering wheel.

"They don't know whether he is dead or alive."

"**Harami!**" Bibi Zahra shouted, reaching into the car to swipe Mahmood across the face. "You want everyone to think that I kidnapped you? That I'm some kind of **dad qalaato**. I thought you were orphaned."

"I never said that, I never wished my mother dead. I said my father had died."

Bibi Zahra shook her head, her antimony-ringed eyes flooding dramatically. "**Weylo o wey**, just because I have not carried a child it does not mean I cannot feel what your mother must be feeling." She clutched her navel and then her breasts. "You are going to go back today. I will give you the money myself."

"No!" Mahmood said, firing up the engine, ready to steal the car if he needed to.

"Come with me," she ordered, beckoning with her long index finger for Mahmood to step out. "You will give life to your mother and speak to her."

"**Hooyo?**"

"Who is it?" his mother shouted down the line.

"**Waa aniga**, Mahmood."

"**Manshallah, Manshallah,**" she cried. "My eyes, my lastborn, my liver, my light. I thought I had lost you."

Mahmood bent his head low to conceal the tears coursing down his cheeks. She sounded so frightened, so old.

"**Hooyo,**" he croaked, he didn't know what else to say, she loved him more than he deserved.

"Are you well, my son? Has any harm come to you?"

"No, I'm fat and well."

"Your brother has married and had a son, I named him Mahmood."

"I am in a town named Dar es Salaam, it is beside a big sea. I am a chauffeur now, and I can speak Swahili. Mahmood? That is an honour, **hooyo.**"

They talked over each other, the line crackly and the conversation bizarre, neither of them having used a telephone before. They had had to send a messenger to fetch her from the shop and bring her to the Post Office. He could imagine her painful lopsided gait, her hand pressing down on her hip.

She shouted a long benediction down the phone, exhorting him to say, "**Ameen, Ameen.**"

"**Ameen.**"

"May Allah let us see each other again."

"Yes, **hooyo.**" He pulled the receiver away from his ear and passed it guiltily over to the operator.

"Now to the train station." Grabbing his shoulder tenderly, Bibi Zahra led him out into the blank sunlight.

Sitting on a wooden bench on Platform 1 of the Central Station, waiting for a train he didn't want to ride, Mahmood picked listlessly at a packet of **chaat** that he had just bought from an Indian hawker. The red flash of his cart squeaking up and down the platforms, having kept Mahmood company over the past hour, now stilled.

The trader stopped and stretched his back, complaining in Hindi as he pressed his thumbs into his spine. "Poor men get no rest till they die, **na**?" he said to Mahmood in Swahili, shaking his head ruefully.

Mahmood shrugged his shoulders; he'd had his fill of rest.

"The Arusha train late?" the Indian continued, eager to give his tongue some respite from the mantra of "one bag **chaat** five cents, three bags **chaat** ten cents."

"I don't know, must be. It was due half an hour ago." Mahmood spread his hands apart and leant back, a picture of lassitude.

"Where you going?"

"Hargeisa."

The hawker lifted his eyebrows. "British Somaliland? Long way." He sprinkled **chaat** from his small shovel into his palm and then threw the mix of spiced rice, nuts and lentils into his mouth. "You should have taken a **dhow.**"

"I will, from Mombasa."

"You have money to burn?"

"I don't, but the woman who bought me the ticket does."

"A real **tajira**?"

"Rich dead husbands."

"Lucky woman."

"Where do the other trains go?"

"Mwanza, Tabora, Kigoma, Kitadu, Tanga, Dodoma, Mpanda. I was one of the men who extended the tracks from Tabora to Mwanza a long, long time ago. There's not much I don't know about this railway. You could go to Tanga, get a **dhow** from there."

"The ticket work for all of them?"

"Let me see."

Mahmood pulled out the flimsy yellow rectangle from his shirt pocket and unfolded it.

Holding the paper close to his eyes, the hawker checked all the details. "Second class, yes, it'll take you anywhere in Tanganyika."

Mahmood refolded the ticket and placed it back in his pocket, beside the ten shillings Bibi Zahra had given him for the journey.

"Maybe I'll go to Tanga, then."

"**Safar salama** either way."

"**Asante.**"

Creaking away with his cart, the Indian had planted a seed in Mahmood's mind. There was no compulsion to do what he had been told; he did not need to go home, or even north. What was ahead of him in Hargeisa? A tearful reunion with his mother, followed quickly by punishment, the mundane routines of the family shop, the long wait for his brothers to marry, one by one, before it was his turn. He wanted to see more beauty, more of the world's strange places, animals and women. He wanted to see palaces, great ships, mountains, fire-worshippers and fire-headed girls. When he thought of Hargeisa it was the sandstorms that came to mind, scratching at his eyes and whipping at his clothes, the **tusbah**-clacking elders calling everything new the work of **shaydaan**, the interminable negotiations between clans over land, women and wells. It was a place for the old, not those just starting out in life.

Hearing the hollow whistle of a train about to depart from another platform, Mahmood grabbed his small cotton bundle of clothes and ran over the bridge towards the shining black train.

"Where you decide, boy?" the hawker exclaimed in delight.

Thick plumes of steam from the squat funnel

shrouded any sign of where the locomotive might be going.

Mahmood turned back and threw his hands in the air before clambering up the steep wooden steps into a carriage. "Only Allah knows!"

The angry bull exhalations of the engine and then the **zug, zug, zug** of the turning wheels as the locomotive jolted the carriages away from Dar es Salaam station gave Mahmood the feeling that he was heading off to war.

Siddeed

[Eight]

"So, what are the men saying?"

"You know what they're saying."

"That I brought this on myself?"

Berlin throws his head back, turns away as if this is not a line of questioning worth pursuing. "It doesn't matter what they think. It's what they'll **do** that counts."

"I don't want anyone begrudging me. If they don't want to help that's their free choice."

"Enough, leave it alone. We can pay for the solicitor and the barrister. We spoke to three barristers and we think we've found the right one. He represented that son of a bitch who killed Shay last year."

"That son of a bitch was found guilty."

"He **was** guilty! The important question is did he hang?" Berlin asks sharply, losing his patience.

"I'll leave it to you, there's not much I can say from here, is there?"

"No. Your case might not even go beyond the hearings, anyway."

"**Inshallah**, we'll all be free of it soon. Tell the men I appreciate their help, truly."

Berlin waves away the sentimentality with both hands.

"What is happening out there, anyway?" Mahmood smiles, reading every part of Berlin's face for some clue to what the other sailors think of his predicament.

"I had a half-caste girl come to the café to sing, dressed like a boy in a baker's hat, straight up and down like a boy too, but she sings like she wants to tear the walls down."

"What's her name?"

"Bassey, Shirley Bassey. She made good money that night, her hat was full to the brim. Her father was that Nigerian that got into trouble with the little girl, but she's doing well enough without him. Dualleh the Communist is in London, meeting with his comrade Sylvia Pankhurst. She's been invited by Haile Selassie to live in Addis Ababa."

"**Ya salam**, Dualleh is trying to persuade her to stay?"

"Something like that. Crazy Tahir's disappeared, someone said they saw him signing on to a ship at the Shipping Office."

"He must have evicted those voices out of his mind."

"Or is running away from something, someone. You can never tell with him."

"Good luck to him."

"He told me that he had been in the shop the night the woman was murdered."

"He told the police?" Mahmood asks, dropping his hands from the back of his head.

"I think so. He was terrified, but I told him he must tell them."

"Did he see anything?"

"I was more interested in asking did he do anything?"

Mahmood pushes his face closer to Berlin's. "What did he say?"

"He bought two bars of soap and left to meet a girl at the Arab café. He rang the bell, bought his things and hardly spent a minute there, he says. He might have a **jinn** in him but I've never known him to hurt anyone, especially for money. You see how he lives?"

"But he must be the Somali they all said they saw, then."

"I don't know, he said another Somali came in after him. A tall, dark young man that he doesn't know. I lose track of all these new Somalis too."

"When is he back?"

"How would I know?"

"Fuck!" Mahmood slams his fist into the table.

"The police haven't stopped asking questions about you, whether you carried a razor, or had ever threatened anyone. They haven't brought up Tahir's name once."

Mahmood laughs incredulously and shakes his head. "How can I shake these devils off my back?"

"It's bad, Mahmood. They're showing your photo to people on the docks, asking, 'Did you see this man near the Volacki shop on the night of the murder?' "

"They can barely tell the difference between us in bright daylight! How they gonna say who they saw in that typhoon?"

"There's the reward to sharpen their eyesight, remember."

"Sometimes, I wake up and I don't know where I am, which bed, which room, which country. I feel out in the deep sea, floating, between watches. It's a strange, strange feeling. I hear the warders pacing past my cell at night, looking in on me in bed, and I think it's my mother coming to check on me and that I must close my eyes. It's made me wonder 'bout Tahir, you know? How sometimes he looked at his hands with such shock, as if he couldn't believe they belonged to him. I can see how men go mad. You open a door in your mind and just step through, easy."

"You're not crazy. Sometimes I've seen you fraying but you've always held it together. Don't let this break you. They always come for us but you keep your **waran** and **gaashaan** up, hold them like this . . ." Berlin pretends to hold a spear and shield tightly in each of his hands, "Vigilance, **sahib**, vigilance."

The doctor's voice drones on, reading the instructions on the black and white form. Mahmood has listlessly completed the first two sections of the intelligence test. It is a simple assault course of numbers, shapes and word games but his mind is elsewhere. Circling what he knows must be the correct answers, he wonders how a month has passed so languidly in prison. "You'll hang, whether you did it or not." Powell's words come to him, clear and sharp; what he had heard then as the arrogance and frustration of a man habituated to throwing his weight around, he now understands to be a sincere threat.

The doctor looks over his shoulder at the answers on the paper and raises his eyebrows. Mahmood had considered hobbling himself, throwing the test so that they would believe they had a simpleton on their hands, but, ultimately, his pride wouldn't let him.

They'd had a conversation about madness earlier; the doctor had been sniffing around, and had eventually asked Mahmood if he could define madness? Course he could. A man was mad when he didn't know what he was doing, or couldn't tell the difference between right and wrong. That's how the courts saw it, and he agreed with that simple definition. He didn't bring up **jinn** possession, or curses, or the madness that seemed to seep into people at sea or in deserts. The doctor wanted to know if he was fit for trial or not, that was the purpose of these chats, but if there was a chance of tricking the whitecoat into believing he was unfit, then the notion never blossomed into action. He can pretend to be stupid, he can pretend to be mad, but why go to such lengths when he knows he's innocent? All he can do is put his faith in the All-knowing, the All-powerful. He has been praying all five daily prayers since Berlin's visit. Trying to fire an emergency beacon out to God through the low concrete ceiling. "**Ibad baadi**, save me, **anqadhani, mujhe bachao, uniokoe**," he chants at the end of his prostrations, pleading in all the tongues he knows.

. . .

The recreation room reminds Mahmood of the Employment Exchange, men shuffling across the bleached linoleum floor, looking for a place to sit or stand idly. The doctor has assured him that there is no risk to his children in mixing with the other inmates, so he has left the funk of his cell. His knees crack and grumble as he strides through the bright room. An awkward smile on his face as men size him up, testosterone charging their glances with electricity. There is one other coloured man in the crowd, his head bent over a complicated jigsaw, and Mahmood approaches him instinctively. The old West African has two short nicks on his forehead and high, sharp cheekbones. He doesn't look up as Mahmood takes the empty metal chair beside him, but mumbles quietly while moving jigsaw pieces slowly around the table.

"You want me to help?" Mahmood asks, noticing the grey whorls in the man's hair and the trembling of his hand.

Silence.

"Take this piece, it goes there . . ." Mahmood tries to place the wood in a space between tree and sky.

"Fuck off, man! Just fuck off!" He thumps his

palm on to the table and pummels the scene until the small pieces pile up like rubble.

"You've gone and done it now, ain't ya?" chuckles a small blond man, sitting behind them. "You can't interfere with Uncle Samson and his jigsaw, it's his life's work, you see."

Mahmood is up on his feet, embarrassed at having gone straight to the madman.

"Pull up a chair here, mate. He likes to be left alone."

He accepts the invitation and moves to the Englishman's table. A draughts board and counters spread out on it.

"Archie Lawson, Esquire," he says, offering a thin, pale hand.

"Mattan, Mahmood," he replies, shaking it firmly.

"You a local boy, then?"

"No. Yes. I live in Adamsdown."

"A veritable hop and a skip. Me, I'm from a land far, far away. My birth heralded by Bow Bells."

"London boy?"

"You got it in one. A cockney by birth and sentiment."

"I stay in London last year, in the East End. Trafalgar Square, Piccadilly Circus, all that too busy for me."

"Old boy, I've had my fill of the Big Smoke

too, it was Samuel Johnson who said, 'When you're tired of London, you're tired of life,' but I've had it right up to here." He chops at his neck while arranging the discs in neat rows on either side of the board. "I'm on my regal tour of Her Majesty's Prisons, I could write a guide book on 'em, if asked. Pentonville grub leaves a lot to be desired, you'd taste better licking the floors, and the sporting facilities? An absolute outrage, an **outrage**, I say."

Mahmood smirks, but the man speaks so fast and in so many voices he struggles to follow. "Prison food is no food," he concurs, finally.

"What's wrong with ya, then?"

"Nothing. They keep me here for nothing."

"Don't complain, least you get your tea and cake in the afternoon."

Under the sleeve of his white shirt, Mahmood sees a coarse bandage wrapped around Archie's arm.

"You know how to play?" Archie asks, gesturing with his chin to the board.

"Sure, every man plays draughts at sea."

"Well, let's not dilly-dally, then."

"How much was in my hands?"

"Two and six."

"Correct, and now?" The doctor turns his closed fists up and quickly flashes them open to reveal a scattering of gold, silver and copper coins.

"One florin, thruppence and two farthings."

"Your memory really is remarkable, Mr. Mattan."

"All my people the same, I told you we keep shop in my country, I learn to count money before anything else."

They have been playing the memory game for the last ten minutes; it's an amusing pastime but only adds to his sense that he is regressing. The jigsaws, picture books, board games and doctor's tests make him feel as though he is in a nursery, the highlight of his day coming at 4 p.m. when the kitchen crew come round with a trolley of perfectly uniform cake slices. Jam sponge, fruit cake, nut spice loaf, oatmeal slice, he is indifferent to what they bring, it's just the melt of sugar on his tongue that he craves, something to remove the lardy, meaty taste of the prison lunches.

"How are you feeling in regards to the progress of your case?" the doctor asks, arranging his coins into columns on the bed.

"I still ain't seen my barrister," Mahmood sits further back on the bed, leaning against the cold brick wall, "and the hearing coming up. My countrymen paying for him, I don't need no legal aid shitty lawyer. The hearing come and then this story come to an end, I walk in the street a free man."

"You sound optimistic."

"Optimistic? You mean cheerful? I be cheerful, I put my faith in God and he don't let no innocent man suffer. You know, I watch a picture once, a cowboy film. I watch every Western they put on at the bug house. I like how in them films every man is his own master, and the deserts and mountains make me remember my old country. Anyway, this film, I forget the name, it have a man new to the town who is accused of killing an old woman and the Marshal, a real nasty man, hate him and want him dead. The saloon man say he saw it, the boy in the stables say he saw the stranger with blood all over him, the whores say he come to them with money, but one by one they kill each other and the stranger prove they lying and he go free, and then the Marshal is taken away for punishment."

"You see something of your own situation in that wild and woolly tale?"

"I do, I do," Mahmood nods. "It show me how the truth kill the lie."

"How goodness conquers evil?"

"That's right, you understand me."

"Well, the Bible tells us so."

"Your book and my book they like this," Mahmood places his index fingers side by side.

"We have one God, and the prophets, Moses, Ibraham, Jesus, and the Devil."

"The Abrahamic faiths can be said to be cut from one cloth, but the crucial difference is that our Lord is one of love and forgiveness. He died for all mankind's sins, yours and mine. The God of the Jews and, correct me if I misspeak, of the Mohammedans is one of vengeance, a slave master opposed to a father."

"No, who tell you that? Your God die. It is impossible for God to die. You tell me that for one minute, five minute, an hour, your God could not see, hear or understand anything? You must have two Gods, one to die and one to bring him back to life. My God is one. He is all-powerful but he all-forgiving too. You call Allah's name the minute you know you dead and he wash you clean, clean like a child freshborn, if you mean it in your heart, in **niyaadaada**, he will forgive you everything."

"That is reassuring to hear." The doctor smiles, trying to let the subject fall away.

Mahmood laughs. "Christians funny people, if your Lord die for all our sins why you have prisons?"

"That's a question for a more philosophical soul than I."

. . .

The unyielding wooden cot is messing with Mahmood's back, sometimes he's forced to get up in the middle of the night and pace the floor, the nocturnal warders snapping open the hatch and barking, "Alright, mate?" He ain't alright. The pain moves up and down his spine, nestling between his shoulders one moment, and then nudging at his tailbone the next. Sometimes he can't get up for hours. This morning, a medical officer gave him two painkiller tablets to take with breakfast, but prostrating for the **fajr** prayer was still a struggle. He'd heard a deep, metallic thump while bending down for the second **rakat**, so loud it had made him jump in shock, even the cement floor had shuddered a little. He realized after the prayer that the chapel bell hadn't rung on the hour this morning, throwing off his usual, clockwork routine.

He changes now from his thin pyjamas into the cotton uniform and combs his hair flat. When he steps out for his morning exercise, the other hospital inmates are gathered in a huddle, all two dozen of them in white shirts that billow in the breeze. It's a pleasant morning; the sun warms Mahmood's face and smooths the appearance of the other men, making them look younger and softer. Archie, especially, looks like a teenager today, the fine reddish hairs along his jaw glowing copper, his big eyes darting this way and that.

"They've had to take his body out for cremation, cos he's a Sikh an' all and they have to do right by him that way."

"Aye, that's proper," agrees Frank, the old Scottish man with knotted, arthritic hands. "It made a bloody racket, didn't it? I thought the ceiling would give way for a moment."

"The gates of hell, innit?"

"You talking about Singh?" Mahmood asks, his mind going back to the disturbed prayer.

"We sure are, the late Master Singh of Bridgend has left our prison fraternity."

"They really did it," Mahmood says, almost to himself. Looking around him, at the waxy ivy snaking through the cracks in the brick wall, at the tall chimneys puffing out thin streams of smoke, at the prisoners on gardening detail carrying hoes and pushing wheelbarrows to the governor's garden, everything looks benign. A man was killed here an hour ago, he thinks, a man like me, who'd worn this uniform, who probably had the same breakfast of salty porridge in his belly as they put the rope around his neck.

"Who did the honours, Archie?" a boy with a bandaged eye asks. "The chaplain said they would move me to another part of the prison if I wanted, but it didn't bother me at all. He killed that girl in cold blood, I said, I'll be applauding."

Samson is on the outskirts of the group, one ear turned towards Archie to better hear him.

"Pierrepoint it was, it's always that bloody bastard Pierrepoint, he's got the hanging game sewn up. I think Allen was the assistant, but don't hold me to that one."

Mahmood elbows Archie to get his attention. "What they do with him now?"

"Bring the ashes back and bury him with the rest. I ain't supposed to tell you," he gestures for the circle to tighten around him, "but they're all under the vegetable patch. We're eating convict-composted spuds and greens, fellas." He bursts out laughing.

"You lie." Mahmood frowns.

"Do I heck! The nightshift warders are my pals, I keep 'em chatting so they won't fall asleep on the job. There's nothing they won't tell me . . . like about Lester the Ghost."

The men groan and fall back from the tight circle.

"Hear me out, hear me out, you know I never sleep, don't ya? Well, take it from me that when you're all snoring like brutes I can hear him, an old stoker he was, a black fella," he nods to Mahmood, "I can hear him shovelling, the pipes knocking as if they're warming up, but touch 'em and they're as cold as a witch's tit."

"You and your cockney yarns." Frank wheezes, his eyes crinkled in merriment.

"Find me a Bible and I'll swear on it, ask any of the old-timers, or the chief warder, Richardson, his dad was the one on duty in the condemned cell when they came for him. Nineteen twenty-something. He had to be carried to the noose in a chair because the silly bugger was paralytic down his left side, had blown the skull off his gal but then turned cack-handed when pulling the trigger on himself. A Jamaican sailor, old Lester was, only young when he died, but getting into his dotage as a ghost, steps through the walls like they're just cobwebs. Listen out at night and you'll hear him, I promise it."

The bandaged boy looks pale now. The others enjoy his discomfort, exchanging mischievous glances as they roll cigarettes and pass around a box of matches.

"You're looking a bit green there, Dickie, your pink-eye bothering you?"

"No, I'm alright, just need to ask someone about something." He slopes back inside, his head downcast.

"Yeah, go to nanny," sneers Archie.

"A stoker?" Mahmood repeats.

"So I've heard." Archie's eyes cross as he concentrates on forming smoke rings with his thick, wet lips.

"They carried him in a chair?"

"You got to admire the diligence of screws, no job too dirty for them. I hope he at least put their backs out, or pissed down their legs, you'd want some sorta revenge, right?"

Sagaal

[Nine]

That disgraceful old bag!"

"She really followed your mother out?" Mahmood blows a sharp arrow of smoke over Omar's head, his hand on his son's round belly, as the boy manipulates the arms of a cheap wooden robot in his lap.

"You bet she did, came chasing after us as we left the Magistrates. We hadn't gone ten yards before she was grabbing Mam's elbow and pulling her aside."

"Tell me again what she said."

"She said, 'If you tell the court that you saw him with a bundle of cash too, we can go halves on the reward money.' Bold as brass."

"What did your mam say?"

"What do you think? She told her to go jump! Then the nasty piece of work starts on with, 'What kind of mother lets her daughter marry a darkie in the first place?' and says that the two of us had gone into her shop ages ago . . . to threaten her! Mam was having none of it, we were in bloody Hull at the time. She gave her a shove, and an earful to go with it."

Mahmood can't help smiling. "They had a fight?"

"Almost, they were separated by one of the ushers, but Mam has reported her and her lies to the police. I don't know what will happen if they see each other again, or if I clap eyes on her, for that matter."

"Keep your hands to yourself, Williams, we can't both end up in this box."

"I can't promise anything, I swear she had my blood seething." Even now, Laura's face has reddened just telling the story, her neck blotchy and streaked where her nails have dragged the skin.

"I saw her at the hearing, a Davis Street special, alright, looks like the marrow suck straight outta her bones."

"A vampire, a real vampire."

Mahmood looks down at Omar, wipes biscuit crumbs from his face, and then reaches for Laura's hand on the table and holds it softly. "I spoke to the solicitor before you came."

"What did he say?"

It had been an unsatisfactory meeting; Mahmood had been waiting weeks to work out a strategy with him on how to get out of this mess, but the solicitor seemed to have already given up. He read out the list of prosecution witnesses, more than thirty of them. Mahmood recognized only four names. Doc and Monday, of course, were singing to the police's tune, but so were Billa Khan and the racetrack man. The rest were either chancers—like the old bigot shopkeeper—informers, or must have been hassled into saying something, anything, by the police because they had dirt on them. The solicitor also reported that the police white-coats had found specks of blood on his boots; spots so small you'd need a microscope to find them. Human blood, they said. He had bought the boots as a favour from Laura's mother. Her brother had found them on a rubbish tip, and as they didn't fit her husband or sons, she had wanted to offload them and get a bit of money in exchange. God knows where they had come from and how many men had worn them before him, **ma'alesh**, never mind, nothing to be done about it now.

Mahmood had said again and again that he wanted to give evidence at the hearing but the solicitor wasn't having it, said it would give away their defence to the Prosecution. Better to hold their cards close to their chest, like in poker? Mahmood had asked, thinking it over. "That's right," the solicitor had replied, but it didn't feel **right**. If they heard him, heard the truthfulness in his voice, they would let him go. He had a low opinion of the police but the courts had been fair to him. That time when he had been wrongly accused of stealing clothes and money from a docked ship in the Bay, the court had thrown out the charges. That time in London, when he'd had an argument with that Warsengali over money, and had been charged with demanding money with menaces and sent to the Old Bailey, they'd taken his word over that thief's and let him go. That was the famous British justice. You had to have proper evidence, or the game was all over: not "I think," or "I heard," or "I guess," none of that shit.

"What did he say?" Laura repeats, squeezing his index finger.

"He said they don't have real evidence against me but it's better I wait for the trial to give my story."

Her shoulders drop. "Wait till trial? But that could be ages. I'm getting tired of this place, Moody, I . . ." Her voice cracks before she can get the words out.

Mahmood raises her hand and kisses it. "I know, my woman, I know. I'm tired too. I am stuck in this cage when I want to be home with you. When I come out we'll live together, yes?"

She wipes a cotton hankie roughly over her eyelids and nods without looking at him.

"From my cell I can see the backyards on your side of the street. How about Friday, you and the boys stand in the yard and I look for you?"

"That's daft." She laughs, her tears not yet dispelled.

"Let it be, I want to see you."

"What time?"

"Noon sharp."

"I'll be out there. Don't stand me up."

"Never." Mahmood laughs, wrapping both of her hands in his and then stroking her forearm as far as her shirtsleeves will allow.

Right on the first day of the hearing they had asked Mahmood what he had to say to the charge of murder. He had put his palms up, and replied calmly, "All I got to say is, I'm not guilty."

Regardless, the witnesses keep coming, as if

they have been dredged up from the bottom of the Glamorganshire Canal and flopped on to the floor of the Law Courts: fat, thin; black, white, brown; swanks and vagabonds; strangers and acquaintances. All coming to drive a knife through his shoulder blades.

"I saw him with a razor, sure I did," says one Nigerian. "He threatened my neighbour with a knife," goes a housewife. The police still haven't found the murder weapon, or any money, so they use these narks to demolish his reputation, make him sound like a man capable of anything. "A desperate criminal," as they call it in the newsreels. So many of them say they saw him walk out of the shop the night of March 6th that he almost begins to believe that he did. They have a West Indian, a Welshman, an Arab, a Maltese, an Indian, a Jew, almost the League of Nations accusing him. He can only stand there in the dock, his lips sealed shut as they drag his name through mud and broken glass. Whose bed did he shit in for them to do this to him? None of the Somalis have given evidence yet, neither for the Prosecution nor the Defence, and he's grateful for that; it would make this circus too fucking real.

His titanic barrister, tall and red-faced, watches the proceedings with unreadable grey eyes. They are yet to exchange a word, but that man holds his life in his hands; Mahmood is beginning to understand that now. As each witness takes the stand, his previous estimation of his own power diminishes. His barrister, Rhys Roberts, looks like a boulder made of the same pale rock as the magistrate and prosecutor; granite hewn somewhere foreign to him, in public school dormitories or army barracks, perhaps. They are gentlemen with signet rings and inherited watches, who speak in a language far removed from his English of engine rooms, factories, quarries, street fights and pillow talk. They mumble and race through the hearing, the routines of it familiar to them but not to him. Questions about him, the defendant, asked and answered before he's even understood them.

When Mahmood had interpreted in court, two years previously, for one of the Abdis who had beaten Shay for stealing their savings, it had seemed easy. Converting convoluted English into straightforward Somali and then forcing the reply back into simple English. He could afford to take the kernel of what was meant and throw away the rest, but now? Now that his own freedom is at risk he needs every distinction. When the pathologist said "contusion" did he mean bruise? When he said "haemorrhage" did he mean some special kind of bleeding or just normal bleeding? The woman was killed from behind, he understood that, and died from one deep cut to her throat, with three other small cuts surrounding it. One second he can understand everything, then they change frequency, like a fuzzy wireless, and go into their university talk, leaving him with only isolated words to hold on to. They think a man stupid because he talks with an accent, but he wants to shout, "I teach myself five languages, I know how to say 'fuck you!' in Hindi and 'love me' in Swahili, give me a chance and speak plain."

Sometimes, he finds himself smiling, overwhelmed by and incredulous at the fictions told about him: the strange costumes the witnesses put him in. What man would ever wear white cook's trousers with a blue Air Force dress jacket? The non-existent moustache and gold teeth they place on his face. The desirable inches they add to his height. They have created a man—no, a Frankenstein's monster—and branded it with his name before setting it loose. Standing there, shoulders sagging, in the Law Courts, in Cardiff, in Bilad al-Welsh, he feels the blows of their lies like a man shot with arrows. They are blind to Mahmood Hussein Mattan and all his real manifestations: the tireless stoker, the poker shark, the elegant wanderer, the love-starved husband, the soft-hearted father.

. . .

It's going to trial. It's going to trial. It's. Going. To. Trial. That's the end of it; the hearing has passed, with all the lies in place. The police have done a good job of fixing him. He needs to save his strength now for the assizes, when he will give evidence, whatever the damn lawyer says. The fact is, he is innocent. "The truth will set you free." He's heard the locals say that many a time, like something they learn in their church.

Standing on his bed, the loose woollen socks on his feet sliding as he tiptoes off the side of the mattress, Mahmood angles his head over the dusty windowsill until he can see more of the Davis Street backyards. He counts down the odd-number side until he picks out the familiar junk abandoned by the Williams family in their weed-strewn garden. A rusty tricycle lying upside down, an old-fashioned pram with large silver wheels and sun-bleached hood, a broken sink, the detritus of a home where nothing with even a notional value can be easily parted with. "I'll fix 'em, I'll fix 'em," promised Laura's father, Evan, chewing his plastic pipe. "I'll buy you a new one," Mahmood had assured her, but everything remained unrepaired and unreplaced. Money coming in and going out like the tide for all of them. His hands grip the windowsill until he's steady, an ache growing in his neck as his crooked body hangs in the air like a question mark, the question being, "Has she forgotten?"

Mahmood waits, a minute passes and then another, he wriggles and adjusts his footing, glad that the miserable cell is out of his sight and that there is still a world out there. The four metal bars on the window throw simple details of life into focus and make them more beautiful. Cars, vans and lorries honk and skid irritably past milk carts and horse-drawn carriages on Adam Street. Black and white specks, crows and seagulls, wheel through the sky, searching for a stray chip or breadcrumb. A ginger tomcat pads along a garden wall, his attention fixed on some unseen target. A stout-armed, hair-netted woman shakes out a wet sheet with a sharp **snap** and then pins it along the washing line with wooden pegs from her wide apron pocket.

She's there, of course, she's there, holding Mervyn on her hip, the breeze flicking her bobbed hair from side to side. The two older boys emerge from the kitchen door behind her, David marching out in his short trousers, while Omar clings to Laura's legs and pulls grumpily at her tartan skirt. She points up to the prison and Mahmood whips his handkerchief from his pocket and waves it out of the window frantically. Laura's face is too far away to see clearly but he catches sight of the moment that she notices the movement and bends down to move David's head in the right direction. Omar spots him without help and starts jumping on the spot, holding his stomach in a pantomime way as he staggers back in glee. They wave, he waves, they wave harder, he waves until it hurts. He wants to holler at them but there is no way his voice can reach them. This fluttering white handkerchief is all he's got. It reminds him of that moment when a passenger ship is about to leave port and the travellers gather on the first-, second- and third-class decks to wave to the masses on the dockside. As the pilot guides the liner out to sea, you have a flurry of handkerchiefs on both sides, like falling snow, shivering until well after the ship's horn has stopped sounding and they are so far out to sea that it looks like the ship could be slipped into a bottle.

Laura kisses her hand and throws the imaginary peck to him, he snatches it in his fist and slaps it against his own parched lips. She had told him once that he was the best thing that ever happened to her. The best thing. He made her feel like a queen, she said. She was a queen, his Welsh **boqorad**, no lie. Her body, her heart, her thoughts could not easily be cut from his; David, Omar and Mervyn's even less so. Their short podgy arms are flagging, but they continue to flap them in bursts of renewed energy. What must it look like to them? The broad, dirty, grey-brown shell of the prison, studded with dozens of rabbit-hutch-sized barred windows; their father hidden, apart from his black hand waving a white flag. Laura had heard David explain to Omar and Mervyn that Daddy was a prisoner in the castle and that the naughty sheriff would keep him there until he'd paid his taxes. His comics, nursery rhymes and imagination filled in what the adults hid from him, but he understood that his father was in trouble, at the mercy of powerful men.

Mahmood stops waving, he wants them to go inside before they catch a chill. Slowly, Laura and the boys lower their arms and turn back into the house. Mahmood watches them until she finally closes the kitchen door and then he stays in place, letting the breeze dry his tear-brimmed eyes. Be a man, he chastises, get a hold of yourself, you spent months away from them at sea, take it easy, look how close they are. This ain't no worse than a ship, you got your bunk, your feed, and you don't even need to fire a furnace. Keep your head together, say your prayers and don't cry like a damn woman.

Toban

[Ten]

Diana waits for the new owner of 203 Bute Street, Mr. Wolfowitz, outside the swept and emptied premises. No longer "the shop" or "home," just "the premises" now. The bundle of keys in her hand range in age from huge, rusted things cut in the 1910s to small shiny ones bought this year. There are some she has never seen or used before. Violet loved locking things; her mind settled by the act of turning a key and checking once, then twice, that it was indeed bolted. She'd read somewhere that in Georgian times the man of the house wouldn't sleep until he had secured all the shutters, doors and windows of the home, and Violet, as "the man of the house," took that upon herself. She also brought home the money that kept them all in comfort, and now with her passing and the liquidation of all their possessions there is a small fortune to divide between Diana and Maggie. Their father had arrived in Cardiff from Russia with just five bob in his pocket, but now Diana has more money than she knows what to do with. Violet had been so secretive and controlling about financial matters that Diana had no clue how much she had made from canny property deals, stocks and gilts. Neighbours are gossiping about their wealth, and she wonders what the worst of them might say about her failure to save Violet from the killer. Money, or even the thought of it, seems to twist people into crooked postures.

"Sorry to keep you vaiting, Mrs. Diana." Mr. Wolfowitz bundles up to her, holding the black **kippah** on his head flat so it's not blown away.

"It's no bother, Mr. Wolfowitz."

He is one of the older generation, his wispy salt-and-pepper beard and twinkling pale eyes hinting at woes and adventures she can only imagine. His accent is fixed in the Pale of Settlement rather than in the Vale of Glamorgan.

"My son come, ve vait two minute, please?" He smiles and, just like with her father, she can't refuse him.

"Of course."

His son is the one she has been negotiating with, and he treats Diana like a fool.

After rooting around in his pocket, Mr. Wolfowitz produces a tin of jewel-like boiled sweets and offers them to her with a small bow.

"That's very kind but . . ." She shakes her head.

"You take, take! Make you even sweeter."

"I'll take it for my daughter, how about that?" she offers.

"Please."

Diana takes a sweet shyly from the tin, wraps it in a clean hankie and puts it into her own pocket.

"Ah, here he come!" beams Mr. Wolfowitz as his bespectacled son saunters down Bute Street, a new-model Kodak camera hanging from his neck.

"I hope you'll excuse the wait, Diana, I had a spot of car trouble earlier," he says unconvincingly.

"Well, you're here now," she replies, with a tight smile that reveals the little creases where her dimples had once been.

"We won't keep you, it's just that my father wanted a little memento of the day, it's the largest store we've bought, you see. You wouldn't mind, would you?" he asks, lifting the strap of the camera from his neck before she's had a chance to reply.

"It's easy enough to operate, ignore all the dials and buttons apart from the top one . . ."

Diana gives him a look that shuts him up, before taking the camera and bringing it to her eye.

Father and son take position before number 203's black front door, adjusting their heads so that the number plate will be clear. "The keys!" Wolfowitz the younger shouts.

Diana throws him the lot and he misses the catch, scrabbling for them on the pavement.

They strike a pose again, each holding the large key ring with a hooked index finger, their free arms tucked behind their backs. They look like a hammy variety act on a poster at the Lyceum: the Incredible Wolfowitzes or the Canton Cantors.

Diana takes one picture, then moves the camera to take another in landscape. She presses the button but the son has leapt out of shot.

"Mind your fingers there," he grabs the camera from her, "it's absolute murder getting the focus right."

It takes him two beats before he realizes what he's said, and to whom, then the where and when of it flushes his face a deep burgundy. He offers a resentful mumble that Diana assumes is an apology.

His father looks back and forth between them, trying to fix the situation but stuck for words.

Diana tucks her chin down, unsure of her expression. Does her face show anger? Pain? Shame? Amusement? Nothing at all? She feels everything at once, but how can she explain that?

"Well, I hope the shop brings you as much happiness as it did us," she says, turning and walking away towards the police station. It's not until she has passed the Cypriot barbers that she realizes that her words sound like a curse.

"Eat up, dearie."

"I'm stuffed."

"So stuffed you can't squeeze in a Knickerbocker Glory?"

"I didn't say that." Grace smiles.

"Well . . ."

Grace resolutely sticks her fork into the baby carrots. On other tables courting couples flirt over stacked tiers of sandwiches and cake slices, and two older women bicker over who should have the honour of paying the two-bob bill.

The Howell's uniform is boxed up under the table: blue tunic, navy blazer, white blouse, khaki-coloured stockings, and old-fashioned bloomers. It had cost far too much but seeing Grace in the outfitters, turning this way and that in the mirror, her small shoulders swamped by the blazer, had lifted a little weight from Diana's heart. She has found a small flat for the both of them near the school, on the ground floor of a tall Victorian terrace and with a half-acre garden. The owners have recently decorated it and its sterility appeals to her. There are no secret childish doodles, no abandoned shoes, no hairs in the drain to remind her that this is someone else's home and her own is three miles away, on the wrong side of the railway bridge. She had shown Grace around the flat earlier in the day, and she had been aggressively positive about everything; the sash windows were lovely, the small black fireplaces lovely, the new russet carpet lovely, and the wisteria-laden pergola in the garden even more than lovely. The child in her is disappearing, obstinacy and egotism dropping away with her milk teeth. A tender bud of a woman is emerging, with two dark scanning eyes searching her mother's face for a clue of what to say, to do, to feel. The tap-dancing Shirley Temple morphing into a silent movie ingénue, eager to melt away into the shadows. "We'll make it nice," Diana kept saying, but the place is too foreign, too quiet, the street outside too genteel and dead. Not one soul has knocked on the door to say hello, and the nights pass by in eerie silence. Maybe it is what they need, a makeshift sanatorium in which to heal.

They never talk about what happened but it's always there, heavy between them, in their silences and distracted gazes. Grace is going to have to give evidence in court. Detective Powell insists on it, saying the jury needs to see her take the stand. It is difficult to argue with him; she ends up wanting to please him rather than demand what she came for, leaving her feeling diminished and prized at the same time. He said they have built a strong case against the Somali, with forensic evidence and multiple prosecution witnesses, but they still need Grace to say he is the man she saw on the doorstep. Powell said that after a bad shock the mind can play tricks on people, wiping some memories away and making others crystal clear, but they need to try harder to remember the attacker's face because all the evidence was pointing to the Somali. The detective showed her the suspect's photo again, Mattan's mournful eyes staring up at her from the table, and told her she had ample time to recollect what she saw, as the trial wouldn't start until the Swansea Assizes opened in the summer.

Leading her out of the police station, he shook her hand. "Let me know if you or your daughter need anything from us, Corporal Tanay. I remember your father coming to the police station to get his naturalization papers in order, all the way back in the twenties. Your family has been nothing but a credit to this town. I'll pray you won't need us for any troubles, but if you ever need a reference or some such I am only a telephone call away."

Spring has no patience for mourning, plants already burst forth from the leaf-strewn borders of the garden. Bluebells, a clump of pink ranunculus, a few late, squirrel-nibbled tulips and tall saffron-tongued irises bring life to the static, grey and melancholic scene. Diana roughly rakes last autumn's brown sycamore leaves on to the scrappy lawn to allow the flowers more sunlight; her own stark white arms warming in the sun too. The temperature is almost twenty degrees centigrade, and it's the first day she's had time to herself since the calamity. Her life is returning to her, the public business of grief taking up less and less of her time: the visits, the questions, the cooing and encouragement, the money, the solicitors, the police. After the trial it will all be over. Straightening her spine, she throws the rake down and takes a cigarette box from her apron pocket. The afternoon sun rests behind two mature sycamores that shield the garden from the railway line, their spindly branches intertwined and glowing like struck matches. Taking a long drag on the mentholated fag, her cheeks pucker, her lungs stretch open and the sweet cool air shoots down all the way to the pit of her stomach. Clarity. Peace. She feels them both for a few seconds. As a child she had enjoyed staring out of the window, pretending to smoke with a piece of broken chalk held between her fingers, her eyes fixed somewhere over the streaming chimneys. "You waste too much time," her father used to chide, idleness a greater sin than any other in his mind, but these moments, when the breeze caresses her hair and carries her thoughts away, pacify her warring soul.

Stepping in from the fresh garden, the kitchen smells so strongly of the new plasticky linoleum that it's enough to give Diana a headache. She pushes open the window above the steel sink and then searches the mint-green cabinets until she finds the flour, butter and condensed milk she'd bought earlier. In two hours she has to collect Grace from her new primary school and bring her to the flat so she can look through fabric swatches and pick her own curtains and bedding. She'll surprise her with a caramel tart, a treat they both love. The ingredients and tools she'll need are basic, which suits her as the kitchen is still rudimentary.

Caramel tarts take her back to her own childhood, to the Lyons' Corner House on the Strand in London. A fine confectionery of a building, with gilt vines and pillars on the exterior and fat samovars and latticed ceilings inside. Tiny chocolates, huge flower displays, ribboned biscuit tins, imported delicacies; it was pure opulence. The counters of the dining hall were jewelled with patisseries so delicate that she felt guilt at the thought of eating them, and plumped for a plain caramel tart and custard each time. A nippy with a white doily hat would take their orders at the smartly dressed table. Her father's voice was stiff, his leather briefcase clutched in his lap as he carefully pointed out their choices from the menu, the solemn High Court having chastened the three girls into silence. Violet and Maggie would order millefeuille, Black Forest gâteau, peach Melba, queen of puddings, or whatever took their fancy, but Diana always took pleasure in the homely comfort of the brittle pastry and the warm custard.

London was an assault on the senses: the merciless crowds between Piccadilly and Oxford Street, who seemed happy to trample a little girl into the gutter; traffic that never quieted; the bellow of newspaper men and flower sellers; policemen blowing whistles. She marched beside her father with her hands up near her ears in alarm. He took them to London two times, for each of the divorce trials. Diana is now the same age as her mother was when her husband, their father, tried to divorce her for the first time. It seemed to come on him like madness, soon after his mother died in Russia, a kind of rage that nothing could cool. He accused their mother of adultery and sued for divorce and custody of the girls. She remembers keenly the hot looks her mother received as they waited to buy ice cream from Salvatore's cart on Stuart Street. An ordeal of whispers and laughter, the divorce splattered across the newspaper, men asking their father where he got the money from, women telling their mother to fall to her knees and beg forgiveness, whether innocent or not. The subtle feeling that all their neighbours were laughing at their father too; at this small shopkeeper from Cardiff who would go to the expense and shame of a divorce. When the High Court, that white castle that replaced any picture-book castle in her mind, rejected her father's petition, he finally allowed their mother to return home. No one explained anything to her; she was ten years old and looking through the school dictionary for "adultery," "clandestine," "impropriety."

Violet kept house and made sure they were all fed and cleaned; if she knew more about the "situation," then she never said. Long-coated rabbis came to the house and holed up in the dining room with their father for hours, counselling patience and trust, but he never looked kindly on their mother again. Less than six years later, he brought a new case of adultery against her and won, exiling her from the home and burning as many of her photographs as he could get to before the girls saved them. The woman he saw in Mam was one they could never see: in the touch of her hands they felt love, while he sensed pollution; in her laughter he heard betrayal, while they saw pleasure; in the distant gaze that he read as slyness, they perceived sadness. She was a tree that he wanted to chop down, and he used the law as his axe. The girls helped her pack her belongings and move to the small house where she died, a few years later, her tears unquenchable. Her whole life was built around motherhood, and then the highest court in the land judged her an unfit mother. Poor woman. Diana still doesn't know what to believe about that time: if the judges were led astray by her father's paranoia, or if their mam really did love a man named Percy. They grew up in a world where the truth was something you needed shielding from.

"We weren't made for an easy life," sighs Diana, as she slaps the dough on to the worktop. She isn't like Mam, she knows that, she doesn't need a man for his money, or as an escape, and she'll make damn sure that Grace won't either.

A few days later, Maggie, Daniel and Diana stand around the dining table, with Grace at its head, her face glowing from the eleven candles on the birthday cake. A large bow on her head giving her two polka-dot rabbit ears.

"Make a wish first!" Daniel calls as she dives down to blow the flames out. "Blow, not spray, don't you be getting any spittle on my slice."

Grace sticks her finger into the icing and threatens Daniel before dipping it into her mouth.

"**L'chaim!**" Diana thrusts her glass of sherry in the air, her voice louder than she intended. "Long life and success, my love."

The adults line up to kiss Grace on the cheek and Diana, last in the short line, can see that her daughter is on the verge of tears. "Hold it back, hold it back," she whispers in her ear, squeezing strength into her.

With a nod of her head, Grace is back to smiles and laughter.

The small party moves to the new sofa for the present opening; the guests sit while Diana and Grace stand around the coffee table, cooing over the thick wrapping paper that each gift comes in. From Maggie and Daniel a whole treasure chest of books, and a pair of red house slippers. Diana leads Grace to the window looking out on to the garden and reveals her present: a blue-framed bicycle with a front basket full of artificial flowers.

"Oh my goodness!" Grace cries.

"What a spoilt girl," Daniel says, shaking his head in mock envy. "When do I get a bicycle?"

"Can I ride it now?" Grace asks her mother.

"Why not?"

She rushes out through the kitchen and into the garden.

Diana tops up the sherry glasses and they all sink down into their seats, the jollity suspended. Maggie looks the most deflated but, always the one to turn the conversation to safe trivialities, she sighs and says, "I can just feel that this year will play havoc with my hayfever. It's come on so strong, already."

Diana hesitates before raising the next subject. "The ground is solid enough to put the headstone on."

"That's good, that's good," Daniel says, looking down at his still-full sherry.

"You picked a nice stone."

Diana had also decided on the inscription—"Beloved Daughter, Beloved Sister, Beloved Aunt, May Her Soul Rest In Eternal Peace"—but it's such a permanent marker, one that will outlive them all, that she keeps wondering if she has chosen the right words. "You're all happy with the inscription?"

"Yes, there is not room enough to write what

is in our hearts, is there?" Maggie twists a napkin between her hands.

"No."

"Not enough ink, not enough paper, not enough time."

"You need my help?" Daniel asks.

"No, everything is finished now."

"It was a nice little party, wasn't it?"

Diana and Grace are snuggled in her bed, their noses almost touching. The candle sputters and shadows wave across the fern-patterned wallpaper and matching curtains.

"Lovely."

"What was your favourite gift?"

"The bicycle."

"Flatterer."

Grace smiles and reveals her hotchpotch teeth, all different sizes and shapes.

"What did you wish for?"

"I can't say."

"Sure, you can."

"No, really, I can't."

"Because it was about Aunt Violet?"

Grace nods.

"Did you wish that she was still here?"

"It's stupid, I know." She holds a hand to her mouth.

"No, you wouldn't believe how many times I've wished the same, Gracie."

"It wasn't right, it wasn't fair, was it, Mammy? There was so much blood."

"She was the best. I don't know why that was her fate. I really don't."

"We didn't hear anything, I mean, what if someone broke in here while we slept or while I was at school and hurt you?" Grace trembles as the fear she has kept hidden so well tumbles out. "It would be better if we had a man in the house, wouldn't it? To protect us from bad men."

"I can protect you, Gracie, I promise that. There is nothing a man could do that I wouldn't do for you."

"But you are just a la-aa-dy," she sobs.

"No, I am a woman, and no man would fight harder for you."

"I don't want to go to trial with everyone there, and that . . . that bad man looking at me."

"It will go very quickly, Gracie, you just have to tell the truth, just say exactly what you saw and then we'll go home and never think about it again. There is no right or wrong answer, just tell the truth."

"They will hang him, won't they?"

"If they prove he did it . . . maybe . . . I don't know . . . sometimes people are reprieved. That's not your concern, you just have to be honest, Gracie."

"I will be, I will."

"I know you will." Diana kisses Grace's black hair again and again until she has quieted.

Kow iyo toban

[Eleven]

"Cocksucker, fuck you!" Mahmood presses his thumb hard against the ringer beside the door, which makes the bell in the corridor clatter.

A warder wrenches the hatch open and bends down to meet Mahmood's face on the other side of the door. "You're asking for a hiding, aren't you?"

"I ask you to bring me water two time already, you want a man to go crazy, you bastard?"

"You really don't know what's good for you. I had a mind to get your bloody water but now you can die of thirst for all I care."

Mahmood buzzes the ringer again and the warder sticks a finger in his ear. "I'll report all of this to the governor, be sure of that, and he'll order us to do whatever it takes to get some sense into your head."

"You touch me with your dirty hands and I kill you all. You think I'm your slave?"

"Threats of violence, too? Nice one, buddy, that will definitely catch the governor's ear."

Mahmood presses the button rapidly—bell, silence, bell, silence—until the warder stops moving his lips and slams the hatch closed.

"Fuck you and your religion," Mahmood shouts after him.

"You a crazy-ass man, too wild," a voice chastises him from inside his skull, "what you get from doing that?" He argues with it silently, "I get my pride, I get my revenge," and he then sits heavily on the bed, his head cradled in his hands. He jerks up again and stands in the direction of Mecca, bringing his feet together and placing his palms over his navel. He takes a moment before beginning the prayer to clear his mind of all the dammed-up thoughts and emotions pressing down on him and then, with a deep breath, he begins. **Allahu Akbar**. Closing his eyes, calming his breath, resting his forehead on the cool cement, his mind slowly lifts away from the prison.

. . .

Mahmood feels a little lighter after the **salat** but there is one particular feeling that he can't push away, an unreasonable but powerful anger towards Laura. He hasn't bothered to wave from the window for four days now, and he watches the hour when they would normally have that brief communion come and go with a sullen desire that she feel as wretched as he does. He knows it's wrong-headed and childish, but he can't pretend that everything is alright and that she ain't let him down. She's already wasted two years of his life stringing him along like some old dog, and now he is locked up because these white **shayaadiin** hate that he got one of theirs. That's what it all boils down to, right? He took one of their women, and for that they gotta punish him. "The blacks take our jobs and take our women." They talk like that in all the papers, and say it to your face if they're feeling bold. They don't see you having the right to earn money or marry whoever you want. The Somalis had tried to warn him, but he was too proud and stupid to listen. These girls will betray you. They take up with any fella that catches their eye. They'll have your children calling any man Daddy, or maybe they'll just abandon them and dump them in a home. He can't look Laura in the eye now, she'll see what he's thinking, she always could see into him.

He'd treated it all like a game, like a cat stalking mice, he'd follow girls into bars and back out again, smiling as they walked away and told him giggling that, "I'm not allowed to talk to black boys." Black stockings, red lips, eyes done up all dark, and high heels, they turned his head every damn time. Their words said no but their eyes said yes, so he'd pick up his step and keep thinking the next one, the next one. The coloured girls had stopped having the same effect, it was too easy. "You don't come all this way for a skirt that looks just like your mamma back home," that's what the West Indian fellas said. The black women knew they had been pushed aside and hated it.

Once, a West Indian woman sheltering under a vast red umbrella had caught sight of him and Laura on the street, she had scanned them both from top to bottom, her nose scrunched up, and asked with a mocking laugh, "You see all that white and think wife, huh?"

He had put his arm tight around Laura's shoulder and shot back, "Mind your own business, gal, I ain't one of yours." What a fool he had been.

Five years. It had taken five years for him to be stripped of all of his delusions about this place. If nothing else, a cell will reveal every last mistake you made. Mahmood stands up and paces the twelve square feet of floor space. That day in Durban, when he had seen his first ship sprawled like a volcanic, steaming island across the water, that was when he was done in. He'd signed on as a pantry boy because they'd said he was too weak for the "Black Gang." It makes him smile, now, to remember how annoyed he had been to work in the kitchens when all his "brothers" were downstairs in the engine room. It was weeks until he realized the "Black Gang" came in all colours and were so named cos they all staggered up from their watch blackened with coal dust. His work was clean, easy and humiliating: "Peel those spuds, Ali," "You ain't got all the grease off these pans, put some welly in it, for Chrissake!" or "I don't give a flying a fuck 'you no eat pork,' get them hams scored now." The stewards had been rough men but not without kindness. One of them, a bald-headed thick-veined Scot, had nearly throttled an engineer for throwing a plate of slimy corned beef back in Mahmood's face.

In his hours off he'd walked every corner of every deck, his legs still used to tramping miles of earth each day, and it amazed him that this **beast**, this steel whale crashing through the waves, had electricity, telephones, lifts, smokeless cookers, flushing toilets, and levers and dials everywhere that did mysterious things. White man magic. It was as if Europeans had remade the world, and they only had to stretch out their hands to bring before them all the wonders of the world. The ship revealed to him the gulf between the life he had been living in Africa and the world beyond. That ship, the SS **Fort Ellice**, might as well have been a rocket ship, taking him to a planet of green gabbling aliens and ice-sheet seas, and the closer they got to their destination, Cardiff, the more Mahmood knew that Africa had become too small for him.

It wasn't until his third voyage, when his muscles were little hillocks atop his fine bones, that he made his way into the bowels of the ship where the real men worked. Still not furnace material, he'd been put to work in the coal bunkers as a trimmer, shuttling coal to the boilers, where stokers, almost limp with exhaustion, threw it into the flames. The coal bunkers were pitch black and illuminated with just a single movable lamp. The floor roiled and pitched with the Atlantic waves, and the trimmers staggered about as the coal slipped beneath their feet. On that ship there had been a fire in the bunker, but not any normal blaze—there were no flames to see or smoke to smell—just a heat so intense, from deep within the black heap, that it forced a bulge in the steel bulkhead. The old Yemeni trimmer, Nasir, who could taste the quality of coal by biting into it, said it happened sometimes when too much new coal was piled on top of old, or when the bunker was sitting idle too long. He spoke of coal as if it was a fond but volatile friend, his bow legs blackened up to his baggy shorts. "**Yallah! Yallah!** No way to put out the fire but to burn it!" he shouted, shoving Mahmood out of the way to rush through with his sharp-lipped wheelbarrow.

They were joined on some watches by a Welshman who sang so deeply Mahmood felt his voice in his ribs; at other times a pair of identical Somali twins from Berbera, Raage and Roble, swung their shovels beside him. Those days when the three Somalis were entombed and fell into the same hypnotic rhythm, the bunker felt almost like a mystical space. Their shovels plunging and flying up to the same beat, old work songs from the desert pulling their hoarse voices together in low, monotonous tones, the sweat, the pain, the heat exorcizing every last thought from their minds, a makeshift **zaar** at the bottom of the sea. He would clamber into his bunk, in a ten-man cabin choked with cigarette smoke and stale sweat, feeling as if he had been battered with hammers, his eyes wincing from the brightness of the light. But he fell asleep still elated, his pulse in tune with the thump of the motors. "**Yallah! Yallah!** No way to put out the fire but to burn it!" Those were words to live by.

Boy, had he burned! There were few sins he hadn't committed. He'd had his first taste of liquor in a small bar on the dockside of Porto do Rio de Janeiro, in a palm-thatched dive where coloured sailors from all over the world gambled and danced with fleet-footed, blank-faced bar girls. The little glass of brown liquid was tea, he told himself, as he took it from the caramel-skinned Brazilian waitress. This had been while he still preferred women who reminded him of home. She was dressed up in a tight black halter-neck top with a red scarf tied around her neck and had twisted her black curls into a pompadour near the front of her head. She watched him as he took his first gulp of rum and giggled as his eyes widened in alarm. He looked around the bar for the other Somali sailors but they were not there, there was no one to judge or restrain him in that dim neon-illuminated space. She said something encouraging in Portuguese and refilled the glass from a heavy bottle. Rain poured down in heavy sheets from the rim of the thatch, cooling the heat of bodies pressed too close together, she took his hand and led him away from the loud jukebox ringing with frenetic samba music. The sky was darkening but the somnolent haunches of the mountains were still visible over the funnels and smoke columns of the port. She pointed each mountain out to him, speaking slowly as if to a child, her feline face silhouetted against a yellow bulb, her tongue making strange, sibilant sounds. He leant over and kissed her powdered cheek, emboldened by the rum, and waited for a slap that didn't come, instead she turned and kissed him unabashedly on the lips. He reached out gingerly for her waist, his mind racing from his mother to the smell of the girl's perfume to a memory of the **macalim**'s cane. Instinct and upbringing clashing just enough that his hands quivered a millimetre above her round hips. What kind of woman does this? his mind said. Who cares? his body replied.

Mahmood's body won the argument that night, and the next and the next, until the coal was replenished and the cargo loaded and he had to wave goodbye one final morning to his bold Brasileira. The gambling came later, when with beginner's luck he'd put in £10 and won £100 at a poker table in Singapore. It was a bigger thrill than even the alcohol and women had been, and he knew he'd found his poison. He'd stayed to watch the other games, promising himself he was done, but then he'd sat down again, placed a tenner on the narrow wooden table, then a twenty and eventually the whole lot. The Chinese cooks he'd tagged along with stayed up all night, fighting sleep with more plates of fried food and thimbles of whisky.

The yellow strip lights buzzed, his brain hummed with exhaustion, but he watched intently as one old chef—with an opium-drowsy **jinu** perched on his knee, rubbing his mottled bald head encouragingly with her long black talons—pulled in a messy heap of cash and jewellery. It was enough to retire on but the old man didn't crack a smile. Shaking the girl off his knee, he passed a bill to each man around the table and then walked stiffly back to the ship along the wide, bare, day-broken streets, his winnings concealed in a brown paper bag. The back room where they had spent the night turned rapidly into a doss house, as the first hawkers cried out their wares outside. He was the only black man there but no one cared or told him to leave. The gamblers flopped on the floor or slept at the tables, ducking their faces into their shirts or crossed arms, like crows nestling under their wings. Mahmood staggered behind the fortune-taker and arrived back at their ship, bloodshot-eyed and empty-pocketed, feeling as if a miracle had been worked.

The need to work for a living was suddenly not an inescapable fact of life. You could earn, or not really earn but pocket enough in one night to put a stop to all the donkeywork, the sour bosses, the four-hour watches, the strikes, sinkings, long workless spells. You could become the master of your own life, go anywhere and do what you liked each day. He had found his new dream but it was one he could do nothing to fulfil, fortune couldn't be nudged or shaken awake, she had to be given her liberty to act when and where she wanted. But damn, the bitch took her time and let a man down too hard. What sense it make for him to be here on a murder charge for something that have fuck all to do with him? What kinda fate is that? When some other bastard can get away with murder and probably win a big race on top of it too. Where is he now? That piece-of-shit killer? Tucked up in his woman's arms, probably, not a care in the world. No chance he's gonna come running, confessing guilt, no, man, no way. Mahmood ain't got no hope of that. He can't rely on no witnesses, no lawyers, no judge, no fate. Just Allah. He has rinsed his soul and can beg God with a clean, true heart for justice. Just justice. He doesn't expect his own sins to be overlooked, only that he shouldn't pay for another man's too.

Even some of his sins feel forced on him by this damn country. He had never taken anything in his life until these bastards made him feel like the shit they'd stepped on in the grass. Old bitches holding their handbags to their chests cos they catch sight of him, or looking ready to cross themselves if his shadow fall on them. "What make you so scared?" he'd wanted to shout many times. "It's your people who easily kill us for sport." You could be the angel Jibreel but if your face dark it don't matter how honest, kind or soft you are, you still the Devil. He'd started walking with crossed arms, as if lashed down, to let them know he wasn't gonna hurt them. His mind was full of **shaki**, he kept asking himself did that woman look at her bag cos she see me coming, or she just needs something from it? Is that man following me around, or just wandering around his shop? Until, one day, he just had **enough**. A woman had given him a real stinker of a look, a real "get back to your mother's hole" look. At him! With his three-piece suit and silk scarf, while the old bat had on a rain jacket that hadn't seen a laundry since the war. It was too much. When he caught up with her, haggling over a cheap fillet with Tommy the Fish, and saw that she had dumped her plastic handbag at the end of the cart, he hooked the strap with a finger and carried it away. It was an act of mischief, of tiny revenge. He had no need of her pennies, but the thrill, the build-up and pleasure of getting away with it, was the same as putting on an outside bet and getting lucky. It happened again and again, when he felt his dignity had been taken too lightly. He would become the devil that they always took him for. Then he got clever and saved his talent for times when he needed easy cash: sneaking a watch here, a coat or wallet there. He watched the experts at work in the pubs, slicing unseen through the crowds, or backslapping and tickling boozers. They each had their own style but it was always like a dance, down to good footwork and knowing how their mark would move, and Mahmood had always liked to dance.

"There's a visitor for you. Are you coming or not?" Matthews, the chief warder, stands in front of the open cell door, his stomach straining against his brass-buttoned woollen jacket.

Mahmood is dressed in his day uniform and had a shower in the morning, but he has left the decision to see Laura or not till the last moment. His heart beating hard, he heaves himself up from the bed and nods to Matthews.

"It will do you good, doesn't fix anything to mope, lad," the warder says encouragingly, slapping Mahmood on the shoulder. "I've seen plenty come and go and I'll tell you this for not a penny, if your mind is a jail then it don't matter where you are, but if you wake up thanking the Lord for the air in your lungs and wanting to make the most out of your predicament, then you're halfway out the prison gate."

They clunk side by side along the gangway. "I want to be all the way out, sir."

"There isn't justice anywhere in the world that is more stringent than the one we have here. I know you claim your innocence, Mattan, and I want to reassure you that the court will give you as fair a hearing as any duke. That is the British way."

"That is what I hear for a long time."

Matthews blushes. "Fair dealing is what we're known for—that and tea, right?"

Laura is alone at the little table, her face turned down and hidden by the sharp lip of her headscarf. A bright red jumper clings to her small conical breasts and lights up the pale, clinical room.

"You didn't bring any of the boys?" Mahmood asks crustily, as he pulls the metal chair back with a screech.

"No, they are not well," Laura replies, looking a long time at his body before resting her eyes on his face.

He sees it immediately. Barely hidden by the hair she has styled forward. He reaches out and with a single finger pushes the strands away. "Who did that?" he barks.

Laura hurriedly looks over her shoulder and pulls the paisley scarf closer to her face. "It's nothing. Don't make a fuss."

"I ask you again, Williams, who did that?" The yellowing bruise spreads from her left ear down to the corner of her thin, pink lips. It is marbled green and purple over her cheekbone.

"Just some cosh boy on the Windsor Road. I was coming back from the shop with David and Omar and I saw him throwing rocks to take out the street lamps, soon as I opened my mouth to tell him off he was on me. Calling me the usual, threatening to bash the boys' brains in, scaring David half to death, poor thing wet himself, but don't let him know I told you."

"Nobody around?"

"There were plenty," she answers bitterly. "One woman washing her front step stopped to gawp, but no one said boo to him. He started going on about how I should move out of Adamsdown, that I ain't got no place being there . . . that they should hang the little niggers along with their dad."

Laura looks furtively up at Mahmood but his face is blank, distant.

"That really cut and, you know, David is looking up at me with his wise old face, asking me if you're going to be hanged. I told this little greaser to go to hell and that I'm not going anywhere and neither are you or the boys. Next thing I see is a rock hitting my face."

"You know this boy's name?"

"I think he is one of the Carson kids but I couldn't swear on it."

"Find out, Laura, and I will fix him when I'm out. I will see him pay."

"Forget it, Moody, we've got bigger worries. I'm just going to keep the boys in until the trial is done. Omar loves to chalk the pavement and chat to old ladies as they pass so he'll probably throw a strop over it. They're only tiny but some people are just so sick-minded, you know? I don't know how some of these teenagers think; if they're not out causing trouble they think they're not living."

"Keep them inside, that's right. Your father not the kind to scare anyone off, so until I come back keep them in the house," Mahmood agrees, shaking his head. The desire to pound that Carson's face to a pulp is so strong it's almost sexual.

"I spoke to Detective Powell this week."

"What for?" Mahmood almost shouts with disgust.

"Hear me out, for God's sake, I was over at my sister's house and Brian said he's working on a building site with this Jamaican carpenter."

"So what? You take any tale to that pig?"

"Listen! You've spent all week ignoring me, the least you can do now is bloody listen."

"Talk."

"This Jamaican tells Brian that he knows you're innocent and he knows who the real killer is."

"Who is he? How would he know?"

"Cover, something Cover. Well, I think he said he was outside Volacki's and he saw two Somalis hanging around outside just before the murder was meant to have happened. I thought the police should speak to him."

"So, who is the killer?"

"He didn't say."

"That Cover, Berlin told me about him, he hates Somalis and stabbed Hersi last year. He's just trying to get us into trouble. Probably covering for one of his own lot. He's wasting everyone's time, you don't know men, they like to talk big and say they know something the next man don't."

Laura raises an eyebrow. "That sounds very much like someone I know."

Mahmood blinks a couple of times and then understands she means him. He smiles reluctantly.

"Detective Powell seemed interested. He thanked me and said that he would follow it up. Let's be hopeful, Moody, this could be the witness you need. Someone knows **something** that could get you out of this place."

He holds his hand out to her. "You are a strong woman, fighting my battles."

She lays her palm against his. "This is my battle too."

They sit in silence for a long time, holding hands, glancing as the metal hands of the broad institutional clock shiver towards the hour, a hubbub of sweet nothings and hushed arguments around them.

"You won't ignore me this week, will you?"

Mahmood shakes his head.

"I know you're angry, Moody, I would be too—in fact, I'm livid—but you can't throw me on to the same heap as the others."

"Me know, me know," Mahmood says abashedly, letting go of her hand to doodle on the table with his clammy index finger.

"We are on one side. Not different ones."

"Me know, me know."

She squeezes both his hands in hers and looks him directly in the eyes, her hazel irises flaring a bright green. "I am not one of **them**, right? I am not one of them. You have no reason to hate me."

"I never hate you, don't say that."

"Well, don't let yourself walk down that road, that's all I'm asking."

Mahmood's hands are limp in her tight grip, he feels cornered and unable to articulate himself. He had wanted to hurt her, he knows that, but he can't confess to it so hides in silence.

"It's time to go now. Next time, the boys will be with me."

"Good, good," Mahmood is finally able to say, his eyes settling one final time on that damning, eggy bruise as she picks her bulky leather handbag up from the floor.

"I'll see you at the window tomorrow, right?"

"On the dot."

"So, you found no witness for me? No one to say I'm a good man or that I stay far away from where the woman got killed? No man or woman at all?"

"I'm afraid not, your defence will rely on the lack of inculpatory evidence rather than the presence of exculpatory."

"What does that mean?"

The solicitor sighs gently and cradles his head in his hand. Mahmood notices the gold wedding band on his finger for the first time; he can't picture him with a woman, all he needs is a cape and fangs and he'll look like Dracula himself.

"It means that we have no way of proving your innocence but, similarly, the Prosecution have no clear proof of your guilt."

Mahmood rubs his hands down his cheeks and thinks. They are seated on opposite sides of his bed in the cell. The late June heat is making him sweat heavily, the stale smell of the room combining with his own odour to embarrass him. He had tidied up before the solicitor's arrival, after days of slovenliness, but shafts of light from the window still illuminate floating pillars of dust.

"There ain't no one to say they saw me in the cinema?"

"Yes, the attendant, but he doesn't remember what time you left exactly."

"And those bastards at Davis Street say I came back later than I said."

"That's correct."

"And Laura's mother say she saw me at eight p.m."

He doesn't bother replying, just nods his long head.

"So you think that the police have nothing on me?"

"I didn't **claim** that, but it's all circumstantial, meaning that the evidence could have different interpretations to those they are imbuing it with."

"Like the old boots they say have blood on them?"

"Precisely."

"And they found no fingerprints, weapon, money, nothing to say I do it?"

"That's right, Mr. Mattan."

"So, why I still sitting here?"

"Because they've managed to find witnesses to put you at the scene of the crime, at the time it's believed to have been committed, and that is no small matter."

"But they are liars, how can I be in two places at one time? I cut myself in two? Stupid."

"Well, that is what the trial will examine."

"No point of trial if people lie," Mahmood says quietly, scratching the wiry stubble along his jaw.

"That is called perjury and is a crime in itself."

"Laura saw me that evening."

"Yes, but they are using her mother's statement against you, because you claimed to have gone straight home from the cinema while Mrs. Watson—excuse me, Mrs. Williams—said you called around and asked her if she needed any cigarettes, as you were heading to the shop. You have also put yourself in two places, Mr. Mattan."

"I don't even remember if I ask her or not, it was a normal night for me. You remember every chat you have? Every minute you come home? Don't make you a murderer if you forget."

"No, but it does create complications for the Defence in a murder trial, Mr. Mattan. We can only work with the evidence and statements we have. Is there anything more you want to tell me? Anything you have omitted or . . ." he raises an eyebrow, "have just remembered?"

Mahmood turns his head sharply towards him. "You think I did it? Ha! My own solicitor think I'm guilty! What funny joke is that?"

Dracula stands, annoyed that he is being laughed at. "I do not think you are guilty, Mr. Mattan, I think the case against you is actually a rather weak one but it **is** strengthening. By being as open with me as possible about your movements you will enable me to find the evidence needed for an acquittal. However, I cannot help you if you decide to be a fool to yourself."

Mahmood holds his hands out in exasperation. "I tell you what you need to know. I am not a Hollywood man. I just go home and I sleep. I never go to school like you but if I kill a woman and steal one **hundred** pound, you think I don't have enough brain to take the next ship out and never come back?" He shakes his head. "You people understand nothing."

"Well, if that is the case, I won't take up any more of your busy time, Mr. Mattan." He picks up his briefcase and wide-brimmed hat and stands stiffly by the door, his back to Mahmood, waiting for the guard to let him out.

They are trying to drive him crazy, Mahmood knows that, it's how they work, how they have Shay's killer sitting in a madhouse in the middle of nowhere, even though when he pulled that trigger he was as sane as any man. Once you crazy they got their victory. Sometimes, he feels like he's half mad already, he can't breathe, as if there is thick, black smoke in his lungs and he about ready to drop.

He is a man who needs to walk, always was, and never sat still from the moment he learnt to get up on two feet. He walked the length of Africa, for fuck's sake. This immobility is what will do him in. Just a few months ago, at the end of January, he had got the train to London and walked from Paddington to West India Quay and back again, just for the hell of it, for a change of scene, just to remember that this body is his and he can do with it what he wants; that he can push it hard and it will do his bidding like an expensive machine. Now, his muscles feel slack, his spine hurts from lying around too much, and his dense dark skin has lightened to a strange dull brown from lack of daylight. He don't want Laura, never mind the children, seeing him like this—a dusty-haired, scuffed, broken shop mannequin.

The sun has slumped outside and the cell glows a grimy yellow from the fat, wide rays flooding it. He's stripped the thick grey jacket off and sits cross-legged on his bed in just the vest and trousers. He's been in that position for so long his buttocks and feet are numb but he is thinking, thinking hard, and doesn't want to break his chain of thought. He needs to plot his way out of this snare. Is it too late to tell them a little more? A little more "well, I did visit Laura's house before going home" and "yes, I did visit

Bute Street the week the woman was killed." Would that help anything now? Or would they just say, "Ha! Now, we prove you a liar"? He is stuck on this little island of his lies and he can't leave because the sea all around is filled with sharks. So be it, he'll just have to brazen it out and put his faith in the all-seeing and all-knowing one. Berlin had said on his last visit that Ramadan was due to begin at the next new moon and he taps his temple to remind himself to check the moon after the sun finally sets. He will fast, that would be the right use of this dead time; one thing he can thank the bastards for is that they have kept him away from all the **belwo** he had grown accustomed to—the alcohol, music, stealing, gambling, women—the five pillars of his old life. He can start to atone for some of his past sins here, in the sterile womb of the prison.

The night comes too late, the sun teasing him and sending the sky all kinds of colours before it tires and finally slinks below the horizon. Mahmood has to crane his head this way and that before he spots the moon, hiding behind a bank of slow-moving clouds. They drift clear and then he can see the sharp sliver of moon settling in for the night. Tomorrow will be the start of Ramadan. He is grateful that he will have something to occupy his mind, even if it is just hunger.

It is an ugly sky tonight, full of gas and smoke. The night skies in Hargeisa made you think of God, while here they are worldly, contaminated by men and their ceaseless chimneys and bright lights. He can see one constellation, its Somali name lost somewhere in his memory, the English never known. In Hargeisa, where sunset meant genuine darkness, you could track the slow movement of stars and planets, glittering and pulling you up into a depthless, shifting sea with its coastline of purple, indigo and black stretches. God reminds you through those night skies of how small and insignificant you are, and he speaks to you clearly, his anger and solace tangible in the rain he sends or withholds, the births or deaths he orders, the long, waxy grass he gives or dead, broken earth he carves. The miasma above the prison, above Cardiff, suffocated Mahmood's faith and separated him from God. He began to strut and bluster his days away and completely forget that this life meant nothing and was as fragile as a twig underfoot. He had needed to be humbled, Mahmood nods to himself, he can see God's wisdom so clearly now. Looking back to the bed, he makes the obligatory intention to fast the next day, using the Arabic sentence—**wa bisawmi ghadinn nawaiytu min**

shahri Ramadan—that his mother had taught him as a child, his sing-song intonation mimicking hers.

Mahmood lies down on his side, his head resting on his spongy biceps, and thinks about shaving the whole of his head, a clean start like pilgrims do after completing the **hajj**, the sins of the old life shorn away. But how would he look? With his broad face and small, jutting ears. What scars and lumps might be revealed? What would a jury think, a white jury already prepared to hate him, if he stood there with no hair to soften him? They would not think of **hajj** or purification, no, they would think him a madman, or a hardened criminal, a wild savage needing the chastening of the law. He can't risk it; he'll neaten up his wiry hair with a short back and sides in the morning, and start pulling himself together again.

Mahmood had joined the queue first thing in the morning, but the line, being one of the few places the prisoners can gather and talk freely, is full of men with closely cropped hair going for their weekly trim. His hunger is manageable, his thirst less so, his mouth already claggy and stale. The other elements of the fast—not swearing, not smoking, not losing his temper, not thinking sexual thoughts about Laura—will be harder for him to manage than the physical deprivation, though. He will go back to his cell and start reading the Qu'ran from the first line: "In the name of Allah, the entirely merciful, the especially merciful." Try to lose himself in the poetry and rhythm of the Holy Book and block out all other thoughts.

It takes more than an hour for Mahmood to shuffle silently to the front of the line and take his place in the barber's seat, where a little mound of ratty hair rests beside his feet, but at least the barber has swept down the chair with a cloth. They exchange a nodded greeting and then Mahmood takes the full measure of the man. He is tawny and frizzy-haired, maybe a Cypriot or other kind of Greek, the wrong side of forty with a round stomach under his blue-striped shirt, and rings on most of his hairy fingers; his clothes have the same sharp herbal smell that his old barber in Bute Street had. Mahmood closes his eyes as, without hesitance, the barber begins running a metal comb through his overgrown and knotted hair, pushing it this way and that, looking for its natural shape. The comb scratches and pulls at his skin, but there is something comforting, still, in the way the barber cradles his jaw with his warm, clammy hand. It's a benign, fatherly touch that allows him to imagine himself back in his real life, sitting in the leather chair in Bute Street, with a scratchy mournful Greek love song on the gramophone.

Mahmood hears the clip of the scissors and then hair drops on to his nose, cheeks. He keeps his eyes closed, leaving the man to do what he wants with his hair. The barber runs the clippers up his neck and around his ears. What difference did he seriously believe a hairstyle could make? If they are gonna hang an innocent man there is nothing he can do about it. A slick of pomade and then the ritual is over, a slap on the shoulder the sign to get up for the next prisoner.

Mahmood lifts a hand to his hair, vanity making him wonder if the barber has done a smooth job, but the Greek blocks his arm and says, "Leave it!" in a gruff, protective bark. Mahmood smiles furtively, understanding the man's pride, and drops his hand. He feels better, that's true, cleaner, lighter, and closer to his real self. He straightens the collar of his uniform and looks for the exit.

"Your mate's in the hospital."

Mahmood turns back, looking to see if the words are aimed at him.

"That's right, your mate Archie's been taken away to the infirmary."

It's the little blond boy who had nearly fainted at Singh's execution. Dickie. He's standing there by the exit, as if he's been waiting for him. "You talking to me?"

Dickie nods.

"Why you tell me? Archie is nothing to do with me."

"Because you might be next, you know." He looks suspiciously around them.

"I don't know what you talking about, boy." Mahmood almost laughs.

"They cut him cos he's a nonce, right, he's been raping girls all over the country and now word's got out and the old fellas have cut him to teach him a lesson." Dickie draws a line from left ear to right, across his mouth rather than neck.

"I never touch a girl like that." Mahmood pulls a sour face, "Why they want to drag me into it?"

"Because they've heard you killed an old crippled woman in her shop. You did, right? They don't tolerate that kind of thing."

"What? They ask you to check for them?" Mahmood shouts. "You tell them I kill no woman, and if they try to hurt me I will hang for **them**."

Dickie raises his hands. "It's a warning, a friendly warning. I was only trying to help."

"You tell them I am **innocent**. I **innocent. Innocent**." He jabs a finger against his heart with every repetition.

Dickie shrugs, eager to end the exchange. "If you say so . . ."

"I say so, you hear? I say so!" Mahmood bellows into his face.

. . .

"You call my solicitor now! You hear me! I want to speak to him now!" Mahmood shouts, pummelling at his door and pressing the bell with mechanical tirelessness.

He had tried to hold it together. Took deep breaths, paced the cell, picked up the Qu'ran, squeezed his head between his hands, but it was too much. These men had taken too much from him. His freedom, his dignity, his innocence, and now his name was finished too, said in the same breath as someone like Archie, the lowest of the low. He had been too meek and they had mistaken him for the kind of man they could do this to. If there was any shred of manhood left in him he would tear this door down, take this cell apart brick by brick, roar and thrash.

"You fucking bastards, you motherfucking cocksuckers, I could kill you." Mahmood drags the thin, rancid mattress that has caused him so much sleeplessness on to the floor and stamps on it. He kicks the bread and milk he had stored to break his fast with; they smash against the walls, the milk cascading down the blue paint. He bangs his head on the window bars and then charges back to the door, throwing his full weight against it, not caring if he smashes his own bones in the process. "You will not finish me, you understand? **Miyaad I fahantay hada?** Do you understand me now? I'll say it in any language you want."

Staggering back in pain but ready to make another charge, Mahmood is startled to see the cell door fly open and a crowd of warders accompanied by the doctor march in, one of them carrying a thick belt in his hands. Their truncheons are withdrawn and Mahmood steps back and stands on the wire frame of the bed, his eyes skipping from one warder to another. One breaks forward and drags him down to the floor, pinning him down with a knee to the chest, then they are all on him. His arms, his legs, his head held in place as they wrestle him into the thick leather contraption. It's only when he notices that one of his wrists has been buckled fast to his waist that he realizes it's a kind of straitjacket, like the ones he has seen at the pictures. He lashes out with his free arm, but they twist it so hard he screams in pain and they take the moment to attach it to the belt too. Lifting him up, a warder's arm locked around his neck, Mahmood flies through the air and is taken out of the cell, through the dark corridor and around a corner.

"**Hooyo! Aabbo!**" he calls, as if his mother or father can help him now, his head becoming lighter and lighter as the grip around his neck tightens.

"Put him in there," the doctor orders, stepping to the side as Mahmood is thrown into another cell, his head bouncing off the door frame. "Be careful, would you? Leave him now, I'd say he needs to be here overnight before he regains his senses." Mahmood hears the doctor's voice drift away before the door bangs shut.

His eyes close, the throbbing around his throat slowly diminishing, but he breathes in greedily, afraid that they will return and choke him again. He reaches to wipe his brow but his arms don't shift, he lies flat on his back, his arms straight and immobile, the body belt squeezing his stomach to the point he feels bile rising up into his mouth.

He opens his eyes, and the first thing he notices is the cell walls, lined with what look like grey mattresses, up to head height. He closes his eyes again, in case his vision is messed up by the knock to the head, but the mattresses are still there when he opens them again. Stained with brown and red streaks in places, and encircled by pale rings where someone has tried to scrub them clean.

"They got you now," Mahmood whispers, "made you into their slave, bound up and out of your mind. Mattan is dead."

"He's in there somewhere." The warder laughs as he opens the door.

"Oh, I see."

Mahmood watches from the gloom of the unfamiliar corner of the familiar cell, hidden behind the door, as two brightly polished shoes step into sight.

"Mr. Mattan?"

Mahmood keeps quiet. There is nothing more he has to say to them.

The solicitor steps further in, walking almost on tiptoe. Finally, the door closes and he catches sight of the prisoner hunkered down where the guards can't see him.

"There you are!" the solicitor says, as if Mahmood is a child playing a game.

The man waits for him to rise, to dust himself off and shake his hand, but he stays in place, looking down at the floor.

"I was told that you had some kind of outburst yesterday. I do hope that you are feeling . . . more yourself now. The doctor told me it was most probably due to the extraordinarily protracted length of time you have waited to go to trial. It is wholly understandable that your nerves would be frayed, Mr. Mattan, but I come, finally, with good tidings. Your trial has been scheduled to commence on July the 21st, at Swansea Assizes. D-Day has arrived!"

Mahmood keeps silent, his eyes trained on his bulbous prison-issue boots.

"I notice that there is an abrasion on your cheek. Shall I take it up with the governor, or not?"

The solicitor glides a thumb around the brim of the felt hat in his hands, waiting for any kind of response. None arrives. He looks for somewhere to sit but eschews the unmade bed.

Adjusting his pose, he straightens his spine and takes a firmer tone with Mahmood. "It really doesn't **do** to be attacking the guards, Mr. Mattan. A man in your situation is truly nothing more than a ward of the State, and in your physical and verbal assault of your guardians lies an insult to the State itself. You will achieve far more with a conciliatory and dignified approach. Mr. Rhys Roberts and I have prepared a strong defence on your behalf, and the Prosecution has not been able to do more than cobble together an assortment of tattletales and what-ifs. I would be gratified if you could express a little more faith in our abilities. It would do you good too to take more air, to eat well, sleep well, build up your morale for the trial," he looks to his watch, "which is less than nine days hence."

Mahmood sinks his head between his raised knees.

"Are you seeing your wife and sons? Maybe that would provide the boost you need? Nothing like the kindly faces of loved ones to remind us that we are not all alone in the world."

The solicitor sniffs suspiciously and sneaks a look at the chamber pot underneath the bed.

"My word. You didn't slop out this morning. What is the matter with you? If you think that all of this palaver will get you declared unfit for trial, Mr. Mattan, you'll have to think again. You passed the Statutory Board and that's the end of it. You'll sit through the trial and the jury will decide your innocence or guilt, dependent on the evidence and arguments. Come what may."

Laba iyo toban

[Twelve]

THE CLERK OF THE ASSIZE:
Members of the jury, the name of the accused is Mahmood Hussein Mattan and the indictment against him is that on the 6th day of March this year in the City of Cardiff he murdered Violet Volacki. To this indictment he pleads not guilty and puts himself upon his country, which country you are. It is your duty to hearken to the evidence and to say whether he is guilty or not guilty of murder.

THE CROWN:

Members of the jury, shortly after eight o'clock on the evening of Thursday, the 6th March of this year, the doorbell of a shop at number 203 Bute Street rang. In the living room behind the shop there were Miss Violet Volacki, who owned the shop, her sister, Mrs. Tanay, and Mrs. Tanay's young daughter. It was after ordinary business hours, but Miss Violet Volacki was never unwilling to do a little more business, and when the shop doorbell rang on this occasion she went to the shop, closing the door between the living room and the shop behind her. Neither her sister nor her niece ever saw her alive again.

MRS. DIANA TANAY SWORN:

Q. Did you at any time hear any stamping in that shop after your sister had gone out?

A. No.

Q. Were there any noises in your own living room?

A. Well, I was playing a little with my daughter, so I doubt whether I would have heard. We had the wireless on.

Q. Just tell my Lord and the jury what form the playing with your daughter took?

A. My daughter was asking me about square dancing. I did not know much about that, but I was going over a little country dancing with her.

Q. Is the door between the living room and the shop a well-fitting door, or does sound travel easily from the shop to the house?

A. No; we had rubber put around it to stop the draught.

Q. Did you see anyone enter the shop?

A. No.

Q. Did you see anyone at the shop door?

A. Yes.

Q. Is that man sitting in the dock today?

A. No.

Q. Would you formally look at that. **(Newspaper handed.)** At the bottom of that newspaper it is quite clear that you and the other members of your family are offering £200 reward for information leading to the conviction of whoever committed this crime?

A. Yes.

(The witness withdraws.)

GRACE TANAY:

Q. Is this man **(indicates)** the same man you saw standing on the porch that night?

A. No.

CONSTABLE ENGLISH SWORN:

Q. Look at photograph number 3. In photograph number 3 do you see the heel of a boot lying on the right-hand side?

A. Yes.

Q. Did you make these marks?

A. Yes.

Q. You were wallowing in the evidence, Constable.

A. At the time I thought the intruder might have been in the back room that adjoins this place.

Q. How long have you been a police officer, Constable?

A. Thirteen years.

Q. Do you not know enough to prevent yourself from making marks like this? What do you think these photographs were taken for?

A. For the benefit of the Court.

Q. And here there are bloodstains from your feet all over these photographs. Did you find it necessary to walk on both sides of the body and round it, Constable?

A. Yes.

Q. Why?

A. First of all I had to make an examination of the body at the time.

Q. What examination of the body did you make?

A. I saw a wound on the right-hand side of the neck.

(The witness withdraws.)

MRS. ELIZABETH ANN WILLIAMS SWORN:

Q. Are you the mother-in-law of the accused, Mattan?

A. Yes.

Q. On the evening of the 6th March did you see Mattan?

A. That is on the night of this affair?

Q. You know the night Miss Volacki was killed.

A. Yes.

Q. Did you see him that evening?

A. Yes, I did see him that evening.

Q. First of all, where were you when you saw him?

A. I was in my room. This man knocked on my door. My daughter went and he asked her if she wanted cigarettes. I went to the door and I looked over her shoulder. He was by the door, and I said, no, I did not want any cigarettes because I had no money, and this time I see him—

Q. When you say "this man," who do you mean?

A. Mattan.

Q. This man here (**indicating**).

A. Yes, my son-in-law.

Q. It would be three or four minutes after eight when he left?

A. That is when he came.

Q. Are you quite sure of the time?

A. Yes, I am positive.

Q. How do you know it was that time?

A. Because my children were all ready to undress and I told my daughter, "Go on," I said, and I got up from my armchair and I looked at my clock. I said, "It's going on; it's gone eight o'clock; let's put the children to bed and let's have a bit of peace."

Q. Your children go to bed to give you a little bit of peace about eight o'clock?

A. Yes.

Q. How long have you known your son-in-law?

A. Going on five years.

Q. Has he ever had a moustache in that time?

A. I have never seen one.

Q. I should like the witness to see the shoes, Exhibit 9. **(Shoes handed.)** Do not worry about those yellow things on them. Have you ever seen these shoes before?

A. Yes.

Q. Were those shoes bought for your son-in-law?

A. No; I had them from my brother; he works on the salvage. He brought them home thinking they would fit my husband. They did not, so I asked the accused if he would buy them for four shillings, and he did.

Q. Can you remember roughly—I do not say you can remember the exact date—how long before Miss Volacki was murdered, if it was before Miss Volacki was murdered, did you sell these shoes to this man?

A. About a fortnight.

Q. And, with the exception of the yellow marks I have told you to ignore, are they in anything like the condition they were in when they were in your possession?

A. I should say they were a bit cleaner now.

(The witness withdraws.)

MRS. MAY GRAY SWORN:

Q. You are a second-hand clothing dealer carrying on business at 37 Bridge Street, Cardiff?

A. Yes.

Q. Do you know the accused man, Mattan?

A. Yes.

Q. Has he been a customer in the shop?

A. Yes.

Q. Do you remember the Thursday night, the 6th March, when Miss Volacki was killed?

A. Yes.

Q. I want you to keep your voice up because those are the ladies and gentlemen who want to hear you. First of all, will you tell us what time it was you saw Mattan?

A. It was just before nine o'clock.

Q. Where was it: where were you when you saw him?

A. He came to ask if I had some clothes to sell.

Q. What did you say?

A. I said, "You have got no money to buy them, so go away."

Q. When you said that to him what happened?

A. He put his hat on the counter and he pulled out a wallet of notes—he could not close the wallet—and a big bundle of money, and he said, "I got plenty of money."

Q. Could you form any idea how much money there was?

A. There was sure to be eighty to a hundred; it was such a big pile.

Q. Just tell us first of all how Mattan was?

A. He was out of breath; he had been running; he looked as if he was very excited, and he was running.

Q. How was he dressed?

A. He had a blue Air Force jacket underneath and white trousers, and dark overcoat, and a trilby hat, and he had an umbrella over his arm, and he had gloves on his hands.

Q. What sort of gloves were they?
A. I went out to the door to see if my daughter was coming from school, and he ran over towards Millicent Street.
Q. I was asking you what sort of gloves he had on his hands?
A. My hearing aid has gone and I can't hear very well.
Q. What sort of gloves was he wearing on his hands?
A. No, it was in pound notes.
Q. What kind of gloves was he wearing?
A. Right over to Millicent Street.
Q. What kind of gloves did he have on?
A. Dark gloves, and they were very wet.
Q. Your business is selling second-hand clothing, is it not?
A. Yes, it was, but I do not sell them now.
Q. You want to make money, do you not?
A. I have wages coming in. I do not want anybody's money. I do not know what you are referring to.
Q. Be good enough to listen to my question before you start anticipating the answer. If you do not want to make money why were you in business the night you saw Mattan?
A. Because if we do not stay in business we have to pay the rent just the same.

Q. You are not in business for pleasure. You are in business to make a livelihood?
A. Yes. But what has that got to do with the case?
Q. Your answer to Jury—
A. You have no right to ask that. I do not want to answer any more questions on that.
Q. I am afraid you will have to. You told my Lord and the jury that you did not sell him clothing and that you told him to go away because he had no money. Is that right?
A. Yes.
Q. Then he showed you that he had money, according to you?
A. Yes, and I still told him to go away.
Q. Why?
A. Because I did not want anything to do with him, as I have had enough trouble with him in my premises, and I cannot understand where he had the money from, because the night previous to that he was trying to borrow a pound.
Q. When did you hear that Miss Volacki had been murdered?
A. Pardon?
Q. Did you not hear my question?
A. Yes, I will answer your question if I hear it.
Q. You were not stopping for time to think?
A. Pardon?

Q. Mrs. Gray, when did you know that Miss Volacki had been murdered?

A. I did not know until the next afternoon when the paper came out.

Q. The afternoon of the 7th March. Did you read about the murder?

A. Yes, I did, and I immediately thought of that gentleman there.

Q. Did you read about the reward—?

A. I did not read about the reward. A reward is of no interest whatever to me.

Q. You did not let me finish my question. Please—

A. I am interested in no reward, no interest at all in no reward.

Q. But although you knew about Miss Volacki's murder the following day and although, according to you, you instantly thought of the man who had come to your shop the same night as Miss Volacki was murdered, you did not give a statement to the police until the 13th, a week later?

A. I waited until the police came to see me.

Q. Did you say that he was cheeky and that you did not like him?

A. I never said no such thing.

Q. You do not like him, do you?

A. He is of no interest to me. I do not want to like him. What do I want to like him for?

Q. According to you, I understand he has been cheeky to you?
A. Yes, and very cheeky, and to everybody else, as far as I know.
Q. And for that reason you do not like him?
A. Why should I want to like him? Certainly not. I don't like him.

(The witness withdraws.)

MR. HAROLD COVER SWORN:
Q. You live in the Docks area of Cardiff, do you?
A. Yes.
Q. Are you a carpenter by trade?
A. Yes.
Q. On the 6th March last, which was a Thursday evening, were you anywhere in Bute Street?
A. Yes, I was.
Q. Did you have occasion at all to pass the shop of Miss Volacki?
A. Yes.
Q. Just tell my Lord and the members of the jury where you had spent the earlier part before you went past Miss Volacki's shop; tell the jury where you had been?
A. It is general, when I come from work, I generally goes to the Mission; I am very fond of playing billiards, and I went in there approximately ten to eight, or a quarter to

eight, and after I went in there the tables were all booked up so I could not get a game, so I stopped and started playing a few games of draughts. On the finish somebody said it was about eight o'clock and I consider it was time to go home. I found I wanted some cigarettes and there was none in the Mission at the time, and I decided to go up to the Club and see if I could get something.

Q. As you approached Miss Volacki's shop, did you pass a Maltese lodging house?

A. Yes.

Q. Did you pass the men?

A. Yes.

Q. When you passed the Maltese and passed Miss Volacki's shop, did you see anybody outside or near Miss Volacki's shop?

A. Actually I seen somebody, but it was not until after I passed Miss Volacki's shop I seen him. It was on the approach of Miss Volacki's shop and the Maltese I see the accused gentleman over there.

Q. When did you first give the information to the police, or when was the first statement taken from you, about these matters?

A. The first night when we were all told about the murder of this woman I was there; as you know, I have seen the accused coming from the shop. Naturally I did not take any notice whatsoever of it, and when I was told of the murder of the woman I still did not believe it would have been a coloured man, until when I came home and I was told in work they were looking for a Somali. I suddenly realized then I had seen this man, and I went up to police and lodged a complaint about it.

Q. When was that—a day later, two days later, three days later?

A. No, I think it was the following day.

Q. As you very fairly said, you had no reason to think it was this man who committed the murder. Had you any reason at all, at the time you saw someone—you say this man—in the doorway or porchway of Miss Volacki's shop, to take any notice of him at all?

A. No, not at all, not in the least, because I know Miss Volacki do sometimes oblige people by selling them certain things at certain hours if they want.

Q. Do you personally know Mattan?

A. Not personally; I have seen him about. At the Colonial Annex Dance and near a Somali lodging house in Bute Street, I have also seen him walking in various parts of the Docks.

Q. Have you seen anybody else who looks like him in the Butetown area?

A. I am afraid I have never been that interested.

Q. It was you who were just passing Miss Volacki's shop and saw a man. Are you positive beyond any shadow of a doubt that the man you saw was Mattan?

A. I am positive.

Q. I must suggest to you that you are mistaken: you may think it is the man you saw, but it is not?

A. If I was not positive I do not think I would be here—I have no right to doubt it or to say anything or come here at all if I was not sure of the man I have seen.

(The witness withdraws.)

WILLIAM REGINALD LESTER JAMES SWORN:

Q. Dr. William Reginald Lester James, you are Lecturer in Pathology at the Welsh National School of Medicine?

A. Yes.

Q. On the 7th March last, at the Pathology Institute, did you carry out a post-mortem on the deceased woman, Miss Violet Volacki?

A. Yes.

Q. Will you tell us what you found and what conclusions you came to?

A. Externally there were several cuts on the right side of the neck extending from beneath the chin to behind the right ear. There was one main cut eight inches long by two inches deep. There were three smaller cuts leading into this and one inch below the main cut, two inches deep. There was a much more shallow cut, four and a half inches long, which had also gone through the dead woman's blouse at the junction of the collar and the shoulder. Over the left shoulder blade there was a bruise approximately two inches across.

Q. How could the bruise have been caused?

A. By any recent pressure by something blunt about the size of one's knee.

Q. Could it have been caused by knee pressure?

A. Yes, it could have been caused by that.

Q. Was there anything noteworthy about the scalp?

A. Yes. On the right of the crown of the head there was a red area which contrasted with the general pallor of the body.

Q. Consistent with what?

A. The tearing of the hair.

Q. The tearing out of the hair or pulling back the head?

A. Pulling back the head by grasping the hair.

Q. Did you form any view as to whether the long main cut or the three minor cuts were caused first, or in what order they were caused?

A. The long main cut was caused first.
Q. Did the major cut result in a gaping wound?
A. Yes, and it involved the backbone.
Q. In other words, you would have an aperture there?
A. Yes, of about an inch and a half wide.
Q. What would the effect of the main cut you have spoken of be?
A. Extreme shock and haemorrhage.
Q. The blood marks on the knees and toes. I think you are about to tell us of those.
A. Yes. There were blood marks on the knees and toes and on the palms of the hands and the knuckles.
Q. Consistent with?
A. Crawling on a bloodstained surface.
Q. What height was Miss Volacki?
A. Four feet ten inches.
Q. And her weight?
A. Ten stone three pounds.
Q. And the cause of death?
A. Haemorrhage due to a cut throat.
Q. How long would she remain conscious after her throat was cut?
A. I would think, not more than three minutes at the outside.
Q. Fit yourself into the theory which I suggest, at all events, you do not contradict at the moment, that the murderer had come back

after hearing Miss Volacki crawling towards him and inflicted the three subsequent wounds. You would expect, would you not, some considerable staining of the feet and shoes and possibly also the hand which wielded the weapon?

A. On the feet and shoes, unless he was very careful where he trod.

(The witness withdraws.)

MR. ERNEST LEONARD MADISON SWORN:

Q. Are you feeling alright?

A. Yes.

Q. I am sure my Lord will allow you to sit down if you want to.

A. Thank you very much.

Q. He has not been well, my Lord. **(To the witness:)** Do you keep lodgings at number 42 Davis Street?

A. Yes.

Q. On the 6th March of this year, the Thursday night that Miss Volacki was killed, did you have lodging in your house the accused man, Mattan?

A. Yes.

Q. And a Jamaican named Lloyd Williams?

A. Yes.

Q. And a man named James Monday?

A. Yes.
Q. Face the jury. Had each of those lodgers a separate room with a separate key?
A. Yes.
Q. Do you remember the Thursday evening, the 6th March?
A. Yes.
Q. In what state of health were you at that time?
A. I was sick, lying in bed in the front room.
Q. Do you remember Mattan coming into the house that night?
A. Yes.
Q. When he came in, what did he do?
A. He come in the front room and he sit down on the settee, and there was James Monday sitting beside him.
Q. I want you to tell us about what time it was that Mattan came in.
A. It was about twenty minutes to nine, or a quarter to nine.
Q. Are you quite sure about the time Mattan came in the night Miss Volacki was murdered?
A. I was under the care of the doctor, and the doctor prescribed to me what time I should take each tablet, and my clock was right beside my bed.
Q. How long did he remain in the front room downstairs with you and Monday?

A. He stopped there until about ten minutes after ten, somewhere after ten o'clock.

Q. During that time how was he behaving?

A. He come into my front room and he sit on the settee, and James Monday handed him the **Echo**, and he took the **Echo** and he dropped it on the floor. He is a man who generally speaks about horse racing and football pools. That night, me and Monday and he tried to speak about the racing.

Q. Usually he was a man who spoke about horse racing and about football pools. That evening, what happened? Monday did—what?

A. After Monday handed him the paper and we were speaking about football pools and horse racing for that day, he took no part in it.

Q. You mean, Mattan took no part in it?

A. He took no part in it.

Q. Was that a usual thing for him to do or not?

A. Very unusual.

Q. Apart from being silent, was there anything else you noticed about him?

A. Yes.

Q. Tell us, please.

A. He was sitting on the settee. I was lying in bed facing him. He was looking, you know, towards the window, very serious, and I have noticed him myself, and I could imagine that the man went in a trance, just like somebody was trying to hypnotize him.

Q. He seemed to you like he was in a trance?

A. Yes.

THE JUDGE: Like somebody who had been "hypnotized." Is that what you said?

A. Yes, my Lord.

Q. Have you ever seen him like that before?

A. Never before.

Q. When he left your room to go to his own room, did he say any greetings as he went away?

A. Nothing at all.

Q. Was that a usual thing for him to do?

A. That was an unusual thing for him to do. He always bids me "Goodnight."

Q. Tell my Lord and the jury quite slowly, and I want the jury to hear every word, what he said about the murder when he spoke to you on the Saturday?

A. I says to him, "Well, Miss Volacki is a very heavy woman and it must be a very strong man to go and hold a woman like that and to kill that woman," and he directly says to me, "That is easy." I says, "What do you mean?" He says, "You can get to the back of this woman and catch her by her throat—that—way."

Q. You are demonstrating by putting your left arm over your face and drawing your right hand across your neck, are you?
A. Yes.
Q. Just tell us this, please: have you ever known Mattan to go out wearing one suit of clothes and, without returning to number 42, appear in a different suit of clothes afterwards?
A. Yes, many times.

(The witness withdraws.)

MR. HECTOR MACDONALD COOPER SWORN:
Q. Are you Chief Security Officer at the Arms Park Greyhound Racing Company?
A. Yes.
Q. Do you attend greyhound meetings at Somerton Park, Newport?
A. Yes.
Q. And at Cardiff. Do you know the accused, Mattan?
A. I do.
Q. Did you have any particular reason to speak to him?
A. Yes.
Q. What did you speak to him about?
A. Begging from patrons.
Q. Did you tell him on one occasion that you had received a complaint?

A. I did.

Q. And did you inform him that if he persisted you would have to ask him to leave the track?

A. That is so, yes.

Q. Do you remember when that was?

A. No, I could not.

Q. Do you remember the 6th March, 1952?

A. I do.

Q. Was it before or after that?

A. Before.

Q. Did you see the accused on the 7th March?

A. Yes.

Q. Was that at Somerton Park?

A. Yes.

Q. Where did you see him there?

A. Just inside the main door between the Tote and the "Pay-out."

Q. Just in case any member of the jury should be unfamiliar with the procedure of the Tote, the "Pay-out" windows are the windows where you draw your winnings, are they not?

A. That is so, if you are successful.

Q. What impression did you gather?

A. Well, on this occasion he was holding a roll of notes rolled up in his hands, and he came from the direction of the "Pay-out" towards the south side of the stadium.

Q. Do you know whether he did bet on any of the races?
A. Oh, he had been betting, yes.

(The witness withdraws.)

MISS ANGELA MARY BROWN SWORN:
Q. Were you, in the month of March this year, employed as a counter assistant at Miss Volacki's shop?
A. Yes.
Q. For how long had you been working at Miss Volacki's shop?
A. I worked for Miss Volacki for sixteen months.
Q. Do you know the accused, Mattan?
A. Only by sight.
Q. Had you ever seen him at the shop?
A. Yes.

THE JUDGE: Can you remember the last time he called before Miss Volacki was killed?
A. The last time I saw him was a few weeks before.

(The witness withdraws.)

DETECTIVE SERGEANT DAVID MORRIS SWORN:
Q. Are you a member of the Cardiff City Police Force?

A. Yes.

Q. On the 6th March last did you go to 42 Davis Street with Detective Constable Lavery?

A. Yes, at 10:25 p.m. I went to 42 Davis Street.

Q. As far as you and Detective Lavery were concerned, when you saw Mattan that same night Miss Volacki was murdered, there was nothing found that night to connect him with that murder?

A. Nothing was found that particular night.

Q. Would you look at the wallet. (**Same handed.**) That wallet which was found in the room was subsequently handed to the Forensic Science Laboratory for examination?

A. I understand it was.

Q. As far as you could see, Sergeant Morris, there was neither a large quantity of money nor any bloodstains apparent to you during your search of Mattan's room that night?

A. The room was illuminated with a low-wattage bulb, and as far as the naked eye could discern there was no blood on any garment.

Q. I am quite sure you do not want to sound grudging. In fact subsequently a complete and thorough search of the room was made by daylight?

A. That is right.

Q. And nothing of evidential value was found there?
A. That is correct.
Q. It is quite clear from the statement that at first, at any rate, Mattan was quite willing to answer your questions: the first part of your interview he was cooperative?
A. Yes.
Q. It was not until about halfway through, when there was mention of a coloured man, that he started to get excited?
A. Really excited, yes.

(The witness withdraws.)

CHIEF DETECTIVE INSPECTOR HARRY POWELL SWORN:
Q. Will you just tell my Lord, first of all: when you saw the accused, Mattan, on the 12th March, had you in your own mind come to a conclusion as to the propriety of charging him with murder?
A. I had not sufficient evidence at all.
Q. Why did you caution him?
A. In fairness to him. If there was something wrong in what he was going to tell me I wanted him to know he was not obliged to answer questions I was asking him.

Q. It was not because you had made up your mind that you were going to charge him at that stage?
A. I certainly had not.
Q. The fact is, Inspector, that you had sent one of your subordinates, Detective Sergeant Morris, to fetch this man?
A. Yes.
Q. Detective Sergeant Morris himself brought him back to police headquarters?
A. Yes.
Q. And thereafter, at whatever intervals and for whatever time it was, he was continuously in the precincts of the police station for seven hours and thirty-one minutes, or thereabouts?
A. Yes, he was.
Q. Did you at any time during that time tell him he could go home whenever he wanted to?
A. I think he knew that—I did not tell him so specifically, no.
Q. At one stage in these proceedings did Mattan give this answer, "If you keep me here twenty years it makes no difference; I tell you what I know, I walk out of here tonight; you get tired"?
A. Yes, he did.

Q. Is it not patently obvious from that answer alone that Mattan was under the impression he was being kept there?

A. I do not think so. He was being kept for the purpose of questioning. There was no question of a charge.

Q. He was being kept?

A. He was not being **kept** against his will. If he had said at any time that he wished to go, I had no option but to let him go.

Q. You and I and his Lordship know that, but did Mattan know that?

A. He said several times something to me about whether he was going to be charged, and I told him I had no evidence to charge him.

Q. That does not appear in your record of question and answer?

A. Maybe not; but there are other things which do not appear there. It is as accurate as possible.

Q. I am not suggesting that your record is in the least inaccurate. You have put down what you consider to be of relevant importance in this case.

A. Yes.

Q. This man is a Somali, is he not?

A. Yes, he is.

Q. And although he has a fair knowledge of the English language, he does not necessarily make himself easily understood?

A. He makes himself very well understood.

Q. And in spite of the fact that he was a coloured man and obviously a foreigner, at no time did you tell him he was free to leave the police station if he wanted to?

A. I did not tell him that specifically, no.

Q. Chief Detective Inspector, have you ever had your attention drawn to another person similar to Mattan in appearance?

A. I cannot remember that. My attention was drawn to a number of people at this time.

Q. Specifically by a prison officer by the name of Smith, in the presence of a salaried solicitor in the employ of my instructing solicitors?

A. I do not think that was me, sir.

Q. You do not think that was you?

A. I cannot remember the incident.

Q. Do you know anybody who looks like Mattan in Bute Street or Butetown?

A. No, sir, not exactly. He has a very unusual appearance for a Somali. He has some of the regular features of the Somalis and some of the features which are not usually identified with them.

Q. Do you know Mr. Hughes, an articled clerk?

A. I think I do. I am not sure of his name. If he is Mr. Morgan's clerk, I know him.

Q. Did you see him in the Main House at Cardiff Prison on Tuesday, the 1st July?

A. Yes, I did, sir.

Q. You remember that?

A. Yes.

Q. And there was a warder present?

A. Yes.

Q. Do you remember anything being said by anybody about someone who closely resembles Mattan standing outside the prison on that occasion?

A. I do not remember that. It might have been, but I cannot recall it at all.

Q. It might have been?

A. Yes.

(The witness withdraws.)

THE PRISONER SWORN:

Q. Is your full name Mahmood Hussein Mattan?

A. Yes.

Q. Mr. Mattan, keep your voice up so that those twelve ladies and gentlemen may hear what you say. Did you come to England in about 1947?

A. Yes.

Q. And have you made your home in Cardiff since?
A. Yes.
Q. Mattan, you are charged with the wilful murder of Violet Volacki. Did you murder Violet Volacki?
A. No, I never did.
Q. Do you remember the 6th March of this year?
A. Yes.
Q. Where were you in the afternoon?
A. I was in pictures.
Q. About what time did you go there?
A. Half past four.
Q. And what time did you leave?
A. Half past seven.
Q. And where did you go when you left?
A. I go back straight to my lodgings.
Q. What time did you arrive at your lodgings?
A. Twenty to eight.
Q. Did you go down Bute Street that night?
A. No.
Q. Do you remember Mr. Harold Cover giving evidence? Mr. Cover said he saw you coming from the direction of Miss Volacki's shop that night. Do you remember him saying that?
A. I do remember he said that, but I was not there; I never been down there.

Q. It was not you whom he saw?
A. It was not me.
Q. Did you see Mrs. Gray at all that night?
A. I doesn't see her.
Q. Did you call at her shop at any time on that day?
A. No.
Q. Later that night did the police officers see you at your lodgings?
A. Yes.
Q. You heard Detective Constable Lavery say that he found a few silver coins and a few copper coins in your trousers pocket on that day. You heard him say that?
A. Yes.
Q. Did you get any money anywhere the next day?
A. On Friday?
Q. The day after the police came to see you?
A. Yes.
Q. Where did you get that from and what was it?
A. It was two pounds three shillings I drew from the Public Assistance.
Q. Now Mattan, when you were seen by the police officers, Sergeant Morris says you were excited after a little time. Is that so?
A. I was not; I was in bed sleeping when he knocked my door.

Q. Were you quite willing for him to come in or not?

A. Well, I was sleeping and I cannot tell you what time it was, but I heard somebody knocking my door and I got out of bed. Before I opened the door I put the light up and I asked him, "Who?" and he told me, "Police." So I opened the door and the Sergeant Morris and the other detective—I cannot tell his name—come in.

Q. Did Sergeant Morris ask you where you had been that night?

A. The first thing he ask me—he tell me, "Something serious happened tonight and we have to see you as soon as possible."

Q. May the witness have Exhibit 10, please. (**Same handed.**) Look at that document. Whose signature is there?

A. Well, I cannot read who is there, but it is my signature.

Q. Do you remember signing that document?

A. Well, yes, I did.

Q. Was it read to you before you signed it?

A. He doesn't read me, and I doesn't read myself; I doesn't read or write.

THE JUDGE: Do you say it was not read to you?

A. He doesn't read me.

Q. Let the prisoner see the shoes, please. **(Exhibit 9 handed.)** Did you use to wear those shoes, Mattan?

A. I did not wear them before; I just bought them a few days before that murder and I never been wearing them since, until the 12th March. I was keeping these shoes for walking purposes; I was not wearing them.

THE JUDGE: Ask him if he was wearing them on the 6th March.

Q. Were you wearing them on the 6th March?

A. No.

Q. Do you know how the bloodstains got on those shoes?

A. No, I cannot tell you, but anyway when he take them off me they were not in this condition.

THE JUDGE: I suppose he is referring to the yellow spots.

Q. I imagine so, my Lord. **(To the witness:)** You are talking about the yellow spots, are you?

A. No. The shoes were cleaner than that anyhow.

Q. The shoes were cleaner?

A. They were cleaner than that.

Q. Did those bloodstains come from Miss Volacki's shop?

A. No, nothing to do with it. It got nothing to do with it at all because these shoes I never wear that day and I never been down there, and I don't know nothing about it.

Q. When were you last in Volacki's shop before the murder, Mattan?

A. As long as I been in Cardiff only once I been to this shop, and it was in 1949.

Q. Have you been there since?

A. I doesn't. I pass the way through, but I never been inside the shop.

Q. Now let us see. Miss Brown is wrong in saying that she has seen you in Volacki's shop since 1949, is she? The assistant of the shop is wrong?

A. I doesn't know her at all.

Q. Your mother-in-law, Mrs. Williams, is wrong when she tells us you went along to her house about eight o'clock and asked her whether she wanted cigarettes?

A. When I been there it was twenty to eight, when I come from the pictures.

Q. Did you speak to Mrs. Williams?

A. Yes, but I got no reason to tell you the business about me and my wife; I got no right to tell you, and I got no right to tell the police.

Q. You see, you are going to answer my question. Just tell my Lord and the jury, are you now agreeing you did speak to Mrs. Williams on the way back from the cinema?

A. I speak to my wife, but I got no reason to tell you that.

Q. Why did you not tell the police: "I spoke to my wife"?

A. I cannot tell police because nothing to do with police; I cannot tell my business between me and my wife.

Q. You are saying you did not tell the police because what happens between you and your wife is not police business. Is that right?

A. I doesn't tell to the police, and I got no right to tell anyone.

Q. Did you mean the jury to understand a short while ago that you did not read that statement, Exhibit 10, because you cannot read?

A. Yes.

Q. You know the evidence is that your regular practice was to go to Mr. Madison's and have the **Echo**. What would you have it for—to look at the pictures or to read it?

A. I just used—if I had it, I never used to bother with it; but if I have a look I used to look partly for the racing and the photos. That is what I used to look for; I doesn't read at all.

Q. Let me ask you about Mrs. Gray. Mrs. Gray is the lady who gave the evidence, the very deaf lady. Have you been to her shop from time to time to get clothes?

A. No.

Q. You have never been to Mrs. Gray's to buy clothes?

A. No.

Q. That means at any time, does it?

A. Any time, because I got nothing to do with any second-hand clothes at all.

Q. Is it right that on the Friday night at Somerton Park Stadium you were there with between fifteen and twenty £1 notes in your wallet?

A. This wallet I never been with since I came out from the sea. It was always in my suitcase, and the police got it from my suitcase; I never use it at all.

Q. Whichever wallet you used, is it right that on Friday night, the 7th March, you had between fifteen and twenty £1 notes in your possession?

A. No.

Q. At the Somerton Park Stadium?

A. No. When I got there all the money I had was thirty-five shillings.

Q. Is it right you were betting on almost every race?

A. Well, yes, because it is only a two-shilling bet.

Q. On the Saturday is it right that you were playing cards for money?
A. No.
Q. Had you on the 6th March no address to which you could slip to change your clothes?
A. I have no other clothes.
Q. You see, Mr. Madison has told my Lord and the jury that on, I think, the 11th March he saw you go out one morning with working clothes on, that he saw you in the city with entirely different clothes on and that later that day you arrived back at number 42 Davis Street once more with your working clothes on. Was Mr. Madison right or wrong in his evidence about that?
A. I am not talking about Mr. Madison.
Q. But you are going to, you see; you are going to.
A. I am not going to talk about him.
Q. You are going to, Mattan.
A. I got nothing to talk about him.
Q. Was Mr. Madison right or wrong in his evidence about you changing your clothing?
A. I am not going to imagine anything about Mr. Madison; I was not changing except when I got change in my own place.

Q. Did not Madison say that it was a funny thing that one person should have been able to kill a short fat woman like Miss Volacki?

A. Me and Madison we had a row on Friday and I never talked to him on Saturday at all.

Q. Are you in the habit of carrying a knife or a razor around with you?

A. I doesn't; I never used to carry one.

Q. Very well; the jury can draw their own deductions from that answer. Harold Cover, you know him, do you not?

A. No.

Q. You are shaking your head again; do you mean "No"?

A. I don't know him.

Q. Do you know him by sight?

A. Who?

Q. Harold Cover, the Jamaican who gave evidence yesterday, Do you know him by sight?

A. I don't know him at all.

Q. The truth is, is it not, that you went into Miss Volacki's shop on the night of the 6th March and murdered her? Is not that the truth?

A. It is not true.

Q. By cutting her throat either with a knife or a razor?

A. Not me.

Q. Is it not true that thereafter you robbed her drawer of money exceeding one hundred pounds?
A. No.
Q. Is it not true that thereafter you made your way up to Mrs. Gray's shop running, and that you tried to get some second-hand clothing from her that night?
A. Not me.
Q. Is it not true that you somewhere and somehow effected a change of clothing before you got home that night?
A. Not me.
Q. You were not wearing—those—suede shoes on that night when you went to Miss Volacki's shop?
A. What?
Q. Let me repeat the question: were you not wearing—those—suede shoes that night when you went to her shop?
A. It's funny thing, but I never been to Miss Volacki's shop and I never been wearing those shoes.

(The witness withdraws.)

THE JUDGE:
Very well; the witnesses may be released. Members of the jury, may I once again repeat my warning

to you. You have now heard the whole of the evidence and tomorrow morning you will have speeches from counsel and then I shall sum up; but you will keep an open mind until you have heard the whole of the case, and whatever you do, of course, do not talk about it to outsiders.

Saddex iyo toban

[Thirteen]

THE DEFENCE'S CASE:
My learned friend, with that customary fairness of his, said that the evidence in this case is wholly circumstantial. With that I, for the Defence, do not seek to quarrel for one moment. It must be apparent, members of the jury, that it is only circumstantial evidence in this case, and you are invited to draw a certain inference from that circumstantial evidence.

Now you may think, too, that the case for the Prosecution was put in a nutshell by my learned friend just now. I forget whether it is thirty-nine or forty-one witnesses who have been called before you, but in effect the sum, substance and pillar of the Prosecution's case are two witnesses only. The one, Mr. Harold Cover, who saw Mattan in the neighbourhood of the shop in which Miss Volacki was so foully murdered at about the time of the crime, and Mrs. Gray, who saw him thereafter with a large sum of money in his possession.

First of all, as my learned friend said, the whole of Mattan's stories and explanations and statements and evidence is riddled with lies.

Members of the jury, as I comment upon the evidence I will ask you to remember and recall that, in addition to denying the things which my friend suggested to him, he has also denied certain pieces of evidence which are enormously in his favour. Why should he do so? You have to ask yourselves this question when you saw him:

What is he?

Half child of nature?

Half semi-civilized savage?

A man who is caught up in the web of circumstance? Who has come under the suspicion of the police and, because he knows he is suspected, has childishly tried to lie his way out of it—**tried to lie his way out of it**. That is how he comes before you today.

I am not going to insult your intelligence, members of the jury, by suggesting that **anything** he has said at **any** time is true. You can see that for yourselves. But to brand him a liar is very far from branding him a murderer. He has lied, no doubt you may think, purely from the fear of consequences. He thought that if he kept on telling lies he would get out of it eventually.

It is quite clear from the evidence of Detective Sergeant Morris and others that he is not a man who likes the police; he distrusts the police. You remember when they called on him that night he started to call the police liars. You may think that he himself is tarred with the same brush, but, members of the jury, this is the first point which I ask you to accept from the Defence, that the Defence in this case does not rely for one instant on **anything** which Mattan has said. The Defence in this case is built out of the witnesses for the Prosecution, and for the Prosecution alone, and I ask you to dismiss Mattan's evidence and the stories of untruth and wrigglings and lies he may have told.

Remember the circumstances in which Cover saw the man he now identifies as Mattan: a casual glance, a passing in the street, at a quarter past eight on a wet night in early March; dark, several people about—in fact, one of the ways he suggests he remembers him is because he stepped back to give him passage. Nothing remarkable about him to draw his particular attention to him. It is only when he hears of the murder later that he thinks back, and says, "I remember a man—yes, it was Mattan; he was jolly close to Miss Volacki's shop that night about that time; I think I ought to tell the police about it," and he does, and in so doing he acts as a good citizen and as every one of you no doubt would act in those circumstances.

How much money can be traced to this man? Between fifteen and twenty pounds at the most, fifteen to twenty pounds being the amount he was seen to have in his possession at Somerton dog track, Newport, the day after the murder. Members of the jury, how did he get it? Here is one of the things which shows that Mattan is lying, surely, because the security officer at the Somerton dog track told you he saw this man coming away from the paying-out window—in his own words, "He seemed to have been successful."

On the matter of the bloodstained suede shoes, do you think, members of the jury, for one moment—you look at the photographs; look at them in all their ghastly horror—do you think that if Mattan was wearing those shoes, and he was the murderer, they would not have been far more heavily contaminated with blood? It is a matter for you, but do you not think so? See how the blood was splashed up everywhere. Do you think that this microscopic quantity on these shoes is evidence which inevitably draws you to the guilt of this man?

The Prosecution invite you to say that something sinister is to be drawn from the fact that this coloured man, admittedly a seaman, carried a knife or razor on previous occasions. You are men and women of the world. Do you know, or do you think it unlikely, or do you think it probable, that most coloured men and seamen who live in that part of the world are not infrequently in possession of a razor? But, members of the jury, in all your experience have you ever heard of a man carrying two razors at the same time, because this razor, which was not the razor which inflicted that wound on Miss Volacki, was found in his clothes the same night by the police. Do you follow what that means? It means this, that there was a second razor in Mattan's possession and he must have been carrying two at the same time.

What else is there against him? First of all, there are the witnesses Madison and Monday—Madison is his landlord, who you may think is not overfond of Mattan, and who was certainly anxious to get rid of him after the call from the police, which is perhaps not altogether surprising. Madison spoke of him when he returned that night as being in a trance-like state, whereas Mr.

Monday, who was the other coloured man who was sharing Mr. Madison's room that evening, says that he was very sad.

This man has been sitting behind me during this trial. I have not had an opportunity of watching him but you have done so. You may have seen his demeanour, not now when I am drawing attention to it, but at other times before I drew your attention to it, or when he was giving evidence in the witness box. In repose his face is, do you not think, a sad face, a face which shows a certain amount of sorrow, and if it is in repose for one reason or another, its natural expression is one of sadness. You may think he has a smile of a deprecating nature which he is constantly using. It may be a question of nerves. This trial, after all, must be something of a strain, must it not? But do you suppose you can connect his sadness on that night inevitably with the murder of Miss Volacki? Members of the jury, that is stretching imagination into the realms of fantasy, is it not?

In terms of Mattan's movements, it is nine-tenths of a mile back from Volacki's shop to his lodgings and you may think that, whether he is childish or a semi-civilized savage or **whatever** he is, he is not quite such a fool that, after having committed a particularly bloody murder, he would travel on a bus where his condition would be noticed, because people have nothing to do except to look at each other in buses. He had, almost of a certainty, if he was there, to get back there wholly on his own feet, nine-tenths of a mile. If you accept the strange story of Mrs. Gray, that he called at Mrs. Gray's shop on the way back to his lodgings, he would have had to walk very nearly a mile and a half because the route from Volacki's shop back to Davis Street via 37 Bridge Street, where Mrs. Gray has her second-hand clothing shop, is about 2,100 or 2,200 yards.

Now, members of the jury, let us consider Mrs. Gray's evidence upon the background of those times. I do not know how it strikes **you**, members of the jury; do you think a **prudent** murderer goes out in a trilby hat and an umbrella, for instance? I do not know; it is perhaps just a background matter. But what do you think about those white trousers? **What do you think about those white trousers?** Is not that small item in itself enough to make the whole of the story look **ridiculous**.

Well, members of the jury, you may take your choice. Consider the way she gave her evidence. You may think that Mr. Edmund Davies was not perhaps raising his voice as loudly as I was, but nonetheless she heard him more clearly than she heard me. You may think her deafness **varied** according to the difficulty of the question she had to answer. It is a matter for you. A few things that you are quite certain of, members of the jury, because she told you so, is this, that she disliked Mattan because he was **cheeky**, and in order to account for the extraordinary clash between the timings of getting from Volacki's shop to her shop after the murder before nine o'clock, you may think that this business of Mattan being wholly out of breath was just a bit of embellishment which was added to the rest of her evidence.

Members of the jury, is she a **satisfactory** witness? Are you going to convict a **dog** upon her evidence, let alone a human being? You cannot, members of the jury. Was there anything which occurred between the 7th day of March when Mrs. Gray says she was suspicious of Mattan and the 13th day of March when she gave her statement to the police? Yes, one thing: the publication of an evening paper upon the 10th March with front-page news about a reward of £200 for information leading to a conviction.

Members of the jury, the Prosecution's case is one of suspicion and suspicion only; suspicion fostered because this **foolish** man has told lie after lie, **stupid lies**. Not once, members of the jury, have I relied, in presenting the Defence case to you, upon anything he has said. I have relied only upon the witnesses whom the Prosecution called to convict him, and they prove louder than any words of his could that he is innocent of this charge, members of the jury. You cannot be in two places at once. He could not have gone all that distance and done all those things and got rid of the money, the clothes and the weapon and travelled two miles or upwards all within thirty-five minutes.

Who, then, killed Miss Volacki? Members of the jury, there is one matter here which is still wholly unchallenged. A man came into Miss Volacki's shop, a man who is not the prisoner Mattan, a man who had a moustache, and no one saw him go out. Was he the murderer who Miss Volacki locked in that night, as a result of which she lost her life? There, members of the jury, is the murderer, not—there—(**indicating**). Acquit him.

The jury retired at 2:36 p.m. and returned into Court at 4:10 p.m.

Afar iyo toban

[Fourteen]

THE CLERK OF THE ASSIZE: Mr. Foreman of the jury, are you agreed upon your verdict?
THE FOREMAN OF THE JURY: We are.
THE CLERK: Look upon the face of the prisoner and say whether he is guilty or not guilty of murder.
THE FOREMAN: **(Turning to the prisoner)** Guilty.
THE CLERK: And that, sir, is the verdict of you all?
THE FOREMAN: Yes, sir.

THE CLERK: Mahmood Hussein Mattan, the jury have found you guilty of murder; have you anything to say why judgment of death should not be pronounced upon you in due form of law?

(The prisoner does not respond.)

THE JUDGE: **(Placing the black cap on his head)** Mahmood Hussein Mattan, the sentence of the Court upon you is that you be taken from this place to a lawful prison, and thence to a place of execution, and there suffer death from hanging, and that your body be interred within the precincts of the prison in which you were last confined before your execution. And may the Lord have mercy upon your soul.

THE CHAPLAIN: Amen.

Shan iyo toban

[Fifteen]

Mahmood had walked on his own two feet to the new cell, the condemned suite, as the warders called it. Through various locked doors, up stairs and down again, along clanking gangways and quiet corridors, the convoy, with him handcuffed and following behind the doctor, had finally reached the isolated place where Ajit Singh had last dwelled.

Following them dumbly, his mind is still inside the court, flashes of it returning: Laura sobbing from the gallery as he descended the steps from the dock, the total numbness he felt on hearing the sentence, the curious black rag on top of the judge's grey wig as he read it out, the pat on the shoulder from the prison officer putting the handcuffs back on his wrists. The long drive back from Swansea in the black van; the forest they passed through, dense enough to hide a runaway; old villages with their grey little churches and low-slung pubs, the red-cheeked children playing in the streets; the bright adverts for fairs and pleasure boat rides, pale skins sprawled out in Alexandra Gardens. He had watched it all impassively until they neared the docks, and he saw the metallic sea calling to him, and then they slipped straight through Bute Street, past the dead woman's empty shop, past the lodging house where he had lived, his Annexe, his barber's, his spice shop, his pawnshop, past a group, including Ismail, gambling on the corner of Angelina Street. Then his heart cracked.

Mahmood is still in the suit he had worn to court; a brown pinstripe that was the least creased from the pile retrieved from the pawnshop. A warder removes his handcuffs and answers questions from the governor and doctor, while Mahmood examines his new holding pen. It is larger than the previous cell and has a table and two chairs beneath the barred and meshed window, as well as a tall cabinet against the wall opposite the bed. He approaches the bed and is set on getting into it, burrowing into it, when a warder grabs his arm and says, "Hold on a second, you need to get changed into your uniform first."

Mahmood shakes away his grip and continues silently to the bed.

"Oh, here we go, he's at it again." The warder exhales.

"You must be firm, Collins, there cannot be chaos, especially in this part of the prison." The tall, white-haired governor turns back from the door to watch.

"Come on, Mattan, be a good lad and get these trousers and shirt on."

Mahmood holds the clothing in his hands for a moment before throwing them to the ground.

"I be a good lad and keep my suit on."

"Warders," the governor says firmly.

The first warder grabs Mahmood's jacket and pulls it off his shoulders. "Don't make me strip you, Mattan."

The doctor steps back to allow two more warders to join the fray and then Mahmood is brought to his knees, quietly struggling as six hands rip off his jacket and pull the buttons off his white shirt. When one of them begins tugging at his belt and trousers, he sees a leg in front of his face and bites. "YOU WOULD NOT HANG A DOG ON HER EVIDENCE." A dog should bite. A dog that you will hang has the right to bite. He remembers the doctor complimenting him on his marvellous teeth and now they are at work, going deeper and deeper into the navy wool and thick thigh.

The warder hits Mahmood on the temple with his truncheon and wrests his leg free. "He's bit me, sir." He runs his hand down the dark cloth, feeling for blood.

Mahmood laughs and pulls his torn shirt back over his chest. There are tears in his eyes.

The governor shakes his head and gestures for the warders to step back. "What do you say, Doctor? What shall be done?"

"My opinion is that he should be left in his own clothes for the moment. He is clearly emotionally imbalanced and there is little to be gained from pressing our authority at this stage. Collins, come with me and I'll examine your leg."

"So be it. Allcott and Wesley, take your places and keep me informed of his behaviour."

They cough. They rock. They talk. They smoke. They belch and fart. They do not leave. The electric light dims in the early evening but they remain. Mahmood refuses the rations they offer and remains in bed, facing the white bricks, while his stomach mewls and pleads. The door opens at around 10 p.m. but rather than clearing out, the warders are replaced by another pair. Mahmood glances over his shoulder as they swap greetings but turns away quickly, before any of them can make eye contact with him.

If they intended to torture him, this is the perfect way; better than any physical pain they could inflict, the loss of privacy makes Mahmood want to unpeel his skin and step out of it. He has an appointment with his bastard solicitor in the morning and he will put this at the top of the agenda. They treat him like this and there ain't nothing stopping him from taking his own fucking life.

He wants to kill them all: Laura's mother with her "that man," Doc Madison's "hypnosis" bull, that lying Jamaican carpenter, and that witch, May Gray, with her crooked, greedy lies. Worst of all, worst of all was that barrister. That red-faced, pot-bellied, pompous son of a bitch, going on about "savages" as if he was marching through a jungle film. "Childish liar," "foolish man," "child of nature," what make him pour all that outta his mouth? And then talk about sad eyes?

Where is God? Where is the God he wasted all those prayers and prostrations on? The most just, the most fair, the most merciful? Why is he so silent? What kind of test is this? Will he let him be put to death by these savages, these cannibals? Who are trying to fatten him up for slaughter. That black cap, that black gown with wing-like folds, sharp grey lips like an evil bird talking. Waaq, the forgotten crow-god of the Somalis, come to life to pluck out his heart, the prayers sent to Allah sticking like arrows in his bitter, proud flesh.

A lesson. His story will go straight to the ears of boys stepping off their first boat. Mahmood already in the past tense. A warning. Don't marry them. Don't live with outsiders. Don't steal from us. Remember what happened to him? The old-timers secretly happy they can now frighten those illiterate boys with his ghost.

"So, what's left?"

"We appeal, Mr. Mattan."

"To who?"

"To the Court of Criminal Appeal."

"And what they do?"

"They can request a retrial or even quash your conviction."

"Quash? What mean quash?"

The solicitor blinks rapidly and plays with the top of his black pen. "It means to overturn, reverse . . . take back. Do you understand?"

"Yes. Just speak plain English to me. I finish with this lawyer English. You know they keep two warder in my cell all day and night? The light burning all night?"

"I'm afraid that is the procedure with all condemned prisoners. It is not personal and it's not just Cardiff."

"But it drive me crazy! What do they want from me?"

"It's intended to be in your best interests, to keep you from harm."

"Harm? They want to kill me in three weeks, what harm they keep me from?" Mahmood slaps his hand on the table, not hard, but loud enough to make the solicitor jump in his seat.

"There is absolutely nothing that I can do about that, or that you can do, so it will be a more productive use of our time to plan the appeal and the limited options we have before us."

Mahmood shakes his head, smiles bitterly. "If they believe all those lies once, what stops them believing twice?"

"Your case will go before the three most experienced and senior judges in the country. They cannot be compared to a jury of Swansea housewives and shopkeepers."

"You think I got a chance?"

The solicitor pauses, looks down at his hands and then somewhere over Mahmood's shoulder. "I don't want to build up your hopes unnecessarily, the figure for successful appeals is not a great one, but it's my legal duty to try every possibility there is . . . to spare your life."

"I sick of saying this, but I'm innocent. I'm innocent."

The solicitor nods gravely. "It was a most unsatisfactory outcome, Mr. Mattan. The evidence against you took a serpentine path that we did not anticipate."

"That mean you did not expect so many liars?"

"The Prosecution is not obliged to share their evidence with us."

"Donkey court." Mahmood looks the solicitor in the eye.

"Well, it is far from that, Mr. Mattan," he sighs, "but justice is reliant on what is brought before the judge and jury, and the Prosecution built a strong case."

Mahmood scoffs. "A strong case? You call one person saying I was at home quarter to nine while the other says I be in her shop showing off money at same time a good case? That I turn up wearing clean white trousers after slitting a woman's throat four times a good case? That I keep the murder razor then hide it in someone's washing during poker game a good **case**? What is a bad case then, mister?"

"You seem to be forgetting your own role in this debacle, Mr. Mattan. I distinctly remember **you** answering numerous important questions with the phrases 'I cannot imagine' and 'it is not for me to say,' In hindsight it **might** have been useful for you to give clearer and more honest explanations of your movements that night," his eyes harden, "because frankly, it was your own performance in that dock that removed any doubt of your guilt from the jury. I can only speak of my own perceptions, of course, but you came across as belligerent and shifty, and you created a mess that I now have to try and rescue you from. I did not want to get involved in mutual recrimination but, Mr. Mattan, you certainly do know how to raise a man's hackles."

Mahmood just shakes his head again and again, looking away from the solicitor's flushed face. Why is it that words seem to create such violence around him? What happens between his mind and mouth that betrays him so deeply? He forces himself to say the word that he hates, that empty English shield-like word, "Sorry."

It works. The shoulders drop, fingers unclench, face lightens. "I'm sorry that you are in this position; it is an absolutely dreadful one. I understand that you have a wife and children that you desire to return to."

"Yes. It has been too long." This is how communication should be, thinks Mahmood, simple and human. He talks too much and forgets that people can't see the fears that he has been goading in the cage of his mind. Evil thoughts that jump from his mouth as snapping, snarling things.

"Your mother-in-law, Mrs. Williams, has agreed to be named as a witness in your appeal, arguing that she should have been called before the jury after Mrs. Gray gave her . . . story. She could have told the court of how Gray had offered to split the reward if they gave the same evidence."

"That is good . . ." Mahmood begins to say something but then thinks better of it.

"Yes, that and some technical points on the judge's summing up will be the basis of our appeal. If you could just sign the appeal document here . . ." He reaches into the yellow folder that contains this whole nightmare, and pulls out a black and white form.

Mahmood takes the solicitor's heavy, expensive pen and waits a moment to arrange his stiff fingers around the smooth metal. His heart begins to race as he forms the jagged peaks of the M, then the H of his signature, before falling into the rhythm of the M-a-t-t-a-n. That is it. He has either signed the last act of his life away, or pulled his fate back up from the depths.

The cell has got so dark that the creamy white walls seem to glow. Occasional murmurs have strengthened and gathered into bad-tempered claps of summer thunder, while brisk slashes of lightning cut across Mahmood's supine body.

"How about a cheese sarnie?" The warder leans over the bed and shakes Mahmood's shoulder. "You gotta have something, otherwise we'll have to get the doctor involved and that's a real palaver. Get up, son, and play cards or something."

Mahmood is turned away, inert, only his eyes move as he follows the cracks in the wall from one brick to another.

"How about a hot cuppa or bowl of soup? We don't have to stick to the timetable in here as such."

"It's no use, Perkins, leave him be," says the other warder from the table, as he counts out cards from a stack.

"We've got to at least try."

"Is it your first time doing this?"

The warder hesitates by Mahmood's side, looking down with concern as his prisoner closes his eyes.

"We should at least order a smaller uniform, he's swamped in the one he's got on."

"He's a difficult one, Perkins, sit down and stop fussing over him like a nanny."

Perkins takes the rumpled blanket from the bottom of the bed and folds it into a neat rectangle before placing it over Mahmood's feet. He sighs and takes his seat back at the table.

"As I was saying, this your first time doing this?"

"That's right, no call for it at Wormwood Scrubs."

"Down your way there's Pentonville, Wandsworth, Holloway . . ."

"Holloway? Never. Don't believe in capital for the ladies."

"You old romantic, if they gab on about equal rights then they can't complain if they're treated equally by the courts. It's the third time I've volunteered and I wouldn't hesitate if it was a bird, neither."

Perkins drops his voice. "Let's change the subject, Wilkinson, we shouldn't be talking about this."

"Alright. Get on and start, then. It's your turn."

"Mahmood-o! Mahmood-o!"

"**Hee hooyo!**" Mahmood is startled by his mother's voice calling him. He jumps from a light sleep and cannot fix where he is or the hour of the day.

"Mahmood-o!" He hears it again, this time quieter, but with the exact tone she had used to call him when he was little, when he would scramble to his feet and thread a needle for her or run to the shop to replenish the tea or sugar tins. "Mahmood-o! Mahmood-o!" Her voice penetrates him.

She will write soon, that's what the voice is telling him, a blue-rimmed envelope with her fingerprints and musk on it, arriving at the bottom of a Somali seaman's trunk. He doubts he will ever hear her words again.

He is half fasting, half punishing himself, it's been two days without food or water and he is so weak he barely tries to move his limbs. He doubts his fast will count if he doesn't eat at sunset, and doesn't even know if Ramadan has already ended, but still he persists.

Trying to carve out his solitude in that crowded room, he won't turn in the bed unless he is hidden under the blanket; he never looks at the warders or talks to them, it's bad enough that he has to overhear their dumb chatter. English is like barbed wire to him now, a lethal language that he needs to keep outta his mouth.

The trial is still ongoing in his dreams and waking thoughts. He plays judge, prosecution, defence all at once, ripping himself to shreds then calling order before arguing his innocence again and again and again. In court he had been copying the barristers' words—their "it may be," "I know not" and "it is not for me to explain"—when he had kept saying "I am not going to imagine" the truth of the statements against him, but from his own mouth it had sounded so different. He should have wept, cried, pleaded, shredded his clothes, told them he was only a savage who had been outwitted by clever Welsh policemen. A sad savage with smiling eyes. A smiling savage with sad eyes.

"You have a visitor, Mattan."

Mahmood opens his eyes, squints at the warder's face . . . yet another new one.

"You should take a look in the mirror and sort yourself out," the man says, pushing the blanket away.

Mahmood unfurls his legs and places his feet on the cold floor. He tries to stand but feels woozy and drops heavily back on to the bed.

"Watch yourself there," the warder says in an accent that sounds almost foreign to Mahmood.

"Where you from?"

"Newcastle."

"Oh, hallelujah! He speaks," exclaims a Welsh warder standing by the door, and that is enough to shut Mahmood's mouth again.

They walk him to an adjacent bathroom with a bathtub, sink and toilet. Mahmood looks at himself in the small mirror above the sink and runs his hands through his linty hair. "**Dibjir**. Homeless man," he says to his unrecognizable reflection, the Newcastle warder visible over his shoulder.

. . .

Shuffling along, his grey uniform trousers billowing around his legs, his hair flattened down with cold water, his regulation shoes held together with a tiny suicide-proof length of shoelace, Mahmood follows the whistling warder into the visiting room. He prays it's not Laura; he's not ready to face her yet.

Berlin stands there. Tall, beautiful, leaning on a black umbrella as if about to break into a song-and-dance number. His pale eyes widen on seeing Mahmood enter the room and he straightens up.

Mahmood takes a long look at Berlin before sitting down: at his gleaming black lace-ups, his grey tweed suit, the fat silver tie, at the jacquard pocket square, at the medals crowding his lapel.

A glass panel separates them. "Eid greetings, old friend," Berlin says, smiling. His face is clean-shaven and glossy, his dark oily skin contrasting with the white hairs running through his black sideburns.

"Eid?"

"Yes, they called it in Cairo two nights ago."

"You had a party at the milk bar?"

"Nothing I would call a party, more a way of passing the time, just Ismail and a few of the other old fellas."

"Big parade to the mosque?"

"Of course, and the sheikh called the mayor and mayoress to eat with him at the **zawiya**, he's big pals with them now. Playing the Welshman."

"That's why they don't give a damn about me. You should start up a Somali mosque, what do you get from them but fighting and politics?"

Berlin looks over his shoulder and eyes the guard, before switching to Somali. The language sounds conspiratorial and intimate to Mahmood's unaccustomed ears.

"We'll get one, **inshallah**. Now, Mahmood . . ." he hesitates, searches for the right words, exhales, "this . . . has gone too far."

Mahmood shrugs despondently.

"We will see you through it, you know that, the money we raised has gone already, we didn't think ahead to appeals or anything like that, but we talked to the Somalis in Newport, South Shields, Hull, Sheffield and East London, and they all say they will contribute. What? Two, three pounds a man? It's nothing. They don't have to reach too far into their pockets."

"I appreciate it, man, I really do. I never had to ask **these** people for their charity and that is **one** good thing."

"I saw it all. I was there at the trial."

"You went to Swansea? I thought you hate to leave the Bay."

"I do, but I got on that damn, stinking train. Thought we needed a man there, an observer."

"And what did you think? Better than the pictures, huh?"

"**Wahollah!** It was a circus, it just needed acrobats and fire-breathers."

Mahmood lets his tense shoulders drop and laughs a loud bark.

"And the lions and women who contort their bodies instead of the truth."

"But she **was** the lion, wasn't she? Didn't you see the grey mane and sharp claws? She did **not** like you. What did you do to wrong her, take her handbag?"

Mahmood puts his hand over his heart, smiling in a slightly manic way. "**Wallahi billahi tillahi**, I wish I knew. She told Laura's mother, to her face, that I stole from her but I was living in Hull at that time. She's that hateful type who just hates a dark face. Now, the Nigerian, the watchmaker, I did wrong him and I can admit that. I took a watch from him, but does that mean I should hang?"

"Of course not, I pray that won't happen." Berlin leans back in his chair, looks around the windowless visiting room. "These people are crazy. It's got even worse in town now, they slam all sorts of doors in a coloured's face. Never mind the usual public houses, poor Lou was even told to get out by the dentist. The papers have riled them up over your case and now they think we're all carrying a switchblade ready for a shopkeeper's neck. How you cope in this place? I swear my blood turns to ice the minute I step through the gate."

Mahmood lifts his palms. "I just live, I wake up each morning and can't believe this is my story, I don't know how it could come to this. Berlin, let me ask you now . . . if they do this . . . you know . . . finish me, I want you to write to my mother and tell her I died at sea, that I went back to the navy and my ship went down somewhere far away. That's all. Don't tell her **nothing** about all of this."

Berlin nods. "Painful either way but I understand you." He nudges his head towards the warder, "They treat you alright?"

"They follow me to the bath, to the toilet, and stand watching the whole time in case I find a way to kill myself. I don't even think about them any more. I can see through them like they're not there, had to learn fast before I go completely crazy. I sit here, thinking about what's happening outside the prison walls. What my boys are doing each day, what Laura is dealing with, what fun you men are having."

"The men are doing what they have always

done: bickering, fighting over money, going to sea. One fella, Awaleh, was sent back as a distressed seaman from Brazil. He's a strange one."

"The same one who was taken sick in Japan? He's just got bad luck like me."

"That sailor gives me a bad feeling."

"Why?"

"I don't want to put thoughts in your head, but you know when you hear whispers and the end of sentences and it leaves you feeling . . . in the dark."

"Yes . . ."

"Well, people . . ."

"People?"

"Ismail. Ismail says the only man who fits the description of the six-foot Somali the police were talking about is Awaleh, the only one in the Bay that night, anyway."

"You believe the police?" Mahmood snorts. "You think they would say it's a six-foot Welshman when they could pin it on a man with black skin?"

Berlin tips his head in agreement. "But, but that's all I can say, something doesn't feel right. I know these Somalis, have lived too long with them, and there is something they are keeping quiet. I've never felt it so strongly before."

"Why? Why would they do that?" Mahmood puts his face closer to the glass, his eyes watching Berlin closely.

"I don't know, man, that's why I can't say anything concrete. If I had real evidence I would take it to your damned overpriced lawyer. Awaleh was definitely here the night of the murder, I saw him in the milk bar that afternoon, but the next day I heard he had gone to Manchester."

Mahmood sinks back into his chair. "So, why didn't someone say something **before**?"

"Because who wants to be an informer? The Somalis didn't say anything about you, and I guess they chose not to say anything about him neither."

They have let Mahmood out into a private yard for his daily exercise hour and he feels brought back to life. The day is warm, almost hot for the first time in a long while, but with the fresh green scent of drying rain still in the air. The light is harsh and washes over the damp brick walls and ironmongery of the prison like varnish. Everything feels new and clean; even the barbed wire above his head glitters with raindrops hanging from the twisted points. Mahmood closes his eyes and lets the sunshine pour over his face like holy oil.

A guard watches him idly from the entrance but Mahmood has space all around him; space to think, to feel, to remember who he really is beyond his prison number. The walls reach just over his head and if he had the courage he would lift himself over and run through the many quadrants, green spaces and gates of the jail and the short distance to Laura and the children. He hasn't seen her for more than a week but knows that she'll be in a worse state than him, full of guilt and fear. On paper he has two more weeks to live but in his gut he doesn't believe it, he feels in his veins and sinews that they have more time, that Laura has time to settle her nerves before facing him. He doesn't grasp where this confidence comes from but it is there, solid and elemental.

It's not that Mahmood believes himself important, the past few months have torn away that illusion, but he is extraordinary, his life **has** been extraordinary. The things he has got away with, the things he has been punished for, the things he has seen, the way that it had once seemed possible for him to bend, with great force, everything to his will. His life was, is, one long film with mobs of extras and exotic, expensive sets. Long reams of film and miles of dialogue extending back as he struts from one scene to another. He can imagine how his movie looks even now: the camera zooming in from above on to the cobblestone prison yard and then merging into a close-up of his thoughtful, upturned face, smoke billowing out from the corner of his dark lips. A colour film, it must be that. It has everything: comedy, music, dance, travel, murder, the wrong man caught, a crooked trial, a race against time and then the happy ending, the wife swept up in the hero's arms as he walks out, one sun-filled day, to freedom. The image stretches Mahmood's mouth into a smile.

Up above, a seagull careens through the midday sky, and from somewhere unseen a crow repeatedly caw-caws, seeming to enjoy the vibration in its throat. Life. Life. It is so simple and beautiful. The waxy leaves of an ivy vine snaking up from the sterile ground, a spider twitching on its bejewelled web, the flow of air in Mahmood's lungs and the rush of blood through his heart—all of it beyond his control, all of it somehow both fleeting and eternal. He, himself, could disappear from the world just as easily as the seagull winding an aimless path in the air, its bones falling apart one day somewhere hidden and mysterious, no one thinking to ask after it. He is a man, and there are other men, just as there are other seagulls, but what he can't shake is the idea that the world will end in a tiny way without him. Everything will appear exactly the same but with a permanent shade where he should be. Laura, alive but widowed, his sons, alive but fatherless, his mother, alive but grieving a child, his technicolour talkie snapping back to be replaced by a black and white, silent film. "We close our eyes and ears to death," the

macalim used to say, "but it is all around us, it is in the air we breathe." While he stands there smoking, a few yards away in one of the streets nearby someone will be drawing their last breath, from disease or a petty little accident. Their possessions piled up around them like wreckage. Like the murdered woman, Violet, and her shop that looked like it held all the world's shoes and dresses and wool blankets.

If, and it's an "if" that he chooses to reject, they go through with the execution, he has so little to pass on to his children. There is his toothbrush, his Qur'an, a few photos at Laura's place, but the rest is with the police, tagged and contaminated by their injustice to him. They will not even have his body, which the courts want to keep here, as some kind of punishment or prize. The only substantial inheritance they will have are his stories, parcelled out by Laura or Berlin and covered in their own fingerprints. They will hear that he was a nomad, a chancer, a fighter, a rebel, but not from him, and therefore they will know the price of being all that, the potion and the poison taken together.

Back in the cell, he agrees to sit with the warder from London, Perkins, and the other from

Newcastle, Wilkinson. The time in the yard has made him realize that for the survival of his soul he must sit up, eat, occupy his time and talk to human beings, whoever they may be. Otherwise, he is only cheating himself of the seconds, minutes and hours that are leased, not given, to any living thing. By nature, he is not a melancholy man, he is someone who has always woken up with a desire to extract as much pleasure from the day as possible, and he can't let the prison change that.

Mahmood sits between them, with the draughts board directly in front of him. Perkins will play against him first and then Wilkinson. He feels like a child between these two large, grey-whiskered men.

"What's your occupation?" Perkins asks, pouring sugar from his spoon into a muddy prison tea.

"In my real life I was a sailor."

"When I was a little boy I wanted nothing more than to sail the seven seas."

"I did that, I sail all seven," he counts them off on his fingers, "Indian, Atlantic, what you call it . . . Pacifical?"

"Pacific, that's right. Artic? Antarctic?"

"Both of them."

"You're a bona fide Phileas Fogg!" Wilkinson says.

Mahmood doesn't know the reference and looks at Wilkinson to explain.

Perkins jumps in. "He's a character from a novel, **Around the World in Eighty Days**, it's by a French writer, Jules Verne. He travels all over the world in eighty days to win a wager."

Mahmood smiles. "I like that idea, you put the bet down, and I would do something like that."

"A betting man? OK, let's play for cigarettes, then."

"These cigarettes hurt my throat."

"Matches, then. Five a game?"

"Deal." Mahmood collects twelve white counters in his hand. "I play with these, the colour black seem to bring too much bad luck."

Perkins gives a false little laugh.

They begin the game in silence, just the clack and slide of counters marching from one side of the board to the other. Mahmood rests his chin in his palm, more invested in the game than he had expected to be. Their skill is evenly matched, unless Perkins is being soft on him. It suddenly feels deeply important to beat this white prison warder at this simple game.

Isn't this what the world is like? Mahmood thinks. With countries and seas instead of black and white squares, the white man spread all over, the black man picked off wherever he might be and left to eke out a life on the fringes of the board, in ghettoes and shantytowns. Not this time, he resolves, jumping over and then slamming one after another of Perkins' counters on to the table. He remembers with fondness the Imam from his childhood and his scheming, winking face; a man devoted to nothing but making life difficult for the British.

Mahmood has breached the last row on Perkins' side. His humble counter now a king, able to move across the board with absolute freedom. He had seen himself that way once, a very long time ago. He was a self-anointed king, far beyond being just a Reer Gedid youth, a Sacad Musa clansman, a Somali, a Muslim, a Black. Those labels so hollow they echoed around him, not stirring any part of his mind or heart. He was cast from a single mould, he had told himself, which is why he struggled to live by the rules other people scrabbled along to. Don't argue, don't fight, don't ask for more than you're given, don't go places where you don't belong. But now those labels are pinned into his flesh: his clan matters because they are few in Cardiff; his Somalihood matters to the West Africans and West Indians who take him for an Arab rather than one of them; his faith matters to the sheikh and the others at Noor ul-Islam who think he turned **kuffar** long ago. And his blackness? Forget it. That was the one he was mad to think he could ever outrun.

Perkins' last counter is hemmed in on all sides by Mahmood's, unable to escape. Game over.

"What I tell you? I play white and my luck change."

Perkins leans back as if he has exerted himself and takes a long slug of his tea. He wipes his upper lip with his sleeve, burps softly and then counts out five matches. "Guess you were right."

Mahmood arranges the counters back in their orderly starting position to take on Wilkinson. He sticks to the winning counters, superstitious as ever.

A question enters his mind but he is unsure whether to even bring it up, whether it will just disturb the little mental peace he has cultivated. He drums his nails on the table and then decides to just ask, fuck it.

"In court, when they ask that man, Powell, questions, my lawyer ask him about a warder who called him to the prison to talk about a man he see, who look like me, standing outside. You know which warder it be?"

Perkins and Wilkinson knot their eyebrows in doubt.

"Not a big thing, I'm just curious, that's all," Mahmood says quickly.

"I'm sure I could ask around . . . being from out of town, I can't say I know that off the top of my head." Perkins looks to Wilkinson.

"Wouldn't be hard to find out. Have to run it by the governor, though. Find out if the solicitor would need to—"

Mahmood cuts him off. "No, I don't want to involve the solicitor, just wanted to say . . . you know . . . that I thank him . . . for trying to help me, for telling the truth."

Perkins pats him on the arm. "Easily done, leave it with us."

Mahmood nods, his mind drifting away to whom the warder might have noticed standing outside the prison gate: an innocent double of his? The real killer come to gloat? Or maybe even Mahmood's soul gone wandering.

"Is it quick?" Mahmood is back in bed, facing the brick wall, taken over by a bone-deep tiredness.

"What's that?" Perkins replies, cracking his stiff spine.

"The hanging."

Silence.

"Yes," Wilkinson says finally.

"How long it take to die?"

"You are out immediately."

"You sure?"

"Absolutely."

"Good," Mahmood says, closing his eyes.

Mahmood hears her deep, musical voice before he sees her. Laura.

Perkins had gone to help her up the steps with the children and he now returns to the corridor carrying the large-wheeled, old-fashioned pram in his arms. Mahmood enters the visiting room and David is standing alone behind the glass and looking nervously at his father, his tongue swiping back and forth across his chin.

"**Aabbo**," exclaims Mahmood, holding his palm flat against the glass, "**ii kaalay**."

David doesn't move.

Mahmood switches to English. "Come to me."

David runs back through the open door and only returns when Laura is beside him, with Mervyn on her hip and Omar clutching the other side of her skirt.

"Beauty," smiles Mahmood, as the sight of them fills up his eyes.

Laura's face collapses from blank repose to slack, sobbing pain.

"Sit. Sit. Sit!" he orders, shaking his head. "None of that."

Mervyn looks at his mother's reddening face

and then, squeezing his eyes shut, begins to wail too, starting a chain that doesn't end until they are all wet-eyed, Mahmood included.

They have clustered close together, steaming up the partition and smearing prints across the clean glass. Small, fat fingers and long, thin ones pressing down, mingling like leaves on a tree.

"**Boqoradey**, my queen," Mahmood says softly, rubbing his nose roughly on the back of his hand.

Laura's chin rests on her chest. Her tears well every time she looks at him.

"It's not over yet, Laura."

Perkins enters her side of the room and places a small white plate of golden digestive biscuits in front of the children. David dabs his hand on them, as if not trusting anything in these strange surroundings, but then passes two to his brothers and puts one to his lips, nibbling at it to savour the taste.

Mahmood watches Perkins as he stands back against the wall and although he is thankful for his kindness, it humiliates him to not be able to give the boys anything, not even a biscuit, to comfort them.

"Laura, listen to me, listen to me." He holds his hand up to the glass as if it will transmit his words more clearly. "I got the appeal yet, they can't do nothing until we hear back from London, from the real judges there."

"I went to see someone . . ."

"What you say?"

"I went to see a lady, that my friend said would be able to see . . . ahead."

"What you mean, love?"

Laura's eyes are on the floral handkerchief that she's twisted between her fingers. "She can read the future, she lives down on the Docks, a Maltese woman."

Mahmood is caught between frustration and fear. "And she say something to upset you?"

Laura wipes her eyes and nods. "I never took that kind of thing serious, you know? But Flo told me of all the things she had predicted that had come true, like the little boys who drowned in the canal and that Flo would marry a Yemeni."

"Everyone say Flo marry a Yemeni, all her boyfriends come from Aden. The Maltese bint just take your money and give herself even odds for getting the answer right."

"No, Moody, she didn't take any money from me. She asked to see me because she kept dreaming of you."

Mahmood tries to smile and lighten her spirit. "She just a dirty old woman, keeping herself warm at night thinking of young men she see in the paper, take no notice of her blabber."

"You told me your mam could read the future in coffee beans."

"She say so . . . but what do I know of it?"

"The Maltese woman was crying, she was really crying, and she just kept saying 'your poor babies, they lose their papa.' "

"Evil woman," Mahmood pulls his hand back from the glass, "who she to call the end of my life? God curse her and the devils she listens to at night."

"I don't mean to upset you, Moody, I just can't shake her words. She looked like someone who would know things. I don't know if it was her eyes or her gloomy, cobwebby home or what, she just did somehow, I can't explain it, but I went from having hope to just feeling like I have a big hole inside of me."

"I am here, Laura, I am still living and breathing and fighting for my life. You have to keep beside me and not fall back. Even your mother is helping with the appeal, after she call me 'that man' in court."

Laura's eyes flash. "My mother, my mother . . ."

David taps on the glass. "Daddy, it's been ages, why won't you just come home? Stop being silly."

"I'm coming home, son, I have to finish my work here, then I come home and sleep beside you. Right, Laura?"

Laura's eyes well again and she looks away from him, stroking Mervyn's cheek. She leaves the question hanging in the air between them.

. . .

"I'm afraid I come back with disheartening news, Mr. Mattan."

Mahmood clutches the thin sides of the table, pushing his flesh into its sharp edges. "They refuse me?"

"Yes, they have." The solicitor watches Mahmood's face closely, studying his reaction.

Mahmood feels a contraction of anger so pure that he has to wince at its intensity, heat spreading like acid along his skin and his stomach turning. He can't deal with what he is hearing. "But you say they are serious judges? The best in the country."

"They have their reasons for coming to their decision but . . ."

"Reasons? I come to a country full of evil people, stupid people, hateful people, that reason enough, I understand."

"It's no easy thing for the Court of Criminal Appeal to overturn the decisions of the lower courts, there must be overwhelming evidence, and in your case . . . they didn't find cause."

Should I just throw this table at him? Mahmood thinks. Should I finish him and then give them real cause to take my life? But then he releases his hold on the table in fright, realizing how easy it would be to do that, how his muscles and sinews are primed like a bundle of dynamite sticks. He struggles to contain his breathing, to slow the ragged pants that come too fast.

"We have one last legal avenue and that is to write to the Home Secretary and ask for a royal pardon."

Mahmood closes his eyes, he doesn't care how strange it looks; he just needs blankness, blackness to envelop him.

"Mr. Mattan, are you listening?"

"How long? How long have I got?" His eyes are still shut.

The solicitor sighs, a long tired sigh. "They have rescheduled the execution for the third of September."

Why does that date sound important? Mahmood wonders, rubbing the heels of his palms into his eye sockets, but he can't remember the answer.

"I will write to the Home Secretary immediately."

"You said royal, is it royal or government?"

"In this matter it's a royal prerogative, or right, exercised by the Home Secretary."

"Just call her, your Queen, and tell her to look at me, look at my wife," spittle flies from his lips as he speaks, "look at my sons, look at the evidence and ask her if I'm fit for hanging? I give up with your judges and politicians, there is no human heart between them." Mahmood meets the solicitor's gaze, his anger dissipating to leave just a dark chasm behind his eyes.

The solicitor looks defeated, as if he is playing to the end of a cricket game that he knows he has no chance of winning, with the rain starting to pour and too few spectators to encourage him on. "There are sometimes petitions . . ." he begins, but looks at Mahmood with his wild hair and sullen, persecuted face and realizes that he is not the type that petitions are established for. "I bid you goodbye, Mr. Mattan, we can only hope that the Home Secretary exercises mercy."

"Goodbye, solicitor, if you try your best, God praise you for it," Mahmood says, putting his hand out.

The solicitor stands frozen.

"Just take it, it might be the last time I see you and I need to start acting right."

Mahmood squeezes the solicitor's colourless, lotioned hand hard. "If you try your best, may God bless you," he repeats, trying not to emphasize the "if."

"The very best of luck, Mr. Mattan." He nods.

"Everything always come back to luck," Mahmood says, standing, preparing to return to the claustrophobia of the cell.

It comes to him later in the afternoon, when he is sitting on his bed, a child's jigsaw splayed over the sheet. The third of September. Mahmood begins to laugh, a bitter, unbelieving laugh blooming from deep within his chest.

Perkins and Wilkinson look to each other in amusement.

"What you cackling over?" Wilkinson asks, his lips twitching.

Mahmood can't answer, he leans back, holding his chest, laughing and laughing.

"Don't do that, you'll get me started too," Wilkinson chuckles.

"Don't keep a joke that good to yourself," Perkins teases.

Mahmood slaps his thigh. "You never believe!"

Perkins and Wilkinson laugh along as Mahmood wipes his eyes.

"You never believe!"

"What?" cries Wilkinson.

"They want to . . . to hang me . . . on my eldest boy's birthday."

Mahmood paces the room, it's making the new pair of guards tense, but they don't try to stop him. He glances up at them; a man with a scorched pink face that seems to glow in the fading light and a muscled, handsome fella with a Scottish accent.

"Take a seat beside them, Queen," he mutters in Somali. "You ever been inside one of your cells? Oh, they love to keep saying Your Majesty's Prison, like it all belongs to you. Like you bought these sheets and those chairs and handpicked all of us that are kept here at your pleasure. What kind of woman gets pleasure from keeping her men cooped up like chickens or goats? The Queen of the English, **malikat al'iinjilizia** to the Arabs, **angrejee kee raanee** to Indians. The little woman in black in the newspapers. I see you now. I see your power, you satisfied? Araweelo the castrator, the indomitable. Somalis were right to overthrow our own evil queen. You have me at your knees. You see that?" He nods to the small barred window. "I could get up on that table and jump and punch my fist through the grille and tear my veins on that glass, I could do that so quickly your guards couldn't do anything to stop me. I still have some power, you understand? I know you but you don't know me. I see you in the papers, in the newsreels, I can recognize your voice on the wireless but you don't know nothing 'bout me. You drink your tea and mourn your father with no knowledge of Mahmood Hussein Mattan, the Reer Gedid man of the Sacad Musa clan of British Somaliland, your Somaliland. You count your ancestors for how many generations? I count mine for sixteen, that good enough for you? I am a descendant of the Prophet Muhammed through Sheikh Isaaq, that good enough? You mourn long enough for your father but you will never mourn for me, I know that. You live your life and I live mine, there is nothing to bring us together. You rich, I'm poor, you white, I'm black, you Christian, I'm Muslim, you English, I'm Somali, you're loved, I'm despised. Fate is wrong to tie us up together when we have no more in common than a . . . than a . . ."

"Why don't you sit down now and rest your legs and our eyes, you've nearly worn a hole in that floor," asks the Scottish warder, keeping his tone jovial.

Mahmood looks straight through him and continues pacing.

After standing out in the yard for his allotted time, hands in pockets, half-smoked cigarette behind his ear, Mahmood turns to see the doctor waiting for him by the door.

"Take your time," the doctor says cheerily, as if Mahmood looks busy.

"How long have I got left of my yard time?"

He checks his watch. "About five minutes, I'd say. Is it spitting rain again?"

Mahmood holds his palm out. "Nothing serious."

"Our notorious Welsh summers, I'm afraid, more benefit to gardeners than anyone else."

The clouds above are dark and marbled, each one self-contained with flashes of blue sky between. It's the kind of weather people in Hargeisa sit out in, when the rain flattens the dust and cools the air.

"I like it," he replies, not closing the twenty-foot gap between them. He fiddles with the end of the cigarette, imagining what his mother might be doing right now: three hours ahead there, the **'asr** call to prayer will be bounding from the mosques to the east and west of their sun-bathed bungalow, his mother not getting up from her kitchen stool to pray but just whispering long prayers under her breath as she washes her home-grown tomatoes or grinds spices from Harar between her wooden pestle and mortar. **Hooyo macaan**, sweet mother, if only you knew the peril I'm in, you would put down your bowls and knives and reach for the prayer mat.

The breeze picks up and splatters his forehead with rain; at home his mother would do that too, sprinkle him with water that she had blessed when he had a fever, using her full voice to scare away any malign spirits. Home. For the first time he hankers deeply for home, the embrace and complicated scent of his mother and the feel of her firm fingers as she grips his head tight to place her dry, feathery kisses on his cheeks. It's been so long, he can't even count the years since he last saw home—ten years, certainly.

"You should come out of that rain now, Mr. Mattan."

Mahmood plucks the now soggy cigarette from his ear and twists it into the ground with his shoe.

The clinic is bright and empty, the large windows bouncing light off the white tiled floor. Mahmood stands on a rubber-clad weighing scale, and pulls his spine straight so that his height can be taken at the same time.

"Curious. You appear to have lost weight but there is a drop of just a couple of pounds. A hundred and twenty-three against a hundred and twenty-five, last month."

"I was fasting during Ramadan."

"I see, and eating at night?"

"A little."

"You have solid muscle mass so you must have lost a little fat."

"And my height?"

He draws the marker down to Mahmood's hair. "Five foot seven and a quarter of an inch."

"Doctor," Mahmood steps down from the scale, "I want you to write my wife a letter."

"Your warders are able to help with that."

"No, I would like you to do it, so I can keep my business private from them."

He puts his hands in his pockets, looks ready to say no, but after stepping about a little, he nods agreement. "What do you want me to say to her?" He pulls his notepad and pen from his coat pocket.

"Just that I say hello, that the Court of Appeal reject my case and that I now have to wait on a pardon from the government. That she should come and see me as soon as she can, but not to panic, there ain't no cause for her to panic, tell her that."

He scribbles with the paper close to his face.

"Tell her that I send my love to her and the children, damn it, send my love to her mother and father too, everyone at Davis Street."

"That all?"

"End with cheerio."

"Not yours lovingly or something of that order?"

"No, cheerio, she like that word."

"As you wish." He puts the pen and notepad back in his pocket and begins to walk Mahmood to the door.

"Doctor, why they care so much about my weight?"

"It's part of my duties," he says, striding ahead.

"It got something to do with the hanging?"

"We have to keep you in good health while in custody."

"But I hear when it was Ajit Singh's time they decide how much rope to give him by his weight." Mahmood is almost chasing after him.

"You shouldn't listen to prison rumours." The doctor holds the door open, his face hard. "I'll send the letter to your wife with tomorrow's post. Good afternoon."

Mahmood hates this time of day, when the sun sets so slowly that blackness creeps ominously up his legs, like a plague with no cure. He sits in a chair, a half-eaten dish of mackerel and cold mashed potato in front of him. A knife and fork lie untouched on either side of the plate, he had used just the spoon and his fingers to eat, with the warders watching him in wonder. One of the reasons he gives up on his meals so quickly is the discomfort he feels eating in front of them, the forced intimacy of it and the shame of being a human animal with base needs and a wet, loud mouth. He had never really learnt how to use a knife and fork and has given up the pretence now, shovelling the tasteless fuel into his mouth the way he had thrown coal into a furnace. They watch him, blushing at his bad table manners, his fingers coated in fish oil and globules of powdered potato. He wipes his hands on his trousers and looks back at them. They had earlier refused him more regular baths. In his own life, with this heat and sticky humidity, he would bathe once in the morning and again in the evening. Just a basin of water would be enough to wash his face and under his arms but "against regulations" they said. He don't give a shit, then, if they think he eats like a savage.

Mahmood swills water around his mouth, swallows and then rises. He paces slowly up and down, stretching his long legs, as the tiny window above their heads begins to glow orange with the final rays of the sun. "I'm a man who can walk non-stop," he announces to no one in particular.

The Scottish warder, Macintosh, replies, "Is that so?"

"Yeah, it is so, if you ask me to walk to Australia I could do it."

"Take you a few years, I'd guess." He laughs.

"No, I could do it in six months."

"Six months! That's optimistic. You know how far away it is? It takes a week by plane."

"I know it. I've been there, more than one time."

"I'll be a Ten Pound Pom in a few years, if everything goes right. Me and the wife are planning on it," replies the other warder, Robinson, as if his already sandblasted skin could stand Australian heat.

"It's a nice country, looks like my homeland."

"British Somaliland? You got those red deserts? Aye, I was in Egypt during the war and they've got those great big yellow dunes, stacked up like castles in a child's sand box."

"Oh, yes, I know Australia. White Australia," Mahmood says, tuning out their voices. The memories come as if on a track, tied together but full of variety.

1947. The broken derrick at Darling Harbour that had delayed departure and felt, even then, a bad omen. The mouth-burning taste of Szechuan chicken from a Chinatown stall that seemed to cook with paraffin rather than oil. The smell of the freshly painted quarters he had shared with seven other Somali firemen. The black sheen of cockroaches scampering over his bunk and tired body at night, the darkness coming alive and swarming around him.

Their vessel, the SS **Glenlyon**, had completely broken down a week into their journey, in the dead heart of the Indian Ocean, far from Australia, Africa or India. He hadn't been in the engine room at the time **alhamdulillah**, but the explosion could be heard throughout the ship. They had passed hard through a long tropical storm, with rain and waves lashing down on to the deck, the passageways beginning to flood and the boilers going billy-o as they tried to power through it. It was only when the storm had begun to lift that the engineers went down to examine a fault the stokers had reported earlier, in furnace three. The engineers had played with it for less than an hour before a loud boom went up the funnel. The ship retreated from a galloping pace to a limp, then the propellers ceased to turn at all, far away from any assistance. You could hear the captain shouting "Christ!," "Fuck!" and "What the hell have you done?" at the poor engineers for hours, but it was no good. There was nothing they could do without a replacement turbine. They could conjure up no temporary fix to take them to a port, only wait for the turbine to arrive on a sister ship. The captain, in a rage, set everyone, high and low, to menial tasks—sweeping, polishing, clearing out, repairing, chipping the inside of the cold boilers—but the ship had come out of dry dock and was in old but tidy shape. Their four-hours-on, eight-hours-off shifts of alternating work and rest came and went with little to do.

The sea had softened but seemed to mock them, tossing the ship lightly about and tugging at their anchor. Time stopped, and at night with no lights alive on the ship and few passing vessels, a strange vertigo set in with sky and sea indistinguishable. He could have been anyone, in any time or place, even at the beginning of history. The breadth of space and depth of ocean reminding him of his own insignificance, as well as that of all mankind. Meteor showers came nearly every night, some of the falling stars so low he could hear them fizzing through the atmosphere, his neck arched back to watch them dance. The First Mate firing flares into the constellations to warn passing ships of their otherwise invisible presence.

The sunbaked deck of the **Glenlyon** became like a city park, with bare-chested men reading, playing cricket and posing for Kodaks. Distinction between ranks faded, chiefs sat down to play against the best domino or card sharks, whether they were galley boys or firemen. It was the first time he had felt any kind of equality on-board a ship, and not just restricted to his bunk or the engine rooms. One night, a message was whispered around the ship that King Neptune would visit the next day, to initiate the Pollywogs who had crossed the Tropic of Capricorn for the first time. Mahmood realized he was a Pollywog too, a novice in contrast to the Shellbacks who had crossed the Equator, Date Line, Meridian and Tropics of Cancer and Capricorn already. The **Glenlyon** was sitting on the Line, drifting on it.

It was unlike anything he had seen before. He

had crossed the Equator many times without incident but now the ship appeared like a madhouse afloat. After breakfast, King Neptune appeared, winched up from a porthole below and robed in a long toga of blue netting. He had a tin-foil crown, trident and a long beard of cotton wool. Whoever it was under the get-up was unrecognizable, and the Captain saluted and transferred command of the ship to him. Buruleh, the bony, fifty-something Somali stoker, arrived after King Neptune, carried on the shoulders of a burly Latvian able seaman. Buruleh was the oldest man on-board and had been given the role of Davy Jones; he wore two steel forks as horns, his shirt stuffed with fabric to create a hunchback, his trousers decorated with fish heads and seaweed, his face powdered and his lips blackened. The third member of the strange troupe was the rotund Chief Steward, wearing a gown of tea towels pinned together and a mop head as a wig, his lips were the thin red of food dye but he had at least shaved his beard. While a sailor played an accordion, King Neptune called forth the dozen Pollywogs and then Davy Jones, to set them the tasks they would need to complete to be initiated into the fraternity.

Buruleh had an evil imagination. He made Mahmood and the others give one hundred press-ups, then made them search through troughs filled with porridge, soggy bread, half-chewed sausage and God-knows-what-else for the pennies he had hidden inside. Their shirts already wet and grimy, the novices then had to drink a brown concoction that tasted how the shower stalls smelled, and then they were dunked into barrels of seawater dyed green. Mahmood was the last to complete, as he had baulked at drinking the concoction, but Buruleh had tripped him up as he ran to the barrels, and poured a glass of it down his throat. Mahmood wrestled with him on the slippery deck, laughing and cursing in Somali, but Buruleh had been fortified by his new role and only released him when the liquid was gone.

It was filthy and joyful at once. They were like children with no worry of rank, or colour, or pay, or jealousy. Each man was just a man with a laughing mouth, flexing muscles, eyes with stories behind them, and a heart that could love as well as hate.

They should have stayed there for ever. Floating near the bottom of the planet. Forgotten. Beyond the reach of the real world. He had married Laura just before boarding the **Glenlyon** but if he had never returned maybe life would have been better for both of them.

. . .

"The governor has arranged for a Mohammedan priest to visit you, he'll be here at noon." Perkins counts out thirteen cards to begin a game of rummy.

"Sheikh Ismail? Or Sheikh Al-Hakimi?" Mahmood gathers his pile into one hand and knocks the cards against the table to straighten their edges.

"I only caught the sheikh part, I'm afraid."

"He shouldn't bother with either. They don't care nothing for my hide or soul. They see me in the visiting room?"

"No, in here, in case you want to pray together."

Mahmood looks around him, at the overflowing ashtray and his bed with the cheap grey blanket and filthy pillow. "It too dirty in here."

Perkins casts an eye over the cell. "I've seen worse, but feel free to give it a tidy if you want to keep up appearances." He smiles.

Mahmood puts down the cards and does just that. He doesn't want either Yemeni to see the level he has fallen to, he won't let them gloat and report back about how bad the Somali thief is living. He shakes out all the bedding and straightens it over the mattress. He takes a small plate of bread crusts and an empty enamel cup to the table; Perkins hurls the contents of the ashtray over the bread and takes all of the mess to the door. He knocks and waits for it to be taken away.

. . .

He appears in all of his entire splendour, Al-Hakimi in a globe-sized turban and sweeping embroidered cloak.

"Abracadabra," whispers Wilkinson to Perkins, stifling a giggle.

Perkins frowns and ushers him into the corner behind the door, to give Mahmood and the priest privacy.

He has brought the scent of their old shared world in with him—incense, spices, **oud** perfume—and Mahmood has to fight the urge to bury his nose in the man's garments.

Al-Hakimi is three or four inches shorter than him, but has thrown his head back and peers down the length of his thin, hooked nose at him. "**As-salaamu Alaikum**, Ibn Mattan."

"**Wa Alaikum Salaam**, Sheikh." Mahmood holds out his hand.

Al-Hakimi hesitates a moment, before extricating his small yellow hand from the heavy folds of his cloak.

They are awkward with each other and the situation.

"Sit down," says Mahmood in English, gesturing to the chairs.

"I have been called to offer you spiritual comfort, but let me say first what an unfortunate, shameful business this is," he begins in Arabic, glancing over his shoulder at the warders and smiling a tight smile. "You must correct your condition before it is too late."

"How?"

"By saying the words of the Qu'ran, 'Our Lord, we have indeed believed! Forgive us our sins and save us from the agony of the Fire.' "

"You think anything else passes through my mind but '**Rabbi inna zalamto nafsi faghfirli**'? I say that both day and night. I know I have hurt my soul."

"So, you admit it?" he says, shaking his head.

"Admit what? That I drank, gambled, stole, wasted time on women? Yes."

"No, the crime that keeps you here?"

"No, I cannot admit what I have not done."

"You cannot ask forgiveness for what you have not confessed to, either."

Mahmood places his left hand over his heart and holds his right hand up, the index finger pointing to heaven. "As Allah is my witness, I did not kill that woman, my blood and her blood are both spilt in innocence. You tell that to everyone. I don't die a blameless man but I die a **shaheed**."

"A martyr?" Al-Hakimi repeats, raising an eyebrow.

"It's the truth." Mahmood keeps his hands in their oath-swearing posture. "I remember **hadith** after **hadith** that my **macalim** taught me as a child. There are many types of martyr: a woman who dies in childbirth is one and her child will drag her into paradise with its umbilical cord—that is from Musnad Ahmed. Another one: 'A Muslim who dies a stranger or in a strange land is a **shaheed**,' as narrated by Ibn Majah. Am I not a stranger in a strange land?"

Al-Hakimi nods.

"And what does a martyr receive?" Mahmood asks, playing teacher.

"**Jannat ul-Firdaws**."

"Yes. The highest paradise. I have learnt much in here, Sheikh. I have learnt the fear it takes to truly beg God for forgiveness, from the **pit** of the stomach. I have learnt how lonely a soul can be when all amusement and kindness and family are taken away. I have learnt how small and fragile this life is, and how everything in this world, this **duniya**, is a mirage that evaporates before the eyes. I have tasted the bitterness of injustice. Have you, Sheikh?"

Al-Hakimi shakes his head, his pale brown eyes fixed on Mahmood's mouth.

"It's like swallowing poison."

"If . . ."

"There is no **if**, Sheikh, **laa**, do not say that word to me."

"Whatever the case, all we can do is pray for

Allah's mercy on you, both for this life and the next life. You have impressed me, Mattan."

Mahmood smiles his indeterminate, mysterious smile. "Do that, and I will return the favour. May Allah forgive you and the other Muslims for abandoning me."

The sheikh leans back in his seat, not breaking eye contact.

"Look at my bones, see how they show through my skin," he lifts his sleeves to reveal his forearms, "know that they will bury me here, keep these bones like loot. No Muslim to wash me, no prayers, no one to rest my left cheek to the soil. Know that, Sheikh."

"We will pray for you. Do not despair, repeat after me: 'Our Lord, in You we have placed our trust, and to You do we turn in repentance, for unto You is the end of all journeys.' Repeat it."

Mahmood repeats the **du'a.**

"**Ameen.**" Al-Hakimi takes one of the long black prayer beads from his richly embroidered chest and lifts it over his head. "Take this, and count the names of Allah day and night, put your trust in the Almighty because the world of men is an unjust one."

Mahmood wraps the **tusbah** around his knuckles.

. . .

Days after the sheikh's visit, there is still a kind of glow around Mahmood, an inner spiritual illumination. Everything is as Allah willed it to be. The warders mean no harm, he realizes, they are only men placed in their stations by divine providence, just like he is. All of them gathered together by a fate that was written before any of them drew their first breaths. This feeling is like being doped, or what he imagines dope achieves; a soft, warm numbness that makes any painful thought or feeling unreachable. He wakes up and sleeps with the sensation of real submission, not having to search anywhere for it, but the feeling lasting and lasting as the days turn over. That train that took him south from Dar es Salaam, that first ship in South Africa, that meeting with Laura in the café, that jury man turning to him and reading "guilty"—all rungs of an invisible ladder that he was climbing up and up towards heaven. The exact date and time of his death already fixed, these ignorant white men manipulated like puppets. There is no one to rage at, or to even blame. He just wishes that he had paid more notice to Violet Volacki, that small, stout, dark-haired woman whose death was inextricably tied to his own. He had never cared to think of her as more than a talking, hard-haggling version of one of her shop dummies. He should have held her hand when she passed back his change, or put a gentle palm on that twisted back of hers. Looked deep into the flecks inside her brown eyes and said, "You and I are joined for eternity. The thread of my life will be cut the moment you die."

Wilkinson whistles. He is a beautiful whistler, trilling through his shift like a caged bird.

"Do 'Mack the Knife,' " Mahmood calls.

With a deep inhale, Wilkinson teases out the first notes, and clicks his fingers as if in a jazz band.

"That's it, you got it," Mahmood says from his perch on the bed, tapping his foot to the beat.

Perkins is moving around the cell, straightening and tidying up as is his habit, but he hums as he does it now, enjoying the moment. He opens the wardrobe against the opposite wall and peers in, finding it empty apart from a wire hanger and a spare blanket. "They'll give back your suit soon, you can put it in here."

"Sure," Mahmood says, swinging his head. "There is something I keep thinking about."

"What is that?" Perkins turns around to face him, and Wilkinson stops whistling.

"If I want to, can I call the police here? To take a statement from me?"

"Yes, that is well within your rights."

"Too bloody right, Phileas," Wilkinson agrees.

"I want to do that. Call him, that lying Detective Powell, and let him take my statement, so the police are not the only ones to write my story. I will have the final say."

"I will send a message to the police station but . . ."

"But what?"

"Don't get your hopes up about it changing anything."

Mahmood flings away the suggestion. "I know that. It's too late for whatever lies or truth gonna come out from Cardiff Police to help or hurt me. Bring him here and I will tell him what I want him to hear."

Detective Powell arrives later the same week, at ten thirty in the morning. His lumbering frame almost too large for the cell, his red-cheeked face damp beneath a felt hat, his black mackintosh dripping rain on to the floor. He greets the warders as if they are old friends, keeping Wilkinson talking about the summer rain before acknowledging Mahmood at all. With narrowed eyes and his arms stiff by his side, he begins, "Mattan, you sent for me?"

Mahmood is sitting down, looking up at him with steady, uninhibited contempt. "That's right."

"Let me get that coat off you before we need to

bring a mop in here," Perkins says, reaching for the detective's shoulders.

"Who said prison warders are the waitresses of the Home Office? Not me," laughs Powell, shrugging his arms out and letting Perkins hang up the coat in the wardrobe.

He dare laugh in my cell, thinks Mahmood, as he watches Powell fold himself down on to the chair opposite him, his knees cracking as he slides his rear slowly into place.

"Is there a sport more vengeful to an old man than rugby?" he asks Wilkinson, who just smiles in return.

"Powell," Mahmood says, reclaiming his attention, "you put me here but it too late for you to get me out, understand? Now, with these two men as my witnesses," he points to Perkins and Wilkinson, "you will hear my word and write it down. You don't write my history for my sons or nobody else, you see?"

"I am just a humble servant of the law, I can't put anyone where they're not meant to be, Mr. Mattan."

Mahmood stares with almost microscopic vision, trying to decipher whether Powell is a real human being with blood flowing through his veins. The fine red lines atop his nostrils and cheeks seem to suggest it, but what fella can sit there with such coolness knowing the lies he has told to put an innocent man to death?

"OK, let's get started, then. Tuesday, 26th August 1952," Powell says, pulling out a lined notebook from his suit jacket.

"I'm ready," Mahmood says, placing his hands on the table and taking a deep breath. "If it is good for the government that the killer is walking around and that I am going to get hanged for nothing—good luck to the government, and I am very glad to be hanged for nothing."

Powell pulls a face but continues to write until Mahmood recognizes a shape that he believes says "nothing."

"I don't want to wait any longer, I want to get hanged as soon as possible."

Powell raises his head from the page and smirks.

"Too many people know about my case in Cardiff, that I am going to get hanged for nothing, and I believe something is going to turn up before long but I want if you find the killer after I get hanged, I don't want him to get hanged at all. Good luck to him, whoever he are, black or white." Damn English, Mahmood thinks, struggling with his words. "Only one thing, I am glad if I get hanged for nothing under the British flag. Good luck to him, because I used to hear that the British Government is a fair dealer but I never see no fair dealing in my case, because I never see anybody in Swansea Court or the Appeal Court interfere in my favour. Only one thing, so far as I am concerned, I am black man and nobody like my favour because my life is buy cheap. I am the first man to get hanged for nothing in this country, and I don't think that anyone believe what I say right now, but before long, one time, you do believe it, because too many people know something about this case and maybe somebody talk later on. Suppose I got a whiter skin, I don't be hanged today for this case, because nobody been hanged for the word 'if' before. I doesn't interfere with anybody else and I don't tell one word lie in my case. I was true all the way."

Mahmood takes a long draught of water from his enamel cup. "The pair of shoes was second-hand when I bought them. I am not going to swear it whether there was blood on them or not but what I do swear is that I got nothing to do with the murder."

Powell writes slowly, his meaty fingers white at the tips from clenching the pen tight as it jerks around in his grip.

"I hope from God if I got anything to do with that murder I never be safe and if I am true I hope my God to save me. That's all."

Powell sighs, mutters something sour, it sounds like "pidgin English." Eventually he finishes writing the statement. "Is that everything?" he asks, scanning what he has written.

Mahmood's mind is whirring. Is it God or Powell who has put him here? Allah or man? He hadn't been planning to say so much, or that he wanted them to hurry up the hanging. What if that might happen now?

"Yeah, that's all."

"Put your signature there, then." He turns the notebook and pen over to Mahmood.

"The last time I write my name." Mahmood states quietly, as the letters form, with a fluidity and elegance that belies his tattered nerves. "You go now," he declares, not looking at Powell as he closes the notebook around the pen and slides it across the table.

Powell stands, casting a shadow over Mahmood before reclaiming his raincoat and silently leaving the cell.

Perkins and Wilkinson look at each other and exhale forcefully.

Moments after Powell's departure, Mahmood realizes with a panic that he has more to add to his last statement. "Mr. Perkins, I got more to say, will you write for me?"

"Of course." There is already a notebook and pencil in his uniform pocket.

"You ready prepared?"

"We have to be, in case we need to record anything important you say or do."

"In case I confess last minute or something?"

"Something like that."

"It will never happen. I go die telling the truth, like I told that policeman."

"I understand."

"You're the first man I've seen who has been unwavering in maintaining his innocence," Wilkinson says, taking the spare chair around the table. "Most want to get it off their chest by the end."

"I don't know how long it will take but, one day, they will know they hang the wrong man. You will see. OK, Mr. Perkins, write this . . ."

"One second. Let me sharpen this pencil." He turns the pencil until the graphite has a spear point. "Ready."

Mahmood clears his throat. "Only one thing I lose in my case. My defending solicitors and counsel been told that I got nothing to say to the Court, but if I put my evidence in front of the jury I would not be here today. But it is no good for me to tell you what my evidence is that I did not put before the Court, because it is too late."

Perkins looks up, waiting for Mahmood to change his mind and say what his undeclared evidence is, but Mahmood jumps to another subject.

"But the evidence you accept of the man Harold Cover, I can tell you something from his evidence, because he was told from the Court he saw me that night by the shop of the murdered woman and also he say there were many people standing in the street, but you can ask anyone from Cardiff what the weather was like that night and nobody would be standing in the street. If there were many people standing in the street, do you believe that anyone would attack that woman? This was not my own evidence but what I heard Cover say in the Swansea Court, and it is up to you, accept it or not. That's all." Mahmood lights a cigarette from a box on the table. "My English gone bad." He smiles, his hand trembling a little as he scratches a dry patch on his neck.

Perkins reads the statement back to him. "Are you sure you don't want to tell this evidence you didn't share before?"

It would only embarrass him now, and achieve nothing to say that all of this had happened partly because he had gone to see that Russian woman and he didn't want Laura to find out. He shakes his head, "Waste of time."

"As you wish." Perkins turns to Wilkinson. "Shall we show this to the governor before sending it to Detective Powell?"

"I expect we should, yes."

. . .

The sweet numbness that Mahmood had enjoyed after the sheikh's visit has worn away completely and he is in bed, under a white sheet, with a kind of seasickness, the walls and floor buckling around him. He clutches his pillow, ready to retch, closing his eyes to focus his mind on other thoughts. He dredges his memory for the names of his old ships and the ports he had boarded them from.

Fort Something. Fort La Prairie. Now was that Cardiff, Newport or London? He remembers sitting, waiting to depart, in a pub full of Somalis with his blanket, bowl and duffel bag at his feet. It must have been the Club Rio where Somalis openly necked their whisky. London.

Pencarron. Falmouth, Cornwall, England's foot.

Fort La Prairie again. London again. Club Rio again.

Fort Laird. London. Stayed away from Club Rio.

Fort Glenlyon. London. Eight months. Laura waiting with a swollen belly when he returned.

Harmattan. London.

Alhama. Glasgow. Only time in Scotland.
Too damn cold and hostile.
Fort Brunswick. London. Meryvn born.
North Britain. Newcastle. Just two months.
Homesick. Last ship.

The sky is red and cracked open to reveal the dark throne of God; a sulphurous substance spreading low over the tarmac and causing Mahmood to hold his nose as he walks towards the Docks. The moon is broken into two jagged halves and is sinking, as are the stars as they plunge one after the other into the Irish Sea, steaming as they slam into the abyss. The factories and warehouses have crumbled into dust. Mahmood walks alone and terrified, weeping like a child. Down past the deserted shops and cafés of Bute Street, which stand intact, the way he left them, skeletons perched behind counters and at tables, Berlin's place as full as a catacomb. There are solitary figures in the distance, walking ahead, but he knows that they can't help him and he can't help them. **Qiyamah** has arrived. Judgement Day. He feels deep in his gut that he is damned, that he will finally face the terrifying reality of God and be shamed and thrown down. He walks as if compelled by a force beyond his control.

Flames spit from the roof of the Volackis' shop and then catch on the clouds, drops of molten gold raining down and burning through his skin. "**Illaahayow ii saamax**, My Lord, forgive me. **Illaahayow, ii saamax.**"

Too late. Too late. Too late.

A hand slaps him on his shoulder. "**Waa ku kan, aabbo**, here you are, Father," says a light-skinned man, the lines of his face oddly familiar. Without speaking another word, he strides away, his figure stooped and defeated.

"David?" Mahmood cries, shrinking away from the fire, kneeling down on to the black tarmac as it roils and splits beneath him, "**illaahayow ii saamax.**"

"Wake up, Mattan, wake up." Perkins shakes him awake.

In the dim cell light, Perkins' pale face hangs yellow and unfamiliar over him. Mahmood pushes the **jinn** away, still caught in the terror of **qiyamah**. He is topless but pouring with sweat.

"You're having a bad dream."

"The world is finished. I see it."

"Let me get you a drink of water."

"Tell him to sit up and shake it off," says Wilkinson.

"I go to hell, I go to hell," Mahmood cries, unable to catch his breath.

"Cool yourself down," Perkins says softly, sitting

on the edge of the bed and holding out a cup. "It was just a nightmare."

Mahmood holds the cold enamel against his head before taking a long sip. "I live a bad life and now it over."

"We all make mistakes, Mattan, and we all do good. It's the way it's always been and God is there to forgive us for being weak, that don't alter, whatever religion you believe in. Now, sit up like Wilkinson says."

Perkins helps Mahmood slide up into a sitting position.

"Take this gazette and fan yourself." Wilkinson drops a thin newspaper into Mahmood's lap before placing the back of his hand against his damp forehead. "Your skin is hot to the touch, Mattan, it must have been an awful nightmare."

That was a **vision** not a nightmare, Mahmood says to himself.

The weak pressure to the taps on this floor means that it takes a long time for the trickle of water to rinse away the thick smear of soap from Mahmood's limbs. He sits in the small bath—his body white apart from some flashes of his real skin—and asks himself what life would have been like if he had been born with skin this white. He would have earned a quarter more as a sailor, for a start, and wouldn't have been limited to finding work in the merchant navy either. He might have become an educated man, able to turn his skills to whatever job he desired, would have been able to buy a decent home for Laura and the children and have old white women commenting on what a lovely family they made. He would know justice too.

The Scottish prison officer stands at the door, his eyes turned up to the ceiling to give Mahmood a little dignity.

Mahmood runs a hand slowly down his arm. This slim, black, muscular body of his has served him well; it's a wondrous machine more finely tuned than any straight-from-the-shipyard steamer. He has banged it about and imperilled it with little care for the generations of men and women who have brought it into being with their greed, lust, courage, restlessness and sacrifice. He has done his duty. There are three boys to carry his **abtiris**, his family line, forward—and may they make Mattan a famous name, a proud name, a name that makes those in power tremble.

Feeling the wet curls on his head, the short flickering lashes of his eyes, the upturned nose and dark wide lips he has inherited from his mother, Mahmood is full of grief for this body that will soon cease to function and begin to rot. This body that has served him so well, that gifted him all five senses and a perfect bill of health. This body that has been weighed, measured, poked, beaten, despised and now is scheduled for destruction, like an old tramper tugged to the breaker's yard.

He moves his hand down his long, arched neck with its pronounced Adam's apple, and traces the thick bones that roll down into his spine, the bones that they intend to snap.

"My love, I don't know what to say. I still haven't heard yes or no."

Laura sits on the other side of the glass with Omar on her lap. She nods. "The date is just four days away. Can they really leave the decision so late?"

"They can give it the night before if they want, and have me ready for eight a.m. in the morning."

"It's torture."

"Yes."

"I wanted to bring you some home-cooked food but they wouldn't let me. You don't look well, my love."

"Neither do you."

She rubs her nose on a hankie. "Oh, it's nothing, I caught a cold from the boys, that's why I didn't bring the other two, they're still sneezing."

"That makes me feel good."

"Why?"

"Because it means you have hope, otherwise you would have brought them."

She shrugs her shoulders. "Maybe."

"I still carry hope, Laura."

"You always did, Moody, you always used to say things will work out fine. Too much bloody hope."

"It just the way I'm made."

"I'll try to think that way too. You have been the best thing to happen in my life, you know that?"

Mahmood sinks his face into his open palms.

"All that petty bickering, squabbles over money or your jealousy, it meant nothing. I don't think I could love anyone the way you have loved me. You picked up this wet-behind-the-ears Valleys girl and made her feel like the Queen of England. I didn't understand why anyone would love me so deeply so I ran away. I was stupid."

"Stop, Laura, the past finished, it don't matter now."

"I want you to know that I LOVE YOU. You hear me? I love you." She almost shouts it. She whispers into Omar's ear and with a smile he rests his palms against the glass and pushes his lips firmly against it. "I love you, Dada."

Mahmood kisses the small print Omar's lips have made. He glances over his shoulder at the Scottish warder, who looks away. "Mummy, give me a kiss too."

Laura rises from the chair and their lips meet on either side of the thin pane, it's the first real kiss since she abandoned him in Hull.

"I always fall in love with you, Laura Williams."

"My name is Laura Mattan."

"Laura Mattan, **qalbigeyga**."

"What's that word mean?"

"It mean 'my heart' in my language. Laura, listen, if they do this thing on Wednesday, if they really go ahead, I want you to keep strong, look after my boys as if you are their mother and father and **don't** let them forget me, tell them when they get older that I died at sea, that's why they don't have no grave to visit."

"Oh, Mahmood, my love." She leans her forehead against the glass and he does the same.

"And listen, if these people in here do kill me, you leave me in here until you find the man that did kill that woman. Even if it take fifty year."

She nods.

"But don't worry, Laura, they won't kill me."

The warders change shift as Mahmood stirs a spoon through the breakfast bowl of porridge, trying to work up an appetite for the grey slime.

"Thought you might like this . . ." Perkins places a white cardboard box on the table.

Mahmood looks from the box to Perkins.

"What for?" he says, reaching with one hand for the lid, his fingers stroking the flashy embossed crest on top.

"Just thought that you've had a steady diet of prison food for near six months and might fancy something different."

Two cream horns sit in the carton, sugar crystals glistening on top of the flaky pastry, thick yellow cream and jam spilling out of the cones. Mahmood's mouth waters at the sight of them but he closes the box and pulls it to his chest. "I eat later, after lunch." He doesn't know whether to say thank you or not—to a Somali he wouldn't—but Perkins stands there expecting something, so he throws him a "thanks!" just to make him sit down and relax. "I play poker against you after breakfast?"

"I don't know if I can handle another drubbing, but if you say so . . ."

"I go easy this time," Mahmood says, drawing the spoon to his lips.

Wilkinson brings in a stack of censored local papers, their pages excised if they mention the murder or Mahmood's appeal.

"You want first look at the racing pages?" Wilkinson says, slapping the **Echo**, the **Mail** and **Times** on to the table. "I'm starting to sound like you now! Good grief, it's bloody contagious." He laughs.

Mahmood chuckles along. "Next, they be calling you a savage too."

A thud of steps rings from the corridor but Mahmood is only half listening to the footfall, his attention focused on the poker game with the warders, who are playing harder than usual. Mahmood has gambled one of the cream horns and is now afraid he will lose it. A few moments later, the door opens and the governor steps in, followed by his pen-pushers.

Perkins and Wilkinson drop the cards they had so carefully concealed, revealing losing hands, and stand to attention.

Mahmood slowly rises to his feet too.

The governor looks him straight in the eye, a telegram in his hands. "Mahmood Hussein Mattan, your appeal to the Home Secretary for a royal pardon has been rejected. You will be executed for the murder of Miss Violet Volacki on Wednesday, third of September, at eight in the morning. May the Lord have mercy on your soul."

The Scottish warder carries in Mahmood's brown suit, the one he had worn to trial, from the laundry. They have put the shirt, tie, jacket and trousers on a frame that makes it seem as if an invisible man is within, supine in the warder's big arms.

"If you want your wife to bring in another suit that's also possible."

"So I look good for death, huh?" Mahmood mumbles.

"You've got your yard time in an hour, remember."

He doesn't feel it's possible, that they can hang him in the morning while still talking softly of exercise and clothes.

The sky is not on fire but the sun is shining, as it has done many other days, with birds trilling callously from lopped-limbed trees. Mahmood crushes a beetle with his boot, grinding its body into small fragments that flicker with the embers of life. "They're doing this because they haven't broken me. If I had lost my mind and sat weeping in my own shit, maybe then they'd be happy to send me to a madhouse like they did with Khaireh. But I still stand and claim my innocence, so they have to finish me to protect themselves. Their lies and evil end with me." He had saved a cigarette to celebrate the reprieve, expecting, despite everything, that it would come through, but now he pulls it out from the foil and clasps it between his lips. He strikes a match against the wall. “If only I could set fire to all your walls,” he says, inhaling deeply from the smouldering tobacco, “I would burn this prison down and let everyone go free, whatever their crime, no one should steal their freedom. Somalis have got the right idea, you wrong someone and you’re forced to look over your shoulder for the rest of your life unless you make amends. You deal with each other face to face. Only cowards live by prisons and cold hangings.”

He can see a pair of hats moving behind a grille on the upper floor of the block. They move left and right, as if by themselves, following his movements, the pale faces underneath criss-crossed by metal.

Mahmood turns his back on his peeping Toms and shuts his eyes. Removing his cloth cap, sunlight warms the bald spot on his crown. Extending his arms in front of him, his shoulders and elbows cracking loudly, he listens to his heart beating out a rhythm. “I will wrap the road around my waist like a belt,” he sings, “and walk the earth even if no one sees me.” Then he holds his palms out as if the sun is a ball he can catch.

Khalas

[Finished]

7:15 a.m. Wednesday, 3rd September, 1952

"No, I won't wear no damn suit," Mahmood repeats, pacing the cell.

He has stayed awake all night, drinking mug after mug of tea. He has prayed only once, in the middle of the night, a long sorrowful prayer with numerous prostrations. But now he feels electrified, unable to pray, sit, or even stand still.

"Mahmood, please," Perkins pleads, unbuttoning his tunic, his face red.

"What? Who am I dressing up for? It ain't my wedding. You should keep me in your uniform if you want to keep my body too."

"Now, Mahmood," Wilkinson barks, pacing along beside him. "If you won't dress, at least sit and eat something, I asked them to sort you out eggs and toast."

Mahmood twists the **tusbah** between his fingers. "You think I can **eat**?"

A knock on the door and a covered plate arrives. Wilkinson puts a hand lightly on Mahmood's shoulder and leads him to a chair. He puts the plate in front of him and lifts the cover. "Have the toast at least."

Mahmood looks at the sickly fried egg and his stomach turns. He covers the plate and gestures to the warders to sit.

He is in the middle with his back to the cell door. "I just want quiet, so I can think."

Perkins and Wilkinson button up their tunics and sit down. It is now so silent that Mahmood can hear the ticking of their watches. "Take off your watches, or stop them. You're driving me crazy."

Perkins and Wilkinson reach for their wrists and pull the crowns up simultaneously. Their breathing takes the place of the **tick-tocks**.

"Stop breathing," he whispers.

Wilkinson's hands are interlocked, his head bowed as if praying.

Time is now a liquid thing, sloshing around between Mahmood's ears, impossible to measure apart from the metronome in his chest. He stares at the dirty cuffs of his pyjamas, at his hands, at the lines branching over his palms, and looks for a clue. Is it too late for a different fate to reveal itself?

The door opens and an old man in a hat enters the cell. He holds his palm out and Mahmood smiles and takes it. "You not kill me," he says, exhaling.

Perkins and Wilkinson stand and step back.

Without a word, the old man claps a thick cuff on one of Mahmood's wrists and then turns him around to pinion both arms behind his back. Men pour into the cell behind him: the governor, the doctor, the sheikh, another, another, another, another, another, another, another.

Two warders grab his arms as the old man leads them, as if they can walk through the wall. 1, 2, 3, 4, 5, 6, 7 . . .

Perkins and Wilkinson heave the wardrobe aside to reveal an entrance to another room. A noose hangs from the ceiling. The familiar cell swims around him and his mind cannot make sense of it. "You are wrong," he cries, struggling to tug his arms free. "You WRONG!"

8, 9, 10 . . .

Perkins and Wilkinson step aside and Mahmood looks back at them for some kind of recognition but they give none.

11, 12, 13 . . .

The executioners drag him to the wooden planks on either side of the trapdoor in the floor, and then hitch him up on to his feet. He holds his bladder tight.

14 . . .

The old man lifts a white hood over Mahmood's head, while his assistant straps his ankles together. "**Bis . . . Bismillahi Rah . . . mani Raheem.**"

15 . . .

It's dark now but he can see the shadow of the noose as it falls over his face.

He sinks again to his knees. The knot pushing against his jaw.

Khalas. It is around his neck. They pull him back to his feet.

Then comes the roar of the world giving way beneath him.

"La ilaha, La
ilaha
illa llah
muham
madun
ru
su
ll
a
h."

Woman Weeps As Somali Is Hanged

ALMOST within a stone's throw of the house in which he lived in Cardiff, Mahmoud Hussein Mattan was executed to-day for the murder of a Jewish shopkeeper at Cardiff Docks.

Mattan, a 29-year-old Somali, lived in Davis-street, less than 200 yards from the entrance to Cardiff Prison, where just after nine a.m. to-day in the drizzling rain a prison officer hung the notices informing the public that judgment of death on Mattan had been carried out.

An hour before the execution took place a woman dressed in a blue raincoat, her head covered by a headscarf, was seen weeping outside the entrance to the prison. She was later joined by another woman and at 8.20 a.m. they left.

Slowly Dispersed

There was a small group of people present outside the main entrance to the prison at nine o'clock, including several coloured persons.

They read the notices which were hung outside shortly afterwards and slowly dispersed. Throughout the morning workmen and passers-by stopped to read the official notification.

Mattan was convicted at Glamorgan Assizes on July 24 of the murder of 41-year-old Lily Volpert and was sentenced to death. His appeal was dismissed by the Court of Criminal Appeal, and a few days ago the Home Secretary announced that he could find no grounds on which to interfere with the course of justice.

'The Shadow'

Miss Volpert was found lying in her shop in Bute-street, Cardiff, with her throat cut. Mattan, known in Cardiff dockland area as the "shadow" because of the silent way in which he moved, was arrested more than a week later.

At his trial his counsel, Mr. T. E. Rhys-Roberts, described Mattan as "this half child of nature, a semi-civilised savage."

At the inquest conducted by the Cardiff City Coroner (Mr. Gerald Tudor) at the prison the jury returned a verdict of "Death from judicial execution."

The governor (Col. W. W. Beak) said the execution was carried out without a hitch.

Epilogue

Laura Mattan was not informed of Mahmood's execution and only found out when she went to visit him in prison. That day was the start of a decades-long battle to clear his name. After the execution the family moved to another part of Cardiff where they experienced extreme poverty and racist violence. In 1969, Harold Cover was sentenced to life imprisonment for attempting to murder his daughter by slashing her throat with a razor. Soon after, Laura, supported by Tiger Bay's Somali community, contested her husband's conviction. The Home Secretary and MP for Butetown, James Callaghan, refused to reopen Mahmood's file despite the similarities in both cases and Cover's hitherto concealed history of violence.

In 1996 the Mattan family won the right to exhume Mahmood's body from an unmarked grave near the vegetable plot of Cardiff Prison and reinter him in the Muslim section of Western Cemetery. In 1998, the Criminal Cases

Review Commission was established to investigate possible historic miscarriages of justice and Mahmood's case was the first one accepted to go before its three Appeal Court judges. With Laura, David, Omar and Mervyn Mattan in attendance, as well as Harold Cover who had been called as a witness, the conviction was deemed to be unsafe and quashed, forty-six years after his execution. New evidence was found that clearly identified Tahir Gass as the Somali man seen by Cover outside the shop on the night of the murder. Cover's identification of Mahmood Mattan as the suspect only came after the offer of a reward, and pressure from the police. Despite Gass's conviction for the murder of a man in Newport in 1954, and his imprisonment in Broadmoor Prison, other suspects were later reported within the Somali community, particularly one sailor, Dahir Awaleh, who confessed to being the man the police were looking for before he fled to Brazil in March 1952.

The wrongful conviction and execution of Mahmood Mattan became the first miscarriage of justice ever rectified by a British court, but the harm it had caused to his family could never be undone. After witnessing her husband's exoneration by the Court of Appeal, Laura told reporters, "If Mahmood and I had been living in biblical times we would have been stoned to death. He was a lovely man. The best thing that happened to me."

In 2003, Omar Mattan was found dead on an isolated beach in Caithness, Scotland, dressed in black with nothing but a whisky bottle in his possession. A few months before his death, Omar said in an interview, "Until I was eight I was told my father had died at sea. Then one day the Salvation Army band was playing near our house and I went out to sing with them. One of the leaders said, 'We don't need the sons of hanged men.' That knowledge felt like a cancerous growth in my head."

Laura Mattan never remarried and died after a long illness, in 2008; all three of their sons have also since passed away.

The murder of Lily Volpert is still unsolved.

Acknowledgements

This novel couldn't have been written without the inspiration, knowledge and humour of Ahmed Ismail Hussein, "Hudeidi." Zainab Nur and Chris Phillips also gave me their time, constant help and encouragement. This is a story that belongs to Butetown and I'm grateful for the generosity I was shown by all the people I doorstepped: Ruth Abbott, Natasha Grech, Mohamed Warsame Berlin, Ismail Essa, Nino Abdi, Eric Abdi, Keith Murrell, Steve Campbell, Betty Campbell, Steve Khaireh, Glenn Jordan, Chris Weedon, Dennis Arish, Abdisamad Mohammed, Red Sea House, the Butetown History and Arts Centre, Hayaat Women Trust.

Thank you too, in London and beyond, to Mayfield House Day Centre, Omar Haji Osman, Cabdillaahi Cawed Cige, Mahmoud Matan, Mohamed Ismail, Fatima Saeed, Michael Mansfield QC, Satish Sekar, Olabisi Oshin, Fadumo Warsame, Said Ali Musa, Mohamed

Ali Mohamed, David Szalay, Gaby Koppel, Dr. Hana Backer, Shani Ram and Marcus du Sautoy, Taiaiake Alfred, Yasin Samatar, Peter Vardon, Kitakyushu Moji Friendship Hospital, Abdirashid Duale and Dahabshiil, Andreas Liebe Delsett, Oslo National Library, the Rockefeller Foundation, Bellagio Center, Rasika, Andy and everyone at Santa Maddalena. The Society of Authors for an Authors' Foundation Grant and Somerset Maugham Award. The staff at the National Archives, Kew, Peter Devitt at the Royal Air Force Museum Hendon, Stewart McLaughlin and Wandsworth Prison Museum, Bodhari Warsame, Mary Actie, Savita Pawnday, and the staff at the British Library.

To my friends, thank you for your love and company over the years: Abdi, Robert, Kim, Danielle, Sabreen, Sarah, Lana, Bhakti, Michael, Aar Maanta, Emily, Amina Ibrahim, Yousaf, Katherine, Ayan, Jama, Zainab Rahim, and most of all, Mary Mbema. To my wonderful team, I'm honoured to work with you: Mary Mount, Assallah Tahir, Chloe Davies, Alexia Thomaidis, Natalie Wall, Shân Morley Jones. To the sublime Caspian Dennis and everyone at Abner Stein, the Marsh Agency, Lubna, Sarah and Brooke, and Maya Solovej at Aragi, thank you. Nicole and John, I owe you so much.

A NOTE ABOUT THE AUTHOR

Nadifa Mohamed was born in 1981 in Hargeisa, Somalia. At the age of four she moved with her family to London. She is the author of **Black Mamba Boy, The Orchard of Lost Souls**, and, most recently, **The Fortune Men.** She has received both The Betty Trask Award and the Somerset Maugham Award, as well as numerous nominations for her fiction. In 2013, she was named as one of **Granta**'s Best of Young British Novelists. Her work appears regularly in **The Guardian** and on the BBC.